Reviews for Deborah Hill's
This is the House

(New Edition)

Hill creates a lush, vibrant landscape in post-Revolutionary Cape Cod with historical details that blend seamlessly with the narrative. What compels the reader to turn the page, however, is Molly's uncompromising will to not only survive but thrive in the midst of her persecution and the country's upheaval. Though the narrative may drag for some who prefer a faster read, others will enjoy Hill's slowed pace that allows for full immersion in American maritime history. Seaworthy historical fiction at its best.

—Kirkus Reviews

Hill's recent revisions have added immensely to the work's clarity and depth. *This is the House* is important and worthwhile, both for helping us understand history and for fostering our appreciation of our fascinating human story.

—Rev. Jeffrey Symynkywicz, author of
The Gospel According to Bruce Springsteen

Those of us who remember Molly Deems from 35 years ago are delighted to see that a new generation of readers will experience her life as a woman living on Cape Cod in the late 1700's. Deborah Hill has captured the essence of the era and has fashioned it into a fascinating novel. Welcome back, Molly!

—Marie Sherman, author of
*Say, 'I Do!' Wedding Tales of a Cape
Cod Justice of the Peace*

D0167041

Deborah Hill weaves a spirited tale of a seafaring community enduring the hardships and uncertainties associated with the War of 1812. Her characters make *This is the House* convincing as well as enjoyable.

—James H. Ellis, author of
A Ruinous and Unhappy War:
New England and the War of 1812

Molly and Elijah Merrick present distinctly women's and men's visions of life in post-revolutionary New England. Skillful, cunning, and caring in their distinctive and often conflicting ways, the couple builds, loses, and struggles to regain fortune, trust, and love. The narrative language faithfully evokes the sense of period and place; the gripping story weaves an enduring portrait of a family and an era.

—Professor Bruce Allen, author of *Voices of Earth: Stories of People, Place, and Nature*, and *Literature of Nature: An International Sourcebook*

Reviews for Deborah Hill's *This is the House*
(1st Edition)

An important discovery in the classic tradition of the novel—long, detailed and full of flesh-and-blood characters. Not only does Molly Deems conquer Cape Cod, but she conquers me as well.

—John Quigley, author of *King's Royal*

Hill writes as knowledgeably about ships . . . and salt vats as she does about the female orgasm, and when it can be said in addition that her characters are human, with faults that make them real people, one hardly knows when to stop praising the story.

—Pamela Hill, author of *The Malvie Inheritance*

Sturdy and well-fashioned, convincing and attractively leisurely, Deborah Hill blends passion, history, and social mores with great skill.

—*Publisher's Weekly*

Molly Deems is a Revolutionary War orphan, and the story of her life, her rise and fall in grace, and the manner in which she redeems herself is fascinating.

—Helen Haggle, *Lincoln Nebraska Sunday Journal*

A huge, roistering novel, *This is the House* is compelling reading throughout its length . . . . And yet it's not history but one of the finest, most unpretentious, complete pieces of writing to bring unusual incidents and characters to compelling life.

—Cameron Parks, *Fort Wayne News-Sentinal*

The writing is so good that Ms. Hill may be forgiven a few purple passages that won't hurt the popularity of the book—or the box office appeal when it is made into a movie, as it certainly should be.

I sincerely hope that Ms. Hill will write many more with the same authority and mastery that she has shown in writing this first one. They should be worth waiting for.

—Marion T. Clark, from the
Baltimore News American (July 4th, 1976)

By the end of the 18th century Massachusetts was well on the way to becoming a maritime center. Her ships sailed around the world and her towns and people prospered. Deborah Hill has used family diaries and papers, combined with extensive research, to produce a fascinating novel of the life in one small

Cape Cod community in the years immediately following the American Revolution. It is a sweeping novel of human emotions as well as social change.

—Connie Granger,
Daily Press, *Newport News*, VA

VOLUME
I
KINGSLAND

This is the House

To Ann

DEBORAH HILL

Deborah Hill
8/15/15

NORTH ROAD
PUBLISHING

This is the
House

Author's Note

It could have happened this way.

This is the House is based on a memoir that I used as a framework for the career of the fictional Elijah Merrick. The personal life of the mariner who wrote it and his responses to the events described in his memoir have been imagined by me, and are part of the fictional world I created 35 years ago. This world was inferred from ancient church records, history texts as well as books written about colonial times in New England. The victories and vicissitudes of Molly Deems and Elijah Merrick are given shape by the events of post-revolutionary America; when seen through their eyes and their experiences, these events are brought to life.

I've been pleased to find that the internet—not available to me 35 years ago—verifies many of the details I discovered when writing the first edition of *This is the House*. It also corrects many. It's been very helpful to have a computer with which to coordinate fiction with historical fact, and new books, like James Ellis's *A Ruinous and Unhappy War*, that describes what went on "close to home" from 1812 to 1815.

With the help of these contemporary tools, fact and fiction blend and blur. It is true that Rockford and Waterford are patterned after certain towns on Cape Cod's north shore where a large population of captains lived. It's also true that I altered certain events that are part of the historical record. I needed a village that would behave as I wished it to, in order to illustrate the customs and conventions of the time. And so the story unfolds . . . .

Did it happen this way?

It could have, in a certain time and in a certain place on the Narrow Land, and *This is the House* describes how it might have come about.

Deborah Hill

Contents

Molly

It was a time of tumult and fear, of mourning and tears. Many men died in those years, and many despaired. But finally, the war for independence from England, in which America rarely won a battle, was finished.

From one village to the next, across the farmlands in the hills of New England, over the gentle rises and falls of the Delaware Valley and the Shenandoah, onto the sprawling piedmont of the Southland, the news of it spread, and thanksgiving rose up. Men embraced, and women wept the gentle, cleansing tears of joy. The farmer might return to his land, the fisher might return to his nets, and a man might speak his mind without committing treason. The old questions, the old loyalties, were laid to rest, and men turned to the business of the new nation, a gathering of sovereign states affirming their right to freedom and self-governance.

In the flood of exhilaration and challenge, they put behind them the devastations of war and their mourning for those who never came home. They chose not to remember their many defeats on the field of battle, or their loyalist neighbors who refused their cause. And they chose not to remember the women who had been left behind to fight wars of their own—against starvation, abandonment and despair.

✦᙮ I ᙮✦

JOHN DEEMS HAD followed Washington to New York near the beginning of the war. With tenderness, he bade farewell to his wife, Hannah, and his daughter Molly, only eighteen months old. He loved them with his whole heart. But he went.

Many men did not go that year. Some never would. There were some who would enlist only between harvest and planting. And there were some who would drift between the lines of battle and home, unable to make a firm commitment to either. But John Deems was committed to the cause of freedom, and so took his little family to his wife's parents, the Pinckhams of Dartmouth, Massachusetts, and went south with the army.

It was an unhappy arrangement for Hannah. Her parents were Quaker and refused to support the war. They upheld their faith with quiet dignity, even at the risk of being labeled Loyalist. Hannah, forced to live with them again, thought she would never be able to summon the restraint needed to be a peaceable member of the household as once she had been.

She had married out of Quaker Meeting; John Deems belonged to the Church of the Standing Order, Congregational. She had become wed to a new standard of values as well, but because the Pinckhams were people who believed in peace, they welcomed her back and forgave any pain she had caused them by marrying Deems in the first place. And of course, they doted on Molly.

Her parents had not berated her, nor had they tried to force her into their beliefs as the price of refuge; since they were Quakers, this would have been repugnant to them. But they stood stolidly in opposition to John's decision to fight, gently firm in their refusal to discuss the war or anything connected with it. They waited instead for the time when their daughter would listen to the voice of the Lord, who, they knew, spoke lovingly to her even if she would not listen. They would know when she had heard, for then she would return to the pacifism of the Quaker faith.

Meanwhile they became poor. Paying the army was not an obligation the Continental Congress could always meet. John Deems' wage lagged. Soon it became clear to Hannah's father that he could not support his wife, daughter and granddaughter by himself. The family savings had shrunk disastrously. Pinckham's little business was bankrupt. As a forger of iron he would do nothing that would find its way to the army, thinking to serve only the people in Dartmouth, shoeing their horses, making nails for their houses, crafting tools for their farms. But they would have none of him or his pacifist ways, and without John's army pay, he was hard pressed.

Hannah saw that she must somehow help. Food for the army was critical, and she found work at the outskirts of town at the farm of George Gorman, who was engaged in beef production. Although his meat was for the army, and the army was an entity her parents would not support, they closed their eyes to the destination of Gormans' produce. They cared for little Molly, now two years old, while Hannah, toiling at the Gormans', brought in the much-needed money. It was heavy work, carrying feed and buckets of milk, churning endlessly for butter, scouring the pails and containers, but she was diligent and the Gormans appreciated her willingness. They often complimented her industry and declared they could never, never get along without her. Hannah began to feel secure; with the Gormans, a small measure of permanence and safety was hers.

Then her father decided he would stay no longer in a place where he was so unwelcome. Most loyalists by then had left the country, fleeing either to Britain or Canada, and those who were not committed to the rebel cause wisely kept their thoughts to themselves. Those who had no commitment because of their apathy were not men of Pinckham's ilk. He eschewed the war because of his religious principals rather than his politics, which were very much in sympathy with the colonials. The strain of being in the minority without having a readily understandable reason for it became a burden he no longer wished to bear.

"Daughter," he said to Hannah, "wherever I go, everyone wants to argue, and I'm lucky if they do not turn their arguments into fistfights. The rebels control our town, and I'm more under fire here than thy John must be facing the redcoats."

"Oh, Father," she said with genuine sympathy. "I'm so sorry!" She could well imagine he felt threatened, for he would probably not have defended himself, even under attack. "Will you go to Jared then?" Her heart constricted with a spasm of fear. Jared was Pinckham's oldest son, and he had settled in Indian territory.

"Aye," Pinckham said. "Will thee come?"

"To Western New York? Father, you are daft! I would sooner take my chances on a battlefield."

"And why is that?" he asked kindly.

"Indians," she whispered. "The Mohawk Indians. They hate whites."

"Jared writes me that he has been getting along with them very well," said her father complacently. "But of course, he holds love for them, great love. And they know it. Love, daughter, is God's way, and it works every time."

"Not every time," she wept. The next day she asked George Gorman if she might live at his house, occupying a room with her little girl. She would need no pay for her work, only her board; her wage had gone to her father for support, but it was no longer necessary.

Gorman, a good man, happy to help when he could, was more than willing for the two to board with him and his family. So again, her security was reestablished. Molly followed her mother from task to task, watching silently and making no demands. Although only a toddler, she seemed to sense that no demand would be fulfilled.

Soon after the departure of the Pinckhams, Hannah received official word that her husband had perished at Valley Forge. He was forever gone, and she sorrowed while recognizing her plight. Desperately, she wrote to her parents; she would take her chances with the Mohawks. But there was no answer.

The path to Western New York was tortuous and time consuming. Hannah was told that it would take a long while for any message to be relayed. Letters depended on those riders of rafts, plying their goods inland over the waterways, who knew the settlements on the rivers and the trails leading farther into the forests. But the Indians were raising havoc in the western settlements, traders from that region told her. They tried, with as much kindness as their sort permitted, to tell her to hope for little.

When definite word reached her, there was no hope at all. Her mother and father, her brother Jared and his family had perished out there on the edge of nowhere in a Mohawk raid.

She tried to stem the welling up of despair. There was no one she could turn to for help; she had renounced the Quaker community of Dartmouth when she married John Deems, and in its turn the Meeting had renounced her. Her father had enraged the citizens of the town and there was no help to be had from that quarter either. She wrote letters to the Continental Congress requesting her husband's army pay, but there was no answer. There seemed nothing she could do except to stay at the Gormans' and wait for John's wage to catch up with her. She told herself there was nothing to fear as long as George Gorman made a profit from the war, and there was no way he could not profit from it, so high was the price of beef.

Another year passed, then a second. John's wage never arrived, and then, one day, the revolution was done. Prices for farm produce fell, and men who profited from the demands of war found themselves without work. Gorman could scarcely pay his taxes; they absorbed all he had saved. Hannah and Molly lived on his charity. Their clothes were threadbare; food was scarce. Hannah's fear grew.

Their situation became intolerable. George Gorman began talking of the widow's vendue—the sale at public auction of bereft women who had no support. It was a practice not uncommon in early days and recently revived as a means of dealing with the helpless. Gorman could no longer extend his charity to Hannah, he explained through his tears.

If the Continental Congress had paid its bills, such measures would have been unnecessary. However, the Congress, with no taxing power of its own, was at the mercy of the thirteen new states. The soaring taxes they levied hardly collected enough to pay the interest on the national indebtedness, let alone the wages of fallen soldiers.

Then, out of nowhere, Seth Adams—lean, short, slightly stooped— arrived on his way back from war. He stopped to ask for shelter in the barn as did many a returning veteran. No one knew Seth Adams, but this was of no consequence. Before he left, he offered to take Hannah away, back to his place on Cape Cod, near the town of Barnstable.

"I am interested in that woman," he told George Gorman. "Who is she?"

"Her name is Hannah Deems. She's a widow. She worked here during the war, while she waited for her husband. But he fell at Valley Forge."

"And what becomes of her now?"

"I wish I knew," Gorman sighed. "For I can no longer keep her."

"I'll take her."

There was a startled silence.

"You'll take her? Just like that?"

"Just like that," Seth Adams said, his mouth curling in a small smile. "My wife run off. Before the war. I don't know where she's at. But I need a woman for my farm—and here one is, all broke in."

"I, I'm not sure of the propriety of it," Gorman said uncertainly.

"If you mean, will I marry her, I can't," Adams said. "I'm married already. I don't need two wives. I need a woman. I'll feed her, house her. What more can she want?"

"She has a girl, nearly seven years old," Gorman said, feeling that the situation was wrong, but powerless to right it in the face of his waning funds. "You will have to take her too."

Adams shrugged. "Why not?" he asked.

Gorman told Hannah she was lucky not to starve. And Hannah saw that there were no alternatives. Only the widow's vendue and the humiliation of it in front of so many folk who scorned her Quaker parents. If Adams was an unknown entity, at least he was there and willing. Bereft of hope and now nearly broken by fear, she went, her only bulwark the child Molly. Whatever the future might hold for them both, it would lie on the Narrow Land.

✦᨞᨞ 2 ᨞᨞✦

During the fifty years preceding the English war, Cape Cod had left the farm, whose earth had been used up, and had gone to sea, fishing. Her people had grown dependent on the sea, and when the waters were barred by the British, they returned to farming knowing the land would not feed them. And the land did not.

Cape Cod, which had not seen a battle or fired a shot, emerged from the war with England as broken as though every skirmish had been fought on her poor soil. Her fishing fleet had disappeared and her citizens had become weak from lack of victuals while trying to provision the army.

The seas were now free; there was no longer a blockade. But neither were there ships. Nor was there money. Cape folk were forced to stay on their farms yet a little while. Food was, for the moment, money enough; corn passed for currency.

It seemed an endless walk from Dartmouth to Barnstable. Gorman gave Hannah a broken-down cart into which she bundled her few belongings—trenchers and porringers her mother had given her, patched clothing, and worn blankets on which Molly might ride when she could no longer walk. By night Hannah cradled the child while they slept under the stars on one side of the cart, Adams beneath his blanket on the other; by day they wordlessly walked the dusty road, on and on, as the land became sandier and the trees took strangely twisted shapes from the winter winds.

After a few days of travel they stopped in Barnstable village for supplies—cloth, thread and needles, food, seed, a spade, some rope. At the edge of the town was a path large enough to accommodate the wagon. On it they tracked into the heartland where they found Seth's isolated cabin at the edge of a sizable clearing.

The door was unlocked, and Hannah wondered that Adams would leave his home without even bothering to secure it. Inside she saw why. There was nothing to take. There was a fireplace in the middle of the room, the frame of a cot without a mattress tucked behind it. A table and chair occupied one corner; rows of empty shelves lined the back wall. Beside the fireplace a ladder reached to the loft and that was all. It was dark and smelled moldy from lack of use.

Hannah tried desperately not to feel that she had been committed to prison. She tried gamely not to be afraid while she waited for Seth's instructions. Under his direction, she unloaded the cart and put its contents on the shelves while he restrung the cot with the rope he had bought in the village. Then she collected wood for a fire, while Molly gathered leaves in a blanket Hannah had hurriedly sewn into a sack. When the makeshift mattress was sufficiently stuffed, they laid it on the cot, and Seth tested its comfort, stretched out his full length and grunted his satisfaction.

"It'll do," he said. "Fix me a bite to eat, woman."

With Molly huddled in a dark corner and Seth napping on the cot, boots on the blanket and a chew of tobacco in his cheek, Hannah grilled a piece of pork. The hearth showed no evidence that a woman had ever used it, with an accumulation of grease no woman would have allowed. She wondered if Seth Adams really had a wife or if she had ever lived here. Once he awoke, she set the pork on a trencher of her own and put it on the table.

When he was through, Seth smacked his lips and belched with gusto. "Perhaps the child had better go look for more leaves," he remarked, "if she wants something comfortable to sleep on."

"I'll help her," Hannah said, taking another blanket off the shelves.

"She can do it herself," Seth said.

"She's too little. It won't take long if I go with her. I'll need some, too."

He left the chair with a swiftness she had not yet seen in him. "I said she's to go by herself, woman."

Hannah stiffened, fear leaping suddenly within her. She spoke low in Molly's ear. "Stay outside until I call you, little one."

Molly whimpered and held back, but Seth raised his hand, and Molly ran out quickly, holding the blanket tight.

The quiet of the cabin was terrible, and Hannah hardly dared breathe. In the dimness she saw he was watching her. Then he threw some small sticks on the fire, and the room became brighter. He moved close and struck her; the blow dashed her against the wall. She wailed in terror, and he struck her again, then caught her wrist and held her fast.

"Don't yell," he said. "I don't want no one running in here, wondering what's going on." Hannah thought desperately of the loneliness of his cabin and knew no one would hear. "I don't want that brat of yours carrying tales to no one either. So you just shut your mouth."

He released her wrist and she sidled away.

"When I tell you to do something, I want it done. I don't want no arguments about it. I didn't bring you here to argue with. I brung you to help me. Understand?"

"Yes," she whispered. He turned away and seated himself at the table.

"Make yourself some victuals," he said, stretching and clasping his hands behind his head. "Feed yourself and the child. Then fix up the attic the best you can for her. You and me will sleep here." He indicated the narrow cot behind the fireplace.

Hannah stared at him, horrified. "I can't sleep with you!" she gasped, forgetting his injunction.

"Why the hell not?" He was sitting in absolute stillness, but she had the sense of his readiness to spring.

"I, I'm a good woman," she stammered.

"You're a poor woman. You're penniless. With a child I offered to feed. You got nowhere else to go." He watched her face. "Do you?"

"No," she whispered. "Nowhere."

"I took you in. Both of you. Without me, you and the child would starve. Ain't that so?"

"Yes," she whimpered. "Please, please, Mr. Adams, pity me. I shall work very hard here to somehow repay you. Please, let my labor suffice."

But her heart grew heavier with each word. It would not work. She should have known that coming with him was, in fact, a bargain that included her body.

"I think I should get a reward for being so nice. I would rather that you gave it, instead of me having to just take it."

He waited while she struggled with herself.

"Let me share the attic with her," she said at last. "You sleep here. I'll come to you anytime you say. She's a heavy sleeper; she'll not know." Hannah tried to swallow something too large for her throat.

"Now," drawled Seth Adams, "now, that strikes me as some inconvenient. Mighty inconvenient. You wouldn't be trying to duck out on me, would you?" He was on his feet, and she drew farther away in terror.

"No, no, I'll do it. I will. I just want her to be a nice girl, Mr. Adams, that's all, so she can get on in this world. I don't want her to learn things too early in life that might make her, well, not nice."

"You must mean I'm not nice," he said, pleasantly enough.

"I didn't mean it like that," she said, and wrung her hands, her eyes filling and her face a mirror of despair.

"Now, don't you get so upset," Seth Adams said softly. He approached her; she was too close to the corner to move away. "I guess I scared you some. I shouldn't have hit you. I'm a man with a temper; you may as well know it. But if I'm content, I ain't so bad. If you make me feel good, I'm even a nice person."

He reached for her, and she shivered and shrank from him.

His face clouded. "Now woman, it angers me mightily to see you try to avoid me. I won't hurt you none if you don't make me mad. All I want is someone to clear up this pigsty. I want someone to do my bidding; a man likes that too."

Again he reached for her and said, "I like a woman to let me have my way. I want that you should obey me. Right now, I want you should hold still."

With enormous effort, she made herself stand quietly, without resistance. He unbuttoned her dress and drew it over her shoulders to her waist, then stepped back to admire her in the flickering light. A tear slipped down her cheek.

"I like it that you don't wear no chemise," he said. "I'll clothe you, but promise you won't wear a chemise. It's nice knowing you got nothing on under that dress."

Miserably she nodded, and Seth, satisfied for the present, turned away. He was canny enough not to press too far. If she became too fearful, he reasoned, she would be unable to give him the sustained pleasure he envisioned. It cost him dearly to restrain himself, but he knew she would pay him in full. For now, the important thing was to show who was the master of the household and of her.

"You can button up now," he said. "Then make the child comfortable. Fix yourself a bed upstairs, with hers. As soon as she's asleep, you come to me. But I warn you, woman, don't make me wait too long."

She ran from the cabin, fastening her dress as she went, and found Molly scrambling among the fallen leaves beneath a nearby maple, pushing them onto the blanket. "Here, my dear one, here I am. I'll help you."

"What did Mr. Adams want, Mama?" Molly asked.

"He said we could sleep together in the attic," Hannah said, steadily as she could. "We'll get lots of leaves and make ourselves a big, puffy bed. That will be nice, don't you think? We can keep each other warm."

"Oh yes. That will be very nice!" Molly set to the leaves with pleasure, but her short arms dropped as many as she gathered.

Hannah drew the little girl to her. "Dearest," she said slowly, carefully keeping her voice light, "you must always do what Mr. Adams tells you. You must always try to help, as much as you can. And say nothing to him unless he asks a question. Do you understand?"

Molly nodded. "Will he hit me?" she asked bravely.

"Not if you do everything as you should. Then he will have no reason to."

"Will he hit you, Mama?"

Hannah blinked and tried to answer in a clear voice. "He may. But you must not mind it, Molly. For he will feed us and give us clothes to wear, so we must be grateful to him. We must try very hard to please him. And Molly, if you should ever wake up in the night and find that I am not there, you must stay in our bed and keep it warm for me until I get back."

"But where will you be?" the little face screwed up in concern and worry.

"I'll be downstairs with Mr. Adams, helping him plan our work for the next day," Hannah lied gallantly. "But you must not call for me or come looking for me. That would make him angry. Do you understand?"

Molly nodded, and the two of them filled the blanket with leaves and carried it up to Seth Adams' attic.

Hannah never let Molly forget who she was and why she was there, and she never let the child forget that they owed Seth Adams their lives.

Molly must work to always please him; she must endeavor never to annoy him; she must perform her tasks well and quickly no matter how her body ached or how much she might long for a moment to herself in the soft air under the brilliant Cape sky. Time for that when Seth was not about. For her part, Hannah gave all that she had to ensure that Seth would keep them alive until they could escape. There was no end of work to do, no end of ways to make herself and Molly useful. They washed the clothes and hung them up in front of the fireplace to dry. They gathered and prepared food, cleaned the cabin, toiling at the same, unrelenting tasks that reappeared at their stated daily intervals, marking the passing of the hours.

Seth was determined to reclaim his land, which had gone to seed during his years at war. Before he left, he had buried all the money he could muster, and his farm tools as well, heavily greased and covered with seaweed. Now that he had a small labor force, he would take advantage of it, and in preparation for spring, cleared and plowed an additional acre. Then he went to the shore to fish and boil sea water to preserve his catch. Since he lived some miles away, he slept on the beach until he had caught and collected enough seafood to supply the little household through the winter.

In the days of his absence Hannah and Molly pretended the cabin was their own, inviolate, where they could live in harmony and peace. Hannah taught Molly the alphabet.

When spring arrived, Seth planted his cleared land and set Molly to scaring off birds that came for the seed. When the plants sprouted and then matured, it was Molly's task to loosen the soil around them and pull the endless weeds. He made it clear that he expected her to work carefully—a willow switch hung by the door.

In late summer, they harvested the corn and helped Seth prepare it for the gristmill. Then they threshed his wheat, though it was a poor crop, and pulled the carrots and turnips, stored onions and herbs in the eaves of the attic. When the corn was ground, Seth traded some of it for chickens, and Molly's new job was picking the feathers off those chosen for dinner and saving the down for pillows. If she dropped an egg when she was gathering them, she learned to hide the remains, lest Seth beat her. She hated him.

Deep winter was the worst. It was simply windy, piercing, without much snow. Drafts scurried into the little house. Seth repaired his tools, worked on a harness for the horse he planned to buy come spring, and replenished the wood supply. The rest of the time he roamed about thinking of little jobs for Molly and Hannah to do and berating them when their work did not please him. There was only one way to truly please him, and waiting for it did nothing to improve his temper.

But wait he did, for Hannah taught him to savor the whetting of his appetite. It was the only way she could devise to keep Seth from banishing Molly to the attic and indulging his lusts whenever the mood came upon him. She hinted that if he let her come to him when Molly was asleep, she would see to it he had no regrets. But he must wait until night.

When he tried it, Seth found the results delightful. He devised varieties of teasing and titillating that he inflicted on Hannah by day when he thought Molly was not looking and that Hannah endured and even encouraged in order to hold him to his bargain. She escaped him in the evening when she went upstairs with Molly and stayed until the child fell asleep. If it were a night that he wanted her, Seth would busy himself by spreading a blanket on the floor Hannah had so smoothly swept by day and building the fire to his satisfaction, the better to see. Then in the middle of the night, the hours passing in their march toward day with a slowness she had not ever believed possible, Hannah Deems did the bidding of Seth Adams for as long as he wanted and submitted herself to his hands as quietly as he required.

Molly, exhausted from the day's chores, slept peacefully through it all.

ᴓᴓ 3 ᴓᴓ

In 1787, when Molly was 12 years old, the American Confederacy gave way to federal government, with the states, however reluctantly, yielding their rights to the superior force of the new constitution. These monumental changes had little effect on the inhabitants of Seth Adams' cabin. But maritime interests, at last given encouragement, flourished almost instantly as the desert blooms the day of a rain. Instead of a few ships struggling in and out of European ports, a whole covey now turned to the continent.

New England started, however slowly, to accumulate wealth. Riches seemed within reach; the men of Cape Cod, fishermen and farmers alike, had only to go up to Boston to find berths on a merchant vessel. If wealth continued to accumulate, servants would again be in demand. So reasoned Hannah Deems and she began to hope again. At least for Molly. The day Seth Adams came home cursing the Quakers, she knew her chance had come. Seth had gone all the way to Yarmouth village trying to sell his sea salt. The Quaker captain, Abel Warden, had been at the general store with his wife. They had not been interested in Seth's salt, which was coarse and, perhaps, had a bit of sand mixed in. They had plenty of money, Seth reported: they bought China tea and Caribbean sugar and a large rug loomed in England. Hannah heard him with a heart that suddenly lurched and left her weak.

"Goddamned son-of-a-bitch Quaker. Rich bastard in plain clothes! Pretends he's so upright. I'll wager he deals in the slave trade. Maybe he has slaves of his own, right there in his fancy house. . . ." On and on Seth grumbled.

He was infuriated that Warden suspected there was sand in the salt. His envy of Warden's wealth drove him to drinking so much that night that he never went to bed at all, but fell off his chair and onto the floor and slept right through to cock crow. Unmolested, Hannah lay in bed beside Molly and thought and planned and schemed.

Quaker.

This Warden was rich and was a Quaker. Perhaps the Wardens, in the name of the Lord, would help. Perhaps they needed servants. Being Quaker, she expected they had no slaves. Might they be willing to train a young girl to be their parlor maid? Hannah Deems was determined to find out.

She waited until Seth packed up and left for a prolonged stay on the beach. He would sleep on the shore as he usually did. As soon as he was gone she gave Molly explicit instructions to stay in the house and keep it neat. The next day at dawn, leaving the girl behind, she walked to Yarmouth. To approach a woman of wealth was a task Hannah could never have accomplished without the aid of her desperation. Every step was accompanied by a prayer, which did nothing to relieve her anxiety. By the time she reached the Wardens' home, six hours later, her agitation was acute.

The hand she raised to knock on the door trembled, and her voice shook as she spoke. Mistress Warden's Quaker heritage had taught her how to listen, and although Hannah did not dwell on the particulars of her situation, Mrs. Warden found it not difficult to guess them. She led Hannah into her keeping room, sat her down, and gave her tea to drink and johnnycake to eat.

"I should like very much to meet your daughter," Mrs. Warden said. She was a handsome woman, wearing a soft gray dress with a white collar and cuffs. An abundance of brown hair was gathered in a knot on her neck, and her dark eyes could be described only as fine, pure and steady as the truth she lived by.

"I am sure you will like her," Hannah said eagerly. "But of course you must meet her. I will fetch her, if you are willing."

"Nonsense," Mrs. Warden said. "It'll take too long." She went to the kitchen stairs. "Isaac!" she called up. "Isaac?"

"Yes, mother," a voice drifted down.

"Have you time to take me to Barnstable in the carriage?"

There was no answer. Instead, the steps creaked, and Isaac, the Wardens' second son, joined his mother.

"Glad to oblige," the young man said. "When would you like to go?"

"Now, this minute," Mrs. Warden said. "This woman," she gestured toward Hannah, "and I have an errand there."

Isaac cast a quick glance in Hannah's direction and then back to his mother. "Certainly," he said, his good breeding hiding his disdain at the sight of Hannah's ragged apparel and his surprise at her presence there. "I'll get the rig." He left the kitchen.

"Isaac is eighteen," Mrs. Warden said. "He drives beautifully. He is home just now between voyages. To tell the truth, I think he would rather handle the rig than a ship." Indeed, there were few people in that part of the world who could afford a carriage; in fact, few had ever seen one. Young Isaac's pride was justifiable.

Sooner than she would have thought possible, Hannah was sitting with Mrs. Warden, watching the road stream quickly past and behind her. Isaac brought them to the rough track that led to Seth's clearing, stopped, and tied the horse to a fence. He escorted the women to the clearing, baking in the afternoon sun. Nothing stirred, only the breeze, starting up from the southwest, ruffling the tops of the forest around them.

Hannah ran toward the cabin. The door popped open and Molly raced to meet her.

"Mama! It's been so lonesome!" They hugged each other and then Molly became aware of the two figures on the far side of the field; a man, tall, and a woman, not tall. It was the first time in years that she had seen anyone besides her mother and Seth. "Who are those people?" she whispered.

"The lady is Mistress Elizabeth Warden, and the man is her son Isaac." Hannah smoothed Molly's dark hair and noted with relief that she was well washed. "I have just met them, and I invited them here for a cup of tea."

Molly was enchanted with the idea of someone coming to tea. "Shall I put the kettle on the fire?"

"Yes, do," Hannah said, watching Molly run joyously back to the cabin, her child unaware she might never live in it again. Hannah returned to Mrs. Warden and Isaac, waiting at the end of the field. "Molly is heating up water for tea. Our place is humble, but she tells me it's clean. Please come."

Isaac demurred. "I'll go back and check on the horse. How much time will you need, Mother?"

"An hour, I should think," Elizabeth Warden said, and started for the cabin, Hannah following.

"Molly may not know what to say to you, Mistress. We have seen no one since we arrived here; she is accustomed to speaking only with me."

"I'll try to put her at her ease," Mrs. Warden said. "Pray do not worry, Mrs. Deems."

They entered the dim interior to find Molly setting out scrupulously clean mugs, dusting a spotless table. Her face was shining with excitement, and Mrs. Warden saw a slim, eager girl, poorly clothed, but as cleanly scrubbed as the tabletop. They sat down and watched as Molly made tea, deftly, as was her habit.

"Thank you for allowing me to take tea with you," Mrs. Warden said to her.

"We're glad you're here to share with us!" Molly beamed in her pleasure and then looked at her mother, wondering if she had been too forward. Hannah did not know, and so only stared at her mug.

"Do you always make such good tea?" Mrs. Warden asked.

"I always try," Molly said seriously. "My mother taught me how," she added.

"Then she taught you well. What else have you learned?"

"I can sew a straight seam," Molly said. "And mend stockings. That's very difficult, but Mama says I do it well." Was she boasting? She wasn't sure, and decided to fold her hands in her lap and just wait to see if she had been offensive.

"Has your mother taught you your ABC's?"

"Yes, she has!"

"Can you read?"

"I know some words. Little words, like dog and cat."

"That's a good start," Mrs. Warden smiled, and turned to Hannah, whose eyes begged: love her. Please, love her. Looking back at the girl, she asked, "Tell me, Miss Molly, do you believe in God?"

"Mama says that God created us," Molly answered in some confusion.

"Do you believe that God dwells in each man?"

Molly looked helplessly at her mother, who looked helplessly back. Hannah had taught her nothing of this basic tenet of Quaker thought, for living as they were, under the heel of a tyrant, made it an impossible belief to hold.

There was silence in the cabin. Finally Molly sighed. "I know that God does not dwell in Mr. Adams," she said firmly.

Oh, no! What would Mistress Warden think? Hannah wondered how to explain it away so that Molly would be acceptable, but her frightened thoughts scattered and drifted in her head like wheeling gulls in the sun.

"I should like to speak with you alone," Mrs. Warden said to Hannah, and a glance from her mother sent Molly flying outside. "I will take her, and gladly, Mrs. Deems. She is delightful. I will, of course, teach her Quaker thought. Do you agree to that?"

"Oh, yes, Mistress," Hannah murmured, tears of relief streaming down her face. "I have taught her nothing, even though I was raised Quaker."

"I think I can understand why you would have found it difficult," Mrs. Warden said gently. "Don't blame yourself. You are too fine a person to live here, Mrs. Deems, and clearly you have lost what is most precious in life. How long has it been since you attended Meeting?"

"A long, long time," Hannah said, her very self far away, at a protective distance from this decent woman, whom she had not told of her voluntary relinquishing of Quaker practice.

"You must leave this place," Mrs. Warden said clearly, her voice strong. "You must come now, to my house, with Molly and me. Today."

"I cannot, Mistress! With me here, Mr. Adams won't go looking for her. If we were both gone, there's no telling what he might do."

"I see." Mrs. Warden took Hannah's hand. Her eyes were irresistible, compelling. "Come to me whenever you see fit. Promise."

"I will," Hannah said, lying blatantly. "I will." She would have to stay, she knew, to keep Molly safe. She bowed her head in order to hide her deception.

"Let's call your daughter back inside. I'll tell her that she's to come with me this afternoon, so that she doesn't hear it first from your lips and think that the idea of separating started with you."

"This afternoon?"

"We don't know when Mr. Adams will return. We only know that he's not here now, and so we must take advantage of the moment. I'll speak with her and then walk out to the carriage. I'll send Isaac to fetch her. Don't come out with her. Let her see that you willingly give her over to us. It will work, Mrs. Deems. I know it will."

Mrs. Warden arose and went to the door, spoke quietly to Molly, then left. The girl hesitantly came back inside, into the dimness that would, Hannah hoped, help to hide the pain that must show on her face.

"Mama?"

"Yes, my dearest."

"Mrs. Warden said that I might come to her house."

"Yes. She has agreed to train you to serve her household. Be her maid. Help in her kitchen. And she will teach you to read and write."

Molly stood silent.

"It's a wonderful chance for you. You'll be able to find work anywhere when you grow up."

"But, Mama," Molly frowned, puzzled and apprehensive, "what about you?"

"I'll remain here for a while. Long enough to be sure you are happy and safe. Then I'll come too, and we'll never see Seth Adams again. But you go now. Ahead of me."

"I will not." Molly stood stiff and resistant. "Not without you."

Hannah's tears fell as an autumn rain, steadily as though pouring from a source unrelated to her voice. She paused, dreading what she must do, and taking Molly's hand, led her back to the table. "Mr. Adams has sheltered us, fed us and clothed us in exchange for the work we do. This you already know. But there is more, Molly, that you do not know." She took a deep breath. "For he also requires the use of my body, which he lays hands on as though I were his wife. Otherwise, he would not have continued to help us these past five years." The expression on Molly's face tormented her. "I have done what I had to, so we wouldn't starve. There was no one to help us, Molly, when your father died in the war. Now, here is Mrs. Warden! She will give you a chance in life. You must take it, Molly. I would like nothing more than to go with you, but I know he would follow us. If I stay, he will not."

But Molly was undeterred. "I can't leave you, Mama," she wept. "I won't."

"You fool!" She shook the girl, hard. "You are nearly a woman now yourself. Don't you understand that one day soon Seth will want to use your body as he has mine? He watches you when you aren't looking. Did you know that?" She waited for Molly to look into her eyes. "You must go, Molly, and I must stay so that he will not try to come after you."

Defeated, the child covered her face and her mother rocked her. They clung to each other and cried, then collected Molly's poor and paltry things and tied them in a bundle. At the last moment, Hannah stuffed her mother's pewter porringers into the middle of Molly's pack. "These are all I can give you, my dearest," she said, "to remind you that you come from decent folk. I wish I had more."

Through the open door they could see Isaac Warden striding toward the cabin. "Here," Hannah said, trying to keep her voice steady. "Take it." She held out the bundle and Molly wrapped her arms around it. Her eyes, blazing green with the hotness of too many tears shed, traveled over her mother's face as though to store its memory forever. Hannah, knowing that Molly would be always in her heart, thought of the short memory of the young. Would Molly remember her? In the years ahead, would Molly be warmed by her mother's love? Hannah wondered if she herself would die of the pain of this parting.

Silently, Isaac stood just outside the door, and Hannah gently pushed Molly in his direction. "You will have to walk through life by yourself now, my sweetheart. Take advantage of any and every chance you have to learn whatever you can. Someday it will all be useful. Someday it will be the key to your life, the key that will keep you from being placed in a position where you are, as we are now, wholly in need of charity to exist. Promise you'll never forget."

"I will not, Mama."

"God be with you," Hannah whispered, as Molly crossed the threshold into the sun. Isaac took her bundle and started across the field. The child hesitated, then followed him. They slipped away, away, and Molly disappeared. And then Hannah waited alone in Seth's cabin to see if he would accept her now-unencumbered self in exchange for making no attempt to find where the youngster had gone.

✦∞ 4 ∞✦

The home of Abel and Elizabeth Warden had been built after the war with England, financed by the extraordinary fur trade burgeoning in the Pacific. The house was designed in the new style and was, as a result, at variance with the dwellings nearby. It rose proudly to two stories, and its hip-roofed silhouette seemed huge and monolithic in comparison to even the largest house of the usual low-swept variety. Its double chimneys changed the manner of living to something before unimaginable, for every room (except for a small one squeezed into an upstairs corner) had a fireplace of its own. The kitchen at the rear of the house was no longer the only comfortable spot; each room in the house could be used whenever its inhabitants wished. As a result, an age of entertaining, of style, of beauty, was made possible.

Such homes had existed before the Wardens built theirs, in the wealthier towns closer to Boston and Salem, but only recently, with the appearance of hard-won money, had they appeared on Cape Cod. Little knowing the styles of living elsewhere, Yarmouth folk believed the Wardens to be well in advance of their time.

Elizabeth Warden brought Molly in through the front door, and the girl was enchanted by the two-story entrance hall that welcomed her, half of it taken by a wide staircase that climbed up and turned toward the front of the house. There were rooms on each side of the front entry. On the left was a dining room with a large polished table in its center, flanked by chairs of the same wood, built-in cabinets that held china and crystal, and a silver candelabra on the mantel.

The room on the right was the parlor. Inside it were shelves of books, plain yet comfortable chairs grouped around the hearth, a table under the front windows that held newspapers and pamphlets. There was a small settee on the far wall. The ladies of the Quaker Meeting gathered here to sew and read the Bible and the writings of Mr. Fox; when the men were home, festive celebrations were held there. In between, Mrs. Warden used it for reading and meditating and planning the events of her family's life.

The beauty and charm of the place made Seth Adams' cabin and her mother seem remote and unrelated to her and helped, immeasurably, to ease Molly in adjusting. She discovered, in an instant, that she loved beautiful things.

Mrs. Warden led her to the keeping room at the back of the house. It was large, the entire width of the house, with a fireplace at each end. A staircase divided the space; on one side quilts were stitched, with wool spun and woven and sewed, for although the Wardens could have bought their cloth, even their clothes, they preferred the simplest fabric available which was, of course, their own.

On the other side of the stairs bread was baked, meals prepared, the weekly bean supply kept warm on a shelf above the embers, water for washing heated. Berries were sorted here in the summer, peas shelled in the spring. It was a busy household, providing for the wants of a variety of guests all year.

The narrow stairs led to the bedrooms in the back of the house, and from there, very, very narrow stairs led to the attic where Molly was to sleep under the sloping ceiling that rose from the eaves of the house to its peak. In it were a commode with Molly's own pitcher and bowl on it, under which she might keep her chamber pot, a chest of drawers for her clothing, on which she could place her mother's porringers, and a bed on legs. Molly had always slept on the floor and was astonished at the prospect of having such a luxury for herself.

The dreadful heartache of parting from her mother was crippling at first, and Mrs. Warden was careful not to press the girl. Taking her around the house, she showed her where the family slept, where the blankets were kept and how to make a bed with linens. She helped Molly start a sampler in order to teach her more the intricate stitches.

"I cannot take your mother's place, my dear," she said, "but I will help you all I can. Be sure you come to me, Molly, if you have need."

Although Mistress Warden was kindness and charity itself, Molly understood, nonetheless, that she was there to work. She was strong and did not tire easily. Her early lessons in subservience stood her in good stead now. She started by working with Ellen, the cook by day who lived in Yarmouth Village and came to the house in the morning, leaving after preparing the day's meals for the housemaid Bethia to serve. Then she returned to her own house and did the same for her own family. With Molly there to help, Ellen's workload was lightened considerably, and if a guest should require an early breakfast, she need no longer come early to prepare it; the new girl was taught how.

Molly was realistic enough to look further than the cook and the housemaid and Mistress Warden. She saw that her position was most clearly defined by the guests of the house. They all knew the place of a servant. Their actions, words and tone of voice put Molly there. Nothing could alter the fact that despite Elizabeth Warden's immense reservoir of kindness and compassion, her attitudes were not the prevailing ones among her associates, even those who were Friends. For everyone but Elizabeth Warden herself, Molly was a mere cipher.

As though to atone for this, the mistress called her to the parlor within a few weeks of her arrival. She sat alone before the fire, and had pulled a small, round table in front of her and a straight-backed wooden chair for Molly.

"Here is a paper and pen," Mrs. Warden said to her. "I'd like to see your letters."

"Oh yes, ma'am!" Eagerly Molly seated herself at the little table, laboriously tracing the alphabet in her finest script. Mrs. Warden made a few corrections and she tried again. They put a few of the letters together to form words, and then made a list of words, as many as they could think of, that could be made from the letters already at hand.

That night in the attic Molly put the sheet of paper on her dresser, with the porringers on either side of it, her candle close by. Her hour of instruction gave her a sense of achievement, and she went over the words she now knew how to spell. She had taken care to be as charming with Mrs. Warden as she could contrive, enticing her as carefully as she would ever one day lure a lover. Remembering her mother's admonition to learn all she could, she had worked hard to ensure further tutoring.

She was successful. Subsequent sessions became habitual on afternoons when the Wardens had no houseguests and were expecting none. Enthusiastically, Mrs. Warden continued her tutoring as well as filling Molly's head with the tenets of the Society of Friends. In light of her recollections of Seth Adams, Molly could only pretend interest in these ideals. But she did closely study her mistress's manner, deportment, grammar and posture. She learned how to read and write Bible verses, and do simple ciphering. "Simple is all I know." Mrs. Warden explained. "It's all I can teach you."

Molly and Elizabeth Warden contrived, without having arranged it, to keep the hours they spent together private, as though both feared that outside knowledge would somehow ruin them. Their secrecy fostered their enjoyment. In between their sessions, in her attic room, Molly studied her spelling and practiced her penmanship so that it was as beautiful as Mrs. Warden's own. Before falling asleep each night, she spent some time in imaginary parlor talk; her penetrating remarks seemed to her brilliant and amusing.

Losing the timidity that isolation and subjugation in the Barnstable woods had fostered, she grew more self assured. Her body matured; she saw her waist define itself and her breasts grow, so that Mrs. Warden periodically set Bethia to making new bodices to put on old skirts, designed so that her lovely bosom would be concealed. "You're growing up, my dear," she comforted the girl, who was embarrassed. "You'll be glad of it later—a beautiful body is a gift from God. But for now we'll tuck it away amid many layers of cloth and keep you safely hidden!"

With the ripening of her body came the ripening of her emotions. Molly's adolescent dreams turned to her mistress's sons. She was hopelessly enamored of them; they were handsome, comely young men and certainly nicer and more polite than the guests who frequented the house.

John, the older son, was a captain already. He was always considerate of her; he never raised his voice. Mrs. Warden told her John was gentle at home because he was harsh at sea. A captain made of steel, she said, like his father, but Molly did not believe it until she saw him upbraid a stable boy for abusing his horse. He did not raise a hand, but his voice was cold and damning.

Isaac was so handsome that Molly was dazzled by him. Her nighttime fantasies now included him. Once, when he had been home from sea, he had ventured out to the kitchen where she was kneading bread, standing on a stool and leaning into the warm mass, turning it, leaning again, turning, leaning. Isaac stood in front of the table and watched until her face became bright red from embarrassment.

"Can this be the girl my mother and I fetched from the woods?" he asked, his voice full of mocking gentleness. She looked up at him and then down, leaned again into the dough. His nearness caused her heart to pound. "There's flour on your nose," he said, lifting her chin and wiping it away with his thumb. His eyes caught hers and held them. "You've become a woman in just a couple of years, Miss Deems, and a very pretty one." And then his glance swept over the rest of her.

"Thank you, sir," she managed to say, and leaned again to the dough. How good looking he was! Shivers chased themselves over her.

And then he was gone again to sea, his laughter gone, his voice gone. She had dreamed of him many times and gradually relinquished him. He would be a captain soon, and would marry a young woman of his station, forever out of reach.

Mrs. Warden set Bethia to training Molly as a parlor maid—opening the door and announcing guests, taking their coats and hats, serving meals and taking care of the parlor and dining room furnishings.

She reasoned that the more Molly knew, the easier it would be for her to get a position anywhere she went. And for her part, Molly willingly absorbed everything offered to her.

✦∞ 5 ∞✦

The day had been hot and she had been kept busy serving punch beneath the trees in the formal garden. Tired and flushed, the heat of the afternoon pulsing within her and sweat streaming down her face, she had at last been given permission to retire. But her attic room held the heat and gave her no ease. She stripped to her chemise and spread a sheet on the floor to lie on, glad to at least be off her feet, happy to rest. The afternoon passed, the guests left, their farewells languid in the distance. They, too, wilted in the suffocating August day.

Mrs. Warden's steps were slow on the stairs, slow enough for Molly to gather up the sheet and hide it under her bed. Her mistress's face, rising as she climbed the top steps, reflected pain and concern. "My child!" she exclaimed. "Surely you will fall ill up here. You'll perish of the heat. Forgive me for not thinking of it sooner."

"Mr. Adams' attic was hot, too," Molly said, wiping the sweat that trickled into her eyes. "I'm used to it."

Mrs. Warden thought for a moment. "I wouldn't take it amiss if you wished to walk in my back garden, on hot afternoons, and wait for the night air to cool things off."

"Oh, Mistress! How kind."

"Slip on your dress, my dear; we'll go there now."

The back garden, behind the formal one, was out of the family's sight and little used by them, though a favorite place of the mistress. It smelled sweet with the fragrance of flowers, and the cool of evening was stealing in. Mrs. Warden steeled herself to tell Molly what she had learned this afternoon.

Hannah Deems was dead.

Mama!

Mama! No! The lost little girl who lived deep within curled up into a tiny ball. No!

"How?" she made herself ask, her voice thin and wavering.

"Her body was found washed up," Mrs. Warden told her. "A clam basket was found nearby. We think the tide caught her unaware." She opened her arms to draw Molly into a loving embrace. "It is hard, so hard, my dear. I am so sorry!"

Molly stepped back. Her eyes blazed with unrestrained anger. "She drowned herself."

"Oh I hope not, Molly!" cried Mrs. Warden. The girl had guessed what she herself had dared not consider.

"So she could get away from that man," Molly continued relentlessly.

Mrs. Warden was weeping now, clasping her hands, despair overtaking her. For she had allowed Hannah Deems to slip from her awareness. She had not sent her sons to fetch the woman. Between them they could have overpowered Seth Adams without striking him. They could have taken the woman away, and Mrs. Warden herself could have found a place for her in Rhode Island, with Friends there. She could have so easily done it!

Now it was too late. "Forgive me, my child," she wept.

It was Molly's turn to reach out, to comfort her mistress. She had spoken the truth too plainly, she thought. "Perhaps it is a mercy," she heard herself saying, and saw that it was true.

Mrs. Warden kissed the girl's cheek, then left her to pray.

Molly understood that permission to walk in the back garden was Mrs. Warden's way of giving consolation for her mother's death and for the way her mother had been forced to live.

It was in the garden that Molly paced and grieved and raged over the unfairness of fate, railing at God. Then, after several nights, she pulled herself up short.

For it was useless to spend her strength this way. There was no God. There was no Divine Person watching over her, protecting her, or failing to do so, just as there had been no Divinity watching over her mother.

There was only herself. And she was not going to wait to see what life had in store for her. She would command her own fate, would never need to take her own life to escape it. She would start now, pursuing her only possibility, marriage. She would find a husband to protect her, provide well for her, make her life pleasant, perhaps even with a servant or two. At this thought, her lips curved up in a small smile.

Yes, she would get what she wanted; she would find a man through whom she could gain her ends. Her total dependence on strangers had taught her to speak low, to curtsy humbly, to cast her eyes down, to guard her words and even the expression on her face while she absorbed through every pore the possibilities of the situation at hand. Now it was time to put those skills into action.

The Warden sons were out of reach, and besides, she had no wish to use the beloved children of her mistress. But John and Isaac had friends who came to visit the house, rising young mariners, lawyers, merchants, on their own road to riches.

There were widowers, too, ripe to remarry. Most were an older, lecherous lot, their eyes hot when they glimpsed the nubile girl in service to their friends, the Wardens. Molly rarely escaped them without a pinch in a place that counted or an attempt to kiss or caress her when they found her alone, polishing brass or washing windows.

To the old, to the young, to those who noticed her and those who did not, to those who were concupiscent and to the ones that kept their hands to themselves, she was pleasant, obedient and ever watchful for an opening into which she might insinuate herself. There must be one man, she reasoned, strong enough to be able to disregard the social handicap she presented, able enough to take her where she wanted to go and lift her above uncertainty, one who could be lured.

And now there were many prospects while before, there had been none. For her mother's death had unexpected repercussions. No one had known of Hannah Deems' presence in Seth Adams' cabin because no one ever went there. Now that her body had been identified, everyone for miles about knew that Adams had kept a woman by his side and in his bed for nearly eight years without benefit of marriage. As a result, there was public knowledge that the Wardens, acting as guardian, had that woman's child in their service,.

There was an advantage to being looked at and scrutinized more carefully than a maid might otherwise be. She was pretty, and she knew it. She had exquisite manners and she was smart, smart enough to know that she must hide this strength long enough to attract the right man.

Once she found him, she had no doubt that she could capture him.

Men believed what they were shown, and she would let her quarry see only a beautiful girl, able to warm his heart and his bed as no other woman could do, docile and eager to please, yet able to understand his struggle in the world of business, for she had learned about that at the Warden house. Let him talk about his challenges, praise him for his cleverness and strength of purpose, which would include giving her the life she would have.

And so it was that when Elijah Merrick next entered the house, Molly, then 16, was ready for him.

CHAPTER

Elijah

✦∝∝ I ∝∝✦

THE REPUTATION of Captain Abel Warden of Yarmouth was formidable. Before the war with England there were many captains from many towns along the Atlantic coast, but the citizenry of Yarmouth knew only Abel Warden and believed him to be the finest captain of any ship, no matter what it carried or where it went. Warden himself knew better; he understood the competition far better than Yarmouth. But he was a competent captain, and he acknowledged that, too.

During the war with England he compromised his Quaker beliefs by smuggling foodstuffs to Washington's army. He refused to fight, and to that extent he compromised the cause of his compatriots, with whom he was in full sympathy. A firm and steadfast father to his sons, Isaac and John, he wished there had been daughters, for his wife would have delighted in them. But the girl born to them when Isaac was still a toddler did not survive the delivery and there were no more pregnancies after that. Later, when the war ended, Abel would take advantage of the Pacific fur trade, collecting pelts from the West Coast, taking them to China and bringing back tea. It was a rich trade, which he seized on instantly, as soon as ships could clear again.

He allowed his sons to believe the local yarns spun about his prowess. It was good for boys to have a legend to live up to. It would call forth the best in them, he believed. Captain Warden ardently hoped they would fill the shoes local legend insisted were his own.

His older son, John, was Abel himself, all over again, with a whole new chance at life. John's calm temperament and astute intelligence were duplicates of his father. The boy also had his mother's sensitivity, as much as was proper in a male, and his wife's appreciation for life's fine things—music, books, and such. Altogether, the captain was assured that his son John would grow up to represent the best of American manhood. Isaac, who was so handsome, was the captain's toy; John, not so beautiful, was his joy.

Like most children of seafaring families, young John Warden, when very small, had little first-hand knowledge of his father and only an imperfect recollection of his face. But he had his little brother Isaac for company. His youth knew no want. The war with England started when he was seven years old, and he was very happy about it because it meant that Papa was home often, in between smuggling expeditions. The child loved his father the better for actually knowing him, and strove mightily to live up to his parents' expectation. Isaac, as though understanding that he could not compete with his brother, continued to learn how to charm his father and mother and indeed his world in order to get what he wanted.

Although they were people of wealth in a locality which had little, the Wardens were eager to mix with all levels of society, as befitted Quakers, who knew that everyone was equal before God. They eschewed the exclusive use of a tutor for their sons in the early years of their formal education. John and Isaac attended district school when it was held. The schoolteacher passed through Yarmouth once a year for two or three months (depending on the weather and how many children would or could come to the schoolhouse). During those weeks, the sons of Abel Warden met and formed friendships with boys unlike themselves in background and breeding. John welcomed these friendships, for until that time he had been confined to his brother and visiting cousins, all of whom he enjoyed, but all of whom had a certain sameness. The differences presented by local boys he savored; they were the salt that flavored his life. As soon as his father saw this, he knew that John would handle men well because of this respect for people, no matter what their background was. Command was clearly John's future.

But Isaac was not so ready to embrace the boys with manure on their boots and calluses on their hands, lice in their hair and patches on their clothes. His good breeding demanded that he be always courteous to them, and he joined games and worked at being a good fellow. He was accepted, but John was loved.

Most of the boys around Yarmouth would head for sea as soon as the war was over. Boys on Cape Cod had always gone to sea in one capacity or another, and became farmers only when they were too old to withstand the rigors of salt-water sailing. This cemented a bond between them all, including the Warden boys. They would go to sea in ships that would carry the world's trade one day, enabling them to bring home the fortune they would deserve. Many would climb for the quarterdeck and stay there, competing successfully in Europe with men from Newburyport and Portsmouth and Salem once the blockade was lifted, the ships rebuilt. But the sea, always the sea, was their future; the sea held their fortune.

In the meantime, as the war continued in faraway places that the people of Cape Cod had never heard of before, they all plied the worn out land, hoping to feed themselves and the Army as well.

∞ 2 ∞

Elisha Crosby's farm lay close by the Wardens' place, and the year that the war began, Crosby took into his home a lad John's age. After many years at sea, he had left it for the land; now his sons were grown and had gone off to fight, his daughters married, and the youngster was no great drain on the farmer's feeble resources. Although the boy was not very strong, he was agile and could bend to the small, low tasks that severely aggravated Crosby's rheumatism. Besides, Crosby wanted to help the child's family, which was destitute and could not possibly feed itself. Elijah Merrick's father perished at sea just before the war when he fell overboard on a trading voyage to Quebec. Although the crew of his small ship could hear his cries for help, they could not see him, and thus could not pick him up.

Crosby had once sailed with Scotto Merrick. It was only fitting to help his widow and family if he could, and so he offered to take the youngest son into his care in exchange for his labor, leaving one less left to feed and the eldest son, Jonathan, then eight years old, at home to help the widow. Gratefully Elijah Merrick's mother accepted and the boy complied. He was determined not to cry over the loneliness and melancholy of being so suddenly orphaned and then abandoned. He fitted himself to the yoke, knowing that he was already taking his place in the world.

But the yoke itself was not especially heavy. Elisha Crosby was as a father to Elijah, and Mercy Crosby temporarily took the place of his missing mother. They were good to the boy, requiring all labor he could give else they themselves could not have managed to eke out their living. But they gave him all they could and shared with him all they had. They taught him to have confidence in himself through their willingness to tell him when his work was well done; they left him alone when he had fallen short, until he had figured out what needed to be done differently. Their reliance on him caused Elijah to rely on himself. They taught him to honor the Lord and his family obligations and sent him to school whenever the teacher was in their area.

It was at school that Elijah met John Warden and it was not long before the two shared a firm and lasting friendship. Although John Warden did not have to work as Elijah did and although he had much more free time in which to amuse himself, he was willing to gear his friendship to the rhythm of the seasons that controlled Elijah's life. The Crosby's, seeing this friendship and happy for Elijah that it was John Warden and not another who sought him out, saw to it that the boys had at least some time to play their games together, to fish, trap muskrats, dig clams and climb trees. Often John would lend his young back to labor on the Crosby farm in order to liberate Elijah from his chores the sooner. Elijah often haunted the kitchen of the Warden house with his friend, pestering the cook for a slice of pie, a piece of bread.

Between their Yankee rearing, their understanding of the necessity to finish a task, and their ability to undertake responsibility, John Warden and Elijah Merrick were being trained for command. One day they would make a fortune. It required only that the war would end, that they would not be too old when it did, and that they would find a ship on which to learn the mariner's craft.

When Elijah was thirteen, the war was over. The day he and the Crosbys learned of it was the day Elijah ruined his chances of immediate departure for Boston and pursuit of a ship to sail on. Although he had not experienced the company of grown men except for Elisha Crosby—a moderate man in any case—young Elijah Merrick found within himself a string of curses he did not even know he had learned until then, when he injured himself in Crosby's field. The stone was too large for him—he knew it the minute he first leaned against it—but he was determined to get it out of that field because he did not want the old man to have to contend with it. With the impatience of youth, he did not want to go all the way back to the barn either, hitch the team to the flat-bottomed sledge and take it all the way out there for one godforsaken rock. And so, grasping it and levering it with his elbows on his knees, he raised it an inch or two, a foot, two feet, and something inside him tore, causing him to drop the stone and then cling to it in anguish.

There Elisha Crosby found him an hour later, crooning in pain. Fetching the sledge himself, Crosby loaded the lad on to it; tenderly Elisha Crosby and his wife nursed Elijah through the worst of his agony so that at least, if he lay still, he did not suffer. Then they waited for winter and the snowfall so that they could carefully slide him home on a sled borrowed from the Wardens.

Lying quietly on a pallet in the Merrick keeping room, Elijah suffered himself to be fussed over by his mother, became reacquainted with his brother Jon, then fifteen, his sister Debby, only seven, Judith who was nine, and Reliance, who was twelve. The little girls were amusing. The local doctor, while willing to mix this elixir and that, was hardly helpful, for Elijah was not a horse.

He thought at length about his future, should the day ever arrive when he could pursue it. He dreamed about the sea and the ships he would sail. At first John Warden came to sit with him in commiseration. The two planned and dreamed together, as young boys will, of the day when both would be captains. Perhaps someday they would hail into a foreign port at the same time; perhaps someday they would own a ship together and share its command. And then his friend left for the Pacific with his father. Because he was the captain's son, he would learn of the sea and ships faster than Elijah would do. If he were good, he would have a ship of his own far sooner than Elijah, who would have to come up from the bottom—if he ever got off his backside!

Elijah fretted. He stewed. He cursed. He chafed under the heavy hand of his mother, accustomed to running her own house, having been in total command there for years, as wives of seamen had to be. She seemed to him overbearing and harsh, for all her good intent. Elijah owed her his respect—this he learned from Elisha Crosby; he owed her his allegiance. He wished, dreamily, that he could do so from a distance, where it would be so much easier. Meanwhile, he practiced restraint in her presence, played Patience with his little sisters, and hobbled about the keeping room, trying to get strength back into his legs. Eventually, with Jon's help, he walked about the town on this errand or that, getting to know it almost for the first time, and soon enough, he believed he was ready.

The doctor agreed he might as well go to sea. "Don't know how you'll make out there," the old man said. "But the sea'll either cure you completely or kill you."

Elijah was more than willing to take his chances! In trepidation, his mother agreed he must go; she had long since used up the cash money that selling Merrick lands had yielded. She had little choice but to allow him to leave for the great city in the company of his older brother who could help him should he need it and who, once Elijah had secured a berth, was to return home in order to be on hand for the spring run of herring. Jonathan was, after all, the man of the house.

It was not an easy journey to Boston, their belongings in a gin case and a bushel of dried corn for money. Jon pushed the wheelbarrow; Elijah struggled to keep pace, and the two of them slept in the fields along the way, assuaging their hunger with johnnycake their mother had baked before they left. In the city itself there were still unemployed men hanging about, hoping to find a voyage. Even with the sea free of the British Navy, it took a long time to rebuild enough of a merchant fleet to use up the pool of available mariners. Jonathan was all for turning around and heading straight back to Cape Cod.

"You can't compete with these men!" he exclaimed. "Look at them! Big, burly fellows—all with years of the sea under their belts. Who'd hire you when they can be got?"

But Elijah was not dismayed. "If you think I'm going home, you're wrong," he said to his brother. "Why give up before you have to?" For Elijah Merrick would never give up before he must, and his determination won that day as it would win many another. He and Jonathan separated to see what the waterfront had to offer.

At a minor and insignificant wharf far down the harbor, Elijah saw the *MaryAnn*, a small vessel that promised little opportunity because she needed so few men to handle her. But her captain was aboard, and Elijah hailed him.

"Where are you bound, sir?"

"Surinam," was the reply.

"Would you be needing a willing hand?"

"I might," was the guarded reply. "Depending on what the willing hand thinks he ought to get by way of compensation."

"Were I found," Elijah called, referring to his room and board, "and given a dollar in advance to invest in cargo, I would ship with you as cook and cabin boy."

"You a good cook?" the captain asked incredulously.

"I don't know," Elijah said. "I have never done cooking, so I can't say. But I can learn, sir."

"Well, I'll need a cook, and it would be a treat to have an honest cabin boy," said the captain. "I have only just arrived in Boston and not yet secured a crew."

"I can find you a strong hand, who will ship for the same wage as I," Elijah said quickly. "If you hire me, you can have him, too."

"Is he a good seaman?"

"I don't know," said Elijah. "He's never been to sea either. But he's strong as hell."

The captain threw his head back and laughed. "You're hired," He said. "And whoever your friend is, he's hired too. Those salts hanging around the wharf—they'd never consent to being on the bottom of the heap. Strong as hell! A mere slip of a lad like you, and already you know how to talk like a sailor!"

Jon was not difficult to persuade. He had been long enough under his mother's thumb. He sent her his dollar to compensate for his absence, justifying it with the argument that he would never produce enough at home to pay for the food he ate.

With Elijah's dollar, the brothers bought salt cod, packed and loaded it and sailed together on *MaryAnn*. When the ship reached Surinam they sold the cod and bought molasses, which they sold upon their return to Boston for twenty dollars. Before shipping again on *MaryAnn*, they used the twenty dollars to buy rum in Boston, sold it in Surinam, and this time they purchased a little molasses and a great deal of fruit, which would be welcomed in Massachusetts. Alas, they were hit by a storm on the return trip, and the delay was sufficient to spoil the fruit. Only the molasses could be sold, realizing about as much as their initial investment, much of which they sent to their mother.

Discouraged, Jon shipped out as a common sailor on a full-rigged ship bound for Spain that would pay a wage he could count on. But Elijah found that his pain had gone; he had filled out and was robust. The small flurry of trade made him yearn to learn the roots of commerce; the captain of *MaryAnn* had shown him the use of a sextant, and he was altogether intrigued with the mysteries of deep-water sailing. To it he devoted the next nine years, patiently and persistently unlocking the secrets of both international trade and commerce and seamanship.

So eager was he to succeed that rarely, in those nine years, did he take the time to go home. He faithfully sent money to his mother and when he visited her, she presented carefully kept accounts of her expenditures since he had been home last. Twice in those nine years he saw the Wardens, but John only once. By default he became a writer of imperfect letters in order to maintain contact with his mother and with Mrs. Warden, and through her, John, who was as much a brother as his own.

It was through these letters he learned his sister Reliance had wed, and then a year later had died in childbirth with her first pregnancy, found out that Jonathan had fallen from the mainmast rigging while his ship was anchored in the Delaware Bay and he would never sail again. When he was twenty-one, it was through Elizabeth Warden that Elijah heard of John's securing a captain's berth; when he was twenty-two, that John had become engaged and would marry when he could afford to build a house of his own.

This news made Elijah wonder if life were not passing him by and if, after all, he were on the wrong course. He was not yet a captain and wedding was so far from possible that he had not considered it seriously. He decided that he must, having been trained for so many years, begin to push in order to find a position as first mate. If he was weighed in the balance and found wanting—well, he would have to accept that. But no longer could he wait for his destiny to catch up to him.

He asked for the first mate's position with Jenks and Company, for whom he had worked the past three years. But Jenks was prospering at such a rate that it had no difficulty securing officers with experience and the company declined to train him. He left Jenks, and was able to find a first mate's berth with Benjamin Fuller of Baltimore. Fuller was a gamble—new to the maritime trading scene—but if Fuller were willing to bet on him, why should he not bet equally on Fuller?

Because he had not been home for a year, he arranged to visit Cape Cod before assuming his duties, and because he had not seen the Wardens for four years, he arranged a long enough leave to see them too. It was a simple matter to take a packet there to see his friends on his way to Rockford. He knew he would be warmly received.

And so it happened that Molly Deems, who had lived with the Wardens all through her maturing years, casting about in her thoughts as to the right and proper man to marry among those who visited at the house, had never once seen Elijah Merrick. And so it happened that Elijah Merrick, working for his future and busy abroad, planned an April visit to the Wardens, knowing nothing of her presence there.

✦∾ 3 ∾✦

The door was flung wide. She stood in the late spring sun that glanced past the fluted pilasters and fell obliquely across her gleaming dark hair, danced in her green eyes and glowed on her skin that was so clear it could have been marble.

"Yes?"

The one word was spoken clearly, her voice perfectly suited to her face and the slight but well-formed figure hidden beneath her gray dress and its white, somewhat rumpled apron.

Elijah Merrick felt the blood in his veins stop coursing. From his sandy straight hair to his large booted feet, he felt his very life drain away. His blue eyes, clear and honest, were puzzled as he looked down on her from his more-than-average height and stared, forgetting for the moment where he was. Molly Deems, accustomed as she was to putting young gentlemen at their ease, being sure she did nothing to slight anyone, lest that one be the person she sought, smiled up at him encouragingly. She moved forward a bit to look at him better through the screen of sunlight, and asked helpfully, "Is there something we can do for you?"

Elijah felt the blood again begin its accustomed round and brought his wits together quickly. He scowled at her. "I should like to see Madame Warden, if she is at liberty. I am Elijah Merrick; she knows me."

"I will see, sir," Molly said. "Won't you step inside?"

She left him in the front hallway and found Mrs. Warden in the parlor, her sewing discarded for a book.

"Mr. Elijah Merrick wishes to see you, Mistress," Molly reported dutifully.

"Elijah! How wonderful!" Mrs. Warden's face lit. "Oh! It's so late in the day! Show him in! Perhaps he'll stay the evening and night." She was on her feet, smoothing her skirt, stacking her books. "Hurry, Molly! I can't wait to see him!"

Molly fairly ran back to the hallway. Again, as she approached him, his heart seemed to falter. Bewildered by this physical condition, he nodded to her absently when she told him he might follow.

Mrs. Warden reached for his hands, kissed his cheek. "Elijah, my dear boy, how wonderful to see you again! It's been so long!"

She could always make him feel welcomed. He expanded now under the warmth of her smile. His grave face relaxed, his continual reach for success temporarily abandoned.

"Too long!" he assured her, "I haven't been home for more than a day since I last saw you. There was no time to go a-calling. Surely you know I would have come were I able."

"Indeed I do. Can you spare me the evening, Elijah? John is home—right now—this day! He'll return very soon from town and would be disconsolate should he miss you. And 'tis already late."

"I'd be happy to, Mrs. Warden," Elijah replied promptly. "Though I must leave at dawn so's to be home with enough of the day left that Mother feels we've had it all. Otherwise, I'm afraid she'll think herself neglected."

"Any mother would," Mrs. Warden said gently. She turned to Molly, waiting quietly by the door. Elijah had not realized she was still there, and at the sight of her he felt the now familiar sinking of something vital within him, like the drawing back of a wave on the beach before the approach of another. He had known only waterfront girls—and precious few of them. A girl of beauty and delicacy left him breathless.

"Molly," Mrs. Warden said, "do tell Bethia that we shall have Master Merrick for supper. Set an extra place at the dining room table, if you please." Molly dipped a curtsy and disappeared without a word. Turning to Elijah, Mrs. Warden saw that he was still staring at the door.

"Molly has been here for four years," she said. "That's how long it's been since you came by! Come now, Elijah, tell me everything you've done. Sit down here beside me!"

Because he knew she cared and was genuinely interested in him, he wasted no time on polite conversation. "I've done it, Mrs. Warden. I've secured first mate with promise of being master soon, if I qualify!" Elijah sat as he was bidden, but his joy could not be contained and he jumped to his feet again. "Jenks of Boston said they had all the skippers and mates they needed for present—if I would be patient with my berth, surely an opening would soon be created or made—but you know, Mrs. Warden, that they have said so for years."

"Indeed I do know!" she nodded.

"So I spoke with Benjamin Fuller of Baltimore, and he was happy to have me. I'm nearly guaranteed a vessel, if I'm good enough. Which, by now, I ought to be!"

Mrs. Warden clapped her hands. "No one deserves it more!" she said happily. "No one. I should so like to hear all your news! Tell me about family! I've been quite swept away and have forgotten to ask about them. How is Jonathan? Is your mother well?"

"As far as I know. There was a letter from her in Boston—I can't read her writing, but I believe she said everyone's fine. Which I expect includes Jonathan."

"And you've been coasting all this time with Jenks?"

"I'm afraid so," he said ruefully. "I know the route to Surinam and Jamaica and all the West Indies so well I could draw maps of it blindfolded, and show the currents and rips as well. Not to mention the ports to our south—New York, Philadelphia, Charleston. Yet they would not promise me command."

"Oh, the scoundrels!" she laughed.

"But with Fuller I'm off to Europe. Two voyages as mate, then, God willing, command. Just in time to reap the harvest. The ports are open. Hamilton is out to protect the shipping interest. The government is at last trying to promote commerce."

"But Elijah!" she cried. "With France in revolution, England and other countries in Europe are alarmed. They might impose blockades. It could prove dangerous."

Mrs. Warden was always current with world affairs.

He laughed. "A little, I suppose, but think of the opportunity. We Yankees will be the only carriers available. At this point I'd welcome a brush with blockades and embargoes. I'm very tired of being safe!"

She regarded him for a long moment and nodded. "I can see that, my young warrior. Perhaps this is your chance after all."

"My mother might accuse me of becoming a criminal," he told her. "But sharp business practice will be necessary, if not outright piracy."

"I'm not worried on that score," Mrs. Warden said. "We all have to fend for ourselves in this life, and I'm sure you can fend as well as the next man—but I know you would never wittingly harm another, so I doubt you'll become a pirate."

"I'll tell my mother you said so!"

"Perhaps you'll be able to see the sights of Europe while you are there," she wondered. "There are machines in England, Elijah, some being used to make fine fabric. You must see them—they hold our future. You could bring some of the cloth back for your mother and sisters. Any woman would appreciate that."

His ears became very warm; he supposed they had turned red. The subject of women instantly put into his mind the little maid who answered the door. "I am not aware of the things that gladden the female heart," he mumbled.

"Perhaps you can learn?" she asked lightly, and saw that his embarrassment was becoming acute. She cast about for another topic. "Well, Elijah, at least you can acquaint me with Fuller's prospects and where you'll be trading."

"That I can," he assured her.

"Captain Warden will be interested, too. Trading in the Pacific does little for his knowledge of Europe and I'm sure he knows nothing of Fuller. I can pass on any tidbits you have to offer when he comes home."

Although few females he had known were interested in such matters, Elizabeth Warden was not the usual female person. Grateful for the difference in this wonderful lady, he said, "I shall be glad to tell you anything I can learn, provided you do not know it already!"

A hearty voice could be heard from the back of the house, teasing Bethia, greeting the maid Molly as it came toward the parlor. "Who is the stranger in our midst? Someone's here. I see his coat on the rack!"

John burst into the room. "Elijah Merrick!" he roared in glee and affection. The friends embraced with delight.

"I heard you went and found a maiden!" Elijah chaffed him. "Did you get lonely?"

"Ah, wait until you meet her! She's an angel! Mariah is her name. I wasn't lonely until I met her, and now I'm lonely all the time. Sometimes I actually wish I were a farmer, so I wouldn't have to leave her."

"Gad!" Elijah exclaimed. "You are love-struck!"

"I am."

"He is," affirmed John's mother.

They sat together until supper, swapping sights and adventures, with Mrs. Warden listening, happy in their youthful and buoyant company.

The meal of young clams, Indian pudding, with coffee afterward, was endlessly enjoyable. Elijah tried diligently to be unmindful of the girl Molly as she moved about serving courses. His very effort made him even more aware of her, but not once did her eye fall on him, he noticed, and indeed, any special attention she gave was to John, in the graceful way that she brought things to him, the extra haste with which she did his bidding. She wished to please him, Elijah could see, but John seemed not to notice these small attentions, nor did he even seem aware of the girl. Elijah found himself thinking that John was profoundly foolish.

When Molly left the room for the last time, Mrs. Warden sighed and remarked, "She is a treasure. She works so hard, simply to please. And she is so bright! I've taught her to read and write."

"Mother!" John exclaimed. "You never mentioned it. Why have you?"

Mrs. Warden looked slightly flustered. "I think she's more than able," she said. "It strikes me as a pity not to develop ability where it lies. And she has taken to it with such relish—I hear her reading aloud in her room in the attic long after everyone is asleep."

"But what possible use can it be to her?" asked John. "Surely it will only make her unhappy. Surely education can cause her only discontent." Molly Deems, able though she might be, could scarcely hope to escape her background!

"Her future? Is that what you are wondering about?" Mrs. Warden's eyes grew soft as she looked ahead to her vision. "I think our country is such, my dear, that the position of one moment need not determine that of the next. Nothing will be the way it has been any more. Molly can be anything, as you can. We are all mixed in a great caldron, all brewing together. Who shall be at the top?"

"Maybe there will be no top," John offered lightly. "Everything will just keep stewing along."

His mother was not deterred. "Granted we have opted for a society without nobility," she said. "But we shall have our native aristocracy all the same. Perhaps, Captains, the giants of commerce, shall be ours."

The idea startled Elijah Merrick, whose legacy in life had been the burden of his fatherless family, one small house, one old cow, one land-holding that had, except for a corner, been sold off already.

"You truly think so, Mother?" John asked. He had always admired her and respected her opinion.

"Surely," she said. "I mean no disparagement, but look at our Elijah, here at our table. In Europe it would be impossible for him to rise to the position he hopes to gain with Fuller of Baltimore, and who is to say where he will be tomorrow? I hope, my dear," she said, turning to Elijah, "that we know each other well enough that I can say this of you. In any other land than ours your only hope of attaining prominence would be to marry it. Here you may earn it. Here you may become an American aristocrat, a lord. And Molly Deems, too, has a chance to rise."

"Hear, hear!" John laughed. He clasped Elijah on the shoulder. "Perhaps Mother would excuse us if we took an evening stroll."

"Of course." She waved them away, and the young men sauntered into the moonlight.

"Let's look at your horses," Elijah said.

"Why not?" They wandered toward the stables. Elijah loved horses, though he had had little chance to ride. John, watching his friend's face in the starlight, saw Elijah's heart. "Let's saddle up," he suggested. "It's such a warm, clear night. It'll be a pleasure to sit astride a horse, pitching to his rhythm, instead of rolling with the sea."

It would not do for Elijah to show his gratitude too obviously. "I'd enjoy a ride," he said. "Tell me which nag I may use."

"That one," John said, pointing to their best filly. "Her saddle's over here. We'll ride to the beach the roundabout way and then swim."

"You're just bragging. You'll never get in," teased Elijah. "But I will. Come on. I'll race you."

They pulled the cinches hurriedly and bridled their mounts, led them out and climbed on, riding crazily down the path and onto the highroad, exhorting each other as they had as lads, then onto a path a short distance from the water.

"I've a little something laid by for occasions like these," John said, and dismounted. Elijah followed. They scrambled over a large out-cropping of rock and there, hidden under a rough fold, was a jug of Barbados rum.

They secured the horses, picked up the rum and started for the beach.

"How long has it been since you were here?" Elijah asked, shoulder-ing the jug. Like any other of his countrymen, rum was his staff of life.

"Since last I swam by moonlight," John said. "It seemed to me the water would feel warmer if I were a little warmer myself. I determined to find out, and the next day I hid this here. But I had no time to use it, until now."

"Well aged." They sat on the beach and sampled the contents of the jug, then ran to the water, throwing off their clothes as they went. April was early for swimming, even in the bay which was usually warmer than the ocean itself, even by men accustomed to environmental excesses. Elijah's body ached with the cold, and he wondered how they could stand it.

John groaned. "My balls is froze off."

"Which way is land?" Elijah gasped. Maybe they would just keep swimming the wrong way, out to sea, to Portugal. It was a pleasant prospect, enhanced by the rum. He laughed unexpectedly, surprising himself.

"Mariah will never forgive me," John announced, his teeth chattering loudly. "There'll be no little Wardens."

"If we swim the wrong way, it won't matter," Elijah grunted. "Rum! I need the rum!"

John laughed. "Follow me."

They swam vigorously, grounded on the sandy bottom, ran out shivering and dressed as quickly as they were able, picked up the rum and went back to the rock, still warm from the feeble spring sun. Leaning against it, increasingly more comfortable as they emptied the jug, they watched the moon rise and the meadows light up. It was late when they returned to the house. They stole quietly from the barn and into the kitchen, up the stairs where Elijah would sleep in Isaac's room, John in his own, Bethia the maid in a small room sandwiched in a corner . . . and upstairs in the attic, Molly.

In the hall they shook hands. "I'll have to leave early," Elijah said, softly so that no one would waken. He looked fondly at his old friend. "I wish you well, John, on your next voyage. Should I be gone when you wed, I wish you well in that, too. I trust there will be little Wardens, despite your recklessness tonight!"

John laughed softly. "I hope you don't get in trouble with your mother for having come to us before going home."

"She'll know nothing about it," Elijah smiled in the dark. "And even if she did, she wouldn't begrudge me a few hours with you and your mother. I'll be on my way at dawn; don't bother to get up and see me off."

"Little chance." John cuffed Elijah's shoulder and they shook hands. "God go with you."

"And with you."

They left each other and Elijah peeled off his clothes, splashed water on his face and jumped beneath the blankets. The night dip's chill now returned as the spirits of the rum subsided, and he lay there shivering until he heard a creaking from the ceiling. The girl. Asleep above him. Perhaps at this moment turning over beneath her covers where the warmth and sweetness of her body would have gathered in kitten softness.

His own warmth beneath his blankets grew and he listened and remained alert for a long time, until the day and evening's fatigue carried him off with the suddenness of a candle extinguished.

Dawn's first fingers poked into the eastern sky as he woke, instantly aware of unfamiliar coverings in a bed not his own, then remembered where he lay. Dressing quickly, he felt his way down the back stairs, edging into the kitchen in search of his coat, which he'd left there the night before. He tripped over a low bench and caught it before it clattered to the floor. As he hugged his shin to ease the pain, there was a rustling behind him and a shadow appeared. Briskly it hustled to the hearth, kindled the coals, and lit a lamp.

"I'll set you out some breakfast, sir," Molly said softly.

His surprise took his mind off his shin. "No need," he whispered. Her face and eyes were clear of sleep, and her skin was fresh and still damp from the water she had splashed on it. "I'll be fine."

But she had already begun before the words were out of his mouth, setting out bread and jam, milk and cold beans and a wedge of cheese. Elijah set to them eagerly. The girl lingered at the edge of the ring of light cast by the lantern. When he rose to leave, she was there again, holding out the coat he had been looking for, her eyes cast down in modest waiting. He took his hat from her hand.

"You've been so kind, Miss Molly," he said. "I thank you."

"I hope it gives you a good start for your day," she answered, and her eyes rose to meet his. But instead of looking to the floor again, she met his gaze and held it, held it with a strength and irresistibility he would not have known existed. Within the green depths he saw, despite her youth, a woman lurking, a woman mindful of herself, a woman who admired him. Rooted firmly there, he could not let go. In his throat he could feel the surge of his beating heart.

"Do captains always rise at dawn?" she asked at last. "You and Mr. John were out so late last night I would not have thought you could waken so early."

"I can always awaken at the time I've decided on the night before." He decided not to correct her mistaken understanding of his status.

"What a convenience!" she smiled softly.

"And you, Miss? Do you always rise at dawn?"

"If I need to. I heard you tell Mistress you'd be leaving then, and I wanted to be sure you broke your fast before you went."

"You're very kind," he said, bowing a little. "No wonder your mistress thinks so highly of you."

"She has taught me everything I know," Molly said. "Including hospitality! She is very fond of you, Master Merrick."

"And I her."

Since he could think of nothing more to say, he let himself out into the morning now blushing, quiet as though holding its breath. The dew on the apple blossoms was heavy, the earth was redolent with lovely smells, and the new leaves on the budding elms of the highroad were a mist of green nearly impossible to see with only the eye.

The sun rose as he walked, and never had a raw New England daybreak in spring contained for Elijah Merrick the warmth and cleanness of that one. The pressingly pleasant memory of Molly Deems followed him, as well as misgiving.

You could have said farewell, he thought. You could have thought of something else to say, couldn't you, instead of just turning and leaving. You are a jackass.

He arrived before ten of the clock. His mother greeted him with smiles and received his hug with such gratitude that Elijah had to work at skirting a guilty conscience for having delayed coming home. Over the next day and a half, he worked especially hard at whatever task needed doing, whether it was helping his now-crippled brother, Jonathan, to repair the barn door or plowing the Merrick vegetable garden or hauling manure for it or cheerfully reviewing family expenses with his mother, to compensate for whatever sadness might have been caused by the delay she knew nothing about. He gave her enough money to see the family through the summer, told her about his chance to rise at last, and did not tell her about the money he had saved from his many voyages and small speculations, a little at a time. She would know about that soon enough.

For he had been working on a scheme. There was no reason to postpone it, now that he was sure of mate's pay. All her life his mother had made every penny count; she had managed well on the allotment he had sent her over the years. But now it was time, he thought, to begin the process that would allow him to decide for himself how his money and his life should be directed, not her. It was not a transition that was ever easy for any woman in her position, he imagined, and he did not delude himself as to her reaction to losing control.

He announced it at the supper table, where he knew he would have the support of his sisters and his brother to help him keep a steady course against the strong tide of his mother's will.

"Are you sure, Judith, that you will wed Stephen White this fall?" He fixed a knowing eye on his sister, who blushed with pleasure.

"Oh, Elijah," she murmured, "I do hope so." They had been waiting to marry while Stephen saved money for their new homestead in Maine. "He thinks that when the harvest is in, he'll have enough. We'll live with his family for the winter and sail down east as soon as the weather permits."

"Well," announced Elijah, girding his loins, "I'd like to have a decent wedding gift for you. I'll have had two voyages by then. We turn around in Baltimore when we get back from this one, and go to England again while the weather's still favorable. Now that I'll be drawing mate's pay, I will have more—much more—to spend and to invest in cargo. What would you like?"

"A set of china?" asked Judith wistfully, her eyes glowing at the prospect of such finery.

"Some people say china makes a dreadful clatter," Debby told her.

"I'd put up with it," Judith said dreamily.

In his mother's face he saw rising apprehension.

"I imagine I can get you china," he said. "And I think I can make enough, the market being what it is, to have something left over, since I can buy more shares in the cargo with my pay raise. That being the case, I would like to commence the building of an addition to our house."

"A what?" his mother cried.

"A little room, off the back." From the fireplace he drew a piece of charred wood. With it he lightly sketched the shape of their house on the floorboards and then drew a small tail attached to the keeping room, where they sat. "We'll build a little chimney here, on the far side, so it'll have heat. We can put in a window—here—and a door of its own—there—facing the barn just like our own back door does."

"Whatever for?" his mother asked, her voice strained. She glared at the mess on her well-swept floor.

"For Jonathan."

The family stared; Jon's mouth dropped open.

"For Jonathan!"

He waited for her to attack.

"Now? This spring?"

"Yes."

"Why not wait until you come back in the fall with the extra money you say you'll have in your pocket?" By then the dear boy might have forgotten this silly plan!

"Because I want Jon to have it as soon as possible," Elijah said firmly. "Our brother deserves the best we can give him." He looked his mother in the eye, daring her to deny it. "His fall in the Delaware was not his fault, certainly, but were it not in an effort to sustain our hearth, he would not have been there at all. While we had nothing more than a shelter for him, that was enough. But I have put aside a little extra; a small room won't cost much, and I am sure Jon would prefer it to sleeping in the borning room, as he does now."

"Hooray for Elijah!" the girls cheered. Jon made a feeble, half-hearted protest. He very much wanted a place of his own.

"Extra," his mother repeated in disbelief. "A little extra!" After all her struggles, making do with so little—he had extra!

"Do you think Pat Mayo would frame it, Jon?" Elijah asked.

"Once the planting is done, I'm sure he would. Right now he's probably busy with his fields."

"Very well. I'll give you what I have as surety. Tell Mayo we'll pay him the balance when I get back. I expect you, Jon, to take care of the details. And as much of the work as you can do yourself."

"I can do a lot," Jon nodded vigorously. "It'll reduce the cost."

"But we don't know how much the cost will be!" his mother cried. "It's foolish to go into debt if you don't need to, Son. Much as I would be happy to see Jon have a place of his own," she amended hurriedly. "But we can provide that later!" It was a stupid scheme, she thought. She was at the brink of seeing herself out from under the cloud of want because Elijah would be drawing mate's pay, and now he would incur needless expense.

But already Jon was sitting straighter, and she had not seen him smile as he was smiling now, not for a long time. Grudgingly, she could not help admiring Elijah's generosity, which impelled him to share his promise of fortune with his crippled brother even before he got it. It made her ashamed, yet did not assuage the anxiety of knowing that for a while yet they would still have no money laid away, nor her anger at knowing that Elijah had withheld part of his pay from her all along.

"Soon as I get back," Elijah promised her, "we'll know how my speculations have fared and exactly how much we'll have to work with. Until then you have enough cash to get through the summer; the garden and root crops will see you through until I get back in the fall. The addition will be mostly completed, and I'll give Mayo what he has coming. The rest is ours, to spend as we see fit."

His sisters looked at him with admiration; Jon could not conceal his gratitude and Mother appeared to have accepted his proposal despite her anxiety over it. What else could she do, really, he thought. Being a woman, being dependent, was an unenviable position, to be sure. He would do his best to assuage her worries.

"I'll write to you often," he promised, "and tell you of my progress. I'll write a letter every time I spot a ship coming to Boston or Providence or New York."

"No, no, you need not," his mother said quickly. "I have confidence in you, Elijah!" There was no point spending even more money on postage! She would just have to endure the uncertainty, as she always had.

The following day, he hitched a ride with Josiah Bradley, who was intent on sailing to Barnstable courthouse. Bradley cordially agreed to drop Elijah off at the Yarmouth wharf in time to catch the packet, and Elijah was delighted not to have to walk. He courteously helped Bradley with the sheets and lines and thought, as they sailed, that it had all turned out very well, very well indeed.

For too many years his mother had been at the helm. Now she must change her ways. If they were able to live more pleasantly now, they would do it, instead of hoarding. When there was enough to do more than feed them, it would be he, and not her, to decide how the money should be spent! For he knew her well enough to understand she would spend none of it.

He had surmounted the first hurdle. The battle for dominance was not done, he knew. His mother could hardly be expected to hand over all vestiges of control without a struggle. Yet one day Elijah would have a family of his own, and it was important to secure his position at home before that time arrived. As well as with Fuller, his new owner. Indeed, if he were successful with Fuller, he could—and would—begin!

And he believed he knew where to start. He thought of Molly Deems and her young, fresh face with its unbelievable complexion and its eyes that held him powerless. There would not be time to see her again, and there was no excuse to do so. But he would like to, yes, he would! He remembered her with a quick, intense and nearly overpowering longing; sweat rose on his brow, and every muscle tensed.

But then he laughed at himself, surprising Josiah Bradley at the tiller, and set to fastening the jib sheets more securely to their cleats. Nothing, Elijah thought, overwhelmed a captain. And since captain's berth was surely next, nothing would be allowed to overwhelm him either. He would think of Molly Deems in a mature and distant manner. Until he could see her again.

✦∽ 4 ∽✦

In the years since the war of the revolution, New England shipping had undertaken commerce unprotected. The new government could hardly maintain itself, for at that time it did not have the power to tax the states and thus could not raise money or build naval force, nor lay claim to international respect.

But now the nation had reorganized itself under a constitution. It supported the Federalist Alexander Hamilton, and gained financial stability and international credit under his leadership. Ports that had been closed to America at last opened. Into these European ports, the Yankee mariner sailed, there to reap the harvest.

More ships were anchored in the harbors of Britain and France than Elijah Merrick had ever beheld, flying flags of nations he had never known existed. There he observed the brotherhood of merchant captains who plied the Continental trade. The captain was truly his own master, making all the decisions, buying low and selling high if he could, his success making profit for the company which owned his ship and his cargo. His share was large, and the more he traded successfully, the wealthier he became. Unless the sanctity of his ship's neutrality was violated by boarding parties, his cargo confiscated by the French, his British-born crew members taken to augment the Royal Navy ....

From his position as first mate, Elijah soaked it all up, watching the spectacle with rising excitement and with an itch to join the fray. Taking an advance on his pay, he had bought French silk. In July the ship put in at the Harbor of Boston on her way to home base in Baltimore, and he sold the silk there at twice the price he had paid for it. Cursing himself for not having risked his whole wage, he soothed himself with the knowledge that the silk profit, combined with the shares in cargo due the first mate, would provide a hefty investment in the next voyage, due to leave Baltimore as soon as the cargo could be onloaded.

There was a small interval of time between arriving in Boston and departing again. It was as an omen, beckoning him south to Yarmouth.

He boarded the packet and set sail on a favorable tide, crossing his fingers that the weather would not delay him on his return. There would be only the next outgoing tide on which to get back. He would have to move fast, and luck had to be with him, but there was no helping it. Despite the shortage of time, he must return and revisit the maid who had captivated him. Hopefully his mother would never know he had come back without seeing her.

In his pocket he tucked a small book for Elizabeth Warden which, he hoped, would provide ample excuse for calling again at her house. It was a first edition of William Penn that he had found in London. Aboard the packet he tried to think of ways he could contrive to see Molly alone.

He could think of none.

Forgoing that, he tried to think of what he might say to her, should he find himself alone with her, what sort of conversational gambit would appeal to her, but he had not been trained in this art and besides, he told himself, how did he really feel about her? Until he saw her again, he would not know. One brief meeting was too insubstantial to give him a true bearing, yet here he was, risking an absence without leave from his ship, perhaps jeopardizing his career. He mentally threw up his hands. His feeling for her, his projected conversation, even the untoward consequences should he miss the return trip—it was distant, too contingent, and Elijah Merrick was not accustomed to distant contingencies. His battleground was the day-to-day decision on tides, on winds, on current, on the prices of goods and did not include women or his own heart.

It was Sunday morning when he arrived—the tide did not wait, even for the Lord! The packet would depart on the ebb, taking cargo and passengers back to the city.

The Warden house was stirring in preparation for breakfast when he knocked. And knocked again. He was crazy to have come! He wished he had not. But he could hear footsteps now, and it was too late to leave.

Elizabeth Warden herself answered the door, her face unbelieving when she saw him. "My dear friend!" she exclaimed, drawing him inside. "I hope you haven't been out here for too long! All hands were busy with breakfast. Molly!" she called, taking his coat. "Set another place. Master Merrick is here."

"Forgive my intrusion," Elijah said uncomfortably. "I found a little something in London I knew you would like. I thought to deliver it myself before I leave for Baltimore."

"And when will that be, my dear Elijah?" Mrs. Warden asked.

"This afternoon."

"Oh," she said faintly, clearly perplexed by this extravagant gesture. "You are a good friend indeed." She paused expectantly.

"Oh, y-yes," Elijah stammered. "Here it is."

He produced the little book. Tears leaped to her eyes when she took it, and impulsively she leaned forward and kissed his cheek. "You knew how much I would love to have it!"

Elijah also knew it was shameful, but he pursued his advantage. "That's why I came," he told her cheerfully.

Composing herself, she took his arm and led him to the dining room, where an incredibly decrepit lady and another of Mrs. Warden's own age awaited them at the table.

"My aunt, Mrs. Sampson. My sister, Mrs. Lewis," Mrs. Warden introduced him. "Mr. Merrick is a special friend of young John's and mine."

Frigidly, the ladies acknowledged his presence, clearly considering him a local product of no importance. Mrs. Warden called for the meal. Elijah did not look up at its bearer, only at the side of her skirt as she passed his place, pouring out his coffee, setting hot bread in the center of the table along with slices of ham and bacon, butter and cheese, fruit and a pitcher of milk.

He tried to listen intelligently as Mrs. Warden told him the news from the North Pacific where Captain Abel had been trading, and from Spain, where Captain John was, and Isaac's news from the China. Dutifully, he recounted his own travels, though he thought them of little interest to the disdainful guests. As the repast drew to a close, he was up against it again and no closer to knowing what to do than he had been when he knocked.

Molly entered to clear the plates and circled the table to stand by her mistress. Dropping a curtsy, she murmured in a low voice, yet one he had no difficulty hearing, "I'm indisposed, ma'am. Would you excuse my presence at Meeting?"

"Oh, my dear, of course." She took Molly's hand. "Why, you are cold! As soon as you're through with the plates, go to bed in Bethia's room; the attic will be too hot. I'm sure she won't mind."

"Then I will," Molly said, smiling faintly. "Thank you, Mistress."

Patting the icy hand, Mrs. Warden said, "Hurry along, my dear. Stay up no longer than you have to." She waited until Molly left the room. "Will you come to Meeting with us, Elijah?"

"Thank you kindly, Mrs. Warden," he said hastily. "I think, begging your leave, that I will walk in the woods, instead. Since I must leave early this afternoon, I hope the good Lord will forgive my absence in His house. It will be many weeks before I see the morning sun in the forest again."

Mrs. Warden, taking this as an excuse not to attend a Quaker meeting, smiled gently and walked with him to the front door. "You are as a son to me," she said, kissing his cheek as he departed. "I can't tell you how much it means to me that you would take so much trouble to come here today."

Awkwardly, he kissed her cheek in return, and smelled the scent of lavender. He would have liked to tell her that the gentleness she gave him made up for what he could not get from his own mother, but this would have been grossly disloyal and was not, besides, the reason for his being here. Instead, he hurried away.

A few minutes later he stopped, and lingered until he could hear, ever so faintly, distant bells from the Yarmouth Church of the Standing Order. Knowing the Quaker Meeting began at the same time, he judged it safe to make his move. Before his mind should change, he raced back to the Wardens' door. His knock was answered instantly by Molly, who did not look indisposed at all.

"Ah, Master Merrick," she grinned. "Have you left your hat?"

He stood, nonplussed, until her smile turned to laughter and coaxed him into laughter, too. "Just checking on your indisposition, Mistress," he said between chuckles. "I trust you have recovered."

"Yes, I have," she said warmly. "I'd invite you in, but I can't, because no one is here."

He bowed. "Mistress, I was hoping you'd walk with me."

She curtsied in return. "I should be happy to, sir. If you would be so kind as to wait while I fetch my shawl."

The door shut abruptly, leaving him to contemplate the cross of its intersecting panels, the closest he would come to religious meditation that Sabbath.

When she returned her color was high, her eyes were sparkling. She looked as pleased as a child, but it was a woman who took his proffered arm with stateliness and grace.

They meandered down to the shore and walked along the beach while he tried to think of what to say. He was not sure where the interests of a young girl lay, nor had he any experience with serving girls. One could not equate her with a waterfront woman or with a daughter of a Rockford family, sedately introduced at Meeting. Finally, he seized on his sisters.

"I have a sister just about your age," he began experimentally, wondering how old she really was. Young, he was sure, but with a body like that, surely none too young. And with eyes that had behind them a certain wisdom and a measure of sadness.

"Ellen tells me you have several sisters," she replied. "And that you take care of them all."

"That's true," he said. "But I don't know them very well. I'm always away, you see, taking care of them."

She laughed as though this were the most amusing thing she had heard all morning. The breeze carried the laugh away.

"Actually, Miss Molly, you could help me very much in regard to one of my sisters."

"Oh?"

"Well, I am working in Europe now, as first mate. My sister Judith will be married this fall and I have promised her a set of English china. But my other sister will need a gift as well—a small one, to be sure—but since I don't know her very well, I don't know what would give her pleasure. Can you tell me what pleases a young girl?"

"Color," she said promptly. "Anything that has color—especially if it can be worn—that would please her, I'm sure." She picked up a shell, its delicate lavenders and purples glowing in her hand. "Like this!" she exclaimed and then slipped it into his hand. "Tell me, Master Merrick, what sort of goods does your new company carry?"

"My company?" he asked stupidly.

"Yes. Your new one. The people you are now sailing for. Are they much different from the old? Is it difficult for you to switch over to their lines of thinking?"

He thought her question very astute and wondered how she knew enough to ask it. "Just now foodstuffs are in terrific demand. The French nation, in particular, is hungry; their revolution doesn't feed them, any more than ours did. And England craves cotton. Being located southerly, Fuller deals more directly with cotton and rice than my Boston owners did, and I have to learn more about that, but trading itself always operates the same old way: buy low, sell high!"

"How much you must know!" she said admiringly. "Here you are not yet a captain, but you already know everything you need, and the subject is so complex. It is hard for one uninitiated, as I am, to understand it at all. For instance, Master Merrick, Mrs. Warden tells me that France needs rice, yet does not like ours from Carolina. So we must grow another kind that suits its tastes better, even though she is greatly in of it need now. Is this so?"

It was a pleasure to talk to a young woman so well informed, who did not ask simply to get a man talking, but who already knew so much and wanted, instead, to understand the deeper ramifications. By the time he told her about the French market for rice, the conversation had swung to his own career, the ships he had known and how he hoped to be a captain soon. The ascent of the sun told him that there was some danger of Molly's being discovered absent from the house. And, of course, he must make haste to catch the packet before the tide fell . . . .

"I've always wondered if mate is not the loneliest position of all," she was saying. "For you don't have the glory of command to compensate for your responsibilities. And you have no companionship, being higher in rank than the seamen, and lower than the captain. All the fault falls on your head, should there be any, and none of the praise, which the captains get."

"That's true enough," he said. "No one loves to be mate. Yet no one ever became captain without having filled that position and done a top-notch job of it."

"I think you must be very strong in order to endure it," she observed firmly. "Very strong." When they turned onto the path that led to town, she took his arm and walked faster. "I fear, Master Merrick, that I shall have to hurry. It would be unseemly were I not resting quietly when my mistress returns."

Her words were demure, but her smile was merry.

"You have been good to come out with me, Miss Molly," he said humbly. "I have enjoyed this morning more than any other I can remember."

"As did I." They were approaching the back of the house now. "I heard you say that you are returning to Boston this afternoon, then on to Baltimore and out again. May your journey be successful. I am sure you'll find the captain's berth you hope for. No one could fill it better than you. Many captains come and go in our house. A servant sees a lot, and I can assure you that you match them in all respects, and you excel in most. But I wish you luck, nonetheless."

At the door, she held out her hand.

Surprised at first, he returned the lavender shell she had given him. Dropping it in her pocket, she reached out again and clasped his hand firmly, warm and strong within his own, although she was so small.

"Thank you," he said simply. "Luck is something no seafarer can do without." He turned away, toward town and the wharf.

"Good-bye to you, and Godspeed," she called.

Yelling at her with all to hear, he felt like a fool but there was no choice. "I'll be returning this fall. May I see you then?"

"You may!" she called back, that clear voice easily heard. "I'll look forward to it."

He ran in order to put distance between himself and the Wardens' house, lest the churchgoers return and find him, and lest the packet should leave without him. I believe she likes me, he thought as he loped along. She likes me! I am sure of it!

The packet was just casting off as he leaped for the deck. The little schooner squeezed out, leaving only inches to spare between the hull and the bottom of the channel. The depth would change, storm to storm. Just now it favored the suit of Elijah Merrick for the hand of Molly Deems, so that although he was late, it was deep enough.

He took this fortunate timing as an omen. He found a spot on the packet where he could compose a letter.

Mistress Elizabeth Warden
The county Rode
Yarmouth, Mass

My esteemed Frend, he wrote, and paused. He looked at it critically, for even a salutation was now of grave importance. Was Mrs. Warden his esteemed friend? Surely she knew how to spell the word. He did not! She

would think him ignorant! When he thought about it, was it proper to
write to her at all? That was the real question, was it not?
He decided to disregard it and plunged ahead.

During my last visit with you I was remind'd of your serving
girl, Molly Deems, and remember your mentioning once that you,
yourselfe, were instructing her. I take this to meen that she is your
ward? As such, I request your permission to call upon her when I
next come home. Not knowing the exact relation of her in your hous,
I sho'd not like to make such a request if you deem it untoward, thus
I leeve the matter in your hands for guidanse.

Once in Boston Harbor, he jumped out and hurried along the wharf
to find the New York packet, which would stop in Yarmouth on its way
south. He tipped the captain to make certain the letter would be safely
delivered. There would be, of course, no answer; not for months would
he know whether Elizabeth Warden would consent to his suit of Molly
Deems. Because of his great respect for her, Elijah would not woo Molly
without her permission, but if Fuller were true to his promise, he soon
would be able to present her with a suitor capable of supporting a wife.
The voyage after this one was his, if all went well. The company would
again send him to England with cotton, rice and tobacco, to see how he
discharged his responsibilities. This time, it would be up to him to fill
the hold profitably for the return trip. If he invested wisely, he could
expect a corner in European trade, staying out longer, earning more.

So long had he been anticipating this, that now it did not even
elate him; instead, it was no different from word from the harbormas-
ter that he might commence a journey. For his destination now was
Molly Deems, and through his promotion, he would be in a position
to have her. Molly Deems was all that mattered. The rest—how to
earn a living—once his only goal—was now just a means to an end.

He knew he would have to make many gestures of courtship.
His letter to Mrs. Warden was the first of those gestures. He sup-

posed Molly would have to be given time to make up her mind—yet he felt he knew, really knew, that with the passing of only one morning he and Molly had linked hands invisibly. It seemed to him wondrous that this had happened. And it seemed equally wondrous that no one else in the world knew that it had! Surely it must show on his face and in his manner. But upon arriving in Baltimore and talking with Benjamin Fuller, he realized that no one sensed the difference in him; no one understood he was not the same man he had been before.

Well, thought Elijah, I must seem no different. But I am.

It was as though Molly Deems had brought him to life. As though he was stronger than he'd ever been, could reach further than he ever had. His quest for a dependable living for his mother and sisters and brother, important as it was, now seemed insipid compared to the new, gleaming and sparkling reality of Molly. Now his old dreams were simply eclipsed by the single fact of which he was certain: he loved her.

✦∞ 5 ∞✦

It was November when he returned to the late Cape autumn. Fortunately, his visit coincided with his sister's wedding, and he had sent a letter ahead to his family that they should expect him for the celebration. But he went first to the Yarmouth Inn, from whence he sent a message to Elizabeth Warden and awaited its answer. When the boy returned with a face flushed from running, Elijah paid him well.

Come at once, I shall be glad to receive you.
E. W.

It was but a short walk to the house, and Mistress Warden herself opened the door. "Hello again, my young friend." She drew him into the parlor. "I thought, under the circumstances, that I'd best be the one to greet you."

Elijah blushed helplessly. He was about to sail as captain of his ship, commanding men and the sea and commerce, yet he was as a boy now, inexperienced and unsure.

"Let's get right to the point, Elijah," Mrs. Warden said. "I'm glad our Molly has struck your fancy. She is a sweet girl, and a very sensible one, considering her age. And intelligent. And pretty. But I have no idea how suitable you might be for her—and I am especially unsatisfied as to whether she is appropriate for you."

"Appropriate?" Elijah asked weakly.

"She is but a servant, you must remember."

"I remember, too, your saying that nothing is permanent in this new nation of ours. I think you said that the position of a person one day will no longer determine his position the next."

"Indeed I did!" Mrs. Warden declared. "Your memory is good; the simple fact that you are interested in her—enough to tell me so— is indication enough that it's true. But there is the other side of it, Elijah—the side your people are bound to take. I can hardly believe that your good mother would look kindly upon your seeing—let alone courting—a serving girl."

"That's a problem, no doubt about it," Elijah confessed. "And yet would you think me insufferable if I told you I believe I have certain prerogatives? That my own well-being, in this case, perhaps comes before my mother's?"

"Hardly insufferable! You are a dutiful son who has taken responsibility early in life. Now you've come to the point where some of its rewards can be enjoyed. Certainly you have the prerogative! If Molly Deems can give you happiness, then, as far as I am concerned, I wish you well. I would only remind you that a suit for Molly will involve some difficulties that you might not know about. And I am obligated to point out that there are other girls you might now be in a position to appreciate whom you haven't considered before."

He smiled. "Perhaps I could appreciate others," he said. "But I have never even noticed them. But Molly—Mistress Deems, I mean— she has . . . awakened me . . . shown me a future I've never dreamed of."

"So I see," Mrs. Warden mused. "You are quite taken with her. Well," she pronounced abruptly, as though closing a book on her meanderings, "I am, so to speak, Molly's guardian—she is only sixteen, and I am responsible for her."

Sixteen. The same age as his sister Debby. But Molly did not seem young. She was a woman, mature, ripe as a woman was ripe, ready, as a woman was ready.

"If, after knowing her better, you decide this is the girl you want, I'll do everything I can to help. But be sure to ask her about how she comes to be here. You'll need that information before telling your good mother about her. I've given her leave to use my back garden. The two of you can meet there. Until you have declared yourself and she has accepted you, that is the only place you may meet. Is that clear?"

"Perfectly."

"I'll call her now, since you are here. But in the future you'll have to come in the mid-afternoon, when our labors are the least taxing and we can best spare her. I can't have you for supper and the night—it would be awkward, so you will have to find somewhere else to stay. The Yarmouth Inn, perhaps. Sundays, of course, we are at Meeting . . . ." Mrs. Warden glanced at him quickly, as though a connection had suddenly come to her mind, and she laughed. "I have enjoyed my William Penn," she chuckled. "Go to the garden now, Elijah, with my blessing."

He nodded and circled around the house, through the formal garden to the one behind it and waited for Molly on an abominably hard marble bench. It was a still day, for November, but with a distinct chill on the edges. His own clammy hands and forehead, cooling in the chill, made him uncomfortable. He stirred unhappily.

How could he woo anybody in a damned garden in November?

The place encircled a young tree, what kind he could not be sure, for Captain Warden had traveled the world over and there was no telling what he might have brought back with him. Large stones were here and there at random, a practice Elijah had never seen, since most stones he knew of were immediately hauled into boundary fences. Flat slates provided a meandering pathway among the rocks and around the centered tree and were cluttered now with windblown leaves.

"It's lovely in the summer," her clear voice said, and he leaped to his feet. She stood where the path from the more formal garden met this one. How long she had been there, regarding his backside, he had no way of knowing. He went to her, searching for signs that would tell him she was glad to see him.

Her gaze in return was steady, her head high, and they faced each other for a long while, simply looking. Suddenly the garden seemed warmer and more pleasant. He burst into a smile, realizing that he must look very somber, standing there and staring at her.

"Let's sit down, shall we?" He led her to the bench, sweating in earnest now. How could she be only sixteen, he thought. She is not a child. She is a woman!

She folded her hands and looked steadily at her lap.

"Miss Molly," he began, and she looked at him quickly. "Has Mrs. Warden told you why I've come?"

Blushing, she looked down again. At the sight of her discomfiture he became more confident. He took her hand, and said softly, "I am unable to cope with this situation as the etiquette of it requires. I have reason to believe that you once found my company desirable. It is my hope that you still do. I should like to impose my company on you more often, and I have asked Mrs. Warden if that would be permissible. She said that it was. Oh Molly"—and his voice became urgent—"Miss Molly, I have never met anyone like you, and I should like to see you as often as I can. Will you permit it?"

She waited for a long moment, then put her free hand on his. "I'm not sure what etiquette requires of me either! But you may as well know I should be delighted." Her green eyes lit, sparkling the way he remembered so well. "I will certainly permit you to keep me company."

Her smile told him that she was mocking herself—a serving girl giving him, a captain, permission to court her, granting the favor he requested as though she were a born-and-bred lady.

He searched his pocket for the small box he had brought.

"I thought of our walk on the beach when I saw this," he told her. "If you will accept it, perhaps in my absence it will bring that walk to your mind, too."

It was a pendant of small enameled flowers that were colored in shades of lavender reminiscent of the shell she had picked up.

She held it in her hand as she had held the shell, cupping it carefully, and then looked up at him, her eyes meeting his in deep understanding. It was as though they had always known each other, and he took both her hands in his own with the necklace nestled in the deep center. She seemed to him fragile, lovely as the shell had been lovely. He thought if he could not take her in his arms, he would perish. But he would have to wait until a suitable time.

He helped her fasten the necklace, then talked a little of his trip on *Chesapeake,* and at length about his promotion and about the French silk he had bought and successfully sold in Baltimore, about Fuller's intention to open an office in Boston. It seemed to him meaningless talk, but he strove manfully on, working up to his real intent.

"My own luck in speculative buying gives me some reason to think I'll do well," he told her. "If things go as I expect them to, I should soon be in a good position to control my own destiny. And then, Miss Molly, I should like to take you to my home to meet my mother and my family."

"To your home." She had said little as he'd talked, but now it was her turn. "To meet your mother. That would make things . . . between us . . . very definite, would it not?" she asked, and he was struck by her directness, her lack of subterfuge.

He pawed at the paving stones. "Yes, of course. I . . . forgive my impulsiveness."

"I didn't say I minded their being definite, Elijah."

They were silent for a while, and the November day surrounded them in pre-winter brightness and quietude while he waited.

"Forgive me if I speak plainly, but I must. In all the world I think no one speaks plainly to anyone about the secrets of his heart. But since we have little time and no place else to go, we may be an exception." She picked and chose her words carefully. "You know nothing of me, and I think before you are ready to declare yourself publicly, you ought to. It could make a difference."

"Nothing would make a difference."

"Perhaps you ought to know who my mother was."

"I don't care who she was."

"And my father."

"I don't care who he was either."

"And why I came to be at the Wardens'."

"I only care that you are here, else I might not have met you."

In agitation, she jumped to her feet, and he followed her as she began to walk the path around the rocks. He caught up with her and took her hand. Her eyes were full of tears when she turned to him, her hand was cold.

"Molly." His voice was tender. "Molly, are you afraid?"

At this, tears spilled over, but she did not wipe them away and only stood quietly, too proud to tell him that, yes, she was afraid.

"My dear, there is nothing to alarm you. I do want to know about your mother and father and how you came to be in your present circumstance. I would like very much to know. But, Molly, do not confound that with caring. I do not care at all. It matters not the least. Molly," he whispered, "you are so beautiful. I worship you."

Her eyes closed for a moment, and then, still holding his hand, she led him along the path. "Mrs. Warden gave me permission to walk here on hot nights when my room in the attic wouldn't cool off," she said. "The paths are like revelations. By that stone will be, in their season, small tulips from Holland. By that one, a wild flower from Maine. Yonder, a mass of little blue things. There yellow. She lets me use it any time now. Mrs. Warden has been so very kind. She rescued me from a man named Seth Adams; my mother was Seth's woman. He bargained for her when she had no place to go, and he owned her as much as if he had bought her." And she told him as much of the story as she knew or could remember.

They walked in silence for a time.

"I was bound out, in a sense, myself," Elijah said after a while. "We were so poor that when a friend offered Mother a bed for me in exchange for work, she was delighted and accepted on the spot. One mouth less made a big difference. And I lived on charity for six years. Are we really so different, you and I? Circumstances pushed us hither and yon. We have both known want, both been dependent on others."

"Elijah, you are a kind man. A very kind man."

"I am not trying to be," he protested. "I only want to make you understand —it doesn't matter to me. I've been poor myself—there's nothing shameful in it. Your mother couldn't help herself any more than mine could—but fate put them in different places at different times."

"I think your mother would not care to be discussed as though she were on the same footing as Seth Adams' woman."

"No doubt she would not. All I mean to say is that I will not have you consider yourself an unworthy person because of a decision of your mother's. Especially a decision she couldn't help making."

She took both his hands in her own. "You make me feel as though I can start over!"

"Already you have done the same thing for me."

"Oh?" She frowned in an effort to understand. "How is that?"

"I don't know." He smiled. "All I know is that it feels like I'm able to see myself and the whole world with new eyes. As though I am awake to everything, living with all my senses. I've never had time, before. You have done this for me, and if I can cause you to take a fresh look at yourself, then I am very glad." He led her back to the bench, sat her down, knelt before her. "Do you think that you'd always feel fresh, with a new start in life, Molly, if you were betrothed to me? Could you consent to marry me? I promise you, I'll see to it that no one makes you unhappy because of your life's trials."

Her eyes were soft, shining, full of wonder. "What a strong man you are," she said quietly, "to know your own mind so well and to pursue its conclusions so steadfastly. No wonder your company wants you to command one of their fleet! You are sure, Elijah, of what you are doing?"

"I am very sure!" he exclaimed. He became subdued as he realized that he was taking advantage of her; her innocence and inexperience were a heavy responsibility, but one he was eager to take on! "I very much—oh, Molly—very much want to secure your favor. Are you willing now or some time soon to declare yourself?"

"I am willing," she said softly. "I am ready now."

Lest he burst out with an undignified whoop, he jumped to his feet. "We'll talk to Mrs. Warden then," he said, pulling her along with him toward the house. "I have reason to think that she'll be in the keeping room, suffering eyestrain, and completely chilled from standing by the window watching her back garden!"

They did, indeed, find her there.

"So you've made up your mind and got her consent already, Elijah?" Mrs. Warden asked archly. "I had thought it would take a little longer."

"'Twas that marble bench that did it, ma'am," he told her. "We couldn't bear to sit on it any more often than necessary."

"A wedding cannot be accomplished so quickly, I am warning you," Mrs. Warden said. "Molly is too young and you haven't served as a captain yet. You still have to prove yourself. But certainly I can appreciate your not wishing to use the garden any longer than you have to! Very well. You may call here, inside, since now you are betrothed, during the afternoon hours that I mentioned before. And you may sit in the parlor when I'm not using it, as long as I am asked beforehand. I really can't think of anything else I can do for you. Time must take its passage; your future must be more firmly secured. I leave it to you." She kissed his cheek and embraced Molly.

"You both look very, very happy. You gladden my heart." She turned to Elijah. "I will excuse you now, young man. You have dominated our scene for long enough today! Go on home, to secure your future there."

As he walked toward the Inn to find a horse, the midday brightness disappeared and a wind took over from the breeze. He held the picture of Molly's face tightly to his heart—the picture of Molly's hands with his lavender gift clasped in them, the look of Molly's eyes when she told him of her mother. He was moved, very moved, by the plight of the hapless Hannah Deems. And alongside this emotion was joy, for there was no doubt in his mind—no doubt at all now—that Molly was his—that he had her heart as securely as she had his—and he reveled in this supreme moment. He would rent a horse for his visit home; he would ride back to Yarmouth in order to return the animal, at which time he would see Molly again. Yes! Was it not a wonderful thing, to have money enough to rent a horse? Was it not a lovely thing, to have wooed and won so beautiful and sweet a maiden? Was not life fine?

After making arrangements for his mount, he slipped into the tavern to consider the task of presenting his mother with the wife of his choice. Knowing Molly's background as he knew it now, he realized his mother would not approve. He had not yet fully established his authority at home. It would be difficult, very difficult, if his mother had heard of Seth Adams. Perhaps she had not! Perhaps that difficulty wouldn't even be mentioned. He thought about Molly, and glowed; he tripped upon the image of his mother, and became despondent. At a small table near the door, he sipped his rum contemplatively, his thoughts alternating between joy and dread.

The more he drank, the higher grew his elevations and the lower his depressions until he was a fit companion for the other loiterers in the place. They gathered him in, ordered supper for themselves and him, and more rum; they played blackjack and ordered more rum, they sang songs and threw darts and drank more rum.

One of them turned to the others. "Men," he said, exceedingly wise by that mellow time. "Men, I perceive that this fellow Merrick has for himself a problem so deep of nature that it will take the counsel of ourselves, and only that counsel, to solve it."

Elijah stared, astonished. "How'd you know?"

"I am clever," his new friend said. "Very clever. Ask these fine gentlemen. Gentlemen," he addressed the others, "am I not clever?"

"Very," they agreed, signaling the innkeeper for more spirits. "If you have a problem you can do no better than to ask advice of Tom

Barslow, here. He has advised us all, one time or another. Out with it! What are friends for, if not help in times of distress?"

"Being on the sea so much," Elijah confessed, "I am unaccustomed to having friends to tell my troubles to—faces change, port to port—the higher a man gets in command, the fewer intimates he has."

"But you are on land now," they observed. "No captains here."

"All fellows together. Jolly ones, too."

"Men," Elijah told them, "it is a matter of the heart."

"Of course it is," they assured him. "There is no other."

"I have found the woman of my dreams."

"A lucky man!"

"Could I but find one, too!"

"I did, once," said Barslow. "But she was already wed."

"Ah."

"Oh, it didn't bother me. But it bothered her husband."

"And herself?"

"Hush," said another of them. "This is not fit talk for the ears of a young man who has found his first love."

"Is she your first?"

"She is."

"Is she—ah—winsome?"

"Very much so."

"And otherwise?"

"Otherwise what?"

"Otherwise—knowledgeable—er, willing—ah, desirous to please?"

"Sir!" Elijah staggered to his feet. "I hope I do not understand the implications of those words."

"Ah, untarnished."

The group sighed and sank into meditation on untarnished womanhood. Elijah sat back down.

At last one of them asked, "What, then, is the trouble?"

"My mother."

"Your mother!"

"I think my heart's desire would not be her own."

"Unfortunate. But does it matter?"

"The young lady would have to spend much more time with my mother than with me. If my mother is set against it, she could make my sweetheart miserable."

"Yes," they assented. "That she could."

"And then my marriage would suffer."

They mulled it over for a while. "Most likely," they agreed.

"But why?" asked Tom Barslow, advisor to them all. "Why would your mother not approve? Aside from the fact that mothers never do?"

"I believe she would desire a young woman of background . . . propriety . . . breeding."

"Your mother's a Tory, eh?"

"Still loyal to the old country?"

"No, no," Elijah protested. "She is a good woman, hardworking, a veritable female patriot—all of that. But we have been poor. Poor a long time; now we will rise, I think, and she would like to have a daughter-in-law she considers—ah—suitable to the station in life we well may occupy." The rum, he noticed, made him eloquent.

"Ah, the young captain!"

"Goin' up in the world, Cap'n?"

"Indeed I am," said Elijah, smacking his tumbler down on the table. "Indeed I am."

"I'll drink to that," said one, and did so.

"The night is young," proposed another. "I suggest this party move to Hallett's Tavern. Halfway between here and the home of Captain Merrick. The closer we are to his abode, the easier it will be for the execution of our decision. If we make one."

"Good idea!" declared Barslow. "And right on his own doorstep, in Rockford, is the finest in these parts—Ben Snow's Inn of the Golden Ox. Wherein we may all find lodging, should the journey back prove too arduous."

"My purse will not take me so far," one of them was heard to say.

"Fine fellows, friends all," Elijah declared. "It sounds splendid to me! Should any of you find yourselves in need of funds by the time we reach Rockford, I myself will pay for a pallet on your behalf. The support of friends is my greatest need now. Greatest, I say. I am in your debt."

"Hurrah!" they bellowed, and trooped out to Hallett's, Elijah on his rented nag, the others riding close by him, full of rum and affection.

At Hallett's the evening was only just beginning; they seated themselves around a large table and swapped tall tales, took some throws at the dart board hanging on the barren and pock marked wall. It was not until they reached the Golden Ox that they seriously considered Elijah's difficulty in a meeting brought to order by Barslow.

"Hear, hear!" he barked. "We are at present in the town of Rockford."

"Fine town."

"My own house is across the road," Elijah told them, waving vaguely.

"I'll drink to that!" They all did.

"Now has come the time to advise our friend on his course of action, as we agreed to do. The hour is at hand. The trump sounds."

"What trump?"

"Are we going to play whist?"

"We have to make a decision, you ninnies," Barslow derided them. "Make a judgment. That trump. Trumpet. Calling for action."

They shook their heads at such eloquence.

"Let's go with him to tell his mother about the young lady," suggested one. "There's safety in numbers."

"We could leave him here and go to her ourselves. We could tell him what she said when we return."

"I think he ought to go alone," another slurred. "We could rest until he comes back. We'd be right here, to receive his news. Or bury the remains." And the author of that suggestion leaned his head on the table and fell asleep.

"Unless he goes himself, he suggests that he is afraid of her," Barslow announced.

Elijah, by now quite drunk, waved a vague hand. "Men," he said, "I am not afraid of her." In his stupor, he was awed by the brilliance of his next insight. "Not only am I not afraid of her, I believe just the opposite is true. She is afraid of me."

"Hear, hear!"

"Keep going, Elijah!"

"I have been my mother's sole support for many years. How, therefore, could I be afraid of her? It must be the other way around. The tail is wagging the dog."

"What dog?"

"I don't see no dog."

"Elijah, my boy." His counselor pulled his chair closer and flung an arm around Elijah's shoulders, disregarding the ongoing discussion about where the dog might be found. "Why have you not said so before? You have no problem, Elijah, no problem at all. You just march in and tell your Mama you have found the woman of your choice—and that's all there is to it. It's all in how you do it. How you say it." He pinched Elijah's cheek fondly. "Just tell her."

"Tell her?" Elijah asked, his nose an inch distant from the other. "Do I just say, 'Mother, I want to get married'?"

"Hell, no," Barslow cried. "All, all wrong. You're a captain, remember?"

"Yes," Elijah said. "I am now. Never was one before, though. Never have had a ship of my own. Haven't had any practice."

"Well, you just remember this, my boy," said his friend. "This captain business is all an act. A man on the quarterdeck is on the stage, and the crew is his audience. Just so at home. In this case, the audience is your mother. You say, 'Mother, I am to be married.'"

"That's all?"

"Substantially. You tell her, you don't ask."

"Bully her?"

"Absolutely."

"Just walk in and say it?"

"That's all."

"By God, I will."

Those in the group who were not asleep rose to cheer him and clap him on the shoulder. "Go to it, Cap'n," one of them said. "Then come on back. We'll toast your success. By then all of us will be awake, we guarantee."

"Drinks on me," Elijah assured them. "If I return successful."

"We'll pray for ye, lad."

He forgot his coat, marching out through the tables of the tavern, upsetting several chairs as he went. The keeping room lights of his house across the road were still burning. This was strange, he thought. Too late for his mother and sisters to be burning oil and candles. But he was glad for it lest he get lost in the darkness. He stumbled through the yard and dimly saw the outlines of the addition he had caused to be built for his brother.

The addition! If his present mission were fruitful, he and Molly would most likely take it, and Jon wouldn't be able to use the room at all. It seemed unfair, and he stopped to think it over. Poor Jon had received so little in life. Drunkenly he thought of the spoiled and rotten fruit he and his brother had brought back from Surinam. It was enough to make a grown man cry! But he did not. Compromise, he reminded himself. We must all compromise. He was not sure of the limits of his own willingness to do so. But he would find out soon enough.

He approached the kitchen door, hammered on its panels before letting himself in. The group gathered sedately around the fire was halfway to its feet, the men reaching for their weapons before they recognized him.

"Elijah!"

"The packet isn't due until tomorrow morning! How did you get home?"

In front of the fire were his uncles from Eastham and their wives along with his sisters, his brother, and his mother.

"What's going on?" he asked somewhat thickly. "Why's everyone here?"

"For Judith's wedding, Son, why else?" his mother said, eyeing him warily. She had never seen him when he did not have complete command of himself.

"Oh, yes, I must admit it had slipped my mind," Elijah confessed, growing confused as this news sprang up to divert him from his task. Wedding. Judith's wedding.

"You forgot!" his mother accused. "Elijah, how dare you? We've all been sitting here waiting for you, thinking you must be making your way home somehow, as you said you would, and all the time it had slipped your mind? How could it?"

He gathered himself. "Easily," he said airily. "I have just become betrothed myself. It tends to make a body forget almost anything."

"Betrothed?" His mother was stunned.

"Splendid!" roared his Uncle Elkanah, rising to shake his hand. Uncle Jeremiah slapped his back; Jonathan pounded his arm "Wonderful," they cried. "High time you settled into a hearth of your own."

"But who is she?" his mother asked, looking bewildered. She cast her mind over all unmarried girls in Rockford and could not think of any he had even met. Clearly he had found one from somewhere else.

"First, a toast," Elijah said. "Surely we must have some rum somewhere to toast me—and my sister as well."

"I would judge you have done considerable toasting already," his mother observed wryly.

Her brothers laughed. "How often does one get betrothed?" they chided. The rum was found and the men broke into it, leaving the women to watch and his sister Judith to wring her hands in vexation at having lost control of her undivided moment of glory.

"Her name is Molly Deems," Elijah told them. "You do not know her, but you will agree with me, when you do meet her, that I am a lucky man indeed."

"Who are her family?" his mother asked.

"Where does she live?"

"Is she pretty?" his sister Debby asked.

"She is a beauty! She lives in Yarmouth. She is a serving girl."

The silence of the room grew more and more profound as the people in it tried to think of something to say. Elijah rose grandly, if unsteadily, to his feet.

"I have seen women of every race," he announced. "I have met women from every country this nation knows of, and some it does not." This was not strictly true, but he was undeterred. "I have met the daughters of respected families and daughters of some families who are not, all of whom were willing—if not eager—to wed." This was not true either, but he liked the sound of it. "And I can tell you that none of them can compare in any way to this young woman. If you will agree to judge her only when you come to know her, you will agree that she is equal to—nay—far above, any person of her age and sex that you will ever be privileged to meet. With the possible exception," he added, bowing low as he dared, "of the maidens in this room. And now I must beg your leave to depart. I have left friends at the Golden Ox who are celebrating with me, and I promised to return to them. Surely," he added, turning to his brother and uncles in what he suddenly perceived as a masterstroke, "surely you will accompany me and drink to the happiness of my future bride and myself."

"Our rum is gone," Jonathan observed. "Wait till I get my coat."

"Jon!" his mother cried. His brothers shot stern glances at their wives, demolishing any possible resistance, and reached for their own apparel.

"Surely we will drink to you and the young lady, Elijah," his Uncle Elkanah said kindly.

Elijah led them back to the tavern without another look at the women of his family. True to the promise of his new friends, those who had slumbered now awakened, rejoicing to see reinforcement to their party, which they proceeded to encourage into their own condition. It was a profitable night for the innkeeper, Benjamin Snow, who by now welcomed Elijah home as heartily as the rest.

It was darkest night when they returned to his mother's house, having bid their new friends the fondest of farewells.

"Almost makes me wish I was young again. How 'bout you, El?" Uncle Jeremiah said.

"Aye," Uncle Elkanah said softly, then cursed as he ran into Jonathan's new back door. "I think we're home."

"Never expected to enjoy a weddin' this much. Mighty obliged to you, Elijah."

"Thank my friends," Elijah said carelessly, all his energy consumed in trying to walk upright.

"Where'll we sleep?"

"Right here in my new room, where else?" exclaimed Jonathan. "We should have brought your friends from the inn, Elijah."

"Good fellows."

"They are indeed." Feeling their way about, the four men found blankets and rekindled the banked fire on Jonathan's hearth. Elijah was given the bed since he was the most recently favored by fortune. The others slept on the floor, as near to the source of heat as they could without scorching themselves.

"When is Judith's wedding?" Elijah remembered to ask, but did not hear the answer as he slid into a spinning vortex of sleep.

The men wakened at varying times the following morning, but they defensively stretched and napped and splashed water on their tight foreheads until all were simultaneously fit to face the ladies waiting in the keeping room.

"Reminds me of the army," Uncle Jeremiah remarked as he watched Elijah struggle with his head and his boots. "Haven't kept the company of men since."

"Let's not talk about the war," Uncle Elkanah said grimly. "Let's talk about Elijah's party. Very enjoyable," he said to Elijah. "Your aunt won't approve of a man my age roistering in a public house, but it was worth the badgering I'll get!"

"Well," Elijah said firmly, despite the pounding of his head, "no one is going to badger me!"

"Have you been troubled by your mother?" asked Uncle Jeremiah. "For all the hard times your family has had, she has always struck me as a patient person. She was ever thus. Don't you think so, Elkanah?"

"Aye," Uncle Elkanah said. "Yet, I believe Elijah has perceived the situation differently."

"There are different ways to badger a man," Elijah remarked.

"Hear, hear," Jonathan cried. "And he not yet wed!"

"I mean my mother no injustice," Elijah said. "She is a good woman. But very careful, to a fault. Very conservative. I'm sure she'll consider the young lady of my choice to be inferior to us. And if I allow her to persist in her thinking, then Molly will occupy an inferior position in our house. I can't allow that."

"He's right," Jonathan said. "Our mother is fairly inflexible in some regards. It's better to set it all straight from the beginning."

"What would you think about supervising more building?" Elijah asked him.

"More?"

"I have it in mind to add a few feet onto the west side of the house. Enough to make a chamber in the front for Molly and me. If we run it clear to the back of the house, the keeping room will be bigger, which I'm sure will please Mother, and this space would still be yours. Otherwise, Molly and I would have to requisition it."

"You are too kind." Tears filled Jon's eyes.

Elijah flung an arm across his brother's shoulders, and the bond of the sons in defense against their mother was sealed.

The men delayed until their hunger drove them into the kitchen world of women who were so absorbed in the details of the wedding feast and the adornment of Judith, that hardly a reproving glance came their way. Nothing was said of Elijah's announcement or of the male abandonment the night before. Not until the following day, with the wedding done and the company gone, when Elijah, in pursuit of his original initiative, flung down the gauntlet.

"Mother, I would have a word with you."

She looked up at him quickly. "Let's go in to the parlor," she said.

He followed her there, where they would be out of Debby's hearing.

"I know I didn't behave in a gentlemanly manner the night before last," Elijah apologized. "I wanted to tell you that I'm sorry about it."

His mother sniffed, and he hurried on. The time had come. "I think it only fair to tell you more about my beloved Molly."

"Yes?"

"She is a serving girl, as I said last night. In the house of Abel and Elizabeth Warden. I met her when I was there visiting John last spring. She is in Mrs. Warden's care."

"You speak as though the young woman were their ward, not their servant."

"She is in a position of a ward at present," he told her. "A responsibility the Wardens undertook voluntarily, I might add. Molly's mother was given to an undesirable person, and she begged Mrs. Warden to protect her child. Which Mrs. Warden did."

"What you do mean, 'given'?" his mother asked suspiciously.

"She was given to a war veteran, who was passing though Dartmouth, where she lived at the time. To look after his house in Barnstable. She had nowhere else to go, as I understand it."

"Elijah, surely you are not talking of Seth Adams' woman. The one who drowned herself in the bay."

"Yes," Elijah said. "That's the one."

His mother looked at him in uncomprehending horror. "You would do this to us?" she whispered. "You would bring that woman's child into our home? It's common knowledge that she was no better than a harlot, Elijah."

"And how is this common knowledge?"

"Seth Adams himself was common knowledge," his mother said. "He was never concerned with cleanliness. What else would he want a woman for?"

"That sounds like speculation."

His mother shrugged. "Speculation or not, everyone knows."

"I had no knowledge of it."

She smiled patronizingly. "You haven't been here, my dear. There are many things you don't know about. You wouldn't even begin to know what it would be like if you married that girl. Our lives would never be the same again. We will lose all our friends. I could never again look a townsman in the eye. Probably she has tricked you, ensnared you. And you, innocent that you are, fell into her trap. Oh, Elijah, how could you?"

She finished in a wail, and he watched her silently as she wept for a while. When she saw he made no move to relieve her distress, Mother Merrick dried her eyes and squared her shoulders. "Perhaps you didn't know about her mother or didn't understand. Now you do. Surely you can see the girl's unsuitability."

"I don't understand at all," he said. "You are willing to pass judgment on a person you have never seen, based on gossip about a person you never knew. I am not interested in the goings-on in other people's houses, and I am not interested in the reputation of a man who doesn't even live in our town. I am interested in the misfortune of a woman left to shift for herself, especially in the daughter of that woman. Molly has told me of her mother's circumstances; they are tragic, but that is all. They are tragic for her, Mother, not for us."

"It will be tragic for us if you insist on linking her name with ours. Of all the women you could have chosen, Elijah, why this one? There are dozens of comely maidens all around us. I'm sure I can arrange introductions, if you'd stay home long enough."

"My choice is made, Mother. You wonder how to meet the eyes of our townsmen? With your head held high, that's how. You are never to talk to a soul—anyone—about your judgment on Molly's mother or even Seth Adams. You are never to behave toward her—anywhere—in any way that implies belittlement. Give no one a chance to tell you their opinion. Tell no one yours. Do you understand?"

"Do you understand," she asked in despair, "that you are consigning me to loneliness, to isolation for the rest of my life? I will lose my friends; no one will speak to me."

"Then you would do well to become Molly's friend," he said to her, "since you are so sure you will have no others."

More tears flowed.

"Mother, your friends will remain true if you hold your head high. But they will not if they believe you are ashamed and consider yourself inferior to them because of the woman your son married. And believe me, you will have nothing to be ashamed of. We will live in style one day, you, along with Molly and me."

"Yes, yes." She sighed. "Yes. One day."

He reached her hand and found it cold. It pained him to cause her distress, yet elated at having mastered her, he plunged on. "You'll like her, Mother. She is different—better than—any woman anywhere. And you will be proud of her. Not only is she beautiful, but very smart, too!" Pausing, he looked around the room. "We're going to enlarge the house. Add twelve feet to the other side, front to back. That will give Molly and me a chamber of our own and make the kitchen much bigger."

"I suppose I am to continue sleeping in the loft."

Elijah rose and bowed. "Unless you'd like the borning room," he said, and left her before she could make further comment.

His sister Debby glanced at him as he crossed the kitchen and let himself into Jon's room to gather his belongings. He sat on the edge of the cot and stared into the middle distance. It was not easy to dispossess a mother, and he was tired and oppressed by it. And yet he was sure—very sure—that if his mother could find it in herself to carry the situation with dignity, Molly would do the rest. With the passing of time, few would remember and none would care where she had come from and what her mother's circumstances had been. Surely a man owed respect to his mother, but how far did the obligation go when it came to his own happiness, with his life ahead of him and his own well-being in the balance? He shook his head sadly and packed his satchel, returned to the keeping room where his family was waiting for him.

"My dear," Mother said. "I was just telling your sister about your plans to enlarge the house. But I forgot to ask you when you mean to begin."

"Perhaps I'd better make a voyage as captain first." He smiled down at her. "Then we'll see just how good I am. And how much booty I can expect to bring home."

"Sounds like you expect to go privateering," Debby said.

"He'll need to," his mother said with forced gaiety. "We'll be so grand here we'll need a privateer's fortune to keep ourselves in our newly acquired luxury."

"I think I shall not marry too quickly," Debby said. "Sounds as though it will be much too pleasant here to want to live elsewhere."

Elijah kissed her cheek and his mother's. "I must be off," he said, his spirits lifting to great heights as he saw that, after all, his mother was going to face the occasion as he had demanded. "I must return my horse and pay my respects to Mistress Molly before the Yarmouth packet comes in." He looked at his mother, at his sister, at his mother again.

She embraced him. "God go with you, Son."

He left for the barn, where Jon was oiling his boots, the clean smells of leather and hay crisp in the November air. "All squared away?"

"It came out better than I hoped," Elijah told him.

"That's a relief." Jon rose to help Elijah saddle the rented horse who had been sharing a stall with the family cow.

"Begin the addition of twelve feet on the west side, toward Sears, as soon as the weather permits next spring. I will write you if I can."

"Aye."

They shook hands and he rode away, waving to his womenfolk as they watched from the back door and to Jon, a small and misshapen figure, growing ever smaller as he trotted, then cantered down the road, the sooner to see Molly again.

The Warden house was quiet as he rode up to the front door and knocked. It was Molly who answered, her face shining and her beautiful green eyes full of warmth and joy.

"They've all gone avisiting," she said, leading him to the back of the house, hanging his coat by the fire and bringing him a hot drink.

"But I may enter all the same?"

"Not for long. Just enough to get warm. When does the packet sail?"

"Not for a while, I would judge from the state of the tide."

She nodded. "How was your sister's wedding?"

"Suitable, I suppose. Everyone seemed satisfied with it. To tell the truth, I was so preoccupied that I didn't notice much, one way or the other."

Her face became solemn. "Did you meet with any difficulty?"

"I met with my mother! As for the others, well—I told my family what I had in mind, and that was that."

She met his gaze, searchingly. "Go on."

"No sudden change comes easily to a woman of forty-five. My mother is at least that old." It was terribly old!

"Elijah," she said quietly, "it is not too late. I won't hold you to words spoken in haste in a cold garden."

His heart fluttered to his feet and he grew numb at the prospect of her backing away. "It is much too late for me, dear Molly. I can't possibly steer another course, now that I know you will be mine. You haven't changed your mind, I hope."

"No," she said softly. "Not I."

In the dim kitchen they lost themselves in each other's gaze, and he rose suddenly. "Let's go for a ride," he said. "I still have my mount."

"Yes, I saw you did. It would be a great pleasure, kind sir!"

She snatched her cloak and led him to the front door and to the rented nag, tied to a nearby tree. After he mounted, he reached for her hand, then swung her up and onto his lap with an arm around her waist. She gasped in surprise, then laughed.

"Master Merrick, you are compromising me," she giggled. "Now you will have to marry me!"

He laughed too so that she would not know he was blushing.

She nestled against him and he rode with her, carefully, into a little-used path that led to the woods, an endless path that wound through the new-growth oaks with their brown leaves whispering, squirrels racing back and forth, crows raucous. Far away the town cannon sounded, announcing the immanent departure of the packet.

"I have to return you, little one," he murmured into her ear, his heart ready to burst with joy at the realization that she was in his arms and all the joy of his life was contained within his reach. He backed the horse into a nearby thicket and tilted Molly's face up to his own, and kissed her lips gently, carefully, so as not to frighten her, caught tight in his arms as she was and unable to escape him. But she did not seem frightened—only very still, like a bird unable to fly, waiting with quietness its fate at the hand of the hunter.

The woods in that moment were intimate and she slowly smiled, a tiny gratified smile, and reached shyly for another kiss.

There would never be anything more that he would ask of life.

The cannon cracked again, and they rode back to the Wardens' house. When they reached the door, she took a handkerchief out of her apron pocket. It was embroidered handsomely with his initials and edged with hemstitching.

"I wanted to give you something of my own making," she told him, looking up at him somberly. Her face wore a small, tight, brave smile. "Godspeed, my captain."

She kissed his cheek, slipped down to the ground, and ran into the house. He turned the horse and hurried to the Inn.

It would be a fast trip southward to Baltimore and then he'd be off to his first command. His feet itched for the deck. Already was he yearning for the ship—his ship—his chance to prove himself, his chance to be able to claim his woman and take charge of his life.

Isaac

✢✧✦ I ✦✧✢

FROM THE SMALL windows beside the door, Molly watched him spring into the saddle. For a man who spent more of his time on ships than off them, he rode well.

She smiled.

Ah, my handsome, my bonnie sailor, she mused, you do very well at everything. You are all you should be, and luckily for me, you are more! Clasping her hands in front of her, she whirled around, watching her skirts flare out, then took another look at the now distant figure. Thank God, she thought, thank God it is he and not another. For she would have no trouble living with Elijah Merrick. Many another hurdle there would be, no doubt. But Elijah would not be one of them. He was a man she could respect. Perhaps, in time, he would be a man she could love. That she did not love him now was not a problem. Marriage neither required nor expected it; love, according to tradition, would come later. Perhaps. His infatuation for her was over and above any girl's expectation at the time of betrothal.

He was almost out of sight and had not turned to look back or wave. She liked that. She liked it that he would set his mind on something and then do it without being diverted. His very determination would guarantee success; from his success would come respect for him in his village, and she would share in that respect. Together they would become to Rockford what the Wardens were to Yarmouth. It would no longer matter that she was a servant, that her mother was, in the eyes of the world, a questionable woman. For Molly would be the wife of the eminent Elijah Merrick, and people would bow to her. She would curtsey back, an elegant curtsey, not the maid-servant bobbing she did now.

Lifting her skirt and dipping deeply, she practiced curtseying gracefully to an imaginary Rockford gentleman who stood by the coat rack in the corner, captivating him entirely.

Rising from her bow, she found herself face to face with Mrs. Warden. "Oh! Mistress," she said faintly. "I was just, just. . . ."

"Practicing," Mrs. Warden said, her eyes gentle. "We have just returned from our visit. Is Elijah gone?"

"Yes, ma'am. Just now."

"It's a sad time, is it not, when they leave?"

She put her arm around Molly's shoulders and walked with her to the kitchen. "So much to hope for, and then there is nothing. But soon enough my dear, he will be back."

Molly smiled. Ah, yes, soon enough he would be back! Before too many departures, they would be wed. And she would be the wife of a captain!

The next morning she was hard at work on the brass andirons in the parlor when she heard the rustling of skirts and looked up. There stood Mrs.Warden, her hair tied back in a handkerchief to keep the dust from it, a copious apron tight around her waist, a pair of faded and scuffed shoes on her feet.

Molly could only stare, her polishing cloth hanging in midair.

Mrs. Warden laughed.

"I can't blame you for being surprised, my dear," she said. "But even I know how to shine brass!"

"But, Ma'am, why should you?" Molly asked with honest incredulity.

Mrs. Warden took a cloth from the pocket of her apron and dipped it into the polish pot. "Well, my dear," she said, rubbing a lamp base vigorously. "I have decided that there's only one way I can give you what you really need now, and that is to work with you in the time we have left."

Molly shook her head. "I'm sorry," she said, "but I don't understand. I wish you would let me do that."

"You were working on the andirons, I believe," Mrs. Warden said dryly. "Pray continue, and I will explain myself."

Hastily Molly bent to her task.

"You know how fond I am of Elijah," Mrs. Warden said, moving from the lamp to its holder on the wall. "And you must know how dear you yourself are to me. Well, Molly, something I can do for both of you is to show you, the best way I know how, all the tricks of housewifery, all the little things that make one woman a better wife than another, a better housekeeper. There are many things that I would teach you, but I can't just sit in my parlor and remember them all. If I am working with you, they will come to me unbidden."

"Mistress," Molly said, her voice trembling with gratitude, "it is too much to ask. What can I say?"

"You need say nothing, my dear," Mrs. Warden smiled. "I never had daughters to pass my knowledge along to. You are a dear, dear child. Life has dealt harshly with you. Perhaps I am God's instrument to rectify that. That you will be Elijah's wife, Molly, is to my way of thinking a far greater triumph than Elijah's becoming a captain. For you to find happiness and fulfillment as his wife and to give him these things in return—that is a triumph of the human spirit. I'm proud and grateful to have a part in it and to help. I believe I know a few things that you don't. Things you should know. For instance, my dear, I believe you are inexperienced as a spinster."

Molly giggled. "I'm afraid so."

"And do you weave?"

"Afraid not."

"Can you make fine dresses?"

"I can sew a seam, Mistress. That's all."

"Well. You will be the mistress of a fine house some day, and you ought to know as much about making clothing suitable to your station as the spinster or seamstress you employ. You should know how to make Elijah's clothes. And clothes for children. You know how to do menial tasks, and you do them well. There has been no chance for you to learn other skills, the more refined ones. So I will help you. Between us, we'll finish these mundane chores quickly and then begin. I have an old spinning wheel in the attic; we'll start this very afternoon."

And this they did, Mrs. Warden teaching, Molly trying to follow the instructions.

"I'll never learn it!" she cried in vexation, hopelessly losing the rhythm required to draw the wool into a strand. The wooden driver, grooved to catch the spokes of the wheel and set it into motion, fell from her hand. The yarn snarled into an impossible knot.

"Not in an afternoon, it's true," her mistress offered.

"Maybe Elijah's mother won't expect me to be good at everything," Molly suggested hopefully, rescuing the driver.

"She probably assumes that you are good at nothing," Mrs. Warden said grimly, then glanced at Molly, looking abashed. "That was an unnecessary comment on my part, my dear, but I think we may as well be honest. Mrs. Merrick knows you are a servant. She'll probably suppose you to be awkward at many of the more refined tasks, and I would prefer to give her an unexpected surprise. So you'll have to spin until you're fairly good at it. There's time, plenty of time. I'll have the wheel brought downstairs, near the fire. On evenings when we have no guests, I'll sit there with you and help you when you need it."

Molly's eyes filled with grateful tears. Mrs. Warden patted her shoulder. "Stay here and practice for a while. I'll hunt up some goods worthy of a dress for you. We'll take a respite this afternoon and turn our attention to dressmaking. Later, after we have the cloth made, we'll take it to the fulling mill."

"I don't know what you mean," Molly whispered, being unable for the moment to speak in a normal voice. "What is fulling?"

"It's shrinks the homespun," Mrs. Warden said, bustling from the room. "Then the weave is tighter and it's warmer." Her words became faint as she descended the stairs.

Molly remained motionless for a long while. It was shame that filled her now. She was unworthy and she knew it. Elizabeth Warden was a saint and Molly Deems was not. Molly Deems was a mercenary, miserable, play-acting fraud.

Then she straightened her back and resolutely set the wheel in motion again. Unworthy or not, Mistress Warden was offering an opportunity beyond anything she'd ever dreamed of. And if she would never have the goodness of spirit that Mrs. Warden had, she would at least learn all she could and make the mistress proud of her.

✦ಜಿ 2 ಜಿ✦

And so the two of them toiled, side by side, both happy in the days that followed. As they worked, Mrs. Warden spoke frequently of her early marriage and the lessons she had to learn then. When a wife should stand firm, when she must yield. How she must defer to her husband's parents and family. When she might sit with her husband's friends when they were his guests in the house and for how long, and how to excuse her presence easily. How to make her husband feel cherished and well cared for without appearing to hover over him, smothering him and making him restive. How Molly might handle Elijah's sister and his friends. And how she ought to manage servants, should she ever have any.

Though she absorbed all of Mrs. Warden's comments as best she could, sure that one day all this knowledge would be used, descriptions about Elijah's family and the town of Rockford interested Molly most. For this was her new field of battle.

They were in the keeping room, sewing the long sleeves of a blue dress, their stitches tiny and precise, when Mrs. Warden said, "You really need to know the background of Elijah's family and how it fits into the town's history. Elijah has told me some of it; the rest I learned from a Friend who lives in Rockford. When Elijah became a close companion of our John, I made it a point to find out more about him."

"Why did you, Mistress?" Molly was puzzled, for the Wardens seemed to accept everybody at his or her own value without being influenced by gossip or local storytelling.

"My husband took a fancy to him and hoped to put him on a ship with John, when they got old enough. Abel thought Elijah was made of the stuff of a captain. He wanted to learn what he could of the boy before taking the time to train him. But then Elijah was injured and sent home to mend. My husband felt, as did I, that he would never be strong enough to pursue the sea."

"What happened?"

"Elijah went to sea!" Mrs. Warden laughed happily and laid the bodice of the dress on the table. "Let's have some tea, and attach these sleeves."

Molly set the kettle on its trivet above the coals. Then she slipped her own dress down to her waist and drew the bodice of the new blue one around her, pinning up the front where the buttons would be.

"Do you think we could put white collars and cuffs on it?" she asked.

"Indeed! Such fine trimmings!"

Molly blushed, wondering if she had strayed too far from the Quaker path. Blue itself was a concession.

Mrs. Warden slipped a sleeve up Molly's bare arm and started pinning. "Everyone in Rockford is, naturally, kin to everyone else," she continued, "just as it is here in Yarmouth. The Merricks came there fifty years after it was settled, but since they were an old Barnstable family, one of the first comers there, they were accepted, and bought land. Where Elijah's mother lives today is part of that same Merrick holding. Over time, bits and pieces of it were sold off, and during the war, the Sears family bought a large portion of it from Mrs. Merrick. Widowed as she was, she could no longer farm it; the money she received from Sears has, I think, largely kept them ever since. She is a careful woman, you can see!"

She is probably a terror, Molly thought, picturing the frugal Mrs. Merrick with distaste.

"Elijah's great-grandfather was called Jonathan Merrick. Soon after he arrived in Rockford he wed Sarah King, Elijah's great-grandmother, little knowing what he was getting into."

Surprised, Molly glanced around her shoulder, where Mrs. Warden was pinning the back of the sleeve now.

"Well," Mrs. Warden hastened to say, "The first King family had built a gristmill on Rockford's herring run. Everyone for miles around was glad for it; the Kings got rich without raising ire or envy. They worked hard, and it was agreed that the Puritan Jehovah had rewarded them." Mrs. Warden's voice did not speed up nor slow down, but Molly knew what she thought of the Puritan Jehovah and imagined a smug little smile curling around her mistress's lips.

"But in a few years, it became clear to the Halls, another large clan in the town, that a profit could be had from a fulling mill. Anyone who wanted cash—and who did not!—could sell their extra homespun to Hall and he'd full it and take it up to Boston to be sold for much more than he paid for it. But the only stream available for power was the one the Kings were already using. This seemed not to bother Hall. He built a dam upstream of the Kings' gristmill and used the water power whenever he had a fulling job to do, without considering any inconvenience he might be causing someone downstream waiting to get their corn ground." She tugged. Molly turned around, and Mrs. Warden slid the other sleeve into place.

"Somehow, neither of them could come to an agreement. By the time the Merricks arrived from Barnstable, the Kings and the Halls had carried their quarrel into the second generation, the third was coming along, and Rockford itself was taking sides on the issue, dividing pretty evenly. Jonathan and Sarah Merrick's son John married Lydia Sears, and their son, Scotto, who was Elijah's father, married Reliance King, the present Mrs. Merrick."

It's a club, Molly thought. One that could deny her admission, if it chose.

Mrs. Warden appraised the sleeves critically. "They'll do." She steeped the tea while Molly cautiously inched her way past the pins.

"So your first lesson, my dear, is to not encourage a friendship with anyone in the Hall family. Your second lesson is to learn the names of each family and their antecedents so you don't confuse them or mix them up and accidentally befriend the wrong person."

"It's hard to believe, isn't it? That they are all still waging the same old war?"

Mrs. Warden sighed. "I have no patience with quarrels of this sort, Molly. I'm not advising you to take part in it. That I would never do. But I am eager for you to be accepted into Elijah's family, and to cultivate a Hall would hardly further your purpose."

"I can see that!" Molly agreed.

"It's not as bad now as once it was. Eventually the Halls agreed to make their schedule public, and promised to stick to it. And did.

"But flour dust is combustible, and the inevitable happened. The mill was badly damaged by fire and the miller, a King of course, was killed. Suspecting the Halls had a hand in the fire, the Kings were enraged, and not long after, a hole was torn—a big one—in the Hall dam. The Kings brought their not inconsiderable weight to bear on town meeting to limit the height of the rebuilt dam so that the spring migration of herring would increase. The Kings implied the Halls' dam caused the run to be the least productive on the North Shore."

"And did it? Increase?"

"Actually the run did become more productive, but there's no way to know the reason. Perhaps it was the Lord who decided the fish should multiply. Regardless, by lowering the dam the Kings always had water to run their wheel and they had bested the Halls after all."

"It doesn't sound to me as though either side was blameless."

"No side ever is," Mrs. Warden smiled. "It was a foolish fight, with only one stream in town, and should never have happened in the first place. Its only effect has been to divide the village and make it even more clannish than would otherwise be the case. Which is why I've told you about it. I would not have you enter the situation blind. Rockford will not be an easy community to join. None of our Cape towns would be, but Rockford least of all."

"Do you think my mother . . . do you think they will look down on me?" Molly found herself unable to ask the question directly, and she stammered to a stop. The pause that followed was a long one.

"I don't know, Molly," Mrs. Warden said at last. "I think fitting in would be difficult, in any case, since you were not born there. You will have to be patient, my dear, and bide your time. Surely it will work itself out. You are a sweet and lovely person. They will see it for themselves, I'm sure, and whether they know about your mother or not won't matter." Mrs. Warden looked into Molly's eager and vulnerable face.

Abruptly she stood up. "There is white dimity in the basket over there. The embroidery floss and hoop are there too," she said. "Best you set to work on the collar and cuffs, and then we will decorate them. I know some very fancy stitches." Her eyes twinkled. "I don't use them on my own garments, but I will show you how to use them on yours. There is nothing like a little worldly glamour to interest a damsel anywhere. Even a cautious Rockford maiden! They will flock to your doorstep to learn your stitches, and you can take over from there."

The two of them sewed in the mornings when the housework was done, and slowly Molly's trousseau grew. They embroidered after the noon meal, and in the late afternoon while Mrs. Warden read to her, Molly spun until her fingers were numb, and her feet ached from the miles of walking, three steps back and one long swoop forward. At first she feared her mistress's idea of enlightened reading was the Bible and William Penn, but Mrs. Warden, instead, read her pieces from the London and Boston and Philadelphia papers, political pamphlets and treatises, analyses of the progress of the French revolution and the results of Alexander Hamilton's financial genius in stabilizing the American economy.

"You know the words of God already," Mrs. Warden said. "It is the world that Elijah is preparing to grapple with that you must learn of now. When you leave me, I will give you a Bible and some of my favorite writings for you to ponder when your time is your own. But just now you must learn of today's world, and the papers and writings of our leaders will keep you current. It's a habit I suggest you continue when you are Elijah's wife."

And thus Molly Deems was well immersed in her training to become the wife of a shipmaster when the Warden household was wrenched from its routine by the return of Isaac, the Wardens' second son.

✦༖ 3 ༖✦

He blew into the house on a gust of January wind, and embraced his mother fondly, bowing briefly to Molly who was sitting with Mrs. Warden drinking tea in the kitchen and discussing the most recent edition of The Federalist. He took his mother into the parlor where they both remained for the balance of the afternoon. The peaceful tenor of the winter days came to an end.

The last time Molly had seen Isaac, she had been kneading bread, and he came into the kitchen and caught her at it. He had told her she was pretty, rubbed a spot of flour off the end of her nose, and then left for his trip. She had girlishly dreamed and dreamed of him, and then her mother had died, her world was destroyed, and she had put both Warden sons, Isaac and John, out of her mind as she searched for security.

Now her security seemed well in hand. Now Elijah Merrick would take the care of Molly Deems from Elizabeth Warden. Now it was safe to bring to mind the smile on Isaac Warden's face. A smile that could weave a spell around any woman. And she was a woman.

Nonsense! Shaking her head briskly, she packed up her embroidery, then set out to do her stint at the wheel.

Alone she spun, watching the sun disappear behind a winter cloud bank and thinking that done by oneself, spinning was surely a dreary, tiring task. When would Mistress Warden think sufficient yarn had been produced so that the weaving might begin? Perhaps weaving would be better than spinning!

Then Bethia began preparing supper. Molly welcomed her appearance at the hearth and happily put aside the wheel to help.

"They're going at it hammer and tongs," Bethia said. "Is the table set?"

"Yes. Who's at it? Who's at it hammer and tongs?"

"Mr. Isaac and the mistress," said Bethia. "She'll never give him leave to go to England, and that's what he wants to do. She'll make him wait until his father returns, and let the master decide. That could be months."

"Why does he want to go to England?"

"To study law, so he says."

"Why should he not?"

"You can make the pudding tonight. Mind you do it slowly, so you don't get lumps. I could about chew the pudding the last time you made it."

"I'll be more careful."

"Can't hurry cooking," Bethia pronounced, and then continued with the subject at hand. "Because London is chock full of young bloods who like their rum and heaven knows what else. A boy like Master John, well, she'd have no need to worry about him. But Master Isaac is a different story. Yes, yes." The older woman grinned knowingly. "She wants him to go to sea, like his pa. Keep him out of trouble, don't you see?"

"How is Master Isaac different from Master John, Bethia?"

It was a question she could not help asking, although there was no reason for her to do so. What did it matter to her who Isaac Warden was or how he differed from his brother?

"He's handsomer, for one," Bethia said importantly. "So he always gets his way. He's spoiled, that one is."

"How else?"

"Well, he just can't keep up with his brother. Ain't made of the same stuff. So naturally he don't want to go to sea. He'll never rise as far as Master John, so if he don't go out, no one will know. That way, there's no way to compare them, don't you see?"

Molly nodded.

"No! No! You're adding the cornmeal too fast!"

"Sorry. I forgot." The subject of Isaac Warden was enough to make anyone forget anything!

"There's other ways he goes about being different too," Bethia continued. "Where Master John is honorable, Isaac is loose. Where Master John does his job carefully, Isaac won't even accept one. And the girls! Well!"

Here Bethia paused for dramatic emphasis.

"Well?"

"He's the very devil!" She hissed. "The very devil!"

Molly, betrothed and a safe distance from the advances of loose men, laughed with Bethia, the two of them amused, as women will be, at the thought of a man making a fool of girls less experienced than they.

But Molly's heart beat a little faster.

That night she served supper carefully, letting no glance of hers stray to the young master.

When the meal was cleared and the dishes done, Mrs. Warden sent for her, stood up beside her, and held her hand. "Isaac," she began, "you may remember Miss Molly from previous times."

Courteously, he smiled. "Indeed I do," he said.

"Well," his mother returned with a smile of her own, "she is in a halfway position in our house. Will you sit down with us, Molly?"

Molly did as she was bid, pretending not to notice Isaac's evident amazement over his mother's servant sitting with them at table. "Molly is betrothed to Elijah Merrick," Mrs. Warden went on smoothly. "And I have undertaken to help her assume the position she will soon acquire. She insists on continuing to serve us, as usual, but in between times, we are very busy, she and I, preparing her for her marriage."

"I see," Isaac. He appraised Molly without appearing to do so. "A novel situation."

"I felt it best to explain it and to explain your presence to her."

"My presence!" He started to rise but sank back into his chair. "Well, I guess you're right, Mother. I do need some explaining." He smiled at Molly. "I am a prodigal, and you might as well know it."

"That's not so at all," Mrs. Warden said quickly, but it was too fast, and Molly caught her concern. "Isaac is unsure how he wants to use his life, and he believes we shall think less of him for that."

"Well, I really do want to study law, Mother," he said. "The sea and ships, well, they are fine. But I am really tired of it all. You must admit I've tried." He turned to Molly. "Don't you think I'd make a fine lawyer?"

"I, I'm sure I don't know," she stammered, made suddenly self-conscious by his attention.

"Well, I do!" he declared.

"We've been talking of it all afternoon," Mrs. Warden said. "And my head is spinning. Let's not speak of it anymore."

"Indeed, Mother." Isaac said, rising and kissing his mother's brow. "It has been inconsiderate of me to belabor you with it this long. Suppose we let the subject drop for a while. I'll go up to Boston on the next packet and buy some books so that I can study on my own until Father returns."

He turned and bowed to Molly. "If you ladies will excuse me now, there are some friends that I need to look up and see if they're still in town."

Mrs. Warden sat silently after he left the room. "Some of us take longer in the finding than others," she said at last. "I think I will go to bed early."

ꙮ✦ꙮ

Isaac told his mother in a dozen different ways that he had tried the sea and forsaken it of his own free will, convinced he had no vocation for it. He had no flair for ships or commerce or command. He wanted to whet his intellect, which was slowly atrophying in the American cultural climate where nothing—ever—stimulated it. Were he not a Quaker he would enter the ministry, he said smoothly, but nothing was worth forsaking his religious life as a Friend. Without the law and the satisfaction it could bring him, he would wither.

Elizabeth Warden had no choice but to accept. She wrote to her husband care of a trading post on the Pacific coast, sent by ship around the continent where her letter would arrive six months later, if it arrived at all, begging Abel to come home soon. She could not let Isaac, then twenty-two years old, go to London with his father's money and without his father's permission. Disgruntled, he went off at once to Boston for law books. Delayed he might be, Isaac declared, but he would nonetheless waste no time.

While he was gone, Molly and Bethia turned out his room thoroughly, shining and polishing and waxing. Blankets, quilts, comforters were shaken and beaten and aired; the feather mattress was plumped up again and again to arrange it comfortably. Mrs. Warden wanted to make her son snug and content so that his stay with her would be as pleasant as possible, even if it were against his will. When the room was well aired and scrubbed and cleaned to her satisfaction, she and Molly turned to the completion of the trousseau.

"I think you have spun enough," the mistress said. "You are quite proficient at the wheel, although there is nothing like years of practice, Molly."

"I am sure of that," she said distastefully.

"You have enough here, I believe, to weave a good sized piece. Why not work it up now? Bethia can help you with it as well as I can, and that would free me to be with Isaac. He's discovered that all of his friends are gone, and he surely needs companionship even if it is only his old mother."

"Old, indeed!" Molly chided.

"We can full what you've woven come spring, and you can make a coat or cape out of it. And we'll start on your bridal quilt. All proper girls come into their marriage with a bridal quilt!" Mrs. Warden actually blushed. "And you can learn to spin flax, too," she hurried on.

"Anything you say, Mistress," Molly said docilely. "Will Master be home soon, that Isaac will be free to leave?"

"Pray God," Mrs. Warden said fervently.

When Isaac returned from Boston the parlor became his study. Doggedly, he sat there reading law, while his mother perused journals and papers. In the kitchen Molly wove carefully under Bethia's guidance.

At the end of January winter hit Cape Cod with unexpected force. The temperature dropped so low that ice choked the bay, rough, jagged, pitted, and potholed, so far out that it seemed to be piled to the ends of the earth. The packets halted, travel stopped, and the Cape folk burrowed into their homes like any other winter animal, living off their fat. It was not supposed to be so cold; the bay was supposed to retain enough heat to prevent such icing, but Cape people were always prepared to hibernate.

With the unusual drain on firewood, Mrs. Warden and Isaac moved into the kitchen with Molly and Bethia. Ellen did not come to them at all; Bethia prepared their meals and everyone ate together before the fire. In those long housebound hours, Molly wove and listened to Isaac and his mother. It was as instructive as outright lessons, to be able to see Mistress Warden's teaching put into action, her questions encouraging Isaac to do the talking while her quiet suggestions steered the conversation to the ideas she wanted to explore.

But it was disastrous for Isaac to be there in the kitchen every day for long hours. As Molly threw the shuttle and drew the beam to ward herself so to tighten the weave, she knew his eyes were on her, appraising her, probing, questing in his own, smooth, sure manner. What maid could resist being flattered by the attention of such a handsome, charming, wealthy man?

She tried not to notice. He said little to her directly, for with his mother ever present there was no opportunity to exchange anything more than daily pleasantries, no reason to be more than casually polite to the young woman betrothed to a family friend. He played his role well, with the restraint required, never indicating in any way that his attention was fixed on the girl so patiently weaving by the fire they shared. But Molly, with the sensory apparatus of the young, knew. When she thought he was watching, she did not lift her eyes, but her color rose despite herself. She worked the loom assiduously and helped with the house chores, there being more of these since Ellen was absent. But her resolve was slowly draining away and she felt increasingly as though her every move in that kitchen were performed only for him, that he missed nothing. When she did raise her eyes to find him watching, a tingle ran the length of her spine.

Abruptly the siege was lifted. The air suddenly warmed, and a land breeze smelling of distant springs pushed the ice out to sea. Everyone walked about outside, relieved for the change. The packet whisked in and out again. Isaac relit his fire in the parlor to resume his studying there.

His departure sealed Molly in a cocoon of preoccupation with him, leaving her to fret. I do not care, she told herself, as she aired out the upstairs bedrooms, whether he studies in the parlor or the kitchen or under the butternut tree. It makes no difference whatsoever, she insisted, putting fresh linens on the beds and airing the quilts over the windowsills, shaking them vigorously before putting them back on the beds. Through the window, she could see Isaac returning from the village store where he had gone to pick up any mail the packet might have brought. It doesn't matter, she repeated. He belongs in the parlor and you belong here, making beds, and stirring pots in the kitchen.

Returning there, she found the object of her mullings waiting for her by the fire.

"Here, Molly, my dear," he said as he held out a letter. "This is for you. I think it's from Elijah."

Who else would it be from, she thought flippantly, but was ashamed, for she had not thought much of Elijah during the siege. She blushed with the anticipation of reading his words, which would be, she knew, ones of love.

Isaac held the letter behind him. "What will you give me for it?"

She stared at him blankly. "What do you want?" she asked.

"Nothing a nice girl would know about," he grinned. He held the letter out and then withdrew it when she reached.

"Seriously," he said, "I would like to be friends."

"I hope that we are that already," she said. "May I have it?"

"Friends do not waste time with manners," he said. "I would know that you are truly my friend, Molly, if you aren't always so dammed polite."

"If you do not give me that letter, I will not *be* very damned polite," she retorted, her face scarlet at her effrontery.

His delight was apparent and she was proud of herself for delivering a clever rejoinder, as well as relieved that he did not consider her impertinent. Chuckling, he handed her the letter and went off to his studies in the parlor.

At the hearth, she sat down to read. Elizabeth Warden wandered in, deep in the many pages of a missive she had received from the captain. Mrs. Warden was fond of walking about as she read.

Molly was deep into deciphering Elijah's penmanship and spelling when Mrs. Warden threw down her letter with a gasp. She looked at Molly as though she were a culprit, at the loom as though it had committed a grave offense, then swept from the room and into the parlor. The door slammed behind her. Such display of displeasure was very unusual.

Hesitating, Molly gathered the dropped pages into a neat pile, reading none of them, securing them on the table under a tea pot, and turned again to her own letter from Elijah, smiling over his tenderness, his hopes for their future, his confidence in his present trip. His profits were good. He had bought and shipped to Judith the long-overdue china he had promised. He hoped to be home in a month or two; he thought they might then plan a time when they could wed. Perhaps the trip after this one? At least by the one after that! He adored her. His heart was ever hers. He thanked God he had found her.

Because they had come from so staid a young man, she knew his words were heartfelt. Guiltily she thrust the letter into the bosom of her dress. No one should feel that way about anyone. It made them too vulnerable.

She thought of Isaac Warden and on the spot dismissed him, hoping it would be permanent. He meant nothing to her, she reminded herself, nor she to him. A fireside flirtation was all he wanted, and as for her, well, Elijah was her own. He was her future. He loved her, and her alone.

The front door slammed, and from the window, she saw Isaac striding away from the house. Mrs. Warden did not reappear, and Molly took up her weaving under the critical eye of Bethia, pausing every now and again to warm the side of herself away from the fire. And then, blessedly, Bethia decided to "do" the parlor, having checked that the mistress was no longer in it. Molly was left alone for the balance of the afternoon.

She looked at Elijah's letter once more, focusing on his plans for their wedding.

> *We shall call on my mother. It is time you met her and she you. Pastur Simmonds lives close by our hous. We might vissit him as well; you ought to meet him, since he will be your minister, and besides, I suppose he will preform our marriage. Onless there is another arrangement you yourself wish to make.*

There were no other arrangements she could make. The only religious services she had attended were with the Wardens, yet she was not a Quaker and so could not be married from their Meeting.

Because of her great respect for Elizabeth Warden, she had been honest about lacking the faith requisite for membership in any church. She was willing to learn Quaker theology, though, both because it pleased Mistress Warden to teach her and because it forged a yet stronger link in the chain of their friendship. And Elizabeth Warden herself was more than willing to wait, for she knew the Lord was also willing.

Now Molly wished she had pretended to religious devotion and become a Friend. It would have been worth it, to avoid Rockford's minister! If Elijah's mother were very much set against their marriage, would she try to convince Pastor Simmonds not to perform the ceremony?

Refusing to risk the possibility, she must see if she could manage an alternative that would rectify the problem presented by having no church or family of her own.

She did not request permission to leave the next afternoon. It was the first time she had ventured from the house without asking her mistress. Ah! When she was married, so many things would change; she would be the one to decide her own comings and goings, for one!

She hurried to the house of Henry Hastings, the minister of the Congregational Church in Yarmouth. Had she been fully aware of the power of this man, the iron rule he wielded, Molly would have been frightened about approaching him. But she was afraid only because she had never approached a man before; she did not understand what it meant to be the spiritual leader of a community that still measured itself according to the yardstick of the church.

Pastor Hastings' house, close by the street, was orderly and well repaired; its winter woodpile, sorely diminished by the recent cold, was even now being replenished by a parishioner who was bringing in and stacking his contribution to the minister's compensation.

The Hastings' house probably resembled the Merricks' homestead, Molly thought, recalling Elijah's description. Two close-set windows looked out beside the door. Its roof sloped to the top of them; a granite stone served as a front step and beside it a lilac bush grew, stringy and sad in the raw winter breeze.

The door it was opened briskly by an immaculate and incredibly old, stooped-over crone. "What is it?" she snapped.

"I wish to speak with Pastor Hastings," Molly heard herself declare steadily.

The old eyes searched her face. "Come in then. I'll ask him if he can see you."

She waited in the miniscule vestibule, trying not to peek into the parlor that opened to her right where Mr. Hastings sat in plain view. But aside from the steep stairs directly ahead of her, there was nowhere else she could look.

Hastings sat with a cat on his lap, spectacles on his nose, beside a small table littered with books and papers. Few folks frequented their parlors; it was considered pretentious, for it was a room used only to receive the minister or one's mother-in-law. But Mr. Hastings was a cut above the average by virtue of his calling. And, accustomed to being received in parlors, he would scarcely have been comfortable in his keeping room at the back of the tiny house.

He watched as the crone marched back to Molly. "He says he can spare you a moment, Miss. Come in." As Molly entered, the pastor nodded and inclined his head toward the old woman. She marched away to the kitchen.

Hastings looked carefully at Molly and smiled politely. "And what may I do for you, Miss?"

He did not offer her a chair, but Molly was accustomed to standing in the presence of her social betters.

"Sir, I have a request. I am betrothed to a young man who lives in Rockford. His family belongs to the First Parish Church there. I live here in Yarmouth, but I do not belong to a church. We would like you to marry us, sir. Can you do that, if I am not a member of your congregation?"

He examined her carefully. "Do you believe in Jesus, young woman?"

"Yes, sir, I do," she lied. "But I have not been free to do anything about it."

"Well!" The old man cleared his throat. "And just how is it that believing in Jesus, you have made no profession of faith?"

It was a tricky question to answer and still win his favor, but she had known he would ask, and she plunged on. "I am a servant in the household of Captain Abel Warden, who, as you know, is Quaker."

"Then you must be young Molly." She was startled that he knew her name, but refused to be diverted.

"Yes, sir. The Wardens have been very good to me. I have not wished to insist on following my own beliefs while in their house and under their care, so I am unchurched." This was stretching the truth of it, but Molly did not care.

Pastor Hastings fidgeted with his pen. "The Wardens, no doubt, have instructed you in their heresy?"

"Yes sir, Mistress has." Heresy! Elizabeth Warden's pure love of God was no heresy! But Molly could hardly argue the point.

"Yet you would join our congregation?"

"Yes indeed."

"Well." He coughed. "I'm delighted to hear it. And naturally I would be happy to instruct you, and should you prove worthy, baptize you."

"I would be very grateful, sir. And then, you will marry us, my betrothed and me?"

"Well! First things first." He waved her to a chair nearby and upended the cat, who wandered into the kitchen. "Ah, yes. Now. We do not practice public confession so very much these days. Only in an extraordinary case of public offense so grievous that the congregation will not tolerate its presence in their midst. I think in your case it would be quite appropriate."

She stared at him, trying to understand what he was saying. He hurried on. "Public confession will reassure the elect, persuade them that I have not become too . . . liberal, in my effort to include you in our communion. Then, after your confession, if the congregation is convinced of your repentance, I will instruct and baptize you."

She felt as though an important part of herself had withdrawn to a private place. "You will have to explain to me what you mean, sir, by confession. Of what do I repent that will so please your congregation?"

He looked stunned.

"You can hardly expect my flock to accept the illegitimate daughter of a whore!" he said. "But if you seek forgiveness, the congregation can hardly hold your mother's sins against you."

His image wavered, dimmed and moved back and then forth, jarred by an inner pressure to destroy him and all he represented. But her voice sounded, to her ears at least, low and calm.

"Do you mean I am to confess my mother's conscience?"

"No, no." He was becoming impatient. "Naturally your mother's error is on her own conscience. But you must confess your bastardy. So that you can be shriven."

"I am not a bastard."

"My dear, my dear," he clucked, a knowing, hennish, between-us-girls chuckle. "Everyone knows who you are. You cannot hide it."

"Nor am I trying to," she said. "My mother was married to John Deems of Dartmouth. I am their daughter."

Hastings shook his head. "Everyone believes you were Seth Adams' child."

"Everyone is wrong. He can tell you I am no bastard of his. Why not ask him?"

Hastings shrugged. "He's gone. Up and sold his place, I'm told. He cannot confirm your claim."

A silence built up.

"Mr. Hastings," she said at last, "I am not a bastard, so I cannot confess to bastardy. There is no need for me to be purified by public humiliation. Will you perform my wedding? Or not."

He looked at her carefully. "Even if I believed you, my dear, my congregation would not."

"But it is the truth! Do they care nothing for it?" Her voice rose. "Is your congregation so hardened to God's love that they cannot extend some of their own? Have they so little regard for truth that I must admit a falsehood in order to be accepted by them?"

"Mehitable!" he bellowed. In an instant, the old lady appeared in the keeping room doorway. "This young woman needs to be shown out."

He turned to Molly. "Feel free to return, my dear, any time you see your way clear to accepting my conditions. It is not up to me to determine where the truth lies. My job is to protect the virgin purity of our church. If you follow my suggestions I will do what I can to speed your acceptance among the membership."

"No thank you," Molly said firmly and resisted the impulse to say more. It was important that she seem cool, poised, if only to salvage her pride. She hastened from the cursed house, down its front path to the street, pulling on her cloak as she went, numb, furious, incredulous, frustrated. Futile hopelessness followed her as she made for the shore and the privacy afforded there. The flats were exposed far, far out; it meant the tide was unusually low and would in a few hours be extraordinarily high. If she ran far enough, fast enough, she would never be able to get back in before the tide overtook her. Was this her only choice? Was it her mother's?

She stopped.

The wind whipped at her hair and clothing, as if determined to hold her back. She stood straight against it, her head proudly high, and then its chill penetrated her cape and drove as an arrow through her body. Shivering, she turned slowly and let it push her back toward the road. Whatever were the hurdles ahead, she was not ready to relinquish the battle. She would not follow her mother.

Elijah will help me, she thought. Elijah would never let anyone belittle me as this man has. I must ask him what to do, how to approach his pastor who, please God, will not be such a son-of-a-bitching bastard as Henry Hastings. I cannot do it alone.

There were no witnesses to the tears that could not and would not be denied as she walked back to the Warden house, her heart as chilled as the rest of her, and took her place at the loom.

Snow fell that night. After Mrs. Warden had gone to bed, Molly crept into the unused guest room across the hall from that of the mistress, too churned up to sleep, hoping the drifting flakes would soothe and comfort and steady her. It was cold and drafty there at the window and she fetched her blankets from the attic and listened as the quiet world became quieter yet, breathless under the fall of snow. She worked at burying the anger of that afternoon, but the anger refused to be buried; it would not admit of fatigue. It goaded her to wakefulness, and she thought she would stay there until sleep overtook her. There was no point going to bed and tossing and turning, waiting for daylight.

Numb from the cold and the devastation Pastor Hastings had wrought, she stared into the pattern of floating flakes, but saw nothing, was alert but thought nothing. The snow stopped, the moon rose up, and after many minutes, the drifting song penetrated her consciousness. In the distance she could make out a person plowing along in one direction and then, in another, tacking toward the house, the song coming closer:

Soon 'twill be morning,
My love, my queen bee,
Soon will be daylight,
And you'll part from me.
So I'll drink to your titties,
And I'll drink to your charms.
Here's a loving embrace 'til
I'm back in your arms,
For a roll, for a roll . . . .

The chorus rambled along, and the first verse began again before Molly came to realize it was Isaac, drunk as only a young lord could be. O mercy, she thought, his mother will die of shame. She watched him ramble further, wondering if she would have to go downstairs and shush him before he woke up the mistress, knowing she should keep away from him, drunk as he was. But there, before her eyes, he staggered, started briskly off in another direction and ran straight into a tree beside the snow-covered road. He sat down suddenly and did not get up.

Molly watched awhile longer and realized he had gradually settled into a heap. Well, she thought, there is really no help for it.

Wrapped securely in her cape, she let herself out into the moonlight and ran for the distant tree where Isaac slumped. Black lines streaked his face, and she guessed they were blood from what looked to be a gash on his forehead.

"Master Isaac. Isaac."

She bent over him, shaking his shoulder, scooped snow and rubbed it on his face. He moaned softly and licked his lips.

"Isaac, you must walk. I will help you." The piercing coldness of the night made her shake uncontrollably, and she pulled desperately at his arm.

"I'll drink to your titties," he murmured, falling in the direction of her pull.

"You are despicable," she hissed, releasing all her pent up anger on his inert form. "You use your dear mother, play on her love for you, and then this! If she saw you, it would break her heart. Help yourself, Isaac Warden. Don't lie there like a besotted pig!"

They were not words a maid spoke to her master, but he appeared not to hear, lying still in the snow with a smile on his face. Her anger slowly seeped away as she looked at him, able to examine his face closely without being thought brazen. Gad, he was so handsome!

Backing up to him, she picked up his booted feet, tucked one under each arm. Holding tight, she began hauling him toward the house. It was hard work. Without the snow, which made it possible to slide him along, she could not have done it at all. She pulled him around to the kitchen door where they would be out of sight, and tugged him through the door.

Leaving him by the hearth, she fetched the blankets from his bed and covered him. Then she collected her own blanket from the guest room and went upstairs to her bed in the attic, hoping to arouse before Ellen came in the morning, and somehow get Isaac up to his room. But her efforts to drag the young master, the exhaustion of the afternoon, and her difficulty getting to sleep in the first place had taken their toll, and she awoke later than usual. She restrained herself from running down to the kitchen, but went there sedately instead. No sign of Isaac was to be seen, only a grim-faced Ellen who seemed less disposed to talk than usual, busy mixing stuff with a mortar and pestle.

The house was silent until Mrs. Warden appeared, her face pale and sober as she seated herself across from Molly at the hearth.

Reluctantly she put the shirt she was mending to one side; Elizabeth Warden, she knew, was awaiting her in Quaker silence.

"Mistress, may I help you in some way?"

After a long silence, Mistress Warden said, "Isaac drank to excess at the Inn last night. I found him here this morning, covered with blankets. Do you know anything about it?"

"Should I, Mistress?" she prevaricated.

"He was wrapped in his own blankets. I think he would not have spent the night down here if he could have reached his own bed."

Molly looked away.

"Someone else most likely covered him," Mistress Warden said gently.

Molly sighed. "It was me. I got the blankets," she said, "then wrapped him up. I was afraid he would get chilled."

"His clothing was wet, the fire low. You should have called me; together we could have gotten him upstairs and into bed and a dry nightgown." Molly tried not to think about removing Isaac Warden's wet garments. "Now he's up there shaking with a chill that is bone deep. He is in danger."

That meant Molly herself had put him in harm's way. "Oh, Mistress!" She bit her lip. "I was afraid you would be distressed to find him .... I didn't want you to know ...."

Mrs. Warden nodded; her face was lined. "I understand. And you're right, I am distressed. How could I have failed him so badly?"

Their months of intimacy caused Molly to lose her restraint. "I'm sure you never failed him, Mistress. Or anyone else."

"But I have." Her eyes filled. "Yesterday's letter was very revealing. Captain Warden wrote to me that he'd sent Isaac home himself. He found him at Macau, if you can believe it, carousing. Only his parents' failure could cause such a thing!"

"Nonsense!" The impertinent word slipped out.

Mrs. Warden's surprise brought her up short. "You're a loyal one," she smiled shakily.

"Mistress, could it not be Isaac's dissatisfaction at sea that so prompted his actions? It must be terrible to be so far from home and hating what you do."

Mrs. Warden thought about it. "It is possible," she admitted at last. "That, and being cooped up in a ship for months. I hear strange things happen to a man after a long spell at sea!" Her eyes, for a moment, recovered their light. "Perhaps I am thinking too much of my own pride and not enough about Isaac. It hurts me, Molly, that he lied to me. He could not tell me what really happened. He hoped he could get away to London before the news of his conduct reached me. That is inexcusable!"

Yes, Molly thought, it was inexcusable. But she understood it. It was something she herself was capable of doing. How weak were the vessels into which Mrs. Warden poured her love!

"Is it not incredible that your husband should find Master Isaac in Macau?" She ventured, hoping to divert her mistress's thoughts. "It's half a world away!"

"Not at all," Mrs. Warden said. "Our men always check on one another when they reach a foreign port. For messages, letters, reports on conditions of trade. And white men always stay together in lands where they are strangers. The only coincidence lies in the fact that my husband happened to put in there at the same time as Isaac."

The diversion worked; Mrs. Warden got to her feet with a resolute smile and went to instruct Ellen to make a broth and toast some bread for Isaac's breakfast.

He did not appear that day or the next, or the day after. Mrs. Warden fetched the doctor. Well, Molly thought, he has probably got himself a catarrh and he deserves it. He'll make her think it's pneumonia, poor thing, until she's so distracted she'll forget what a blow he has dealt her.

In her secret worry over him, Molly herself forgot the duplicity of Isaac Warden.

The house became hushed as the women busied themselves nursing the fallen lord. Mrs. Warden wore herself out within a day, running the stairs to his room, back down, back up. When his condition became critical, the mistress gave in to common sense and stayed in his room with him. It was Molly, on tiptoe lest she disturb the quiet, who did the running with buckets of hot water and buckets of cold, compresses, syrups, and messes of poultice, slops, and food. The procession was endless, the silence oppressive; her body ached and her eyes were heavy, but worst of all was the terrible anxiety, the fear that due to her own error in judgment, Isaac might die.

Night was the worst; Molly took her mattress to the kitchen so that she could keep the fire higher and be better able to help her mistress should she call. The house, the world, were hushed; lying downstairs, Molly could hear the wracked breathing of Isaac Warden, who struggled for air, weak and wasted and fighting for his life.

In those fearsome days, all the women of the house wrung their hands in despair and kept his stifling room hot and filled with steam, and plastered his chest with evil smelling things.

At last he could breathe more easily. Then his fever dropped, and he was able to stay awake long enough to smile his thanks and eat some of the food they offered him.

The crisis was past. The women sang about their work.

Not long after, when Mrs. Warden was out, Molly, at Bethia's instruction, took a tray up to him and learned that he was recovering more than his health.

"Pray, stay and talk, Molly," he coaxed after she had placed the tray across his knees.

"Me?" Her old admiration caused her heart to leap.

"And who else?"

"Talking will tire you, Master Isaac." His attention was heady.

"But I have so many things to ask you. About Elijah, for instance."

Was he stalking her, using Elijah as bait? Her excitement mounted. "You are too sick to spend time asking questions," she said evenly. A fireside flirtation, she told herself. That's all it is. It's Elijah who loves you, she reminded herself. She turned to leave.

He caught her wrist with a sudden grip so strong it wrenched her, yet did not dislodge the tray on his lap. "Sit and talk," he commanded. "I am lonely."

It was clear he would not release her. With the hand that remained free, she drew a chair up to his bedside and looked at him inquiringly. She tried to remain calm in the face of the challenge he presented. Oh, why was he so handsome?

"I am interested in why you wish to marry Elijah," Isaac said softly so as not to overheard. His face was flushed and his eyes were bright, but his voice was clear and strong. How sick was he?

"I am fortunate that Elijah wants me."

"You could do better."

"You forget that I am but a servant, Master Isaac."

"But a very comely one. You could have the world at your feet."

She stared at him; his hand on her wrist loosened its hold and moved upward; his thumb moved along her inner arm in a caress. Fear began to rise in her.

"It's true, Molly. A beautiful woman can have everything she wants. Not here, in this backwater, but out in the world, where beauty is appreciated." He released her and nonchalantly began his breakfast. "This porridge tastes wonderful. I must be getting better."

"How nice." Offering a smile, she rose from the chair. Quickly he reached for her again and the tray slid off his lap, spilling the hot tea. Cursing, he flung back the blankets and leaped out of bed.

She fled to the kitchen. Soon she heard him calling and hid in the privy, leaving grumpy Bethia to clean up the mess.

The confusion he thrust upon her mounted. Unwillingly, she dreamed of him, of his magnetic eyes, of his touch, of the cool appraisal in his glance and the smile at the corner of his mouth as he spoke.

In her bed at night, she became restless when she thought of him, and by day, he hovered in her mind as she went about household tasks or made clothing for her trousseau. She struggled to put him from her thoughts, yet she had only Henry Hastings to replace him. Isaac was infinitely more attractive!

As he recovered his health, he became restive. He complained about losing time with his law books; he begged his mother to read them aloud and, when she tired, requested Molly to take her place.

There was no way she could refuse to read. Mrs. Warden thought he was doing his best to get along in the world, and it was up to them all to support his efforts.

The next afternoon, the mistress came to her with Isaac's book. "He has been resting since I read this morning," she said. "Now, if you would take a turn I would be very grateful. I confess it is heavy going."

"Perhaps I am not well-enough schooled yet," Molly protested, feeling somehow that there would be no escape for her, no matter what she said. "I may not be able to read most of the words, Mistress."

"It will be a challenge, most certainly." Mrs. Warden smiled. "Do the best you are able, my dear. It will be a great help to me. Right now, I must take a posset to Mistress Farnsworth—she's been unwell. Ellen has gone home, but Bethia will be here, should you need anything."

"Very well," Molly agreed, and full of trepidation and excitement, went upstairs. Isaac's room was bright with the winter afternoon's light. Quietly she let herself in, hoping he was still sleeping. He was not; he watched her approach, settle herself in a chair well out of reach of his bed and open the book. If he were a cat, she thought, he would watch a mouse like that.

Without addressing him, she read a line.

"Come, Molly," he said softly, persuasively. "Why don't you move right over here"—he patted the bed beside him—"so I can see you better?"

"I'm sorry your illness has affected your vision," she said. She read another line.

"So you're quick as well as pretty," he interjected. "I deserved that. Read on."

For another five minutes, she read haltingly, then paused to catch her breath, listened to Bethia's bustling about in the kitchen below.

"It's true about Elijah, isn't it?" Isaac asked in a low voice, lest the older woman should overhear.

"What is true?"

"That you don't love him."

"Why would you think such a thing, Master? He is such a decent man, how could a woman help loving him?"

"No woman ever loved a man because he was decent."

He watched her, his gaze steady, and she could feel her color rising. Quickly, she looked down and tried to find her place in the book, wishing she could remain calm. It was infuriating to be so flustered by him.

"I owe you an apology for my crude behavior the other day," he said before she could go on. "I am not normally so rude. Perhaps I can blame it on my feverish state. Will you forgive it?"

"Of course." She nodded and read a line of gibberish.

"Master Isaac?" Bethia's voice came up the kitchen stairs. "I'll be out at the hen house for a bit."

"Very well," he called down. "Do you know why I think you do not love him?" he asked, as though their conversation before were uninterrupted.

"Please don't," she begged. "Please stop badgering me."

"I am not badgering you, dear Molly." His voice became urgent. "I am trying, though you will not let me, to tell you that I understand you, just as I believe you can see me for what I am. It is not often that any of us can be honest with one another. We must ever pretend that we are something we are not. But you need not pretend with me, Molly. I would not try to make you into something you are not, as my mother is doing. Nor would I demand you play a role that suited me, as you will have to do when you wed Elijah. You know that I am a vain and foolish and perhaps lazy man. Is that not true? Can you accept that? And if you can, how difficult is it to imagine that I can accept you, just as you are?"

She stared at him for a long while. It was as though he were giving her the right to be herself. It was as though a sharper, stronger, clearer Molly were emerging from under his gaze.

"I am almost afraid to ask what you have seen in me," she said, her voice barely audible. "From your actions, Master Isaac, I assume you think I am a whore."

He had the decency to blush.

"From my actions, I think you can assume only that I am a clod," he said. A long silence gathered. "I believe you are a woman who can face the truth. You are not, nor will you ever be, a whore. You are too clever. There is no future in such behavior, and you will do nothing that will not forward your future. And you will marry for the same reason. Am I right?"

"What are you trying to do?" she demanded, her anger rising. "No decent woman would admit to such accusations. May I be excused?"

"I'm only telling you that I see you clearly. And that I accept you for what you are. I admire it. You should be flattered."

"I am not," she said hotly and ran from the room and down the stairs. With a flounce, she seated herself at the loom, hoping a stint would calm her ire.

How much cloth had she made? She checked. Hopefully there would soon be enough to take to the fuller and she'd be done with it. If weaving was better than spinning, it was not better for long! They were both dull, dull, and would cause her to be dull, too. Elijah must do well, so that she could buy goods ready-made!

An involuntary flush spread across her cheeks. That was the sort of thing Isaac knew she would think, and it was indecent of him. He should not know such things! Yet had she not seen him for what he was, at least sensed it, from the moment she first saw him? Might he not be equally attuned to her? Perhaps their spirits were kindred, after all.

He was right, she thought suddenly. She was forced by Elijah, and even Mistress Warden, into an act. Everyone and everything forced her into an act. Everyone but Master Isaac. She could not help smiling: Isaac Warden and Molly Deems were two of a kind, and he had seen it long before she had. He is dangerous, she thought suddenly. He knows too much. He is quick. Too quick for me.

In the days that followed, she tried valiantly to read law while he tried valiantly to coax her to him, his voice low and confidential so he would not be overheard, pulling her ever so slowly from her protective veneer of submissive innocence, gradually building a feeling of camaraderie that she denied to herself and, by her studied composure, to him. In the process, her role as a servant was slowly changing into one of an equal.

"I admire you very much. You are the greatest little gambler I've ever known," he said one afternoon. It was the last she would read to him, for his doctor told him he might rise on the morrow.

"And what do you mean by that?" she asked archly. "Gambler?"

"You are staking your whole life on one throw of the dice," he explained. "When you marry Elijah Merrick." He had not thrown

Elijah up to her in many days, preferring instead the more usual games of wordplay.

"Then that is a gamble I'll choose." In order to put him off the subject, she laughed, then closed the book and prepared to leave the room.

Suddenly he was out of his bed, pulling her to him.

"Aha, I have you now," he mocked, his eyes merry, yet penetrating, too.

She froze. "Let me go, Isaac," she whispered. She could feel his body quivering with his effort and she could feel his heat rising as well. "You will injure yourself. You are too recently ill."

"It's in a worthwhile cause," he murmured, kissing her throat. "Shall I play the required part? Long have I admired you from afar." He swayed.

"Please." She could not help but giggle. "If you swoon, I should not know how to explain it."

"Just hold me upright!" He tipped up her chin, covered her lips with his own. His embrace was not boorish; it was, as he was, tantalizing, teasing, promising. The blood beat heavily in her ears as he drew back. "We're good together, Molly. I can show you pleasures you never dreamed of."

"Don't," she begged before he kissed her again, and again, until she felt she was smothering, until she knew, without meaning to, that her lips were answering his.

"That's right," he breathed. "I can teach you how to love. I can teach you so much. How lovely, how lovely you are." He stepped back at last, and drew her with him. "Help me back to bed," he commanded. "I fear I cannot make it alone. No, no," he hastened to say, "I will not drag you into it with me. I have wanted only to show you what I can offer. Think of it, Molly." He lay back on the pillows, his face white, a mist of sweat on it. Still holding the hands that had helped to steady him, he looked up at her. He was at once handsome, and helpless, and all together the most searing force she had ever experienced in her waking life. "I can tease you and touch you in delicious ways you don't even dream of now. I can make you nearly faint with pleasure; all you have to do is ask."

She felt the flaming of her face. Isaac's talk excited her, but she knew it should not. "You ought to be ashamed," she chided helplessly, "speaking like that to me."

"You should be complimented," he said. "Not one woman in a million could I say such things to. They would pretend to be aghast, even while they were titillated. They would banish me from their presence, even though they might long for me. You are so much more real than that. I hate to think of you submerged forever in the bog that is Rockford. For submerged you will be."

"Please, Master Isaac. Don't say such things. You only make it harder. For I must and I will marry Elijah. You can't even begin to understand why. But my mother was used, enslaved, if you will, and Elijah is my promise of not being enslaved too."

"Marriage for a woman is slavery of its own kind."

"I suppose it is," she said slowly. "If you look at it in a certain way. But surely, not even you could believe your father enslaved your mother when he married her."

"This is fruitless," he said. "I had hoped to make you understand, but you do not."

The stark certainty of her situation rose now so sharply and clearly that she spoke she spoke to Isaac as a woman, not as a servant. "I understand that you want to put me in bondage to you, but you do not want to pay for it."

"What do you mean?" he asked, a certain admiration lighting his eyes. So young a woman, yet so acute!

"You will not marry me yourself, will you? You will not provide a future for me! It is only the present you want. You would hold me to you with a promise of pleasure. You would coax me from Elijah, but offer no alternative to him."

"The present is delightful," he smiled roguishly. "It is ruined if you look so far ahead that you can take no pleasure in it."

"A rich man's son can say that," she retorted. "But a poor man's son knows better."

"And if I said I would marry you? What then, Mistress Molly?"

"You are only teasing," she said, and went to the door. "It is unkind."

"Well," he shrugged "It's a possibility, is it not?"

She backed from the room. Marriage? A possibility? To Isaac Warden?

Hardly!

But she shivered when she thought of his lingering lips and the promise that they held. This was disgraceful! She was betrothed to a man she had carefully snared. And now here was this one. To think that only a short time ago her prospects were negligible, and now they were bounteous.

Then she sobered. Isaac was not a prospect. He was diverting, stimulating and enormously flattering. That was all. No woman in her right mind would take him seriously. And she did not. Resolutely she put him from her.

The next evening there was a small book of poetry on her bed. Inside the cover was written:

Let us not to the marriage of two minds admit impediments.

Isaac.

❊❊✦❊❊

It was only a matter of days before Elijah was expected back. Molly and Mrs. Warden assembled the trousseau to show him, putting final touches on the dresses they had made, on the aprons to which they had added bits of embroidery, on linens they had hemmed.

Captain Warden had returned, closeted himself with Isaac, and emerged, finally, having decided that the young man might go to England after all. Isaac had done what his father had requested. He had shipped as a sailor for nearly nine years, and if he had botched the job, he had at least done his parents' bidding. "And should I hear of any philandering while you're abroad, son," he said, "I will send for you at once, and you will go to Philadelphia. Some of our own staid aunts and uncles can curb you while you study at Ben Franklin's college. But I'll save that for a last resort. Perhaps the London social scene will be sufficient to keep your energy in bounds. I'll grant a ship tends to make it more explosive."

"Forgive me, Father, if I have embarrassed you," Isaac said sincerely. "But I hate the sea. It is so senseless, driving men day after day simply to shave a few hours from running time."

"None of them object," his father said brusquely. "They know their pay will be higher if they can beat the next incoming vessel. But just because the mariner's life is one your brother and I have chosen doesn't mean you must so choose. Let us part in peace, Isaac."

They embraced and the house breathed a sigh of relief.

Mrs. Warden was eager to spend all her available time with her husband and their friends who congregated for endless hours in the parlor. It was natural that she would appoint Isaac to take Molly to the mill. "I'd like to have your weaving fulled before Elijah gets back, my dear."

Molly looked at the material with misgivings. "I'm sure his mother could have done it better."

"Mrs. Merrick ought to; she's done it all her life," Mrs. Warden retorted. "For a first effort, it is very, very good. I should know!"

Against her will, Molly looked forward to spending the day with Isaac. After he had recovered and was up and out of bed, sitting by the fireside with his books, there was no chance for them to converse. But his eyes told her he had not forgotten their hours together or their embrace.

After getting the carriage ready, he helped her into it, climbed up himself and set the horse to trotting down the sandy road. "I'm glad of the chance to be alone with you again, Molly," he said. The sun beat on them with warmth and comfort, and she relaxed in its caress, happy to pretend that she belonged in the carriage with him and always would.

"It is a lovely day for a ride," she said languidly. "See how the sun shines on every pine needle. And look there—that willow is nearly greening."

"It is lovely indeed," he said. "And made more so by your presence."

The carriage veered sharply off the road and onto a cart track. When she stared at him, he laughed and then stopped some distance from their turning.

"We will probably not have another chance to be together," he said. "Perhaps you would once again permit me to kiss you. A farewell token." He asked so earnestly she could find no words to refuse.

"I think it is hardly proper," she murmured. "There is no gain in it for either of us."

"My clearheaded, hardhearted Molly! How you have captivated me! How I wish our circumstances were different!"

Cupping her face in his hands, he kissed her carefully.

Ah, she liked it. She could not help liking it. She had thought so often about the earlier kiss that this one was almost a continuation of it. Her heart beat loudly in her ears.

"We would be so good together, so good," he said at last. "Molly, Molly, no one will come this way. Come into the woods with me, that I might hold you closer."

"Your attentions flatter me, Master Isaac," she demurred, completely flustered by the terrible excitement surrounding them both. "But I think we should not go there."

"A pretty place lies behind that stand of pine. I'll show you."

In an instant, he was out of the carriage and around to her side; he lifted her to the ground gently but insistently. His strength had clearly returned.

In a small clearing carpeted with dense moss, he drew her down beside him. They kissed again, and then again before she reluctantly pulled away.

"If I have to walk to the mill, Master, I will," she said defiantly. "I think we should leave."

"Don't be alarmed," he cajoled. "You would not disappoint me, would you, Molly? I have awaited this moment for so long. There will never be another!"

"Then this makes no sense at all. It has no meaning, Isaac. Come, let us be on our way. We can enjoy this beautiful day, can we not? Isn't that enough?"

"No," he said flatly. "It is not enough. Pleasure has no meaning. It doesn't need any. It justifies itself. You'll see."

He nuzzled her ear, her throat, and he kissed her again, the kiss becoming more and more urgent. Before she knew it, his hand was cupping her breast. She drew back but he followed her, his lips pursued hers.

Relaxing his hold, he said, "Has a man ever touched you, Molly? I would be willing to believe none has." He began unlacing her dress.

"No one. No one. I wish you would stop, Isaac. Please." She tried to refasten the laces. Her torn self, wishing he would stop, wishing he would go on, made her fingers clumsy.

Gently, he captured her hand. "Let me show you what a wonderful thing a woman's breast is, Molly. Why, you don't even know." He stroked her softly. "You have beautiful breasts, full, soft. And look, my sweeting, they stand out just ever so much, all by themselves. And when I touch here," his fingers caressed the nipple beneath her chemise, "you will feel—ah! Already! A tightening, a pleasurable sensation elsewhere. Is it not true?"

"Yes, yes," she cried in wonder. His eyes, intense and magnetic, fed her lonely soul with loving, with admiration, with understanding.

"Even nicer," he said, slipping the chemise down her shoulder, "when there is nothing between you and me."

She let him slide the undergarment off her other shoulder, let him kiss her bared and lovely breasts until her nipples were small and tight and hard beneath his touch. It was delicious, just as he had promised. Leaning back, she submitted herself to him, shudders traveling the length of her and a curious fullness gathering, which throbbed and pulsed and which she did not understand.

Then, in a deft, strong motion, she lay beneath him. He rose above her, his forehead beaded with sweat, his eyes burning. "You know what I'm going to do, don't you, Molly?" he said quietly. "You know I intend to have you."

It was as a dash of cold water, chilling her instantly, making her heart turn cold, heavy. Dear God, she thought, what have I done?

"No! No! Please no!" she cried. It would ruin everything! She tried to push him away, but he held her easily with his weight and lifted her skirts.

"You are beautiful . . . , vibrant . . . , warm . . . ." He parted her legs with one knee, then the other.

Elijah will never marry me, she thought wildly. "Oh, please, Master Isaac," she moaned. "Let me go, oh please do."

With all the strength she could muster, she twisted, she writhed, but could not escape him. She was sick with the sudden realization that he had trapped her and that his strength was beyond breaking.

"I have admired your beauty from the beginning," he said in short gasps, somehow undoing his breeches and holding her tightly at the same time. "Now you will wed that ridiculous, sanctimonious fellow, and I shall never have another chance. So I shall help myself first."

Something hard, something hurtful, probed the soft wet flesh between her legs, something that bore down on her, relentless. Oh, God, her thoughts whirled. Is this my punishment? Oh, God, that a man should so use a woman! For the first time in a long time she remembered her mother . . . .

The probing became agonizing. "Please don't do this to me, Isaac. Please!" she begged, but he did not hear. His eyes were closed; he would not look at her; his words continued as though she had not spoken.

"I would have preferred softness; I would have preferred a whole day, a whole night, to caress you and you me, until this point. Relax, Molly. Don't fight me. Then you will like it. You will!"

Then, having found what he sought, he entered her and covered her mouth when she screamed. He paused, thrust. Tensed. Shuddered.

And then it was done. He rolled to her side, staring up at the trees as they sketched themselves with spring delicacy against the sky.

She wept.

She wept from pain. She wept from humiliation. She wept for her dreams, scattered and lost. He has taken me, she thought. He has gotten what he wanted. I am no longer a virgin. Everything is gone, gone. She lay still and silent and miserable, her groin aching, her flesh burning, her skirts crumpled and flung up to her waist.

An interminable time passed. Brown oak leaves, clinging tightly against the onslaught of the swelling season, rustled secretively; a bird called, an animal nearby scurried from stump to log; a twig far away fell. The dampness of the earth seeped into her clothing, but she was heedless of it. Her silent tears soaked her hair.

Isaac rolled over, propping himself on an elbow, watching her face and tears for a while. He was inscrutable; there was no expression in his eyes, just watchfulness. "We will have to make haste," he said at last. As she lay there, limp, he drew her dress down over her nakedness and touched her cheek with a knuckle. "You are beautiful, beautiful. I will never forget this day."

Just like that, she thought bitterly. Just like that, he has taken what he wanted and then will set me on my way. Oh, God, she thought, her heart breaking, oh God, how can I go on?

He stood up, adjusted his clothing. The sun struck him full through a gap in the forest overhead, his blond hair flashing, and he was, of an instant, a golden god.

"Tidy up, my love," he said, looking down at her. "'Tis still a beautiful day, and a nice one for a drive." Nudging her with the toe of his boot, he directed, "Now."

If I just lie here, she thought, he'll not know what to do.

But she struggled up, rearranging her chemise. Drops of blood were sprinkled here and there on her clothing; she was sore, and it was no easy task to crawl up to the seat of the carriage. The package of homespun lay on the floor where it had fallen so long ago, and she put it on her lap and waited for Isaac to get in. He turned the patient horse, and they regained the highroad.

"See?" he said. "Is it not a lovely day?"

She turned stricken eyes on him, full with unshed tears, and then looked at the road again without answering.

He shrugged and, clucking to the horse, urged it to a faster pace.

✦ↄↄ 4 ↄↄ✦

The note was delivered by a panting, small boy.

> *My deerest—*
>
> *I am in Rockford and will come to the Wardens tomorrow. I will bring you back to mete my mother and return you to Yarmouth by suppertime. Impachently awaiting the moment when I can see you.*
>
> *Elijah*

When she showed the note to Mrs. Warden, her mistress hugged her tightly. "Oh, it's such an exciting time, my dear! It's almost like courting again, for me. We will have you both for supper, whenever you get back. Abel, is it not sweet?"

"It is, it is," he agreed, and turned the page of the newspaper he was reading. "I hope Miss Molly will feel comfortable at our table. We'll help her to, all we can."

"Thank you, Captain!"

She tried to say it with gratitude and with the happiness she knew she should be feeling. It was difficult, and she wondered how her poor performance could possibly fool them for even a minute; she wondered, for that matter, how any of her actions of the last four days could conceivably have fooled anybody.

But they saw only what they wished to see, and as she went about her tasks, polishing silver and dusting the dining room—by herself, for Mrs. Warden did not share the household tasks now that the captain was home—she began to see that she had more self-control than she had realized. She could smile and laugh at the required times, set her feet to flying as though they had wings. She could lay impassive eyes on Isaac when she served at table and look right through him whenever he entered the kitchen. All the while she wondered how she could contain the pain of betrayal, endure her own contribution to that betrayal, stupidly enjoying those fatal kisses that led to being trapped. Constantly she remembered moment and pain when Isaac entered her very flesh, and its anguish. But worst was the sure and certain knowledge that for all his love, Elijah would have only a virgin for a bride.

When he discovered, once they were married, that she had been used already, his pride would forbid him ever to love her, ever to do for her all the wonderful things she had envisioned. He would hate her. And he would have reason.

It paralyzed her, not knowing what move to make next or, indeed, if any such move existed. Then, last night as she lay sleepless on her bed, it had suddenly caught her in an enormous wave that crashed onto the shore of her consciousness, the sudden realization that she could no longer lie there, submissively letting herself be lacerated by her misgivings, her conscience, her aches, her woes. Her sorrows had so overwhelmed her—her greatest difficulty being how to present Elijah with her lost virginity—that she had not even considered this final, totally demolishing, possibility . . . .

She could be with child.

So far she had only reeled from one torment to the next. But now she knew she would have to act. Somehow she must cajole Elijah into marrying her now, on this trip home. It was too big a gamble to wait and hope nothing had happened, for by the time she knew she was pregnant, Elijah would be gone. And if they could marry now, somehow, perhaps before a civil officer, the problem of the church and its cursed ministry would no longer matter, either.

Well, she thought grimly, at least if I marry him now one good thing will have come of this disaster. Pastor Hastings can go kiss a pig.

She turned from this gratifying image to the problems at hand and the possibilities of solution. Since she had had her body so recently used by another, it occurred to her that she might try to stir Elijah to the point where he could not resist and would be impelled to marry her immediately in order to have her. But she knew she could not make herself do it. Although she did not love him, still she cared too much about him for that. Besides, she thought, he was no Isaac Warden, indulgent, pleasure seeking. He was far more controlled, and, she suspected, far more strait. No doubt he had experimented sufficiently at ports of call to know all he needed to. But she guessed he would not have done so out of simple idleness. Only from necessity. Here she sighed. The plain fact was that she did not know how to seduce him, even if she would.

She rejected telling him outright, for if he did not abandon her, he might well feel compelled to defend her integrity and his own by killing Isaac—this would, in fact, be expected of him—but it would so injure Mistress Warden that Molly discarded this notion as she had the first. Besides, it might be wishful thinking. Maybe he'd kill her, instead.

She reread his note and his other letter to her. Surely if he loved her so much . . . .

Perhaps he could be made jealous, she mused, be made to think that Isaac was his rival. Perhaps that might cause him to act on impulse. Jealousy could drive any person to extremes, even Elijah Merrick.

It depended, really, on how possessive he might be and if his possessiveness could be made overwhelming. Beneath his restraint, she thought, there might be a whole hotbed of raw, tightly checked emotion. If it could be released . . . .

She gnawed on her lip, thinking.

Late that night, while everyone in the house slept, she crept down the attic stairs, candle in hand, and went to Isaac's room. Her trembling caused the hot wax to drip onto her fingers. It burned but she paid it no heed.

Slipping inside, she closed the door quietly behind her.

"Who is it?" he murmured.

His voice startled her, for she thought he would be asleep. At least she was spared having to shake him from slumber; she did not want to touch him.

"It's Molly," she whispered. "Let me light your candle. Mine is nearly gone."

"Oh. Yes, I see," he yawned, handing her his candle. The room leaped into light as she lit it and set it on a table. "I little dreamed, though I hoped, you might come to me, my Molly." He moved over and patted the vacant space beside him. "There's room for you right here."

How can he be so boorish, she wondered, a flare of anger shooting through her. She fought it down in order to keep her head clear.

"I need your help." She drew up a chair and blew out her candle. Her desperation had turned her to steel now, leaving no room for panic. There is nothing left that he can do to me, she thought.

"Only ask," he said, a smile on his handsome mouth, his eyes wandering provocatively over her.

"Elijah must marry me now. And you must convince him to do it."

"If I should tell him what I know of you, my love," he drawled, "Master Merrick would hardly be capable of containing himself. Why, he would marry you instantly."

"There is a way to persuade him to change the plans he has made already," she continued, not allowing him to trigger her anger. "You must convince him you intend to marry me yourself and that you plan to take me to England with you. If he believes it, I think he won't go out on his next trip without making sure I am safely his."

"I am sure he would not," Isaac agreed. "Perhaps it's a good idea. Would you enjoy England?"

She stared coldly at him.

"You are so delectable, Molly. I could arrange passage to England for you. I would do so willingly, in order to keep you by my side. Not as my wife, of course. That is unthinkable, for I am a Warden. But when I depart, whenever that is to be, you could just . . . disappear. I could meet you in Boston, or New York, and arrange your passage from there."

"Isaac, you're not listening! He must marry me now!"

"Why the haste?"

"In case . . . ." Her face reddened and she wondered if he could see her blush in the candlelight. "In case I am with child."

"Oh," he said. "So that is what is worrying you."

"Yes," she said flatly. "That is what worries me."

He picked a small clump of fuzz from his blanket. "Well, in that case, Molly, I rather have you where I want you, do I not?"

She watched his eyes unclothe her as he rolled the ball of fuzz between his thumb and forefinger. Incredible, he was. Unbelievable.

"No," he said slowly. "No, I think I would prefer that you came to England with me. In case you were, er, um, with child, I could arrange a way to fix it. In the meantime, there are many delightful hours to be had." He discarded the fuzz and made as though to reach for her.

"I'm going nowhere with you, Isaac Warden," she hissed as she quickly rose and moved out of range. "You are going to convince Elijah that you are out to marry me, so he'll take me away with him. And you are going to do it now."

"You are hardly in a position to make demands."

"I certainly am," she snapped. "And I shall. How do you think your mother and father would take it, should I tell them that you raped me?"

He stared. "You would not."

"Oh, but I would," she said. "I know your mother, probably better than you do. I should not like to tell her, for it would hurt her badly if she knew the truth about you. But I will if I have to. And what is more, Isaac, I am sure, once your parents knew what you did, there would be no trip to England for you. Do I make myself clear?"

He looked at her coolly enough, but she could see a pulsing vein in his temple. "I think you really would tell them," he said at last, when she refused to drop her eyes. "But what makes you think they would believe you?"

"They know you lie. Neither your mother nor your father would believe your denials. And they know I would have nothing to gain by such a deception. If Elijah does not marry me on this leave, be assured that I will tell them, Isaac, whether I am with child or not. I hold England for you, and you hold Elijah for me. You must come up with a plan, and it must work. Do you understand?"

His face and voice were cold. "Oh, yes," he drawled. "I understand." He thought about it. "We will have to convince him that he has a serious rival in me. Of course, you will have to do your part. You will have to make him think that you could be persuaded."

"Don't worry about me," she said. "I have the little book you gave me, which will be a good start. But I'll need something more. Another token of esteem. A piece of jewelry, or something like it."

"Quakers are not accustomed to giving and getting jewelry," he said sardonically. "There is nothing I can give you."

"You can find something somewhere, I'm sure," she said evenly. "It's up to you to get it. I trust it will not bother your conscience too greatly, if you were to deal for only a short time with an ornament."

She lit her candle from his, then went to the door. "I will somehow convince Elijah that I am interested in you, and you will let him know it is mutual. It's up to you. For Isaac, make no mistake, I shall tell should you fail."

Somehow she made it back to her room without stumbling or knocking against the walls, her welled-up tears blinding her. When she was safe behind her own door, she let them go without restraint. How very handsome he was! How wonderful a lover he would have been . . . .

✕✕✦✕✕

When she saw Elijah, mounted and trotting toward the house, she was nearly giddy. She was not sure how a proper young maiden greeted her betrothed after a long separation. Not sure how a proper young maiden, in love, acted in the company of her betrothed. Nor how that young maiden would act if she were being drawn away from her betrothed without herself knowing it. Innocent, she decided dryly. Innocence should cover it all.

As she had that first day, she met him at the door, with the sun on her face and hair. As she smiled, she spoke to him in her heart. Love me, Elijah Merrick, she said fiercely, love me and I will repay you in the only coin any man ever wanted. Love me, and you may ever have your will with me.

For the occasion, she wore one of her new muslin frocks with white collars and cuffs and delicate traces of blue embroidery. Playfully, she curtsied and swayed to show him its full skirt and then drew him into the hall and stood there, holding both his hands in hers, tilting her head up to reach his gaze, looking deeply into his eyes. The knot of tension loosened as she sought his love there. In that moment she could recall who and what he was, a man so different from Isaac Warden. It would not be difficult, she saw in that instant, to know how to act. Elijah himself, open and honest, assuming that her love was his, had cast her into the mold expected of her and would give her the cues she needed.

And so she abandoned herself to him, and in that moment cast the die of her future for his love and protection, staked her life on his mercy, on his lust, and gambled all she had that she might win the future of her dreams.

The Quarry

SHE WAS LOVELIER than he remembered, glowing, vibrant. It seemed to him that she surrounded him with love, for just one glance told him of her trust and faith. He forgot the opening words of greeting he had rehearsed. They were not necessary.

"My Molly," he said, his eyes taking in her whole self. "How lovely you are!" He reached for her hands and pulled her toward him and kissed her forehead, then each flushed cheek. How he longed to enfold her in his arms, but dared not! He stepped back, ostensibly to admire her dress. "What a pretty frock!" he exclaimed. "The color becomes you well."

"Mrs. Warden and I made it. I'm glad you like it!" She set her skirt to swaying again, proud and pleased.

"I do indeed. You should always have lovely things to wear. You do so much for them!"

"Oh, Elijah," she smiled, "I'm very happy you are back."

And then he did embrace her, chastely, a quick hug in which he could glimpse a small ear through her hair, on which, with great restraint, he dropped a quick kiss. My God, he thought. I will go mad!

"Mistress says we may sit in the parlor." She took his hand and led him there.

It was delightful to take his ease in the Wardens' lovely sitting room with just Molly and himself chatting in an unhurried fashion.

She sat a proper distance from him on the horsehair settee, and sternly he commanded himself to make no move toward her. He would obey the courtship protocols if it killed him.

"Elijah, you wouldn't believe everything my mistress has done for me since you left. She has taught me so much, as though I were her daughter." She cocked her head and shot him a mischievous glance. "I will make you a far better wife, knowing all the domestic arts and not just how to polish silver."

His heart went out to her at her pleasure in learning skills other girls would acquire as their birthright. "You would make me a good wife in any case," he said. "But I'm glad, very glad, Molly, that Mrs. Warden has given you so much and made you so happy."

"You, my dear Elijah," she said softly, "it is you who will give me the most joy."

They gazed at each other for a long, deep moment. Then there were sounds in the hall—a loud male voice, a light womanly one. Mrs. Warden and the captain entered the room, laughing. The young people leaped to their feet.

"I hope we have announced ourselves sufficiently!" Mrs. Warden said, and gave Elijah's cheek her welcoming kiss. "I'm so glad to see you, my dear boy! And I expect Molly is, too."

"She gives me cause to think so," he said, shaking the hand of the captain and reseating himself.

It had been years since he had seen Abel Warden, and the man's charm was as compelling as ever it had been when Elijah was a callow youth and the Wardens had interested themselves in his future. Their continued goodwill was warming, and he felt himself at home.

"Tell us about your voyage, Elijah. Or shall I call you Captain now?" Abel Warden teased.

"Yes, I am finally a captain," Elijah grinned. "It was a very good voyage. You should really reconsider the European ports yourself, sir. There's a wealth of opportunity in them."

"I'm pretty well confirmed in the northwest routes by now, my boy. But I'd like to hear about Europe nonetheless."

"This evening, dear. I think they want to go to Rockford this afternoon." Turning from her husband, Mrs. Warden proposed, "We can all have supper together here when you get back. Will that be agreeable, Captain?"

Elijah made no response.

"Captain?" Mistress Warden repeated.

"She means you, Elijah," Molly whispered.

"Oh! Me! Yes! Yes, indeed!" he floundered, having forgotten his new status.

"And since the hour will be late, I see no reason why the captain—meaning you, Elijah—might not stay the night here. Do you, my dear?" she asked her husband.

"Goodness no. No reason at all," Captain Warden said. "We'd be happy to have you. 'Twould be like having another of our sons home."

"Another?" Elijah asked.

"Isaac. It has been quite awhile since you've seen him. He'll be happy to know you're here."

Elijah covered his disappointment quickly. "Oh, yes. Yes, I shall be glad to see him too." Isaac had never been one of his favorite people in their boyhood. Perhaps he had improved with age. But Elijah could not help wishing it were John instead.

"It will be a full day—you'd best be starting out. Get your cloak, Molly," Mrs. Warden said.

With a smile Molly slipped out of the room, and he watched her go, marveling at her grace.

"After supper, perhaps you can see some of the things Molly has accomplished in your absence," Elizabeth Warden suggested.

"I was just trying to find the words to thank you," he said, "and you too, sir, for all you have done for her. It was the first thing she told me and it has meant a great deal to her."

"I have enjoyed it," Mrs. Warden said simply. "She is a dear girl."

"So few people would have . . . ." he began, fumbling for the words to tell this fine woman of his gratitude.

She hushed him. "We Quakers have not the impediments that blind many of our fellow men," she said quietly. "When you see everyone as the possessor of the Divine, it makes no difference where a person comes from, or what their background is."

"You make me wish to know more about your faith, since it gives you such a sound moral guide," he said stiffly, beginning to feel out of his depth and wishing fervently that Molly might return. The Church of the Standing Order, Congregational, might do little to change men's hearts, but it was where he belonged.

"Before you leave, I'll give you one of my books by William Penn. He explains our faith very well. Should you wish to talk of it more someday, then I should be happy to do so."

"His thoughts are of marriage, my dear," her husband said. "Not of sanctity."

Elijah looked sharply at the captain, wondering if the older man was able to read his mind. Abel Warden's eyes twinkled in amusement.

Molly reappeared miraculously, and no further comment was necessary. Recovering his composure, Elijah bowed himself and her from the room quickly.

The air was warm and sweet, with a salt tang to it. They breathed it deeply and he swung her up on the saddle, happy to have her again in the crook of his arm. Her hair brushed his cheek.

"I hope you will not be uncomfortable," he said. "Hector has not the smoothest gait I have ever ridden, but he is adequate on the short haul."

"Why, he has a name!" she exclaimed. "That must mean he is yours! When did you get him, Elijah?"

"My brother, Jon, bought him. He decided if we could afford an addition to our house, we could afford a horse, too. He found Hector at a very reasonable price in Harwich."

"Congratulations," Molly said coyly. "I am happy to see that you are coming up in the world, Captain."

Elijah received her words seriously, without understanding that she was teasing him. "I must come up in the world, my sweet, so that I might give you all that my heart desires for you," he declared heavily, blushing at his own pomposity. Curses, he thought, I am not at the headquarters of Fuller or on the quarterdeck impressing my sailors. "It takes awhile to get to my house," he tried again. "But we can stop and stretch whenever you wish."

"I hope it takes forever to get to Rockford," she said wistfully, and the side of her face that he could see held a small, frightened smile. "I admit I am nervous about it, Elijah."

"I can't blame you," he confessed, somewhat dreading it himself.

"What shall I do? What shall I say?"

"I'll help you, Molly. Just follow my lead."

He would have gladly given everything he possessed or ever would possess to ease her way and lift the troubled frown he saw now on her brow. They bobbed along on Hector for an interminable hour and then dismounted by the Rockford mill stream.

It was small, as streams went. The road crossed it in a rock-lined ford that was easily passable all year. Incredible that so much power could be generated from so small a brook, but the chain of ponds beyond and out of sight ensured a steady flow. Two mills stood confident, the gristmill on the bay side, downstream, the fullery up toward the ponds. The stream was in spate, tearing around and over boulders, tumbling to create small waterfalls, eddying into backwaters before rushing out to join the bay a mile distant, winking blue in the sun.

The trees overhanging the banks, even though not yet in leaf, made the Rockford mills a beautiful place despite the noise of the grinding wheels and fulling paddles. Elijah took Molly's arm and led her well beyond the gristmill, downstream toward the bay where the business of the mills subsided and the peace of the sunlit day was restored.

They looked for the herring that should soon begin making their spring pilgrimage to the upstream ponds where they would spawn. "Isn't that one?" she called, running farther down the bank.

"Looks like it," he said. "And here's another."

They watched the fish work their way by. "I used to catch them for Farmer Crosby," he told her, remembering those wet, happy afternoons that, while they lasted, freed him from the farm.

"Isaac brought me to the Yarmouth mill just a few days ago," she said. "But there were none there."

There was a timbre to her voice that he had never heard before. He turned to look at her. "Why were you there with him?"

"For the fulling. I haven't had a chance to tell you. Mrs. Warden has taught me to make cloth, and Isaac was kind enough to bring me to the Yarmouth mill. To get it shrunk. So its weave becomes tight."

In her eyes was a certain inscrutability that chilled him. "Did it turn out well? The cloth, I mean?"

"We'll see when I get it back. The process takes a while. I'm sure your mother wouldn't think highly of it," she said with a frown, "though Mrs. Warden says it shall be passable as a first effort."

Her reference to his mother was a welcome diversion. "Listen, Molly." He drew her to a log beside the path and sat down there with her. "You must not worry so about my mother."

"I can't help it," she said, and he saw her lip quiver. "I want her to like me, and I'm afraid she will not."

He was quiet for a while, listening to the stream. Above them the swirling gulls called, also watching for herring making their way to the ponds. It was pointless to evade; he wished he could say nothing and spare her. He wished there were no need to give her counsel. Yet, he thought, all the alternatives weighed and found wanting, directness was what she needed and would want. He must risk hurting her though he hated it. But Elijah Merrick was not one to evade things he hated.

"Let me be honest," he said at last. "I hope I don't wound you. If what I say changes your feeling for me, I shall always regret it. Yet I cannot let you walk into my house unprepared. My mother will be civil, but I fear, Molly, that she will not give you a warm welcome. She is a country woman, set in her ways and unaccustomed to visitors she doesn't already know. She may look askance at you. A stranger. A girl she knows has been a servant. That being the case, I think you might try being somewhat high-handed, if you are able."

"High-handed!" she gasped, and then giggled. "Me? High-handed?"

"Yes, and why not? You are virtually an adopted daughter of the Wardens. Except for their religion, no one could have a higher or more respected position than they. So why not pretend you are a Warden? Born to wealth and bred to gentility. It will do you as well or better than meekness. Naturally you must be respectful of my mother—I'm not suggesting impertinence or anything like that . . . ."

He stopped, wishing he could avoid being so garrulous, then tried again. "If my mother thought she could trample on you, I'm afraid she would. Not while I'm around, of course, but later, when I'm not. If you let her know, nicely but firmly, right from the start, that she cannot intimidate you—well, I think you should."

"I have no practice at being high-handed, Elijah!" Yet her eyes gleamed; he thought she almost welcomed the challenge.

Grinning, he encouraged her. "I think you can do it."

"She wouldn't be so unwelcoming if I were a member of the King family, would she?"

He was startled. How did she know about the clan feud in Rockford Village? "Yes, that's true."

"And is it possible that even a daughter of the Halls would be more welcome than I?"

There was a long silence before he said at last, "I suppose it is, Molly." He sat miserably, hating this for her, and his misery must have shown, for she put her hand on his cheek and turned his face so he must meet her eyes.

"I care for your sake, Elijah, not for my own. You are quite sure? I mean, sure you want to marry me?"

"Molly, Molly, I am certain." He nearly shouted in his desperation. "I love you!" He shook his head. There was nothing else he could say. "I love you," he pleaded abjectly.

She jumped to her feet. "Then we'll practice being high-handed. Come, give me your arm."

Mystified, he complied and walked with her back up the path toward the gristmill.

"Ah!" she exclaimed, with an artificial song in her voice. "I espy an old friend. Pray, my dear Elijah, let me introduce you." She led him close to the stream where a rock impeded the flow of water. "Mistress Gurgle, I should like you to meet my friend Captain Merrick. He has recently returned from Europe. Captain, this is Mrs. Merrily Gurgle."

He bowed, and the brook babbled in acknowledgement.

"And there! Yonder I see the Twigs." She pulled him toward a small clump of scraggy bushes. "Captain, may I present Mistress and Master Twig?"

He bowed again.

"Oh, yes," she rolled on, "this dress is the latest fashion in London just now. The captain keeps me well informed. Perhaps, my dear, you would enjoy it should I show you the collection he has brought me." She looked the bushes over. "'Twould bring some light to the provincial clothespress, I might think."

Laughing despite his concern, he looked down at her fondly. "You are a lively sprite, Molly!"

"Well," she shrugged, "we might as well get some fun out of it." She looked at him with pleading eyes, and he took a kiss from those trusting lips. He had to use much Merrick restraint to bring it to an end; this was, after all, a public place. Despair and the height of affection struggled with one another.

"Your humor will save us all, Molly," he said. "I do love you so."

"And I love you, Elijah."

He took her arm and led her back to the horse, he bowing and she dipping to the trees they passed in continuation of their charade.

The Merrick house was a short ride away. At the barn, he lifted her down and unsaddled Hector. She held the bridle and patted the soft muzzle.

"I should admire to know how you keep your skin so soft, my dear," she told the horse. "Though perhaps you could take a lesson from me as to the cleaning of the teeth."

Laughter came from the barn. She whirled around and saw Elijah and his brother watching her.

"That nag could stand it!" Jon limped over to take the reins. "Good day, Mistress Deems!"

"I'm so pleased to meet you, Jonathan," she said evenly, schooling herself not to call him master. "Elijah has told me so much about you!"

"Seems I have heard of you too, Ma'am." He bowed "Excuse me while I walk the horse." He clucked to Hector and led him around in a few circles before taking him to a hollowed log to drink.

Elijah took her hand and led her to the front of the house where the unfinished extension held dominion. "We're going to use the parlor today," he murmured. "That's how important this meeting is!"

His mother, who had been waiting, opened the door casually, as though she often entertained in the front room.

The sun did not grace her as it did Molly; her aged skin and its creases were magnified under its midday glare. Her clean apron and dress were aggressively unwrinkled; her hair, drawn to the back of her head in a knot, was lusterless.

"Mother, here's Molly," Elijah announced unnecessarily.

The hand that met Molly's already outthrust one was heavily veined and thin. "How do you do, Mistress Deems?"

"Mrs. Merrick, I am so happy to meet you." The girl's eyes met her gaze steadily and Mother Merrick drew back. "Pray enter."

They did so, though there was hardly enough room for all three of them in the small entryway.

"You'd think we were herring in a bucket," Elijah said.

"We've just been at the brook," Molly explained. "So we have ale-wives on our mind."

"Are they running?" Mother asked, ushering them into the parlor. The south windows let in the sun, and the simple pine furnishings gleamed, without a hint of dust. The air, however, held the mustiness of an unused room.

"We saw a few." Elijah replied.

"Jonathan hopes to gather some this year," Mother said.

"He wasn't well enough last spring," Elijah explained to Molly. "It was colder than this, and his wounds bother him when it's cold."

She nodded, casting an eye over the plain plaster walls, the chairs placed at precise angles, one by the hearth, where Elijah's mother was seating herself, the other two in each corner. The parlor was very small, just as it was at Hastings' house.

"I trust the travel to Rockford has not tired you unduly," Mother Merrick said, glancing at Molly.

"No, indeed, it's a splendid day. I enjoyed the journey." After a small pause, she ventured, "I think Rockford is a charming village, Mrs. Merrick. Perhaps you could tell me something of it as long as I'm going to be living here."

Mrs. Merrick stared at her. "Yes, I suppose you will," she said at last, while Molly continued to look at her expectantly. "Son, what have you done with the horse?"

"Jon is looking after him."

The old woman nodded.

"We haven't had a decent mount of our own until recently," he told Molly in explanation, feeling sweat break out on his brow. "So we concern ourselves overmuch with his welfare."

Mother Merrick folded her hands in her lap and was silent.

"Let's start with the house across the road," Elijah said. "Perhaps you could tell Molly about our King cousins, Mother."

The woman shifted in her chair. "Melissa King is my cousin; their son Nathan is a good friend of Elijah."

"Nate's older than me, and has been at sea longer than I have," Elijah added. "He got his start as cabin boy before the War forced him ashore, but he's been a captain for several years now."

"And the inn on the far corner, yonder?" Molly craned her neck to look out of the window closest to her.

"Snow's Inn. They have called it the Golden Ox for years, trying to be fancy. Tavern below, rooms to rent upstairs. Their own house is just next door to it, farther down the road. They run a store there."

"And they are your cousins, too?"

"No, they are not," Mrs. Merrick said with some asperity. Her brittle words seemed to snap on the mold-scented air.

Goddamn you, Mother, Elijah thought.

"Then," Molly said lightly, "I take it they are kin to the Hall family."

Elijah laughed. He guessed he was seeing a little high-handedness.

"It seems that you know something of Rockford already, Miss Deems," Mother observed dourly.

"Truly, I know only facts about Rockford. What I don't really know are its ways, what its expectations are, how people get along, things like that."

"Well, you will, I expect," Mrs. Merrick said. "I'll tell you anything you need to know when you need to know it."

Enough of this, Elijah thought. "Molly, let me show you the new addition to the house."

"Oh! I'd love to see it!" He led her across the tiny entry hall and into a barn-like structure, 12 feet wide, running from the front of the house to the back.

"This end will be ours. The back will be part of the keeping room. There'll be a door between them." He leaned toward her in mock seduction. "That we can shut, if we like."

"Master Merrick! Watch yourself, sir," she teased.

He blushed and took her back into the parlor, through and into the kitchen where his mother waited with Debby. His youngest sister smiled and extended her hand. "I'm Debby," she said. "Welcome!"

"Oh, I'm so glad to meet you! Elijah told me you were pretty. I see he is so right!" Molly took her hand and let Debby draw her into the kitchen where tea was steeping and little cakes were waiting on a platter.

"And you, Miss Deems, are far more lovely than even he said."

Mother Merrick, who had been following, made a sound resembling a snort. "We'll have our refreshments here. Pray be seated, Mistress Deems."

"We can't all fit into the parlor," Debby explained.

"No, it would be a little snug in there," Molly laughed, and the two girls giggled at the picture of all four of them, five including Jonathan, stuffed into the small space.

"Fetch your brother, Deborah."

"We'll do that," Elijah interjected, took Molly's arm, and left the room without a backward glance.

They fled out into fresh air and sunshine, breathed deeply. "Anyone else could have said the same things and they would have sounded different," he said with anger. "I hate to think of leaving you with her when I'm gone."

"She was civil, as you said she'd be," Molly remarked. "And your sister is charming. Your brother seems well disposed toward me, too."

"They are stout fellows," he said. "They won't let us down." Inwardly he seethed. "Let's let Jon show you around the barn. It would give him pleasure, and you'd get to know him a little better."

He left her with his brother and Hector and stomped back into the kitchen. Having lived nearly half a year with the lives and destiny of a whole crew entirely in his hands, he was not now going to let himself be undermined by his mother. He was a captain! He would let her know it! No one was going to come between him and his goal—no one.

"I won't have it, Mother. You will behave better than this. And you will do so immediately."

She turned from the hearth and wiped a wisp of hair away from her forehead. "I told you I would be polite, and I have been."

"There is more required here than civility and you know it," he retorted.

"There are so many decent girls you could have chosen from," she whined by way of apology.

"Our family needs fresh blood," Debby said. "The town needs it. We've been marrying each other since the start."

"We do not need your opinion, Deborah."

"She's right," Elijah declared. "But that's not the point. Molly is my choice, and if you cause her unhappiness because you don't like my choice, you will reap it for yourself. I swear I'll have Mayo put up a shed for you behind the barn, and there you will stay."

Debby gasped.

"You're all against me," his mother whimpered.

"We won't be if you will show Molly some kindness, for Christ's sake!"

Rarely did he take the name of the Lord in vain; never had he spoken to his mother so vehemently.

Jon led the object of the discussion into the kitchen and the five of them looked at each other.

"Well, well, well!" Mother exclaimed heartily. "Here we are!"

"Won't you sit here, Molly?" Debby said, indicating a place at the table. "And Elijah, why don't you sit next to her! And Jon, you sit on her other side. A little tight, but you'll be brother and sister one day!"

He was relieved to feel a certain festivity among them, at least between his brother and sister, himself and Molly. Granted his mother was quiet, but she smiled some of the time, nodded occasionally when an observation was made that she could agree with, and the rest of the afternoon passed easily. Elijah knew his mother was chafing to return to her chores, yet she could not abandon her children to the influence of this new threat. It was clear that Jon and Debby liked Molly enormously and Molly, completely at her ease with them, was enjoying herself in the company of her contemporaries, as she had never had a chance to do before. Elijah had the opportunity to lean back and watch her, and his heart filled with joy at the companionship in the room. Companionship was not a commodity he had had much of in his life.

Perhaps, he thought, perhaps she will bind us into a happy family. Perhaps her youth will give Mother a chance to enjoy herself once again. But a glance at his mother's face was not especially reassuring.

"We could walk with Hector a bit," he suggested, once they were outside and ready to return to Yarmouth. "I could tell you who lives in the houses we pass, and something about them."

"Oh, yes, Elijah, I would like that."

It was his effort to make up for his mother's lack, and if it seemed to him clumsy, she accepted it and seemed happy. He remembered his own advice about attacking broadside and decided to try it. "I admired your restraint in the presence of my mother's formality," he said. "It would have been easy to become angry, but you did not."

"It was scarcely my place to become angry!" she exclaimed.

"Or downcast."

"Oh, well—you warned me about it, did you not?" She smiled up at him, and the need to kiss her rose sharply, and to touch her, and to let her know in these ways how much he worshipped her. "Was my behavior acceptable?"

"Why, yes. Courteous. But without yielding what is rightfully yours."

"Then never fear, Elijah. I can do it."

They circled around a hog rooting in the highroad. "As Mother told you, the business establishment across the corner belongs to Benjamin Snow. Snow's wife is a Hall, so my mother has never cultivated their friendship."

Molly shook her head. "Hard to believe that quarrel is still alive."

"Well, it's really not a quarrel anymore. All that remains is an attitude. Strong yet in my mother's generation, but not nearly so strong in mine."

"An attitude." She appeared to be thinking it over, and then she nodded, apparently coming to a conclusion of sorts. "And there is the King's house." She pointed to it.

"Right." They proceeded west, toward Yarmouth. "I haven't seen my cousin Nathan since I was thirteen and spent half a year in bed. He came to visit me a few times then, when he was home."

"Six months in bed!"

"Afraid so. I'll tell you about it, sometime. Right now, let me tell you about the Kings. They were ruined by the War, just like the rest of us. Cousin Nathan's father joined Washington's army, closing up the farm and sending the family down to the South Shore to wait out the war with their kinsmen. Nate earned some money for them all by smuggling. Then, after the war was over, he went back to sea and became a captain in continental trade, and did well, so the family could afford come back to the North Shore. That's what Uncle Elnathan, Nate's father, most wanted—to see his farm again, and see it worked. So Aunt Melissa keeps it going with the help of relatives who come up from the South Shore when there's too much for women to do."

"And your uncle?"

"Badly crippled. In constant pain. He gets into a chair every morning, with the help of my Aunt and the girls, and he stays there all day.
Tells everyone what needs to be done and when. Then they take him
back to bed at dark."

"That is so hard!" she exclaimed. "Those poor people!"

He was afraid she would cry, and quickly pointed to the neighboring place. "Next door to the Kings is the family of Jabez Denning. See
how far back their house extends? Two of the Denning sons share the
place with their parents, and both of them are running rum and molasses all over the world. The households share and share alike while the
sons are at sea. There are dozens of people living in there!"

"Friends or foes?" she asked mischievously.

He was puzzled for an instant, then perceived her meaning. "They
aren't Halls," he laughed. "Their family was originally from the South
Shore, like the Kings. But they've managed to stayed out of the feud
by marrying girls from Eastham. There may be a Denning girl about
your age, Molly."

They led Hector farther along. "And there is the house of Mr.
Simmonds, our minister. I wrote you that I thought we might visit
him while we were in Rockford. Would you like to do that now? There
is time . . . ."

When he looked down, her face was filled with panic. He stopped.
"What have I said?" he asked gently. "You are shaking."

"Nothing at all! Nothing!" she exclaimed hastily. "I think I must
be tired, is all."

"We can visit Pastor Simmonds another time, if you like."

"Yes, yes, that would be best." She nodded vigorously.

"Here, let Hector do the work. It's his job, after all!" He climbed
into the saddle and helped her up. "Besides the Kings, there are the
Grays, related to Kings by marriage, but not to us, if that makes any
sense," he said, changing the subject with as much ease as he could.
"They live a little way from the center of town. Hope is close to your

age, and the Snows have a daughter that age too, named Olive, although you might hold off on her for a bit, to see how the land lies on this ridiculous quarrel. Olive Snow is a lively lass and I'm sure you'd enjoy her. Really, Molly, there are many pleasant maidens in Rockford."

She was still trembling slightly, and his heart went out to her. He went on describing the town, trying to soothe her. "All farm folk used to live on this shore, the soil being better here. The fishermen always lived on the south side, where they can get in and out without having to wait for the tide."

She leaned her head back on his chest. Surely she could feel the heavy beat of his heart! The road veered, and a pond came into view. He stopped beside it and together they watched the reflection of the sun and clouds in the calm water.

"Molly," he whispered into her luxuriant dark hair, "Molly, have I told you I love you?"

Her face turned so that her cheek nestled against his shoulder, smiling at his ardor, totally relaxed and trusting in his arms. "Wouldn't it be grand if we could just stay here, always?" she murmured. "And I would always have your arms around me, and I should ne'er fear a living soul."

"I will make sure you are never afraid," he said, aching from his love of her.

They watched a while longer and then, reluctantly, he urged Hector forward.

"John Warden bought this land," he said, indicating the meadows and woods surrounding the pond.

"Oh! Then Master John and his new wife will not live in Yarmouth with the mistress and the captain?"

"Mariah will stay in Sandwich with her parents until John can build a house here. When I saw him a month ago in London, he told me he would establish himself here in Rockford rather than in Yarmouth. That way he won't be confined by his father's reputation."

"How confined?" she asked. "In what way would his father confine him?"

Elijah chuckled. "He wants to leave the faith of his parents and join the Congregational Church, but he does not wish to cause an uproar. So he'll do it and far enough away so as not to cause them embarrassment."

"Surely you must be pleased to know he'll be nearby one day."

"I'm delighted," Elijah said. "With Nathan King and John Warden close, I am assured that you will never be in want, should any misfortune arise."

They were approaching the mills again.

"This is Hall territory," he explained. "The families who still have an interest in the mills live nearby." He pointed out the modest cottages scattered here and there. "Halls own both mills now and run them too."

"From the sound of it, they must run the town," Molly remarked. "They own all the business establishments."

"They are shopkeepers," he said, trying to put the smugness out of his tone. "And as such will always succeed, but we on the high seas shall soar!" Suddenly his spirits rose with his words. "And you and I will soar, too!" he cried, and dug his heel into the startled Hector. They flew down the highroad fast enough, he hoped, to outdistance the impulse to duck behind the nearest bush and embrace his beloved in a manner befitting a deepwater captain.

Back at the Wardens, it was inevitable that he must describe to his host the intricacies of the contemporary European market. Commerce was the captain's lifeblood, and he was eager to learn what Elijah could tell him. He launched the topic on the way into the dining room and plied it through the meal.

Politeness as well as respect required Elijah to report everything he had seen and heard, judgments he had formed, consequences of the new Federalist policies as he had observed them. The whole meal was a monologue and he was desperately trapped by it. He heard his own voice droning on and on and on, and Mrs. Warden listened as attentively as her husband did, but Isaac, he could see, had little interest in the talk. And Molly—he was unable to tell whether or not it interested her.

She was seated beside him and he could not see her face, only her profile. Opposite her was Isaac. The two of them, excluded by default, formed a small society of their own, which seemed to him somewhat intimate, complicit. It was as though Molly had temporarily slipped away. Isaac sent her signals when he thought no one was looking: a rolling of the eyes, a tilting of the head, a little smile.

Elijah wondered about the trip Molly and Isaac had taken to the Yarmouth mill, about the past winter Isaac had spent here, in this house. He was a handsome man. He was far more witty than the pedestrian Elijah. Entertaining, certainly. Persuasive, surely.

Thankfully, Mrs. Warden suggested at last, "Why don't you two go on up and take a look in John's room? We've laid out the things Molly's been working on. Mind you don't spend too long, or we'll be obliged to come and fetch you." She laughed and disappeared into the parlor with Abel. Isaac held the door, and Elijah watched a signal pass between him and Molly.

What does it mean, he thought. She is mine. He knows it.

His heart filled with hatred. As he passed Isaac, he ignored the bemused look on the fellow's face as best he could. Following Molly up the stairs, his anger cast a deep shadow before him, and he tried valiantly to shake it off. The bed in the center of the room was covered with delicate items, practical items, some of color and others of plain Quaker gray.

"Hah! What have we here!" His voice sounded too hearty in his ears.

She seemed nervous; she ran to the garments and began fussing with them, talking quickly. "My trousseau! Is it not lovely, Elijah? Mrs. Warden has taught me many things. See this embroidery." Dutifully he examined it. "We have made some dresses for me, and here is an apron so I need not use your mother's." She lifted it by the hem, and a silver locket fell out of its pocket. She looked at it as though she had never seen it before.

"Hah! What is that?" he said genially, reaching for it. Opening it, he found it empty, clicked it shut again. "Where did you get this, Molly?"

"Why, Isaac gave it to me. I'd forgotten I put it in this apron."

"Isaac? What is the son of a Plain family doing with such a thing?"

She shrugged elaborately. "He told me he had gotten it at one foreign port or another and wanted me to have it."

"Why?"

"I don't know, really." She shrugged again. "Perhaps because he is a Quaker and has no use for it."

Elijah clenched his fingers over it. "What did he say when he gave it to you?"

"What . . . ." She stopped short of repeating his question. "Why . . . he said he wanted me to have it. He thought it was pretty, and he wanted me to have something pretty."

"It is not fitting that you receive gifts from another man," he said flatly.

"I am sure he meant no harm," she said. "He wanted me to be pleased, to remember him. That is why he gave me the book."

"Book?" he asked stupidly. "Isaac gave you a book?" He knew he must remain outwardly calm, lest he frighten her.

"Yes. From his own library. He didn't buy it for me. Is there harm in that?" she asked, her eyes wide.

"Fetch it."

"The book?"

"Yes. I want to see it."

"It is only a book, Elijah."

"I would like to see it, Molly, if you don't mind." His voice was cold, and he could see that she felt its coldness. He was too angry to care.

"Surely."

Nimbly she ran from the room and up the stairs to her own quarters in the attic. He paced, picking up this piece of finery, then that, turning the locket over and over. Molly seemed to have nothing to hide, but he did not like Isaac, never had, and he had not missed those provocative glances showered on her through the evening meal. Bastard, bastard, his mind said over and over. But by the time she returned, he was well in control of himself, though he could feel a pulse start throbbing in his temple when he turned the title page of the book and saw Isaac's inscription.

"Molly," he said quietly, after a long pause, "Do you realize what this looks like?"

His quarterdeck control had returned. The problem was defined; now he would attack it, whatever the cost. First her, then later, Isaac.

"What it looks like?"

He persisted. "How do you feel about Isaac?"

"Oh, he is pleasant, certainly. Polite . . . ."

"And handsome?"

"Yes, yes. I suppose so. Intelligent, certainly."

"Molly, do you . . . like him?" His heart dropped as he asked, but he would not back away from it.

"Surely, and why should I not? See this little pretty thing, Elijah? It is a chemise. I have embroidered flowers on it. Perhaps it's immodest of me to show you, but I'm proud of my stitches!"

"You have certainly done them well," he said in some exasperation, which he tried to conceal. "They are lovely."

She took his hands and turned him toward her.

"I see you are disturbed, Elijah," she said. "I am sorry if I have done something wrong. Had I known you would look amiss on it, I would surely not have taken those things. But, Elijah, how could I refuse? He is the son of my patrons." Her face was innocent, her eyes trusting. There was nothing he could say. The discussion now belonged elsewhere, and he would not belabor her with it longer.

"How, indeed," he said, lightly kissing her forehead. "I surely would like to hold you, Molly. Do you think it would be improper?"

His need to reaffirm her love was enormous.

"I think not, if only for a moment." She slipped willingly into his arms. The softness of her bosom, the smallness of her waist were finally his. He did not release her until he heard Isaac's voice down the hall.

"Here I come, you two. Here I come. Mother says that's long enough."

With an impish grin on his perfect face, Isaac poked his head around the corner. "I think the captain has something to say to you, Elijah."

They had separated quickly as soon as they heard him, and each stood watching, masked and expressionless.

"I'll return these things to my room so this bed will be free for you tonight, Elijah," Molly told him. "Go ahead downstairs; I'll join you later."

He followed Isaac, swamped by the frustration of having to release her, by the fact that it was Isaac who forced him to do so, bewildered at Molly's acceptance of Isaac's gifts, enraged at Isaac's offering them. She was an untried, innocent girl with no real exposure to society; she would be unaware that there could be any implications drawn from her accepting the locket and the book. That cursed book with its cursed inscription: *"Let us not . . . ."*

The sea, European markets, hostile foreign governments, indecision within the Republic and the weight this imposed on a captain—piracy, confiscation, capture—the quarterdeck seemed a haven of security compared to this tangled mess! But just as it was on the quarterdeck, so it would have to be here. He would take command, let Isaac know his gifts were out of line and had to stop. If necessary, he must use force and he must do it tonight.

Captain and Mrs. Warden wanted to discuss a dowry. "So she'll feel she's a person in her own right, not simply an object handed back and forth from one house to another," Abel explained.

Their concern touched him. What fine, generous, godly people! A dowry for a penniless maid! He expressed his thanks but could say no more for then Molly entered the room and everyone discussed what a fine day it had been and what a lovely sunset had presented itself that evening.

Finally, leaning forward and slapping Isaac's knee, he said, "Old boy, I would toast your fortune, your future. Will you let me buy you a toddy at the Inn?"

Isaac's eyes lit as he jumped to his feet. "I should be delighted. And I will offer a toast to you and your future." Glancing at Molly, he added, "It is a rosy one, with such a lovely lass in the offing." He bowed to her.

Elijah could only attempt a smile, rising and bowing in Molly's general direction, too.

Mrs. Warden said, "I'm sure Isaac would enjoy the chance for male companionship—he's had little of it these past months."

"I must return to Rockford by midday," Elijah said, "So we can't be out too late."

"Be off, then," said the captain. "It's time for the girls and me to retire anyway." He winked in Molly's direction. "So you'll be sure to wake up in time to bid your beloved goodbye."

She nodded acquiescence, shot a look at Isaac, curtsied to the group, and withdrew. That left Elijah with a chance to speak up. "Captain Warden, the matter you brought up, sir, the, er, dowry, I beg leave to think on it further. I would not have you think me ungrateful, but I need a little time with it."

"Think all you want, my boy," the captain said. "Doesn't matter. My mind is already made up. Go on, now—the Inn is awaiting."

They let themselves out into the evening and set off to the center of the village. For the life of him, Elijah could think of no direct way to begin what he was determined to do.

"The herring are starting to run in Rockford," he said finally. "My brother plans to go out soon." Anyone could always talk about the annual migration. Like the weather, it was a universal conversation opener. For his own situation, as it turned out, the herring worked beautifully.

"There weren't any in our run a few days ago when I was there," Isaac returned.

"Yes, Molly told me you had taken her there."

"I did. A fine outing it was. She enjoyed riding in the carriage."

"Mmmmmm." Elijah wished he did not envy this young man his wealth and the impression it could create. He must watch himself very carefully. It would simply not do to murder Isaac Warden.

"After Molly and I stopped to check the run," Isaac said. "I took her for more of a ride, as it seemed to give her such pleasure. It was a pleasure for me, as well." They paced along in silence. "I showed her around the mill and Mr. Sherbourne, the fuller, explained the process to her. It's doubtful he knew she is Hannah Deems' daughter. I'm not sure he'd have taken so much trouble if he had figured it out."

Now he is belittling her! How dare he! Elijah fumed.

They gained the inn and found a table. The place had many patrons and its noisy conviviality was pleasant and relaxing. They ordered rum.

"Not much of this carousing left for you, old boy," Isaac said. "Soon you'll be snared at home."

"Not necessarily. I should think many men here right now are married."

"No captains, though. These are farmers. Fishermen. Shopkeepers. Men who are here day in and day out. When a man is gone most of the time, as you'll be, his woman doesn't look kindly on his leaving the house unnecessarily. I think Molly will be as possessive as most. Maybe more."

"More? What makes you think so?" Elijah glared at him over his glass.

"Oh, I don't know." Isaac leaned back expansively, beckoned the innkeeper for another rum. "I think she is hot-blooded, and I think she will keep you busy at her side and would regard it an affront if you took an evening away from her. As though her charms were not sufficient."

Elijah listened carefully to this effrontery, attempting to detect hidden meaning. "I wonder what reason you have to say so."

"Come, come, Elijah." Isaac sipped the new rum that had been placed before him. "I have been in the same house with Molly for months. My mother has welcomed her into our family circle. I'd wager I know her far better than you do. Certainly I've seen more of her." He leaned over his drink. "And I can tell you I certainly like what I see. Hot-blooded? Why, she is. I can cause her to blush by merely looking at her. You know what that means, don't you?"

"I think you are about to tell me."

Isaac waved Elijah's words away in the same gesture his father was fond of using. "Now, now, Elijah. You're getting upset, I can see. But I'll tell you anyway. She knows that when I look at her, it's as though she has nothing on at all. That I am seeing her white skin, those marvelous tits, those pink nipples like early primroses. It causes her blood to rise—and so she blushes without even knowing she's doing it. I tell you, Elijah, you are lucky. The girl is hot-blooded."

Elijah leaped up, his chair scraping the wooden floor in a piercing screech. "You apologize for that," he shouted. The room was hushed, eyes turned to him as he rocked there in his rage.

"I do. I apologize. Profusely," Isaac said smoothly into the silence. The noise of the place resumed, and Elijah reluctantly sat down.

"Captain! Captain!" Elijah looked up to see his former drinking friend, Tom Barslow, thrusting out his hand. "Remember me? From that night we spent here and in Rockford?"

He accepted the hand, his relief making him almost giddy. A diversion from Isaac was a godsend. "I do! I certainly do, Tom! Good to see you! Sit right here!" He did not care if Isaac found it offensive to sit with a common man whose hands were calloused and whose boots were muddy.

But Isaac seemed not to mind at all. Greeting Barslow with the warm companionship of shared alcohol, he ordered a round for all three of them. He monopolized the conversation, coaxing Barslow out of any awkwardness he might have felt in sitting with a Warden, whose fame and fortune were well known around the town. Elijah listened to them, brooding over his rum and refusing yet another round that Isaac ordered.

Scum, he thought. For all his mother's a saint and his father's a man of integrity, Isaac is scum, and a man like Tom Barslow dirties himself by sharing a table with him.

But Barslow, from the evidence, did not think so. He expanded before Isaac's well-trained hospitality and grew garrulous under the influence of his rum. "Has the captain here ever told you about the first time—the only time, really—that I met him?"

"Nooooo, I don't b'leive show," Isaac answered, his words starting to slur.

"Well, me and my friends were here one night, and in he comes, looking like a hurrycane. So we thought we'd cheer him up. Seems he was worried about his old mother. Right, Captain?"

"I've got to pee," Elijah said gracelessly, and made his way to the privy behind the inn. It gave him time to think of how to deal with Isaac and Molly.

When he returned, Isaac was well launched into an escapade of his own in China. Elijah listened without hearing. It seemed to him that Isaac was far from sobriety, with Tom not far behind. For himself, he had never felt more clearheaded.

"Now I'll visit the privy too. So mush rum!" Isaac laughed and was gone. Elijah found Tom's eyes on him with a look that he turned to read a second time. Some moment of silence followed.

"He aims to have her, Captain," Tom said thickly.

"What?"

Barslow blinked and cleared his throat. "Young Warden, there. He aims to have your girl."

"Molly would have none of him, you may be sure!" he blustered.

Tom shrugged. "Who can say what a woman will do? Anyway, I wanted to tell you, Elijah. That's what he said to me while you were out. That she had accepted his gifts and he had told her that if it were not for you, he would marry her himself and that it was not too late. And that she heard him out. He thinks if she would even listen, then he has her where he wants her."

It was outrageous, and he knew it. But it ignited the tinder within him, and his jealousy leaped into raging flame.

"I'm going to thrash that son-of-a-bitch," Elijah seethed.

"As well you should," Tom cheered. "But what will happen after you leave? That bastard will still be nearby her."

"I'll . . . I'll take . . . Take her away . . . ." He thought a moment. "Do you think you can keep him here a while, Tom?" He marveled that his voice sounded so calm.

"Glad to help." Tom beckoned to a man in the corner, who approached them eagerly.

"You don't know my friend Enoch Knowles," he said, introducing them. "Neither does Warden, I should think. Perhaps a new face and more rum will induce Master Isaac to stay put."

Elijah laid some notes on the table. "See that he does," he said roughly. "By foul means, should fair prove inadequate."

He all but ran out the door and, once on the road, sorted quickly through his plans. At the Wardens', he circled the house, ascertaining that the lights were all extinguished, then let himself into the shadowed kitchen, lit vaguely by the glowing coals of the banked fire. After finding a candle, he took a light from an ember, set it in a holder and crept up the two flights of stairs to Molly's attic room.

He knocked softly and heard the rustle of her bedclothes.

"Yes?" she called softly. A moment passed, and then her face appeared in the crack of the slightly opened door. "I think it highly improper to let you in, sir."

So distressed was he that her arch and impish smile did not slow him down in the least. "This is no flirtation, Molly. I must talk with you."

"All right." After more rustling around she opened the door wide with a blanket over her shoulders. Her eyes were bright, suggesting that she had not yet slept. "You smell of drink," she whispered, wrinkling up her nose. They were only inches apart, in order to hear each other.

"Do you love me?"

"Did you get me out of bed simply to ask? You know I do!"

"I got you out of bed to see if you love me enough to come with me to Provincetown."

"Provincetown! Now? In the middle of the night?"

"Yes. We can catch the next packet to New York and then one to Baltimore, where we can be married before my ship sails. Will you, Molly?"

Her eyes became somber, looking closely into his. "Why the haste?" she asked at last.

"I'm due to leave within a week. You must know a wedding cannot be arranged in that time here on Cape Cod. No minister could marry us that fast."

"I know it well," she said grimly.

"But in Baltimore, we can be wed in a civil ceremony within just a few days. I know Fuller's people will help us, especially if I slip them something for their pockets. Then we'll sail to London. . . ."

Molly interrupted him. "On your ship? You mean to take me with you on board? Are women permitted to sail on merchant ships?"

"It's been done before," he answered brusquely. "Not often. But I think it had better be done now."

The hand she held out to him was cold. He took it in both of his. "I must know why, Elijah," she said with quiet dignity.

"Do you not trust my judgment?"

"I do. But you must have a reason for wanting to marry so quickly, and I must know what it is."

"Isaac," he answered firmly. "He has given you gifts, and you have accepted them. He has showered favors on you for months. You must know his actions are not just tokens of brotherly esteem."

"It would be presumptuous to think anything else."

"Presumptuous!" he snorted.

She said simply, "I am a servant."

"And he has not told you that he wants to marry you?"

There was a hesitation before she said softly, "I am betrothed to you!"

"And you have not told him that yes, you will marry him, once I am out at sea?"

"Elijah! Of course I have not! Did he tell you such a thing?"

"Not in so many words," he hedged. "But I cannot leave you here, Molly. If you love me, you will come with me now. It will ease my mind. I don't mean to say I don't trust you, but I most certainly do not trust him, and he has his eye on you. I know that for a fact. Besides, Molly, if we get married now in Baltimore, when we return it will be not to Yarmouth, but to Rockford. As husband and wife."

"Ah," she breathed. "That is a very pleasing prospect!"

"Will you do it?"

She pressed her temples as though trying to clear her thoughts, and the blanket hid her face. Then she looked up, smiling. "Certainly I will go, Elijah. And you're right; a civil wedding would solve quite a few difficulties."

"Gather your things, then," he said, kissing the tip of her nose. "I'll return within the hour."

There were certain insults a man could not tolerate. There were certain injuries he could not sustain. There were certain limits beyond which restraint was not possible. Elijah Merrick returned to the Yarmouth Inn, there to seek Isaac Warden and, in the bushes behind the privy, there to thrash him senseless.

It would have been a tedious, endless ride had it not been for Molly, pressed against him as they rode through the night. Dawn broke in its loveliness as they journeyed through Wellfleet, and morning was upon them in Truro. At the Provincetown wharf, Elijah found a boy who would deliver a hastily written note to the Wardens, and another to his mother, along with Hector, saying that because of the strength of their affection, he and Molly wished to be joined together as soon as possible. He bundled his beloved and her parcel and his own bag onto the packet, and within an hour they were sailing for New York. What a delight she was! Her fresh face was rosy and clear; she had never sailed before and the breeze rushing past them exhilarated her. Perhaps she would be a good sailor, he thought. He surely hoped so. It would be difficult, cooped up in his cabin with a seasick bride—but no matter! She was his, all his! No one could take her away from him! And soon they would be wed, and alone, and they could rightfully come together. He tingled. All the hotness and drive of his twenty-four years surged and pulsed and urged him forward, toward the haven of his vessel and the privacy of his wedding night.

❧❖❧

The civil ceremony was come by as he had hopefully supposed; his friends proved their worth and smoothed the way. They had secured a room for Molly and another for himself until the following morning, when in the eyes of the state of Maryland, they were wed. He hustled her aboard his vessel, *Brave Voyager*, and into his cabin, now familiar from his last trip. After hurriedly kissing her, he bade her stay where she was, to get some rest if she could while he set about procuring his papers and hiring his crew, loading the cargo of rum, dried fruit, tobacco, cotton, and stores for the cook. He thrilled at being in complete command! Never had his touch been so sure! It was magic! The world was his, all his! His excitement rose, mounted, flooded his very being.

Finally, it was night. They were due to sail at noon the following day. He dismissed the watch, usually aboard when the vessel was loaded; the men went joyfully now to the nearest tavern to celebrate. From an inn nearby the wharf, he procured supper and a bottle of wine, and had everything packed into a basket that he took back to *Voyager*. And then they were alone, the creaking ship and restless lapping of the water on the wharf and against the hull their only companions. Nearby, other vessels lay at anchor, only their anchor lights visible from the tops of their masts.

It was apparent that she was terribly nervous. She leaped from the captain's chair, where she had been sitting, her instant smile too quick. He set the basket on the table bolted to the cabin's center and unpacked it, talking as he did so, hoping to ease her.

"Quite a day, my bride!" he said heartily. "I trust it hasn't been too tedious for you. For me, it has been the most successful day of my life. Here is roasted chicken for our supper, and here's some cheese and a bottle of wine." From the corner of his eye he watched her watching him, and continued with his monologue. "You can get good wine in Baltimore; they import it from France, whereas we on the New England shore are too cheap to do that and instead stick with rum. To our loss, I might add! But the Wardens used wine, did they not?"

"Yes," she whispered.

Pausing, he leaned on the table to look intently into her eyes. She glanced away as a tear spilled down her cheek. It was natural she should be apprehensive, he told himself. He must move forward calmly, he thought, without hurrying her. Yet without faltering either, so that she would know what to expect. He wondered if he was equal to the task.

"It hasn't been an ideal wedding day for you, my darling. I hope you have no regrets."

"Oh, no, Elijah," she protested in a quavering voice. "No regrets at all."

He reached out to her gently. "It's a man's world here, my dear. Perhaps in the morning I can go into town and find things that will occupy you while I am busy. I would not have you be lonely and bored."

She seemed to perk up. "I'd enjoy doing some embroidery, and I'd like to make you a shirt, Elijah—a silk one. 'Twould give me pleasure to work on it while you are tending the ship."

"Good enough!" He pulled up the cabin's extra chair and turned to the meal.

"I could hear your voice all day," she said, her own voice steady now. "Tell me how you command so many men and know so much about the goods you are onloading."

He poured them both some wine. "I've been learning how to buy and stow cargo for a long time. For nine years I've watched captains managing men." He sipped. "Right now, the biggest challenge, as I see it, is speed."

"Speed? But you already make very quick voyages."

"Yes." He poured her more wine—she would need it—and went on with the discussion that, at the moment, held not even the slightest interest for him. "More and more men and ships will sail as our commerce expands, more and more companies will be competing. So the best and fastest will take the cream, earn the most profit, be in the highest demand. I would like to be among that group."

"You will be, I am sure."

"Only if I am willing to drive my men to the limits of their endurance, and myself as well. I've learned how to set the pace; now the challenge is hiring the men who are willing to meet it." He refilled her glass. Time was passing with satisfactory speed. "Foreign trade is not entirely a question of speed, though. It depends somewhat on international politics and how well a man can smuggle. Of course, we of New England are pretty good at smuggling—we've been doing it for years!"

She giggled, and he emptied the bottle into her glass. He continued with an air of nonchalance, though his blood was beginning to run faster. "Now, my dear one, suppose you drink this up while I fetch you a bucket of water." Her eyes flew open, wide and frightened. He pretended not to notice. "You may refresh yourself while I take some air on the deck. I'll wait there until you are prepared to retire. Then you can call me."

"Very well," she said faintly, and sat where she was, unmoving, until he brought in the water. Out on the deck he could hear sounds of her washing and moving about, and he paced feverishly until she called, "I am finished." He forced himself to walk into the cabin slowly. She had put out the candle, the little minx! The cabin was too shadowed to see much. Casually, he removed his clothes, dropping them in a heap on the floor.

"Where did you leave the bucket?" he asked softly into the quiet.

"By the table," she whispered back.

He splashed himself, dried himself with his shirt, then felt his way to the bunk. Sitting on the edge, he waited until his eyes accommodated themselves to the darkness. At last he saw the outline of her dark hair on his pillow. Tomorrow, he thought, I must remember to get another pillow. It won't do to share one indefinitely. But tonight sharing one was a delightful thought!

He stroked her arm gently, picked up her hand, kissed the palm, then the smooth inner wrist. "A man and woman may come together when they are married, Molly," he said. "Do you understand what that means?"

"I . . . think so," she said haltingly.

"Are you willing?" He heard her draw a deep breath.

"You are my husband, Elijah."

"Oh, my dearest!" Such a sweet and docile answer! He lay down beside her, pulled her close, nuzzled her throat and kissed her, his embrace more and more powerful. And then he became aware that her body was tense, stiff as untanned leather, and he made himself stop. "Forgive me if I am too quick," he begged, his breathing heavy. "I have longed for this moment, my own darling; I'm afraid I'll be too hasty. I don't wish to frighten you, Molly. I love you so."

She clasped her arms around his neck and drew him toward herself.

"Do what you need to do, Elijah. I love you too, and I trust you."

He loosened one of her hands and guided it. "This is my manhood, Molly. It is meant to enter you. It may cause you pain, though I would not wish to hurt you. In a while it won't hurt at all, but tonight it probably will."

"Only show me, Elijah. I have no knowledge of these things."

Releasing her hand, he cradled her and showered her face and throat with kisses. Never, never in his life had he been able to show love like this; never had he so much love to give. It was as though she unlocked him, set him free. "You are perfect . . . you are everything . . . the source of my strength . . . I adore you."

Lying there beside him, shyly returning his kisses, she seemed very small, so finely made that he did not see how he could enter her without injuring her. He ran his hand along the curve of her thigh; he worked her nightgown up so that it would not impede him, reached under it to the fullness of her breasts. Oh, how smooth! How soft! Heat from within him seemed to sear his very flesh, and he was overtaken by the irresistible demand to have her. He must not rush, he told himself, but it was too late. His need of her caused all thought, all awareness of responsibility to be carried away in a flood. Her hotly delectable, engulfing womanplace surrounded him and he was lifted up in an agony of passion.

She was his! His! Oh, the warm welcome of her, oh, God, he would die of her, oh, Molly! He gasped in his release. "Molly," he murmured, lying still atop of her. "Molly," he whispered, remembering to roll away before he fell into numb and happy slumber.

When he woke again, there she was beside him. Slowly, he lifted back the blanket and looked at her, able to see quite clearly by the predawn light. The low neckline of her white nightgown revealed the swelling of her breasts and the rising and falling of her breath. He watched a short while, then gently pulled her toward him.

"I fell asleep," he whispered. "I'm so sorry, dearest. I didn't mean to leave you all alone. Can you forgive me for hurting you?"

"Oh, yes, yes," she whispered. "I'm really your wife now."

"You are! You are! And since you are, will you do as I ask?"

"Of course," she answered, though he detected apprehension in her voice.

"The gown is very lovely, I'm sure, but I wonder if I may take it off you."

"Oh, no!" she said. "I'll take it off myself!" Then she knelt before him, drew the nightgown over her head, her nakedness slowly appearing as in a dream. He drank in her loveliness, and reached out to caress her, to fondle her, to lift her over himself, to penetrate her as she straddled him and to lift her up and then back, up and then back. This time he delved deeper and exalted higher and was able to hold himself in check while he luxuriated in her, consumed by her, until suddenly it was done.

His happiness was complete. There was no more he could ask of life—but his duties called, his ship awaited. He slipped out of the bunk, every muscle in his body fine tuned, his confidence at its peak. Dressing quickly, he kissed his wife, tenderly touched her cheek, and strode off to his command and his future.

CHAPTER

The Wooing of
Rockford

❖❀❀ I ❀❀❖

MOLLY HAD LAIN beside him, staring at the tiny
windows of the stuffy cabin without seeing, a quiet
witness to the dawn she did not watch. She had listened to the harbor
and the gradual increase of activity on the wharf without understanding what it meant and without caring. Her husband breathed deeply
while she lay quietly with her suffering.

She watched herself submitting to Elijah Merrick, knowing there
was no way to resist him, steeling herself so that she would not draw
away. Muffling her involuntary cries, she had endured him unflinch-
ingly when he found her, did his will with her.

When he was done and asleep, she had slipped out of the bunk. She
had tucked a piece of broken glass inside her bundle of clothing, and
with it inflicted a small wound near her groin. Blood would be present
in their bed, come morning, and Elijah would have no doubts about
having deflowered her.

Would she feel as distant from him, as defiled, when the pain subsided and intimacy again took place between them? It would happen
tonight, she knew, and the night following, and the night after that,
.... Night after night of submitting to him, gratifying him, spreading
her legs for him. For the rest of her days she must carry on the façade

of loving Elijah Merrick, tantalizing and tempting him whenever he was home.

Then near dawn, he stirred and held her, spoke words of heartfelt love and devotion and a request to see her naked. Kneeling before him in the bunk, she slowly removed her nightgown and arched her back so her breasts would stand up and out—a living figurehead—hoping her actions were bewitching.

They were. She had captivated him entirely. Because of the dimness of dawn, she could not read the rapture on his face, but his hands told her of it as he fondled and kneaded. Though his passion consumed him, he was less hurried. He was intent on a more lingering pleasure, and the cut she had inflicted on herself became hot and throbbing. How it had hurt! And then he was done and gone to meet the arriving crew.

Now all she could do was lie here, sore and soiled as a whore, forgetting for the moment that she had chosen him in the first place, had chosen him because of his ability to put her exactly where she was—in the captain's cabin.

Burying her face in the pillow, she wept until she fell asleep. The clattering of his boots on the cabin's bare floor awakened her and she saw he'd brought parcels and a pillow for her. He leaned over and softly stroked her cheek. His eyes shone with love, and she strove mightily to put the same expression in hers as she roused from slumber. "Good morning," she mumbled.

"Good morning," he whispered, and pushed the blanket aside, ran a hand across her breast, her belly. Then he stopped, for he saw her blood on the linens. "Molly!" he gasped. "Oh, my God, Molly!"

She tried to look at him, but could not meet his gaze.

"Do you hurt?" he asked.

She nodded.

"Oh, my dearest! You should have stopped me when I . . . Why did you not say something?"

"I wanted you to be . . . be happy." It was not difficult to squeeze out a tear. "But now I will be in agony if we . . . come together . . . until I am healed."

He mastered any disappointment he might have been feeling and embraced her gently until she stopped crying. "We have a whole life together," he comforted her. "There is no hurry, none at all. And Molly, you must learn to tell me when there's something I should know. Agreed?" Smiling, he coaxed her to smile back. "Stay right there in bed," he said. "Pretend you are royalty, and need not arise until you choose." Pulling the blanket up to her chin, he tucked the new pillow under her head. "Forgive me, beloved!"

And then he was gone.

Relieved, the pressure off, she sighed and rolled over and was asleep instantly. When she awoke, the ship was under sail, slowly rising and falling. Holding onto the bolted-down bunk, then onto the nearby captain's table, she investigated the parcels that Elijah had bought for her in Baltimore—the womanly entertainment she had asked for—silk for a shirt to sew, needles and thread and scissors.

Refreshed by her long sleep, her youth worked for her, healing much of her distress. Her despondency was gone, although not her soreness, and she wondered how long she could hold him at bay. A woman did not have to love a man in order to make him happy, she knew now. And she would make Elijah happy if it killed her! But she would, if she could, give her self-inflicted wound a chance to heal, and give herself a chance to master her shock and confusion. Then perhaps she could go through this voyage with a degree of relative pleasure, and through the rest of her married days, too. She needed time, and she would gain it with tears, pretended ignorance of his intent, feigned slumber.

For a week, she delayed him, amusing him with her chatter and her shirt-making industry, clinging to his every word so that he would be forced to treat her gently in order not to demolish that admiration. When she thought she could stand it, she invited his attention, continuing to react as though she were tender so that he would not linger. And that was very helpful! If she did not have to endure prolonged love play, she could manage the rest. She could meet the daily challenge of being the new bride, making Elijah happy and pleased with his apparent domination over her, blindly unaware that she did not love him.

As she began to feel more secure, she was able to remember all the reasons why she had chosen and pursued this man, all the things she could gain by being his wife, at his side in Rockford, important because he was important. Gradually, she became the Molly of old.

She enjoyed London and the shops there, buying an extravagant nightgown to help secure her future, and a few everyday dresses to wear at the inns and taverns where Elijah took her for their meals. The city scene thrilled her, where the wealthy rode about in carriages, wearing and gold-encrusted garments festooned with lace. Molly imagined herself an aristocrat, lounging in the captain's cabin, eating confections and reading newly purchased novels by Mrs. Radcliffe while the vessel was being loaded and the papers processed for the next leg of the trip.

Then nausea struck.

At first she thought she had succumbed to tainted food. But the nausea continued, and became worse. There was no escaping what now she knew—she was pregnant.

It was bad enough to be sick, but worse was the tension of not knowing whether Isaac or Elijah had fathered the child. Sleepless and ill, she became pale, great dark shadows appeared beneath her eyes, the luster left her hair.

The thought of lying with Elijah in that cursed bunk, of his hands on her, of his possession of her—it was enough to make her flesh crawl. She could not let him know, lest he be offended, but she could not stand him. Suffering the marital bed as long as she could, Molly did the only thing left to her. Nothing. Nothing at all.

When he tried to embrace her, she was unresponsive. The morsels he brought to tempt her remained untouched. Though he tried to talk with her, she did not speak. She only watched him with huge shadowed eyes whenever he came into the cabin to sit with her and hold her hand, to worry over her and, to her very great relief, leave her alone.

✦✦✦

When Elijah brought her to Rockford at the end of August, she was weak and wasted. The extra twelve feet added to the house was complete, though the family purse was thinner and his mother anxious about money. Nonetheless, she helped Elijah move Molly into the new room. Whatever anger she harbored over their unorthodox wedding (and it was considerable), whatever misgiving she might have had over the entrance into her family of a serving girl of questionable parentage (this too, was considerable)—all of these things she put aside in the face of Molly's pregnancy and its untoward and unexpected complications.

Elijah gave up Europe and took a vessel in the coasting trade so that he might return frequently to sit with his wife, trying to amuse her and coaxing her to eat.

In the new chamber, Molly watched the shadows and the shifting light of the sun's travel across the sky outside. She waited as the season wore into autumn. Elijah came and went.

She often looked at the gleam of the pine chair beside her commode, its richness soothing in her diminished world. Beside the bed was the chest in which her personal belongings from the Wardens' had been placed. But she had no will to unpack it. Mother Merrick had told her that the trunk held a note from Elizabeth Warden but Molly did not read it. In fear she waited to see if the child would give her away, if Elijah's affection and protection would be lost after all she had done and given to secure it.

Throughout, Elijah came and went.

❧❀❧

And then it was time. He was gone acoasting, and Molly was grateful. She did not want him near, did not want anyone near. Even as her contractions became more severe, she did not call for help, enduring them through the long night. But in the morning an involuntary cry escaped her and brought Elijah's mother running.

"You should have called!" she exclaimed, and ran from the house in search of the midwife. They moved Molly into the freshly scrubbed borning room, whitewashed and pristine. In the keeping room, they built an enormous fire and brought rags to soak up the waters and the blood. The women worked quickly, just in case she was the sort who delivered quickly, but she was not. Molly's firstborn took its time arriving, and stretched to breaking on the rack of labor, she was left there to suffer unendurably for the rest of the day and the night following, each contraction a tightening of the wheel, pulling her apart.

Within the rising crescendo of pain was the knowledge she must utter no word lest she give away her secret. This she clung to as all other needs were obliterated, as the ordeal of confinement drowned all other things, all horizons, all realities. She screamed as she was driven by the scourge of delivery past the fear of death until she reached the ultimate fear that she would not die, that she would live eternally in this hell. But she was wordless to the end when, at last, Sarah arrived, resembling neither Isaac nor Elijah.

◌◌✦◌◌

When her husband came home just after the birth, Molly was weak—never had she been so weak—but she knew she would soon be well and would stay well. She was unable, as yet, to feel the love that a mother should have for her baby, but was grateful that Sarah looked like only herself; the threat the unborn child had posed was gone. Replacing it was the memory of her tortuous labor and the challenge of facing her husband.

When at last they were alone, she met it head-on. "My dearest," she told him, "it is over! I believe that soon we can be husband and wife together!"

His cheeks became very pink, his eyes very bright, and if she had been able, she would have been his wife right then, mending the fences her distracted pregnancy might have broken. All the revulsion brought on by that mysterious use of those mysterious parts of men and women receded as though it had never arisen. He was hers. She had fought for him, suffered for him, and now she had him. Soon, she hoped, she would grow to love little Sarah and perhaps even Elijah himself.

❖⧓ 2 ⧓❖

As soon as she could, she struggled out of bed to begin the long process of getting her strength back. Her legs trembled as she staggered to
Sarah's cradle, then the door, and finally, the keeping room.

"Well, young miss! We wondered if we would ever see you!" Mother
Merrick greeted her.

They were not unkind words, nor were they said unkindly, yet Molly
sensed the anger behind them. As she was up and about for longer peri-
ods of time, she looked to see if anyone was glad at her presence, but if
they were, they covered it well. Mother Merrick urged Molly to rest,
to take her time regaining her strength after such a strenuous delivery.
She spoke only of Molly's health with scrupulous manners, and without a vestige of warmth. Debby, Elijah's sister, never said a word, only
answering any questions Molly put to her, politely and shyly. Jonathan
was tongue-tied and spent most of his time in the barn in any case.

And, the most troublesome, was her exclusion when Mother's friends
appeared at the house for tea or gossip. They bowed to Molly when they
arrived and when they left, but they never asked if she would come to
their homes and drink tea with them. They did not say they would enjoy
seeing her again. She could sit with them in the keeping room, invisible,
or retreat to the new bedchamber and wait for them to leave, but regardless, she was ignored. It was such a monumental rebuff that at first she
simply observed it, then as she grew more robust, endured it. But when
she was fully mended, she had had enough. She began to scheme and
devise ways to break out of the cocoon Mother had woven around her.

There was nowhere to start but Meeting, given Mother's reluctance
to introduce her to Rockford folk. Surely young women her age would be
there. But the thought was daunting, for at Meeting there would also be
Pastor Simmonds. He would have heard about Hannah Deems—everyone had. Would he refuse her daughter entrance, make a public spectacle
of Molly, pointing his finger and declaring her unfit for the company of
saints? Henry Hastings would have done so!

This was daunting enough, but there were other considerations as well. The Congregational Church was a new experience for her. She had never seen the inside of their meetinghouse. Church was not part of life at Seth Adams' farm, and while she lived at the Wardens', only Quaker meetings were available to her. How did one behave at the Church of the Standing Order?

She closeted Elijah's sister, seeking advice. What should she do if the baby cried? How would she know when to stand up and when to sit down again? How long would the service take?

"We have our own pew where no one can see you," Debby explained. "If Sarah cries, you can nurse her right there, covered with a blanket."

"How is it that no one can see?"

"The bench is enclosed with a wooden wall so high (Debby indicated a height of four feet) around it, that has a little door. When the family is inside with the door closed, there are no distractions and it's warmer in winter. We take a pail of coals in with us, to heat it."

"So I can stay seated, and no one will think ill of me."

"You can," Debby agreed. "But you won't. Those benches are pretty narrow, and your back will ache if you sit there too long. But you need not worry, Molly. I'll make sure you aren't standing when everyone else is sitting."

"Thank you," Molly said humbly. Encouraged by Debby's willingness to advise her, she pushed on. "I confess that I'm a little worried about going. Can just anybody attend?"

"Of course!" Debby assured her. "For all we know, you are one of the elect."

"How could I be?" Molly wondered. "I've never even been inside your church."

"That doesn't matter. If you're one of the elect, God chose you even before you were born."

"Really! How do I know if I'm chosen or not?"

"You wait for the voice of the Lord to tell you so."

Molly remembered Mrs. Warden talking about God's voice, although there was no mention of being chosen. But this did not concern her just now. Her only interest was finding a way to break through her isolation.

"I'm hoping that I'll meet other young mothers there. Will you introduce me?"

"Well," Debby hesitated. "We don't linger between services. People go home for their noon meal and then hurry back for the afternoon lecture. Those from farther out go to friends' homes near the center of town. There won't be much time for introductions."

"No one has been to our house between services since I've been here, and we're quite close to the meeting house."

Debby squirmed. "The folk who usually eat at our house haven't been here because you've been so unwell. I don't know whether they'll come back to us now that you're better, because they're accustomed to going elsewhere by this time."

They had probably not been urged to return, Molly speculated, for if they did, they would meet the dreaded daughter-in-law.

So. There would probably be no conversing with young women between services, if she understood Debby correctly. But she was determined not to give up. In her gathering loneliness she thought about Meeting with longing; she dreamed of walking into the hall behind Mother, her head high, Sarah in her arms. They would seat themselves in the mysterious pew and once settled, she would look up to smile, but only slightly, as befitted a meetinghouse. Everyone would be watching her with curiosity and interest, since she was new. Perhaps they would smile too. Rockford's citizens would crowd into Mother's parlor between services to say hello and welcome her to their village. They would not be Mother's friends. They would be hers.

Molly knew the scene was unlikely to unfold in this way. And she was right. Not a soul knocked on their door.

She had dressed carefully and now wondered if it were too careful. She had combed her hair elaborately, and now she wondered if it were too elaborate. She sat attentive and still and made sure that little Sarah was quiet, but nothing she did, or did not do, appeared to make any difference. A few of the younger people watched her curiously, but never did they approach her. For she was a stranger in a place where all were kin. And worse, she was a questionable stranger.

Through another week, through another Meeting, and yet another, and another, she waited. Once John Warden's wife, Mariah, spoke pleasantly to her, and Molly's hope rose a little. But the new Mrs. Warden was only visiting Rockford that day. Mariah did not yet live in her new house, although she expressed the hope that she would see Molly once she settled in the town. But that was too far in the future to do Molly any good now.

❈❈❈❈

It had been over three months since Sarah's birth. Mother's occasional tea-drinking friends continued to do nothing to include her. Elijah wrote to say he would be detained; he cursed the fact that this would be the longest separation they had yet endured, but his was a new command, and Fuller wished him to depart immediately for the West Indies.

Bleakly, Molly saw that the pattern of her days was being set indelibly. As one followed another, she was close to despair. Clearly, she would have to be bold. With this in mind, she spoke up one afternoon. The household tasks were done; all three of them sat around the hearth, Mother mending, Debby knitting, Molly sewing a little dress for Sarah.

"Mother, I think that I've fully recovered. I feel strong and full of energy, and I'd very much enjoy meeting women my own age. Do you think you could find time to take me visiting? Some of your friends must have daughters, is that not so?"

Mother's expression of horror would have made Molly laugh if she had been disposed to do so.

"Perhaps you are not busy, my dear, but I am," the old woman responded. Debby looked up, looked back down at her knitting.

"Perhaps Debby, you could take me to meet some of your friends."

"She is busy, too," Mother said with a quick glance at her daughter that warned her to remain silent.

"Well, then." Molly maintained a pleasant voice at great cost. "I am quite capable of going alone. How about the Winslows? Did not Mrs.

Winslow mention a daughter when she was here last, visiting you? Might I not start with her?"

"Mrs. Winslow does have a daughter," Mother said reluctantly. "But she would think you brazen if you went to her house by yourself."

"It would be brazen," Molly nodded. "But I'm willing to risk her displeasure. Shall I go tomorrow, in the afternoon?"

"You should not go at all," Mother said coolly. "We have our own ways here in Rockford." She pressed her advantage. "I would not have you blunder in your haste."

"I have been cooped up here a long, long time," Molly said, matching Mother's coolness. "I have been inside this house since last August. Some of the time ill, I grant you. Now I am well, and if I remain cooped up, people will think I am hiding, as though I were afraid to go out. Or as though you are afraid to take me out. We would not wish them to think that, would we?"

"Of course not," Mother said very quickly.

"Surely we do not want anyone to think you are ashamed of me?"

"No, no indeed," exclaimed Mother, her advantage obviously waning.

"If you do not yourself take me out, that is what it will look like, I'm afraid," Molly said sweetly. "Where shall we start?"

Across from her, Debby could barely conceal a smile.

"I can assure you, my dear, that simply going to visit a neighbor won't open the path to friendship. Not in Rockford."

"And why is that?" Molly asked, still sweet, but determined to have it out.

"It is not our way," Mother said noncommittally.

"So you would have me just sit here and wait?" Molly asked, knowing that her voice was getting shrill. She held herself in tightly; she must not give Mother Merrick the advantage of her own anger.

"For a while," Mother said smoothly. "Perhaps another week or two."

"Or three."

"Or more." Mother smiled smugly, and went to fetch water from the well by the kitchen door.

Yet, the next morning, the old woman knocked at Molly's chamber door. "I apologize, Daughter," she said with great effort. "You are right. It is time to take you out."

Molly was propped up against the headboard, nursing Sarah, a quilt drawn up around them both to keep off the chill. Had Mother been struggling with her Puritan conscience? Or was she worried about Elijah's wrath when he learned the truth?

"I cannot guarantee the results, as I told you yesterday but let us go when you're done feeding Sarah."

"Very well," Molly nodded.

Tense now, and anxious, her milk was no longer flowing. Although Sarah seemed satisfied, Molly did not want Mother to think the infant had been hurried in order to take advantage of an offer that should have been made weeks ago. Without haste, she changed Sarah's wrappings and bundled her securely, put on the apron from her trousseau, combed her hair carefully, fetched her shawl.

When she emerged, Mother was waiting, her foot tapping impatiently.

Molly reminded herself to be civil. "I would like to visit the Dennings," she announced. "There are a lot of them, Elijah told me. I've seen a daughter among them who seems to be about my age."

"They are good folk," Mother said. "Fine people."

"Well?"

"I would rather start with a different family," Mother said after some hesitation.

"Don't tell me they are Halls!" Molly exclaimed. She knew they were not. Elijah had said so.

"No. But they are really South Parish people, and I would sooner wait before cultivating their friendship."

"What is wrong with South Parish people?"

"Well, they are fishermen, and very different from the farmers and merchant seamen of the North Parish. By the nature of their trade, fishermen have a lot of things strewn about—nets and dories and traps and flakes and such. On the North Side, we take pride in being ship-shape. Everything in its place."

"And the Dennings have all manner of refuse in their dooryard?"

"No, they've been very neat. But I don't know them well. I would rather wait until I can be sure they are North Siders at heart and not just South Shore fisher folk masquerading."

Time was passing. "How about the Grays and their daughter. Elijah has mentioned them."

"Hope. A lovely girl. In fact, perhaps her brother, Tony, will one day be a match for our Debby. He needs time to settle down first, but our Deb is still quite young. Yes, Hope Gray would be fine, but we'll have to go another time. Their house is quite distant and we'll need to take turns carrying Sarah, you and Debby and I. And Debby is fetching some wool for me from Mrs. Mayo. She won't be back in time."

Molly knew a stone wall when she saw one. "Does anyone live nearby who is suitable?" she asked, trying to keep the impatience out of her voice. "Olive Snow lives right across the street, does she not? I'm quite sure she is nearly my age."

"The Snows are part of the Hall family," Mother said with finality. "I cannot take you there."

But I can go by myself, you witch, Molly thought. And one day, perhaps very soon, I will! "How about your King kin across the street then. I know you visit them sometimes. Elijah said they had lived on the South Shore, so I suppose their standards are low, but I know they have girls my age."

"My cousin Melissa King was at the South Shore only for a few years during the War!" Mother cried. "I assure you there is nothing wrong with her standards."

"Wonderful!" Molly declared. "I am ready."

Mother was forced to relent. "I'll carry Sarah."

Suddenly nervous, Molly hastily gave Mother the baby and wrapped her shawl around her shoulders. The house across the street seemed a long, long distance away. Mother looked neither left nor right, but marched across the road and around to the back, rapping on the door, then letting herself in, as was the custom among neighbors and kin.

The young girl standing within must have been watching their approach from a window. "Auntie!" she cried, though Mother Merrick was not her aunt, but rather a cousin, perhaps a second one, somewhat removed. "How nice to see you!" She did not so much as glance at Molly.

"We've been wanting to call," Mother Merrick said brightly. "We've been so busy that it's taken a while. Here's the baby! And Molly."

It all ran together in an incomprehensible stream that the girl seemed to understand.

"This is Thankful," Mother told Molly, and Molly smiled and ducked her head in acknowledgement. She recognized Thankful from Meeting. About her own age, she thought, and attractive enough.

"Sit there," Thankful said to them both, indicating a bench near the fire. "You're just in time for tea. We've been cleaning the barn, and we needed an excuse to stop." Through the back door, she bellowed, "Tea's ready!"

The family came trooping in, hot and steamy. Each one stopped when she saw Molly, causing a pileup at the door, with bumping and scolding until the scolder saw the cause of the commotion and fell silent. Melissa King was the last into the room.

Here it comes, thought Molly. If I can get past this one, there should be no trouble. She rose gracefully to her feet as Mrs. Warden had taught her to do in the presence of her elders.

"You're leaving already?" Melissa asked.

"Well, no, I was only . . . ," Molly stammered.

"Sit down, for goodness sake!" Melissa stooped to kiss Mother Merrick's cheek and retrieve Sarah, all in one motion. "Let me have that baby! Oh, how precious!" She showed Sarah to each of the girls, then sat her massive bulk down and examined the infant carefully. Her daughters, like a flock of chicks, jostled and shoved for a place at their mother's side. Thankful brought mugs of tea to everyone.

The conversation languished. Molly sat in uncomfortable silence, determined to do nothing to call attention to herself. If they wished to speak with her, she was here to do it, but they did not. Instead, Melissa talked with Mother and the King daughters listened.

"Farming is too heavy for a clutch of females," Melissa said. "I don't know how much longer the girls and I can do it."

"How is Elnathan?" asked Mother.

"Poorly. And the more time goes by, the less chance there is that he'll get better. He's too old, and I'm getting too old to do his work."

"No, Mama," cried the chicks. "You are not old at all!"

"Elnathan is crippled," Mother told Molly. "Has been, since Monmouth, in the war."

"I'm sorry to hear it. What shall you do?" Molly inquired of Melissa out of courtesy.

"We must pray for a good voyage," the woman said piously. "One more like the last and our Nathan will have made enough money that we'll need not farm at all."

"Hear! Hear!" the chicks murmured.

"Nathan is Elijah's cousin," Mother explained.

"Elijah's turn will come one day soon, too," Melissa told Mother, ignoring Molly completely. "And then you can rest. We'll all live easier when our young men have made their mark."

"You mean we'll only spin the flax? We can hire someone else to hatchel it?" one of the girls asked laughingly. No one liked to hatchel flax.

Molly saw her chance to make a move. "If you're wealthy you won't even have to spin. You'll be able to buy your thread and your cloth ready-made."

"Already spun?" asked one.

"And loomed?" asked another.

"Yes! Wouldn't that be wonderful? There are machines in England that do it now," Molly explained knowledgably, "and if we get very, very rich, we can drink tea while others make our new dresses for us."

"I doubt Nathan and Elijah will make that much money," Mother Merrick said tartly. "Cloth is very expensive, my dear."

"That is because the English overcharge us," Molly replied. "But there are water-driven looms of our own being built now, in Rhode Island. When they produce enough, the price of cloth will be so reasonable that we will never buy from England again."

"Really?" one of the chicks asked disbelievingly.

"How do you know these things?" another added.

"Through the Wardens of Yarmouth. They have many Providence kin and get newspapers from them, so Mrs. Warden has a lot of information on doings there and everywhere else."

Molly sensed, but did not look to confirm, that Mother's back was becoming straighter. Well, she thought, there's no sense avoiding it. They all know where I come from.

"She must be a great lady," a King daughter said. All of them knew who the Wardens were. There was no one in Barnstable County who did not.

"Yes, she is," Molly affirmed. Now was the time to follow Elizabeth Warden's advice. "And very clever, too. She was a good needle worker. She knew all the fancy stitches, and even though she didn't use them herself, she taught me how to do them."

"Oh?" they asked.

"See this trim on my apron?" Molly held the hem of it out toward them. "She taught me how to do that."

"Oh," they breathed, all leaning in to look.

"Come to our house," Molly said to them. "I'll show you all the things Mrs. Warden helped me to make. And I'll teach you her stitches if you wish."

"Oh!" they exclaimed, and in unison looked at their mother.

Molly could tell that Melissa King knew a bribe when she saw one. "Just now, we are busy here," she told her daughters. "Very busy. And will continue to be, until Nathan returns."

"Oh . . . ," they breathed. "Yes. Of course. Much too busy."

Taking their cue from their mother, the chicks looked away from the apron and said nothing more.

Had Melissa allowed these five stupid young hens to learn fancy embroidery, they would have been easily wooed and won. But instead, they ignored her for the rest of the visit. Melissa and Mother talked to each other of one thing or another, none of their conversation directed toward Molly, while the girls watched her being monumentally snubbed.

Finally, Sarah cried for her next meal. Molly snatched her up, excused herself, and fled. She hid in her chamber until the baby was content and asleep in her cradle and she, herself, was calm, then went out to help with the kitchen chores.

"I hope you're satisfied," Mother carped from the pot she was stirring. "And don't ask me to take you out again. Fancy embroidery, indeed!"

So, Mother had flung down the gauntlet!

Clearly playing the gentle, passive, sweet young wife and daughter-in-law was not going to work. Molly would have to ride roughshod over them all, and by now she was well prepared to do so.

Her chance, her plan, rested with Elijah. He could not cause the townsmen to love her, but his wealth would earn him political power in village affairs. He would have prestige, and through him, she would have it, too. Rockford would be in awe of her, its women would vie for her attention. All she needed was his continuing success while she showed him how well she loved him, how much she would do for him. Would he not, then, do much for her?

They had not lain together since London. When he had been home last, after Sarah was born, she had suggested that intimacy might well be in order soon, and she had no doubt it would be easy to enthrall him. Letting Elijah see her nakedness, as she had done before, would probably ensure his continued devotion. And besides their actual coming together, she would demonstrate how much she cherished him with little kindnesses and coddlings, small intimacies unseen by anyone else, and then describe exactly how he could help her.

✦∽∽ 3 ∽∽✦

Whenever she could, Debby went to the landing to meet incoming packets. Secretly she was looking for Tony Gray, Molly suspected. Might her sister-in-law forewarn her if Elijah was on board? Debby agreed, thus assuring Molly that she would have a chance to ready herself, grit her teeth, and throw herself into her wifely role.

The packet was a service directed by Benjamin Snow, proprietor of the Golden Ox and owner of the store adjacent to it. When a ship was sighted, he fired an old and moldering cannon located on a hillock behind his place. Beside it was a flagpole, and on that, once the cannon roared, he hoisted an empty barrel that announced incoming goods and passengers. When the packet was due to depart, the cannon would roar again, and a flag would be raised, notifying those wishing passage to the world outside that they should gather at the landing. Benjamin Snow, a Hall, was an entrepreneur like other Halls who ran the fulling mill and the tannery, and all of Rockford depended on him.

On a day not long after the disastrous visit to the Kings, the packet was announced by the firing of the cannon and hoisting of the barrel. Passengers were coming in and Debby went to meet them as usual, then came flying back to the house to tell everyone that Elijah was home.

Molly found her heart beating fast as she hurried to change her housedress for one she had made at the Wardens. It was unpretentious, but its skirt was cut a little fuller—the better to curtsey, Mrs. Warden had said. During her rest and recovery after Sarah was born, Molly had cut the slightly scooped neckline a little lower and had embroidered a wreath of leaves around it to complement the lavender enameled necklace Elijah had given her in the Wardens' garden. It was fetching, she thought, without being ostentatious. Dashing water on her face from the pitcher on her commode, she rubbed it vigorously to make her skin glow, fastened the necklace with shaking, cold hands and snatched up the baby so that she would be calmly waiting by the hearth. The perfect wife and mother.

"Just come and see how much your little daughter has grown!" Mother Merrick led Elijah into the kitchen, followed by Debby and Jon. "Isn't she precious?" Mother took the baby from Molly, and stood between her son and his wife, cooing at Sarah. But Molly was far from excluded. Elijah's eyes found and held hers, and she put into her own gaze all the ardor and magnetism that had once engulfed him at Elizabeth Warden's house. They stood, invisibly linked, the world receding like an ebb tide.

"Is she not beautiful?" Mother settled the child in Elijah's unaccustomed arms. Awkwardly he held the baby, inspected her and allowed his mother to position Sarah more comfortably in the crook of his elbow. Then she led him to the bench beside the hearth, where he could hold his little daughter and converse with his family without the possibility of even kissing his wife's cheek in greeting.

Molly retreated to the chamber door where she could tease him with provocative glances as he listened to his brother's news. Jon was describing a forge he had made behind the barn, powered by a bow he had mounted in a tree just above. "All I have to do is give it a little twang now and then, to make the bellows fan the fire. I can make almost anything!" A foot treadle was difficult for Jon to manipulate, due to his crippled leg, but this invention made it possible for him to work with iron. He showed Elijah some of the nails he had made, which he had arranged for Benjamin Snow to sell in his store. His pride was clear to see.

"Pastor Simmonds' sister came to call the other day," Mother told Elijah, in order to continue holding his attention. "It was a great honor. Usually it is I who call on her. To be called on by her . . . ."

Sarah was squirming and getting ready to cry. Molly came forward to retrieve the child. "I'll take her, Elijah, and nurse her before our supper."

She suckled the baby in their chamber, listening to the chatter on the other side of the door. Elijah's presence reminded her of how terribly lonely it was when he was away, living in this house where no one cared. She thought of Elizabeth Warden, who had loved her, and her eyes filled. But succumbing to self-pity would only deter her, and she fought her tears. It was to the present she must address herself, and that meant Elijah!

The door burst open and her husband strode into the room. Sarah started and squalled, and he took her while Molly fastened her dress. Patting the child's backside, which placated her, he watched with loving adoration. "Good God," he sighed. "Life is not worthwhile if a man isn't given a chance to say hello to his beloved!"

She kissed his cheek and whispered, "Welcome home."

Carefully he laid Sarah in her cradle and returned to enfold his wife in an embrace and a kiss meant to last the rest of the afternoon, deep and full of longing. Molly willed herself to submit to him. Sarah did her part, and was silent.

"I've looked forward to this moment so much, Elijah."

"And I," he responded fervently. "I could hardly believe what was happening out there in the kitchen, Molly. Does my mother always go out of her way to exclude you?"

"She tries," Molly said slowly, as though she were loath to admit it.

"I will not stand for it!"

"We can talk about it later, my love. Supper is nearly ready, I'm sure. Soon enough they will all retire and there will be plenty of time for us. And then . . . ."

"Yes!" His color was high.

Mother cast smug glances at Molly as they set the table. Her son had returned, and it was his mother with whom he had spent the most time.

Poached fish with old turnips would grace the table this night, for there had been no time to kill a chicken and roast it. Debby had made Indian pudding, and it served as treat enough.

Jon brought in some rum from the barn. He and Elijah made good use of it after the meal, while the women drank tea and Mother recounted all the doings around town that she could think of. Elijah's enormous yawns suggested a lack of interest that she pretended not to notice. Then he was obliged to discuss household accounts with her while Molly sat close beside him on the hearthside bench, noting his trust in the old witch. Watching them, she thought, I must be careful, very careful not to speak disrespectfully of her lest I offend him. How can I get him away from her?

But Mother took care of the situation entirely by herself. Long after Debby retired and Jon fell asleep in his chair, Mother talked on and on, faster and faster, and Elijah's face grew blacker and blacker. Molly could fairly feel his tension as they sat together on the bench until abruptly he stood up.

"Well!" he exclaimed heartily. "This is very enjoyable! How wonderful, to be back, with everyone who means the most to me here by our hearth!"

"It is wonderful," Mother simpered. "I haven't felt so content in a long time. There's still so much to tell you . . . ."

"And I'm eager to hear!" Elijah assured her. "But now I am weary, and here is our poor brother whom we have so rudely prevented from getting his rest." He picked Jon up, one arm under his knees, the other cradling his shoulders and head, as though his brother were a babe. Without so much as staggering, he carried him, sleeping soundly, into his little back room.

"I'll bank the fire," he told his mother when he returned, and waited for her to leave.

"Oh, why, yes! I'm so used to doing it myself. . . ."

"Goodnight," he said, shutting off further remarks.

"Goodnight." Mother docilely climbed the ladder to the loft.

"I thought she'd never leave," he breathed when at last he closed the chamber door.

"It's her house," Molly said simply, wishing to subtly impress on him the terrible undesirability of living here. "She has her own ways."

"Well, I maintain it," he pouted. "I support her."

"Indeed you do!" She lit a candle from a coal and carried it into their room. After banking the kitchen fire, Elijah followed.

"Perhaps you ought to build a little fire in here, so the room will be warm." She smiled, and modestly turned her back. He was watching, she was sure, as she slipped the dress off her shoulders, off her hips, and onto the floor in one flowing motion. Beneath it, despite the chill of the spring evening, she had worn nothing at all. With her back provocatively turned, she took up her nightgown and slipped it over her head, then folded the discarded dress neatly while he ignited the kindling and a blaze leaped up.

She turned around. The front of the nightgown was not as chaste as the back. With creamy lace around its low-cut neckline, it seemed to nestle her bosom in a lather of foam. The long, close-fitted sleeves, also lace-trimmed, were a demure contrast. He stared, as she had meant him to do.

"It's lovely," he whispered. "Wherever did you get it?"

"We bought it in London, but I got sick and never wore it." The fine lawn of the gown was sheer enough to show the darkness of her nipples, the black patch at the joining of her thighs. "I'd hoped to please you."

"Please me!" He took her hands in his own, turning her this way and that. "I can't believe it. You are like a dream, Molly." Gently, he drew her close. "Will I hurt you, dearest? It has been so long . . . ."

Oh, it was hard not to be afraid. "Perhaps if we proceed slowly?" she murmured, trembling despite her determination to be bold and flaunting.

Very carefully, he lowered the bodice of the gown so that he could kiss her breasts, large and firm and round with nursing. "Molly, Molly!" he whispered, "you will drive me wild." She could see that he was striving with all his strength to be careful.

Go on, she urged herself. Get it over with.

"Now." She stepped out of her gown. "Come to me now."

Throwing his clothes on the floor, he took her into their bed, a man beside himself with the urgency of his need. She welcomed him, although it did indeed hurt, and she bit her lip to keep from crying out. When he was done, she cradled him in her arms while he slept the instant slumber of a man satisfied.

There! It wasn't as bad as she remembered. In fact, except for the pain, it was easy, and Molly expected the pain would diminish soon. Relieved, she knew she could carry forward as she had planned, instead of simply steeling herself to endure him. How nice knowing that her destiny was now in her hands, lying before her limitlessly, sleeping beside her peacefully.

The late spring night was cool and raw beyond their window. Time passed as she dreamed of the future. In the distance, the peepers called the hours, their cries spaced more evenly as the darkness settled itself to wait for daybreak. She dozed.

Sarah cried sharply, her wails cutting decisively through the room. Molly hastened to retrieve her from the cradle, changed the wet swaddling clothes and settled in beneath the blanket, gave her suck. Elijah woke quickly and rebuilt the fire. He watched as the room became warm again. Beyond the windows, early dawn lifted the darkness.

"You are so beautiful," he said softly. "You are all things. If you could see what you look like right now, you would know what holiness is. To be so lovely and at the same time to give life and breath to another human being . . . ."

He stopped as he choked up. Respecting his emotion and a little ashamed at playing on it, she murmured, "It's I who have received of you, Elijah. You have made it all possible."

He edged in behind her, wrapping his arms around her and the baby. "We, ah, must consider . . . , ah, discuss, how I can best provide for you and the little one," he said hesitantly, then added, "It is a large responsibility, being a family man."

"You have provided already," she assured him, "in all the areas where you can. There's nothing you can do about the situation between your mother and me—that's not part of your job, in any case. As a captain, you've done very well!" She kissed his cheek.

"As a father, too," he said proudly. "Our family will grow. One day we'll have to add on to the house so that the maid I will get you, to help you with all the children I plan to beget, will have a place to sleep. Then there's Mother. Perhaps a separate house for her?" They laughed quietly.

Sarah was asleep again. Molly returned her to the cradle and crawled back in beside him. "I must tell you something, Elijah. I hope you won't be angry." She held her breath, hoping her timing was right.

"Of course I won't be angry." Then he added, "As long as you won't be mad with me when I tell you something that's on my mind, too."

Concentrating so hard on her mission, his words did not register and she plunged on. "I am nearly at my wits end. In all the time I have lived in your house, no one, not a soul, has made a move to befriend me. No one will speak to me; I am nearly convinced that no one ever will."

"Molly!" he exclaimed, dismayed. "Surely you have misunderstood."

"There is nothing to misunderstand," she told him. "There isn't even anything to wonder about. Your mother has introduced me only to your King cousins, and only then because I demanded it. They never came back to offer me their friendship. She hasn't taken me anywhere else. In fact, she refuses to do so."

"That's something I can fix," he declared. "I'll speak to her, Molly."

"My dear one, I don't think you can change her. And you certainly can't change Rockford. Your townsfolk would leave me to rot." She watched him closely. He appeared puzzled, but certainly not annoyed. "I feel the lack of friendship sorely," she added.

Shaking his head, he said, "I find it hard to take this seriously. My mother promised, and I am sure she will make her promise good eventually. These things take time. You haven't lived a year in Rockford yet."

"It won't matter how long I live here, Elijah," she insisted. "I am alone."

"Would it help if I gave you some money to spend?" he asked. "If you could go over to the store and buy a trifle, now and then, it would get you out of the house and give you at least some pleasure. I'm led to believe that women like trifles." He smiled kindly, leaned forward for a kiss.

"That is very kind. It wouldn't solve my difficulties, but it might prove a diversion."

"How about, ah, a dollar?"

"That would be lovely, thank you," she answered politely.

He must have heard the politeness. "Two?" he asked anxiously.

The flames glistened and sparkled through the prism of her rising tears as she saw he did not understand. Time to approach the matter more directly, advice he'd once given her himself.

"But there is a little hope. John Warden's wife lives in Rockford now," she said. "She moved into their new house three weeks ago. Last week I saw her at Meeting, and she told me all about it and invited me to visit her."

"There!" he exclaimed. "You do have a friend, after all."

"I think she might become one, if I were able to get to know her. Mariah is not a Rockford woman; perhaps she's as lonely as I am. But Elijah, I can't reach her! She lives too far away for me to walk to her house, especially with Sarah."

"How does she get to Meeting?"

"On John's horse."

"Umm."

"Elijah," she went on breathlessly, before her courage failed her. "Elijah, will you buy me a carriage, so that I might visit Mariah? So that I might escape the bonds your mother imposes on me?"

"A carriage!" He was amused, but shocked too. "So that you may visit Mariah Warden? You must think you are Lady Washington herself," he teased gently.

Molly smiled and waited to see what he would say next.

"A carriage!" he exclaimed again. "I've just finished expanding this house. What makes you think I can afford a carriage, you little minx?"

"You can do anything, once you set your mind to it." Coyly, she patted his cheek. "If you wanted me to have a carriage, you would find a way to get one."

"That's not fair," he said. "You know full well I'd like to get you whatever you want."

"Wonderful!" she laughed softly. "You can start with a little one. I think it is called a chaise." She looked closely to see if there was any hope.

"No one has a carriage in Rockford, Molly." He was serious now and clasped her hands in his own. "A wagon, maybe. But not a carriage."

"Why not?"

"We are not a rich town—only the richest people have carriages. Why, I'd guess there are only a hundred in all of Boston."

What difference did that make? "Well, of course my knowledge of such things is not from Boston but through the Wardens. They have a carriage."

"The Wardens are one of the wealthiest families in Barnstable County," he told her. "They can afford a carriage. We cannot."

"Do they cost so very much? Even little ones?"

He scratched his head. "Well, they cost enough! You have to import them. From Haverhills of London." He sighed. "Cost isn't the only reason we won't have a carriage, if you really want to know."

"I do want to know."

They pulled up the blankets to keep warm. "It's the showiness of it. None of us wishes to appear ostentatious, even if we could afford to be. But you, Molly," he nibbled on her ear, "you wouldn't mind being ostentatious! Am I right?"

"If I admit it, will you get me one?" she giggled. "People may think it unseemly, but they would envy me, Elijah. And I don't think Mariah Warden would consider it ostentatious. Her husband's family has one, after all."

"You think that this is the solution to your problem?"

"Yes. I will have something no one else in Rockford has. Some people will wish to know me better, so they can ride with me. Once they do, perhaps they will see me as I am, and will like what they see."

"Oh, my darling." He cuddled her close. "I'm so sorry you feel you must induce them to like you."

"As long as some of them do, Elijah, that's what's important."

He sighed again. "Then I'll get you a chaise. You'll have to help though. I don't have that kind of money yet. But I think I know where I can get it."

"Where?"

"Europe. It's time to get back into Continental trade. I've been gone long enough. If I continue the West Indies route, I can't agree to buy you a carriage. But I can guarantee one if I return to Europe."

"You mean I would have to exchange you for a chaise?"

"Not quite," he laughed. "But close."

"You would be gone always."

"I would be gone a great deal," he agreed, "which is far from pleasing to me now that we can really be together. That has been the one advantage in working the coast and West Indies route, to be able to come home often. Seeing more of you makes the route bearable."

Bearable? "What do you mean?" Now that her need had been addressed, she could attend to his.

He buried his face in her hair. His muffled voice said, "I long for deep water."

"Pwader?" she asked. What ever did he mean?

He could hardly stop himself from laughing. "Deep water! The ocean, you ninny!" They laughed aloud, then waited to see if Sarah had heard. The cradle was silent. "I long to take a ship out of sight of land again, and sail it to the ends of the earth. And I long for the challenge of overseas trade, where I can really make a profit."

So unaware had she been of his wish, that she was stopped completely, unable to believe this vast lift in her fortunes. He would be gone and he would be making money! Lots of money! Here she was wondering how to ask for a carriage, and all the time he would have the means to buy one, because he'd be sailing the European route, apologizing because it was his dream!

"I don't know why deep water lures me so," he said. "I don't think anyone who loves it knows. The call of the sea is either there or it's not, and if it is, you will go out however you can, just to be there."

"Well I don't know about sailing." Tenderly she touched his face. "But I can understand wanting something so much that you never let it out of your sight."

"Like a carriage?"

She could not yet tell him her heart's desire, for it was too soon. But she could see it with her inner eye—a house that sat where Samuel Sears' place was now, on land adjoining theirs, facing the low road. A house with two full stories and two chimneys, one on either end, and a fenced porch on top of the roof where the bay could be seen and the packets sighted long before Benjamin Snow's cannon roared. The front door would have carved columns beside it and a graceful fan of glass above. It would show the world that its owners were people of means, and no one would dare to look askance at Molly Deems Merrick, a stranger to Rockford, the wife of the esteemed Elijah Merrick, master of the European market!

"A chaise is a start." Throwing off the blanket, she bounced out of bed. "It's morning, lazy bones! The day begins now!" She pulled on yesterday's dress, with nothing beneath it as a way of reminding him that she'd be waiting for nightfall. She grasped his hands and drew him up. "I will sacrifice you to European trade, and you will get me a chaise. I'll accept rejection by your mother and the indifference of your townsmen," she lifted his hands to her lips, "if you promise that you will not forget me when you go so far away."

"Hardly," he said, pulling her to him roughly. "I could never, ever forget you."

◖◗✦◖◗

A week later the packet was already coming about on the afternoon tide by the time Molly arrived at the shore. She stood on the bluff, watching the usual crowd gathered below, waiting for news from Boston. Mother Merrick slipped into their midst, greeting her friends and being greeted by them, disappearing much as the old apple tree in their field slid quietly into the fog on misty mornings.

But this was a bright day. The whiteness of the sails far out in the bay and the whiteness of the gulls gliding in the blue sky were nearly reflections of each other, one above, one below. Entranced, Molly concentrated on them and waited for her personal tide to turn. Once, she would have gone down to the beach with Mother Merrick, to mingle, to smile, to listen to the talk and pretend to be interested even if none of it were directed at her. She had put up with it so that Mother, walking back home, would not have the chance to open and read letters from Elijah that might be addressed to his wife. Now, however, tired of being ignored, she simply waited on the bluff.

The packet anchored near shore in the shallow trench dug out for it. Its dory was dispatched with passengers and the mail, and she hurried down to the beach, to be on hand when it landed.

As it grated to a halt at the water's edge she prayed fervently for a letter that would show them all that Elijah remembered her before he sailed from Boston. And she was gratified—nay, ecstatic—when, besides a letter was a package, wrapped in canvas and tied with twine knotted in the intricate manner of a sailor. In that moment, she could no longer be ignored; she was important. Even Melissa King, hoping for a letter from Nathan, could see that Molly was singled out by this token of devotion and followed the Merricks back up the Rockford Road and to the house, curious to see what it was. Jonathan was seated at the kitchen table, drinking a mug of milk and sorting blueberries he had picked that morning. Silent by habit, he only nodded at Melissa, showing no surprise at her unexpected presence. Debby sat opposite him, knitting as she invariably was, rocking Sarah's cradle with her toe to persuade to the baby to stay asleep.

"From Elijah?" Debby's excitement over the package was obvious.

Molly nodded. Without a glance at either Melissa or Mother, she hurried to her room, hoping Sarah would not claim her before she reached the haven of privacy to see what the parcel contained and what the letter said.

She unlaced the twine. Within the canvas lay countless yards of soft-as-dawn sea-green silk. Taking up an edge, the silk spilled effortlessly across the bed, whispering its loveliness. *It remindes me of yore eyes* a note read, written in Elijah's hand.

He had thought of her, and he had done something to show her that he had. Sitting in the midst of the silk, her imagination instantly fashioned a gown, finer than any she had ever worn or even seen. The green of her eyes and the green of the dress would set off her dark hair to perfection, and her skin would glow. She would wear it to receive her guests once she had that two-story house with the porch on top! Between now and then, she would wear it when she went riding in her carriage.

Amid the billows of green, she nearly forgot his letter. Quickly, she opened it.

Boston

My deer wife,

It is just as I thought. Fuller has a ship here, Monsoon, which he has loded with flour and wants taken to Amsterdam, and a cargo of tea and woollens from London brought back. It is an easey trip, just to get my hand in, so to speke. I know you wanted a chaise soon, but I cannot take so much money out of my captain's share yet as I believe the profit will be modest. I am worried about you; I know you are lonely and I am afrade I have disapointed you. I hope that the little packag which will arrive with this letter will ease your sore harte.

Elijah

Molly could feel her color rising, her body filling with heat.

He would buy her off with some green silk! He would not get her a chaise, even though she needed one desperately. Captain's share, indeed! It was only because he did not wish to appear ostentatious, she was sure of it! He thought he could distract her, hope she'd forget about the chaise.

Sulking in the cloud of silk, a wry smile slowly arose. No, she would not forget, nor would she be fobbed off like this! For there was still a way to get the chaise, and she would pursue it as soon as the house settled down for the night, writing to Haverhills of London herself. She would order the chaise and ask that it be delivered to Captain Merrick at the London waterfront when the *Monsoon* arrived there after departing Amsterdam. Elijah would pay for it and bring it home.

There. That would take care of everything!

She dismissed her misgivings. Elijah would not like her taking the reins from his hands; she understood that. But he had promised her a chaise. Wasn't she just seeing to it that he kept his word? There would be many captain's shares, after all, but a chaise was important now.

The next afternoon she left the baby with Debby and slipped out of the house as soon as Mother had disappeared down the road to have tea with Pastor Simmonds' sister.

Her heart beat rapidly as she approached Snow's store. She had been there before, with Mother, but it was Mother who had dealt with Benjamin Snow and mighty quickly at that. He was a Hall by marriage! Now Molly would have to deal with him herself, and she could only hope that he would not assume that she, too, was an unfriendly King. Besides, his daughter Olive had long been of interest to her. Perhaps she would be at the counter, too.

The store was wonderful, with its piles of ships' gear and fishing tackle, flour and sugar, leather and hardware, fruits in season and smoked herring out, seed and farm tools, coffee and tea, candy and rum. Its smells, its stuffiness, its riches enfolded her in the luxury of abundance.

Savoring the aroma of the store, she took a deep breath and commanded herself to be calm, unhurried. "Hello, Mr. Snow! How are you today?"

"Mrs. Merrick, I am fair. Fair," he answered, appraising her expressionlessly and looking much like a turtle that would quickly disappear into its shell should the world, or Molly herself, not meet with his approval.

In the dimness of the store she sensed, rather than saw, that other patrons had stopped what they were doing and were watching. Here was the daughter of Hannah Deems, now Elijah Merrick's wife, who had received a package only yesterday. She had rarely been seen out except for visits to the packet landing, and never unaccompanied.

"Could you arrange to have this taken to Boston and then to London?" she asked as she handed him the letter she'd written. "Very quickly?"

Snow balanced it in his horny hand. "Might be able to give it to young Tony Gray. He's due to leave from Long Wharf tomorrow. If anyone's a fast sailor, he is."

"That would be wonderful," she exclaimed, holding out a coin Elijah had given to her. Snow rummaged in his cash box and gave her change. Very casually, she slipped the coins into her apron pocket, as though she were entirely accustomed to handling money.

"I am desirous of making thread to match this color." From the opposite apron pocket she drew out a piece of the silk, large enough for any onlooker to see it easily. "My husband sent me this material, and I wish to make a gown with it."

He took it reluctantly, feeling it carefully. It snagged on his rough hand. "No, can't imagine that I would," he said, and handed the silk back. "I don't deal in fancy stuff, and that there's a fancy color."

"Fancy?" The girl Olive popped in from the back entrance to the store. "So that was the package you received yesterday!" Lightly, reverently, she touched the silk. "How fortunate you are, Mrs. Merrick! It is lovely! Perhaps, Father, we could find some tint that Mrs. Merrick could mix. A little blue, a little green, maybe a bit of yellow to brighten it?"

He thought about it. "Aye. You'd have to experiment, Mrs. Merrick, to find out the right balance."

"It sounds like fun," she smiled up at him.

Olive came from behind the counter and began to squirrel under a table that held canvas and twine. "I think the tints are under here somewhere."

Molly knelt beside her. "Let me help you, Miss Snow."

By now, old Benjamin had come to the table. "Here, here. I'll move those bales of cotton out of your way." He shoved the bales to one side and unearthed the dyes. "Try this, and this," he said, pulling out two packages. "And here's yellow, in case you'll need it."

He handed them over and put the bales of cotton back in place. Molly placed the coins he had given her on the counter. "I hope there's enough here."

"Oh, yes. There's plenty, young lady." There was a twinkle in his eye as he took some of the money and pushed the rest back in her direction. She rather thought she had charmed him.

"Would you enjoy seeing the whole piece, Miss Snow?" Molly asked the girl. "Perhaps you'd have an idea of how I might best use it."

"I can do better than that," Olive Snow said with a glance at her father. "I have a fashion book. It would give you all kinds of ideas."

"Oh, I'd love to see it," Molly exclaimed, her delight growing and crowding her heart.

The girl turned to her father. "Papa, may I show Mrs. Merrick the book?"

"Fashion!" he snorted. "Sounds frivolous to me."

"I think it was you who gave me the book, Father," Olive said sweetly.

Snow looked them both over carefully, very carefully. Both young women stood still as deer pursued in the woods. Would he let his daughter offer her friendship to the wife of a King?

"Don't take too long," he said, and smiled. Clearly he could refuse her nothing. "I'll need your help here, Missy."

Olive Snow took Molly's hand and led her to the back of the house and up the stairs to a small chamber with a narrow cot and a commode, and to a table upon which the cherished book was opened.

"I look at it often," she explained, and pulled the table up to her bed so that they could both sit and look. It was lovely to page through it. Molly had only ever seen garments so elegant when she was in London, and told Olive so. Olive had never seen anything as elegant as Molly's silk, and told her so.

"Will you come to our house to see the whole piece?"

"Certainly," Olive agreed, and paused. Her gaze was steady and strong. "You do realize that your mother-in-law will not approve of a visit from me."

"She may not like it, but I don't think there's anything she can do about it," Molly returned, relief flooding her, that someone should say it! "And what about your Mama. Do you think she will approve your coming to my house?"

"I doubt it," Olive giggled. "But maybe I can slip away when she's not around. How about Tuesday?"

"Perfect. I thank you," Molly said softly.

She could hear Sarah's bawling halfway home. In the kitchen, Mother was walking the baby up and down, patting her back, while the child howled harder and harder. Molly reached for her, opening her bodice as she did so, and put the babe to suckle on the way to her chamber. The house was quickly peaceful, and into the peace Mother Merrick said, "Feeding her is your primary job, Molly. It was irresponsible of you to just go off."

"Time went by faster than I realized," Molly said over her shoulder, and quickly shut the door on further discussion. Nursing Sarah, she remembered each detail of the afternoon visit with Olive Snow, and each detail of Olive Snow's countenance—her small turned-up nose, sparkling dark eyes, glossy brown hair. She was pretty, full of life, and Molly knew they would enjoy one another. A friend, at last!

Then, without enthusiasm, she went into the keeping room to help with supper.

"Where were you?" Mother asked, the shuttle on her loom passing back and forth as she wove sheeting.

"I have had the afternoon with Olive Snow," Molly said, unable to keep pride out of her voice.

Mother Merrick's hands became still on the edge of the loom, and Debby, hemming a newly woven sheet, looked up.

"I thought I might be a good neighbor," Molly said, stirring the pot that hung over the flame in the fireplace. "So I introduced myself to Miss Snow."

"You just walked across the street and said, here I am?"

"Yes," Molly said, her back turned as she scraped the bottom of the pot. "Yes, that's exactly what I did." It was easier to let Mother assume the situation rather than to describe the give-and-take. Finished with her stirring, she turned. "I thought it in the best neighborly tradition of your family."

"*Our* family, Molly," Debby murmured.

"Our family," Molly repeated. "Don't you agree, Mother Merrick?"

"It would have been more seemly if you had been introduced by me," Mother pronounced.

"That would have been preferable," Molly nodded. "But you were not here, and my time is very limited, what with a baby to nurse and all. I didn't know when another occasion might arise."

"I suppose she will be running in and out whenever it suits her," Mother remarked. "I suppose you told her to drop in any time at all."

"I told her she might call next Tuesday. I hope that meets with your approval."

"There's nothing I can do about it," Mother snipped, "since you have asked her already."

"I can return and tell her it isn't convenient for you."

"Hardly," Mother snorted.

"Is she nice?" asked Debby.

"Very."

"I'd like to know her better than I do," Debby ventured.

"It looks as though you will," Mother observed. "Thanks to Molly."

"Surely, Mother, you are not reproving me," Molly challenged. "Surely you would like me to have at least one friend."

"Of course. I don't mean to suggest otherwise. I'm thinking only that she is not . . . appropriate."

"Appropriate? What do you mean, Mother?" Molly asked innocently.

"You know. You know who she is."

"She is a Hall," Molly answered. "Is that what's troubling you?"

"The Kings have not fraternized with the Halls for more than a hundred years!"

"It's about time they began, then, is it not?" Molly asked.

Debby giggled despite herself, and quickly returned to her hemming as Mother glanced menacingly in her direction. "I wonder why Benjamin Snow allowed it," Mother mused as the shuttle resumed. "He must have had a reason. He must feel we're getting above him, or are about to do so. Why else would he countenance his daughter's befriending you?"

"Perhaps he feels she is old enough to make up her own mind," Molly retorted, stung.

"No Hall would allow a child of his to befriend a King without reason," Mother said firmly.

"Perhaps it's the other way around," Debby suggested without looking up. "Perhaps it is we who have been carrying the quarrel."

"That is enough, Deborah," Mother said.

The room became quiet. Molly felt her determination rising and the words spilled out. "The past is a broken-down nag," she declared. "It is a broken-down, swaybacked old nag. You and everyone else in this backwater ride it, using the sway in that old back to keep you from falling off." She congratulated herself on her calm voice, for these must be words of reason, not of anger, words that would free Debby from her mother's influence and make an ally of her. "The Kings were prominent here a long time ago, Mother. They cannot do you any good now. Only you can help yourself, and the only good you can do for yourself is to turn this backwater into a town you can be proud of, and that our new nation can be proud of!"

"The Kings founded Rockford and made it what it is. They are a noble clan, and I, for one, am proud to be one of them."

"Noble they may have been, but if Rockford is going to move forward, it cannot be run from the grave by its founding fathers."

"You wouldn't understand," Mother sniffed. "You'll never understand our heritage."

"It doesn't matter whether I understand it or not. What I do understand is that your heritage is preventing you from moving with the times. I assure you, I will not be prevented by it."

Mother Merrick stood with clenched fists. "That is an attitude I expected from you, Molly. That is why I was eager for Elijah to marry a Rockford girl, who would know these things."

"A Rockford girl might well know," Molly said firmly. "But that doesn't change anything. A Rockford maiden might perpetuate these myths and do nothing to help bring the town forward and into the present. I think Elijah knew that very well when he married me. He knows I'm not bound to the past, and that I shall not allow myself to be bound, even for the sake of his mother. So there you have it. If Olive Snow wants to be my friend, I, for one, am grateful. There might not ever be room on that swaybacked old nag for me, and I am not going to wait any longer to find out."

The two of them faced each other, their heads high, their cheeks flushed, neither giving ground until Mother sighed and reseated herself at her loom. "You are very impetuous," she said. "Perhaps you will be more content if Debby and I take you to the Grays someday soon. Their daughter Hope is very pleasant. Their son, Tony, is at sea just now." She glanced coyly at Debby, who blushed. "He's a great friend of Elijah. The Grays and the Kings have been closely united by bonds of friendship for many years."

"I would like to meet Hope. That would be very nice. Thank you." Molly slid in beside Debby on the bench and began hemming the opposite side of the sheet. "Tony Gray isn't at sea yet, by the way. He won't leave Boston until tomorrow."

"And how do you know this?"

"Mr. Snow told me." Take that, you old bitch, she thought. She turned toward Debby and said, very softly, smiling, "Olive Snow has a fashion book." And if you are nice to me, she added silently, we will let you look at it with us.

How dear Olive was! How much Molly enjoyed her!

The following Tuesday, watching eagerly from her chamber window at the front of the house, she saw the girl crossing the highroad and leaped for the door.

"The front door?" Olive laughed incredulously. "I believe I have never been let into anyone's front door in my life, Molly Merrick!" Beneath her arm was the cherished fashion book.

"Pretend you are the minister," Molly giggled, and whisked Olive into the new chamber. She had set a small fire on her hearth in case Olive might wish tea. And she had brought in a plate of sandwiches in case she and Olive might desire refreshment. The baby was already asleep, a pile of fresh swaddling clothes nearby her cradle. There would be no need for Molly to go into the keeping room where she knew Mother Merrick would be waiting, probably nearby, the better to eavesdrop.

"Why does everyone use the back door?" She took Olive's cloak and placed it neatly on the room's only chair, then reached for the book.

Olive gave it over and shrugged. "I suppose it's because the family is always by the hearth, and the hearth is in the keeping room, and the keeping room is at the back. So no one uses the parlor—except his majesty, the minister."

Yes, she was going to like Olive very much. "The house where I lived for several years was built in the new style. Because the parlor was always used, so was the front door, believe it or not. I suppose the style of a house makes a difference."

"The style of the people in it, too," Olive remarked dryly. "You have moved to a provincial town, Mistress Merrick. We have no style here."

"We will, one day," Molly assured her. "Starting with the wearing of magnificent gowns." She handed a length of the silk to Olive, who sighed deeply as she closed her eyes and drew it slowly past her cheek.

"It's like air," she whispered. "So light, so cool." They seated themselves on the bed and together paged through the fashion book. "Oh, I admire this one."

"Do you agree that it would be suitable for the silk?"

"Definitely," Olive said. "Do you like it?"

"I love it."

"Then let's get started."

"You mean you'll help me with it?"

"I certainly will."

"That's very kind of you."

"Well, I have my reasons," Olive said. "May I speak frankly?"

"Of course." Molly studied the picture, then cut two pieces of silk for each of them. Both set to their seams with green thread Molly had dyed.

"So that you'll know I am being honest, I'll tell you my most important reason first," Olive said. "It's name is Tony Gray."

"Tony Gray!"

"Keep your voice down!" Olive hissed. "Else Debby will come running in here and tear my hair out by the roots. I think she wants to marry Tony herself. Is that not so?"

"I think she does."

"Have you ever met him?"

"I've only ever seen him at Meeting a couple of times."

"Have you seen enough to know that he is very good-looking and has a delightful way about him?"

"Well, I wouldn't know about the delightful part," Molly said grimly, "Since I've never spoken to him. But yes, he is certainly good-looking."

Olive laughed with pleasure at thinking about him. "I was hoping you could tell me when Tony comes to call and how I might intercept him, if such a thing is possible. Like you, I myself have only ever seen him at Meeting," she admitted. "He is a Gray, which is the same thing as being a King. So no one will formally introduce us, and there's no way I can make him aware of who I am, being a Hall. I want to find out if he's got more to offer than just a charming appearance. Charm is very pleasant, but I would never marry a man for it."

Molly appraised Olive's intelligent, sensitive and somewhat wayward face. "What you mean is, you want to see if he is worth fighting for?"

"Something like that." Olive grinned mischievously.

"He hasn't actually come calling on Debby, though both she and my mother-in-law are awaiting the day he does. But I'm not sure they would tell me, even if he were planning to call. They'd probably not even want me in the house. I'm not exactly an accepted member of this family, or the community for that matter. So far, I haven't been introduced to anyone but Elijah's King cousins, who disdain me."

"Actually, you've led right into the second reason I am here," Olive said carefully. "By now, I suspect you're getting a little lonely."

An unexpected lump rose in Molly's throat, making speech impossible.

"I thought I'd like a new friend," Olive went on matter-of-factly, overlooking the sudden silence. "I long for the companionship of a girl who doesn't view life as her grandmother did."

"You've come to the right place," Molly smiled shakily. "I never even knew my grandmother. But Olive, do you dare risk having me for a friend? My mother's reputation, undeserved but well known, precedes me."

"I do dare. And I would be honored, Molly, if you would return the favor."

The eyes of the young women met, a pledge exchanged. Embarrassed because she felt tears rising, Molly hurried to cut more silk. "You'll be glad," she said flippantly. "Elijah is going to buy me a chaise and since you are my friend, you may ride in it with me."

"A chaise!"

"We can drive over to Tony's house and kidnap him," Molly teased, her mood light now. "Once we have compromised his reputation, he will force you to marry him."

Olive laughed so loudly that Sarah awoke with a start and demanded to be fed. Molly nursed her while Olive prepared tea. They stuffed themselves with sandwiches and spent the next hour figuring out how they would cut and stitch the bodice. Promising to return, Olive left, but allowed Molly to be temporary custodian of the fashion book so she would have a picture of the gown to guide her needle.

A friend! Molly was content in the happy cheer of carefree affection and companionship so long denied her and now, at last, rightfully her own and available just across the street. Olive had style, and was the sort of person Molly wanted for her future social circle. Debby would have to be included too, for ballast and to reassure the rest of Rockford that the new society of younger people was respectable. But Olive would provide the spice, and between them, they would attract the girls Molly wanted.

She would woo wide-eyed Debby with the fashion book, sharing its illustrations and designs whenever Mother was elsewhere. She would see Olive on Tuesdays and they would finish the sea-green silk gown. And then there would be nothing left to do but wait for the return of Captain Merrick and the arrival of the chaise, fresh from London.

✦∞ 4 ∞✦

How splendid he was, driving down from Boston, rolling into Rockford with a flourish and a great snapping of his whip over the ears of the trotting horse he had bought just for this purpose.

It was a warm October day, and everyone in Rockford ran to the Merrick barn to admire both the horseflesh and the chaise itself. Happy to stand back and let Elijah bask in the center of attention, Molly smiled, privately, of course, at the answer to her dreams, small compared to the Wardens' carriage, yet exactly perfect for her needs and without any question, the answer to her predicament.

Olive went racing by with her mother, giving Molly a wink as she went. Elijah stood in front of the barn for a long time, answering the questions of the crowd, talking carriage construction and horses. After a while, she realized that although they had not seen one another for five months, he had not once looked her way. With a heart that suddenly plummeted to her feet, she understood he was angry. She had never seen him so and became afraid.

"I'll sell this nag to the highest bidder," Elijah cried, his voice rising above the hum of the gathering. "Starting at fifteen dollars. It's a good horse; she brought me here from Boston in only three days, and you can see for yourself that the journey hasn't bothered her a bit. What do I hear?"

"How much for the carriage, Merrick?" a voice from the crowd asked. A laugh followed, and then a chorus of catcalls as Elijah held up a hand.

"Fellows, the chaise is not for sale. It is for the use of my wife."

The gathering, as one, turned to look at Molly standing on the doorstep with her head high. She disdained to even glance at the crowd that now regarded her with such open envy. Within it were people she had seen at Meeting who had refused to associate with her. There were many she had seen at the packet landing, who never found time to speak. A pox on them all!

"Now, what do I hear for the horse?" Elijah called, and the attention of the group shifted away from her and back to him.

The horse was much prettier than Hector, and Molly would have loved riding around Rockford with such a handsome animal pulling her chaise. But there was nothing she could do about that, and she dismissed the thought immediately. Other things were more important.

"Fourteen dollars," someone offered.

"Fourteen and a half," another said, the men getting down to business.

With the bidding now in progress, Molly helped Mother set out the noon meal. Through the open door, she could see sunbeams caught in the golden shafts of the chaise, glittering on its red painted body and shining on its black hooded top. It was beautiful, and its elegance helped her to steel herself for the inevitable encounter with her husband.

As soon as the crowd dispersed and the chaise was pulled to the side of the barn, Elijah appeared, standing for a moment in the doorway to survey the meal preparations.

"I would talk with you, Molly," he said firmly.

She found within herself the determination not to show fear.

"My pleasure," she said demurely. "And I'm glad to see you, too."

"Dinner is nearly ready!" Mother protested, but Elijah waved her aside.

"Get your shawl." Inwardly quaking, Molly complied and followed him out the door and into the back pasture, down to the little brook. Hidden from public view, he wheeled suddenly.

"Do you know what the word *obey* means?" he asked. His voice was cold. "You promised you would obey me when you married me. Do you remember?"

"Yes, of course," she said steadily. "Of course I remember."

"Ordering a chaise behind my back is not obedience, Molly."

"It is not disobedience, either," she said bravely. "I gave you a chance to keep the promise you made to me, and that's all I did. I don't call that disobedience, Elijah!"

Astounded by her temerity, he took a step back, the better to look at her. "I never promised you anything."

"Indeed you did!" she retorted, determined to have it out. Timidity would make her look guilty, and she was not! "I told you how much I needed a chaise, and you told me one was possible if you went to Europe again. And you went. Here I was, alone again, with no way to escape my isolation."

"But Molly!" he protested, caught off balance by her unexpected accusation. "To just go ahead and order one—that isn't what a wife should do! You had no right!"

"Why did you bring it home, then?" she asked. "If what I did was so wrong, and the chaise is so awful, why did you drive it down from Boston like the King of England? Why did you not send it back to Haverhills as soon as you saw it on the London docks?"

"Because I would have looked like an ass if I had let everyone know that my wife forced my hand." His anger returned as he spoke. "It will take a good voyage, Molly, a very good one, to make up this loss. I should whip you. Many a husband would, believe me."

She stared at him. It was not uncommon, she knew, for a husband to chasten an erring wife. Still—whipping? Never once had she considered he would do such a thing! "But Elijah," she cajoled, "I believed you didn't really understand this was the only way for me to escape imprisonment at your house. I never meant to be a bad wife."

They stared at each other, helpless to resolve their conflict. She allowed herself a tear. "For so long, I've hoped your leave would be a happy one. Made even more exciting because we can ride around town like royalty. And I even made a surprise for you, too. You'll like it." She looked up at him imploringly, with all the admiration and longing and loving she possessed. It must work. It had to work! "Will you let me show you my contrition, dear Elijah?" she murmured. "If I have done wrong, will you forgive me?"

She watched as he struggled with the complexities of the situation. In the autumn sun, the tufted marsh grass was yellow as wheat and glistening, lifting and falling in the intermittent breeze. Bowing to the inevitable, reluctant to forego his anger and equally unable to hold onto it, Elijah gestured his helplessness.

"What can I say, Molly?" he asked, his palms up. "It is clear you thought you had just cause. And I suppose I was unfair, after all, to postpone getting a chaise when it seemed I had promised one." He moved closer. "If you want to make me happy, you can prove it by kissing me. And I'll kiss you back, to show I bear you no ill will."

It was as graceful a way out of the impasse as any and she admired his ability to defer to the inevitable, to turn the situation to his own advantage so that he did not seem defeated by it. The kiss was more healing than words, and Molly gave a great deal to it. If she could keep that up throughout his leave, he would not even care that the chaise was not his own idea!

She set to pleasing him with all her concentration.

∞✦∞

Hector, the family animal, paid no more attention to the chaise shafts than he did to the plow. The elaborate decoration on its wooden work seemed to inspire him, and he held his head a bit higher, lifting his old hooves from the sandy track in front of the barn with more spirit than he had ever shown before. His tail and mane floated in the breeze of his own making, and he shook his head and snorted as he pranced.

Molly clapped her hands gleefully. "You've given his life a whole new meaning."

"See if Deb will mind Sarah," Elijah called down to her. "We'll ride out together."

Lifting her skirts, Molly dashed to the house to arrange for Sarah's safekeeping. Within sat Mother at her loom, glowering. "Never will I ride in it," she said balefully. "The Lord gave me legs, and I shall use them."

"He gave Hector legs, too," Molly retorted, and ran off.

Ah, the wind on her face! To sit at ease and see the road slipping by. It was good! It was! The road, of course, was not well adapted to wheels, and so bumps and hillocks challenged them, but no matter! They drove to the Rockford Mills, splashing through the ford and throwing sheets of water high up on either side. They turned around and splashed through again, waving at the varieties of Halls who ran out to see the sight of a chaise in Rockford. Then they headed back toward town, swinging into the circular driveway of John Warden's square-rigged house. The sight of it made Molly, for just a split second, doubt her senses and think her dream had materialized right there on John's high land overlooking the bay.

Dismounting, they called on his wife, Mariah, who was delighted at the prospect of Molly coming to see her soon and of riding with her in the chaise.

Speeding off, they grandly passed the door of Pastor Simmonds, who could be seen watching them through his parlor window, no doubt wondering if the fancy cart were the Lord's doing, or the Devil's.

They turned onto the low road, two ruts, really, past Samuel Sears' place, his back fields adjacent to the Merricks' own. Sears was mending the fence in front of his house, and they stopped to chat with him. Then taking the highroad again, they swept past their own house, past the center of town, to the south, and then along a track deep into the woods where Elijah stopped the chaise and embraced her, his passion rising higher and higher. Content to let him have his will, happy to please him, her joy in her victory made it easy to contribute to his well-being.

"Oh, Molly," he panted, nearly falling out of the chaise in his ardor. "There was never a woman such as you. My dearest, I will never get enough of you."

That night she modeled her surprise for him—the green silk dress she and Olive had made. Everyone had gone to bed by then, and Sarah was asleep. She took him into the parlor, which she had readied and dressed up with a few articles of her own to give it the air of gentility: leather-bound books from Elizabeth Warden on the mantel; nearby the two pewter porringers from her mother, rubbed to gleaming; a small round rug filling the middle of the room, braided by Olive from wool pieces left over in the scrap bag at Snow's store. Molly's gown and the room itself were demonstrations of the kind of life she would create here in Rockford when she was allowed free reign.

The dress enchanted him entirely and Elijah watched her as she handled its long folds and curtseyed to him, a curtsey that revealed the admirable fullness of her bosom, the dainty smallness of her waist. She spoke with him intelligently about his voyage and about her progress here at home, due largely to her friendship with Olive Snow. Did he approve of this bold step she had taken? Did he, too, wish to end this pointless division between the leading families in Rockford? Of course, she had no desire to do anything he disapproved of. . . .

Of course he approved!

Molly was sure, by the time they returned to their own chamber across the entry hall, that he had forgiven, or else forgotten, that she had ordered the chaise. The next morning Sarah was at her best with him, smiling now in response when he made faces at her. His mother nodded dubiously as he expressed his view that ending the old feud was long overdue. The few evenings left, spent in the privacy of their own part of the little house, were enough to bewitch him completely.

✤∞ 5 ∞✤

Several weeks after his departure, Molly realized she was pregnant. It was Sarah, complaining and fretting over the waning milk supply, that first told her. Drat, she thought, it's not supposed to happen to a nursing mother! Fate ever ran against her. But then, she decided, it was part of the bargain, and it would hardly do to complain. With a sigh, she prepared for a new baby.

It was an easy pregnancy, once the initial fatigue passed. She remembered that her first had not been so uneventful. Not only had she felt wretched, she had also been flat on her back, so preoccupied with her anxieties that she had all but starved.

No need to worry this time! It was Elijah's child she was carrying, and no one else's. And now, on top of that lovely certainty, she could ride about in the chaise to her heart's content, as long as the weather permitted and Hector went slowly so that the rutted roads did not jostle her into a miscarriage. Often she took Olive with her, sometimes Debby. She visited Mariah Warden in her grand house. Once she and Olive and little Sarah went to the South Shore, an all-day trip. About the fishing shacks was strewn the debris of the trade. Women mended nets, children played among the trailing lines, stacks of buoys, traps, and upturned dories. It was a sunny scene that contented their hearts while offending their destiny. Homey, yes, but indeed, it was not for the denizens of the North Shore and their progress toward gentility!

Now that she had the chaise, Molly's dreams moved to the house she wanted: a fine captain's house, like John and Mariah Warden's, built on the land of Samuel Sears. This goal never left her mind as she rode about the village with Olive.

"I really love this," her friend exclaimed. "It must be like Boston!"

"I wouldn't know," Molly told her. "But it is like London, where the aristocracy never, ever walks anywhere! Surely your father doesn't like it, though," she went on. "Wouldn't he prefer you to stay at home rather than riding with me?"

"So far he hasn't said a thing," Olive told her. "I think he feels that Elijah is going to do very well, and he would rather not be on record as being uncooperative."

This accorded with Mother Merrick's estimate of the situation, but Molly did not let that bother her in the least. If old Snow thought his business would grow because of cordiality with Elijah Merrick and his wife, she had no objection. In Olive she had found a real friend—her first—and it didn't matter what the motivation of Olive's father was as long as he stayed out of the way.

"What of the friends you already have?" she asked Olive. "Surely they resent me."

Olive shrugged. "They'll get over it, I am sure," she said "My friends and I have never spent too much time dallying over tea like you and I do. The Puritan in them disapproves of idleness. But we will change their minds, in time."

Her heart sang with these words. Content in Olive's companionship and working carefully to inspire the growing confidence of Debby and Mariah, Molly made no gesture of friendship to another soul. They must be absolutely convinced, she thought, entirely sure that her company was both desirable and difficult to attain. And so she spurned the few overtures that were made by some brave souls and slowly maneuvered her husband's sister and John Warden's wife into the social position she was arranging for them.

✦

The pregnancy advanced. After months of snow and bitter wind, a taste of spring blew in. Molly invited Debby to accompany her in the chaise.

Debby looked at her askance. "Do you think you should be out around town, looking like that?" she asked. "It is considered unbecoming, Molly."

"Who considers it so?"

"Why, why everybody!"

"Does it matter what people think?"

"Of course it matters!" Debby was shocked. "You do want to be liked, don't you, Molly?"

"I don't even care," Molly answered gaily. "And if you do, then you had better not be seen with me." Though spoken lightly, it was a test. Would Debby pass or fail?

Debby only looked embarrassed. "I can't blame you for feeling that way."

"I'm glad of that, since we are sisters of a sort," Molly said gently. "But I would not have you suffer because of me, Debby. You need not come with me."

"Oh! Please! That's not what I meant!" the girl replied. "I love riding in the chaise. I love going to Mariah Warden's beautiful house as though I belonged in her company. I love being with you—you're fun!"

There had not been much fun in Debby's life until now.

"And I like having you with me," Molly soothed. "I like your company, and I need someone to hold Sarah. But I can get Olive, should you feel more comfortable."

"No indeed," Debby said hastily, anxious not to be preempted by Olive Snow. "Unless you prefer her company."

"It's not a matter of preference," Molly prevaricated. "She's willing to befriend me, though I am new here, and I'm eager to please her. But there is no reason why you and she cannot share the chaise. If you like."

"I like," Debby grinned, passing the test beautifully. "I'll ride out with you whenever you'll take me."

On those occasions, she hurried past her mother, without asking permission. Mother, disdaining even a glance as they pulled grandly away, grimly peeled potatoes or plucked chickens or wove cloth or went to drink tea with her cousin Melissa or the sister of Pastor Simmonds.

ⓧⓧ✦ⓧⓧ

"Tony's home!" Debby's excitement and pleasure glowed on her plain face. Along with the rest of Rockford, she had gone to meet the Boston packet. "He says he won't be here for long, but hopes to call on me before he goes back. He said he might even visit later today."

"How nice!" Molly exclaimed. "I know that would mean a great deal to you, Sister."

"Well," Debby sniffed, "he'll be sorry if he doesn't come by. I won't wait around forever!"

She liked pretending she had a choice. Molly was almost pained by her joy because of what was going to happen next.

She found Olive, and quickly they moved to carry out the plot they'd contrived. Gathering up Sarah and hitching Hector to the chaise, they drove toward the east of town and then slowed to a walk, as though eager only for the spring air and sunshine. Not far from the Gray's house, they saw Tony on his family's horse, trotting badly toward them. Men of the sea were often poor riders.

"Ready?" Molly asked. "Now's your chance."

"Ready." Olive settled herself.

Molly pulled Hector to a stop.

Tony came closer, then stopped, too.

"Good luck!" she whispered to Olive. "Good day, Master Gray!"

He swept off his hat. "Good day, Mistress Merrick. I'd heard that Elijah bought a carriage! It's a beauty." His was a merry face, full of life and reflecting his pleasure with the world. "And good day to you, Miss Snow."

"Master Gray, good afternoon," Olive responded softly in a voice Molly had never heard her use before. She turned in surprise, then quickly covered her amazement by concentrating on Tony.

"Where did Elijah get the chaise?" he asked.

"In London. I couldn't get around town very well, so he brought it home for me to use."

"So my mother told me." Reaching out, he touched the shining paint.

"Maybe you should try it, Master Gray," Molly suggested.

"Try what?"

"Driving the chaise," she said, though she truly did hate letting anyone use it.

"Why, I'd really enjoy that, Mrs. Merrick," he beamed.

"I cannot go along though. Should you overturn it, I might lose my baby."

"I did not realize . . . ," he said, turning scarlet.

"Olive, why don't you go, too? Someone needs to show him how to manage the reins. Sarah and I will visit with Master Gray's mother and sister."

Tony turned his horse and accompanied them to his house. He helped Molly down and drove away very quickly with Olive lest his family see him with someone from the Hall clan. Carrying Sarah around to the keeping room door, Molly presented herself to Tony's startled mother and his sister Hope, two visiting aunts and one sister-in-law. She explained that Tony had coaxed her into letting him drive her chaise and that she herself was very thirsty and would beg of them a drink of water. And a bit of bread for Sarah, if they had any.

It was one of the more enjoyable moments she had known in Rockford up to then. She explained that Mother had been too busy to bring her by before, to meet them, and wasn't it a fortunate thing, to have seen Tony out riding? Regally she sat in a wing chair by the hearth, sipping the water, cuddling Sarah and feeding her bits of bread, directing the flow of conversation as any playwright might do with strokes of his pen. Tony's sister, Hope, watched the performance quietly from the corner of the room where she was making thread. Molly, very much aware of that scrutiny, showed Hope plainly the sort of person she was and would ever be—a social leader, a beggar to no man, a woman filled with vitality, sparkling and vibrant. Could Hope follow this lead? Indeed, did she want to?

Much, much later, the chaise pulled into the yard and around to the kitchen door. The womenfolk swarmed out of the house to admire its gleaming beauty. Olive was not present. Curious as she was, Molly had no opportunity to ask Tony where they had gone and what had happened to her friend. It was not her business, and if she knew nothing, then she could better handle Debby's complaint that Tony had not come calling after all.

She never asked Olive about it either, and went out of her way to be kind to Elijah's sister after that, sharing needlework secrets and reading newspapers and pamphlets to her, procured at Snow's store.

After her seventh month she stayed home. The confinement made her restless as a cat, irritable and weepy and determined not to show it so that Mother Merrick would have no opportunity to complain about her. Nor did she show her fear, so that Mother would not be able to belittle her lack of courage. But she was afraid. Like most every woman, Molly dreaded to distraction her second labor, for she was left with memories of horror surrounding the first and there was no way of knowing if the second would be any better. She suffered her anguish alone.

Then she started to worry when she realized they had not heard from Elijah. He had been gone the entire time of her pregnancy, but a round-trip voyage to Europe could take anywhere from three months to ten, depending on how much trade a captain could find when he got there. It was not especially unusual to have had no word from him before now, but surely soon? She shut her eyes to the natter of Debby and Mother Merrick about his safety. Resolutely, she made clothes for the new baby, walked in the summer fields with Sarah's little fist in hers and taught her the names of things they saw.

Her eighth month passed, and then the ninth, and then her time came and in July she delivered, with as much agony as before, but much more quickly. A lusty male child, wrinkled and howling and looking unmistakably like his father.

Of course, he was named Elijah. She studied him. So unlike Sarah, who did not resemble Elijah at all. As their little girl grew older, Molly wondered if she did not somewhat favor Elizabeth Warden. Fortunately, few people in Rockford knew what Elizabeth Warden looked like. And to avoid any comparisons, Molly occasionally exclaimed over how much the child resembled her own mother, who was unknown to everyone.

The baby was a month old when the packet brought Elijah's letters. The whole family sat at the kitchen table while Molly pored over his labored writing. Mother was nearly in tears because there was no letter for her, while Molly received six.

Piling them up according to date, she read them through, taking her time and making sure she skipped nothing despite the awkward spelling. Mother was enraged at being made to wait, but as Molly read, she saw that a problem more important than Mother had arisen and she was no longer interested in besting the old bitch or trying to wrest control from her. She schooled herself to remain calm, willed her face into immobility, commanded her hands, suddenly cold, to remain steady and without tremor. For Elijah was at the mercy of the revolutionary French.

"You must have read each one twice," Mother remarked peevishly, unable to conceal her impatience any longer. "You might tell us what he says."

Daylight was fading fast and Debby went to the mantel for the candle, lit it in the coals and brought the light to the table.

"Bring another, please," Molly told her, and stifled Mother's protest at the extravagance. "I don't want to make a mistake in what I tell you because of not having enough light to read." Supper shriveled in the fireplace, unnoticed. Sarah, napping in a heap by the hearth, sucked her thumb noisily, an indulgence Mother usually complained about. Nearby, Jon jiggled the cradle with the baby 'Lije in it.

"He is in France. Their government has captured his ship and cargo."

"Captured!" they all exclaimed.

"It's a revolutionary government!" exclaimed Jon. "They're a bunch of criminals!"

"Criminals?" his mother quavered.

"Wait, wait. Please." Molly smoothed out the letter she was reading. "They have promised to pay him. For the cargo. It's flour, which the French people desperately need because they are starving. But he is having trouble getting his money out of them."

"Brigands," Jon said mournfully, forgetting the French contributions to his own country's revolution.

"Oh," moaned Mother, her head in her hands. "We shall never see him again. They will murder him, rather than pay. I know it."

"Murder?" Debby asked in horror.

"Elijah never was very careful," Jon said to the andirons in the fireplace. He had forgotten 'Lije, who started to fuss. The jiggling resumed, the baby quieted.

I should have been more concerned before this, Molly told herself. Instead, all I could think of was delivering a child again. I never really thought of Elijah at all. Only of myself.

She refused to consider the possibility of his dying. "I believe he is in some danger," she said to Mother, "He's been told he must travel from the port to Paris, which is 600 miles distant, in order to collect what he is owed. And the French countryside is a poor place to be roaming. It is lawless just now."

"Oh, God, oh God, help us," Mother groaned piously.

His life, Molly thought. Oh Jesus, his life! Without him, I am lost. The letters were weeks, some of them months, old. Anything could have happened in the meantime, but she refused to let his family mourn him. It was senseless to bury anyone before it was necessary. And perhaps even bad luck.

"I don't think the French people would harm him on purpose. They appear to have a high regard for Americans. Elijah says here: *They spoke the name of Washington as though he were God almighty. They call out "le bon Georges!" whenever they find out I am not british.*

"And so what happens when he gets to Paris?" queried Mother.

"They will compensate him for his cargo. And then he'll come home."

"I wish he would just forget the money and come home without going so many miles to get it," Debby said.

"He can't, Deb," Jon said. "That ship, everything on it and in it, is his responsibility. Not being paid for a cargo is like scuttling it. 'Twould ruin his career."

It was too shattering to contemplate, nearly as bad as if Elijah were killed. Molly refused to consider it. "I shall think only of his homecoming," she told them. "And I would suggest that you do, too. It does us no good to borrow trouble. We must act as though we expect him to walk through the kitchen door tomorrow. And that could happen, as you know. He could already be en route. The French will pay, I believe, in order to keep their credit good, just as we had to pay our war debts in order to trade in Europe."

This reference did not comfort the family, for they had not read of Alexander Hamilton's policies that would establish American credit abroad.

She prepared to take the letters to her room, shoving them into the safety of her apron pocket, gathering baby up on her hip, cradling his tiny head in her hand, taking a lit candle with the hand that was free. "We must look ahead eagerly, and not with dread."

Leaving them sitting mournfully in the kitchen, she closed her chamber door on their premature sorrow. She put 'Lije on the bed, changed his nappies, nursed him and reminded herself to think pleasant thoughts and not borrow trouble.

When 'Lije was done and asleep in the cradle with his little arms flung up beside his head, she took the letters out of her pocket, stood near the candle on the mantel, found the one she wanted, opened it and read it again, and then again, and then again.

My deer, if I can collect this damned money, it will be worth hundreds of purcentiges more than when I went away. We will be rich! Your hartes desire will easly be gained, no matter what it may be. If you wish a larger carrage to ride about Rockford like Ladie Washington, you have only to ask. You shall have jewls and a palase if I can get the money, and I shall not leave until I do, never fere!

Defiantly she pushed Elijah's troubles from her mind and allowed herself to consider only his probable success. And the jewels. And most important—the palace.

It was time to direct her energies to the goal that her imagination had seized and held ever since the day she and Elijah had driven about Rockford in the chaise. A goal she could see from her chamber window. The farm of Samuel Sears.

Her palace, in the form of a captain's house, would sit perfectly on Sears' land, once the present cottage was dismantled and its lumber used to make barns and sheds, replacing the ones that were there now, rickety, and in some places, falling down.

The land had been part of the original parcel owned by Elijah's grandfather, sold by Mother to put food on the table. It held yet an aura of destiny for the Merricks, attesting to the proper order of things. That aura, she was sure, would work in her favor as she moved forward. Forward now, while the time was ripe. Now, before her husband returned with his habitual caution, before he could dismiss the idea as imprudent or extravagant. Now was the time to strike a bargain with Sears.

Bringing out her ink and quill and paper, she wrote: *My dearest Mistress.* It sat ill to ask a favor of her beloved guardian when the intent was to further material gain, something Elizabeth Warden would have considered unworthy. But there was nowhere else to turn.

I risk offending you; please do not think ill of me. I am in need of money for a short time, until Elijah returns from Europe. I have the opportunity to purchase the land of the Merrick First Comer to Rockford. Elijah's mother was forced to sell it when his father was lost at sea. Elijah will repay you as soon as he comes home, but I am fearful that if I wait, the opportunity will be lost. Will you, dear Mistress, help me?

At Snow's store the next morning, she dispatched the letter. The post rider would deliver it that afternoon or the next, and she waited feverishly until, three days later, Olive came running toward the house with a small, neat parcel in her hand. Molly swept her friend into her room and broke the seal. Inside were ten golden dollar coins.

"Ah," Olive breathed, impressed.

They had been wrapped in a letter, which Molly read now:

My dear child,

Remember that God is interested only in your heart and your soul; do not confuse what is real, in this world, with what is not. If the Merrick land is part of His will for you, then I am glad to be His instrument. Take the enclosed coins with our blessing. Use them to show your intent to secure the land until Elijah returns.

She could not contain the tears that spilled down her cheeks. Alarmed, Olive leaped up. "Molly, is something wrong?"

"No, no," she shook her head. "The money is from my mistress, so that I can make an offer on Samuel Sears' land. What do you think of that?"

Still the tears came, for she was ashamed at using Elizabeth Warden's trust.

"No doubt Mr. Sears will be happy to get it, knowing the state of his credit at the store," Olive remarked. "I didn't know you had this in mind, Molly."

"It just came to me, like a revelation," she laughed, wiping her tears away. "It's the perfect place for a captain's house, don't you agree?"

"One like Mariah Warden's?"

"Indeed, yes."

Olive hugged her. "Good luck," she whispered. "It's certainly the right place and exactly the right house for your green silk gown."

Molly unpacked the dress and hung it on her bedroom wall, a tangible symbol of her dreams. It whispered to her every time she passed by: Queen of the castle. Queen of the castle.

"Why anyone would want such a garment, I do not understand," said Mother, her hands on her hips as she stood critically inspecting the offending dress. "I'm sure you look lovely in it, but it is dreadfully out of keeping."

"I wore it before, to welcome Elijah home, and I shall again, soon."

"Well, I think you will look rather foolish, eating baked beans in your finery," Mother sniped, unappeased by Molly's optimism. "That's all we'll have, by the time he gets back."

"Oh, Mother, I didn't realize there was so little left." She tried not to think of the Wardens' money hidden in her trunk. "Is there anything I can do? I think Mr. Snow would extend us credit if we asked."

"He would do so, I am sure," Mother said stiffly. "But I would rather borrow from Melissa than from Mr. Snow. We can get by for now with turnips from the garden and stewing up the old hens. I should not have mentioned our want."

Molly knew she had done so only to take pleasure away from the green dress. Going to Debby, who was kneading bread, she said, "Unfortunately, I must make the dress bigger. I wonder, Deb, if you will help me."

"Gladly," said Debby, deliberately ignoring her mother. "Once I get the flour off my hands! I'd love to work on it, just to touch it!"

Mother refused to countenance such heresy, and went out into the garden with her hoe.

"If you would let the two side bodice seams out, and the skirt seams where they meet, I think there's enough material to make it fit." Molly had designed it with generous seams, just to meet this challenge.

Debby set the dough to rise, then took a look. "Yes," she said. "You're right."

"When Elijah comes home rich, we'll make you a gown, too. What color would you like?"

Debby laughed, fetching her sewing basket. "A gown for me! To wear while I weed the garden? Eat baked beans?"

"No, you ninny! To wear when you are the wife of a captain and the two of you go out in your carriage."

"I never did hear from Tony," Debby said wistfully.

"There are other captains. Rockford will be chock-full of them soon. Then you can take your pick!"

"Well, for now I'm happy here with you," Debby rejoined. "Bring me the dress."

Molly did so. "Are you sufficiently happy here so that you'd watch the children for an hour?"

"Of course. While I work on the seams."

The nicest thing about Debby, besides her docility and her acceptance, was that she never, ever, asked where Molly was going.

With a racing heart, she let herself out the front door so that Mother, still in the garden, would not espy her. She hastened down to the low road and to the house of Samuel Sears, and then to its keeping room door at the rear. Its panels were split, and she knocked on the frame for fear of further damaging them.

"Come in," a woman's voice called. "Oh! Mrs. Merrick! I thought you were Eliza Stone, come to return my pie tin. But she wouldn't have knocked . . ." Mrs. Sears was flustered at the arrival of her uninvited guest and fluttered about the table, looking unsure of whether or not to ask Molly to seat herself. "I feel very shamed, Mrs. Merrick, that I have not come to your place before this, to make myself known to you."

"It is difficult, I know," Molly said politely, restraining herself from fidgeting in response to the fidgets of Martha Sears. "It's hard to find any extra time."

"Yes, yes, that's so. I'm already late with my churning."

"Oh! You must have a cow!" Molly smiled, hoping to put the woman at ease.

"No, I'm afraid not. I make butter for Mrs. Browning, who has two cows and more milk than she needs. She gets half, I keep half. What may I do for you, Mrs. Merrick?"

"It is your husband with whom I would speak."

"My husband? He is in the back field. Finishing up the hay, I expect. But I don't know when he'll be in."

"I'll go to him, if you just point the way."

"You'll walk out there? 'Tis some distance."

"The exercise would be enjoyable," Molly said blithely. "I do ride about quite a lot, and walking would do me no harm."

"I would not walk a step farther than I have to," Martha sighed and retrieved her butter churn from behind the stack of wood near the hearth.

"You work so hard, Mrs. Sears," Molly said. "There must be little room left for pleasure when you work so hard." To her own ears she sounded wise, like Elizabeth Warden, and it pleased her.

"Well, we like to eat," the woman said dourly. "So we work."

"I have an idea things might change for you, depending on the outcome of my discussion with your husband. For many of us, life might become a good deal easier if we take the opportunities that come our way."

Mrs. Sears shrugged. "What opportunities?" she asked her butter churn.

But Molly was not going to tell her. "You'll soon hear about them from your husband." She had planted the seed and was content. Thanking the woman for her directions, she set off through the farm. The Sears' farm. But perhaps, someday soon, hers. Hers and Elijah's.

The fences were in poor repair, she noticed. The kitchen garden was forlorn. An enormous heap of manure was piled pungently near the barn. Behind a hopeless orchard of worm-struck apples lay a gentle rise that, she knew, would run toward the shore on its far side, just as did the Merrick's.

At the top of the rise the bay glistened as a mirror in the distance. Molly looked about in a passion of exhilaration, in the freedom and openness of the fields stretching to the shore. A tangle of bleached timbers could be seen near the beach. Sears must have once set up vats for making salt, encouraged by the need brought on by war.

Not so distant, Sears himself swung the scythe, stepping rhythmically to its sweep. *He is probably cranky and short tempered,*

Molly thought, itching from chaff, sweating and hot. This is not the place or the time to talk with him. Yet there might be no other.

And so she walked on. When she had covered half the distance, he noticed her and stopped his labor, leaned on the handle of his scythe, waited.

"Good morning!" she called when she was suitably near.

"Morning."

"I would speak with you, if I may, Mr. Sears."

He appraised her with suspicion and with curiosity, too.

"I am Elijah Merrick's wife, Mr. Sears. You may remember meeting me when my husband was home last, and we were out riding in our new carriage."

Sears watched her for what felt like a long time.

"A-yuh," he acknowledged at last. "I never seen a carriage before."

"We are most fortunate to have one," Molly observed.

"A-yuh," Sears agreed.

"Do your crops grow well here?" she inquired, as though she were merely being polite.

"Nope," he said. "Land's used up. I been on this farm fifteen years, and your husband's family farmed it before me. I don't think they did much better with it than I do."

"Well then, Mr. Sears, I am wondering if you might enjoy trying something else besides farming."

"Something else? Mrs. Merrick, there ain't nothing else."

He turned a bit to look out over the bay.

"My husband, as you know, is in European trade and doing fairly well with it," she said chattily.

"A-yuh," Sears grunted.

"We're thinking that if you sold your farm to us, then perhaps you'd have enough to take care of yourself and Mrs. Sears without farming."

"Sell it?" He turned to her. "Why'd you ever want to buy this godforsaken place?"

"To have a home of our own, Mr. Sears, and now we have the means to do so," she said sweetly. "Elijah has invested in a large share of the cargo on his ship, and it's worth a good deal more than anyone thought it would be, because of conditions in Europe."

"That so?"

"Naturally we are grateful for his mother's help when we needed it and while he was working to establish himself, but we'll be able to build a place of our own when he gets back. If we settle right here, we'll still be close enough to his mother that we can care for her, should she need it. And nothing could be more appropriate for us than the land of my husband's forefathers. Your land."

"A-yuh."

"Elijah asked me to approach you, should I find an opportunity his mother wouldn't know about."

"And this be it?"

"It is. I was able to leave the house without her noticing. But I must hurry back now, else she'll discover I've left. She doesn't know about our plans. We don't want her to know until we're sure of them. Old people do get so upset at the idea of change."

"A-yuh," he nodded. "Mothers are like that."

She nodded. "Elijah is sure you'd never regret it.."

"Sounds too easy," he observed. "But I am tired of farming, and I'm not young no more. Will Elijah pay me three thousand dollars for the place?"

Molly did not know the value of the land, and was caught red-handed in her ignorance. She managed to say, "No. But we will pay you two thousand."

Was it reasonable? Was the land worth that much?

"It's worth three," Sears countered, but unconvincingly. "Got about 75 acres, with two ponds that are good for ice and some fish too."

"The ponds are certainly valuable. But as you say, the land is used up. And my husband would never allow me to offer more than two thousand," she countered, disregarding the fact that her husband would not have allowed her to offer even one dollar.

"That probably ain't enough for us to finish out our days some-wheres else," Sears objected, "depending on how many days there'll be." How much would he need for his old age? she wondered. Was there something that would reassure him? Then it came to her. "Mr. Sears, perhaps you have heard that some townsmen invest in a ship's cargo. When the vessel returns, they get their money back and a decent percentage of profit on it. You could use some of the money from the sale of your land to invest in cargo on Elijah's next ship."

He chewed on this for quite some time. "I know Ben Snow has done that and it worked out just fine for him. So, Elijah could invest in his cargo for me?"

"Most certainly," she assured him brightly, despite her doubts about Elijah's willingness to do anything of the kind.

After studying his hands for a while, he asked, "When are you planning to do this Mrs. Merrick?"

"Well, naturally I am prepared to give you some money in advance, enough to show our good intent. We can spare only a little at this time, as our funds are largely tied up in cargo. We can offer you ten dollars in gold. Talk it over with your wife and let me know."

"We'll talk on it, sure," he said and returned to his labor. Elated, Molly bounded back to the house she despised.

There was much to do. First, she would finish the dress so that it was wearable again. Then she would ask Benjamin Snow, who was the town clerk, to help her prepare a buy-and-sell agreement. She would furnish the parlor as she had when Elijah was last home, and invite Sears and his wife to the house when Mother went to the par-sonage for tea. Debby would take the baby and Sarah over to the Kings while Molly, in her green silk gown, would meet with the couple, surrounded by her simple but elegant props that would show them the Merricks were not only on their way up, but halfway there already. If they had any doubts as to the Merrick's ability to pay, that would help allay their concerns. And they would see what might be gained from investing in Elijah's cargo.

And then she would wait for the return of her husband, and her fate at his hands. Resolutely she put out of mind the possibility that he might be angry. The truth of the matter was that she had run him in debt for a Cape Cod farm, and if he disliked being forced into buying a chaise, he might be considerably angrier at having to buy the Sears' place.

Refusing to consider his rage, banishing the thought that he might at that moment be dead and buried in French soil, she continued to nurture such stature in Rockford as she had, up to that time, acquired.

Ladie Washington, indeed!

The Land

THE WIND WAS RIGHT, the tide was right, the day was right. But if the goddamned customs officials didn't get off this goddamned tub, the tide would not be right and another day would be lost! Sweat beaded the brow of Elijah Merrick and his fists were clenched, though he tipped back his chair as if he had not a worry in the world. On the decks and in the hold he could hear the French officials yapping, their voices sharp with frustration. Jack Pollard, Captain James Jellison's first mate, peeked in.

"They're going over the ship a second time," he whispered, then winked and was gone again.

Elijah waited.

The officials were no longer jabbering. Perhaps there was cause for hope? Yes—through the little cabin window he saw them depart. One of them turned and gestured obscenely toward the ship. Grinning, Elijah returned the gesture behind the safety of the cabin walls. He remained out of sight while the ship was freed from her moorings and the pilot edged her into the channel. At the harbor's mouth, Captain Jellison put the pilot off and took the ship out to sea.

Then, Elijah guessed, it was safe to emerge. Clumping out of the cabin, he watched the crew going about its business. The breeze picked up a trifle from the northeast quarter. At the rail, he looked ahead into the rising and falling sea, judging the reach and fetch of the waves. The sturdy ship sailed them easily. Had she been his to command, he would have pressed canvas, for *Susannah* could easily take more. But he was only along for the ride. As Jellison was kind enough to provide a berth and share his cabin, the least Elijah could do was to forgo second-guessing him. Jellison was old for the sea, and his age betrayed itself in his manner of sailing. He would carefully bring his cargo, crew and vessel home safely, while a younger captain would be concerned with speed at almost any cost. A younger captain like Elijah Merrick!

"Ready for breakfast?" Jellison asked, joining him at the rail.

"Anytime you are, sir," Elijah replied with the courtesy always due an older mariner. "'Twill be a pleasure!"

Together they squeezed into the cabin where the ship's boy set out their breakfast of ham and eggs with mugs of coffee. Jellison tucked his napkin under his chin and wasted no time. He motioned Elijah to begin eating. "Now that we can relax, I'm hoping you'll tell me what you've been up to. I've seen you conferring with my first mate on more than one occasion, and I've a suspicion something's going on between the two of you."

"It was better, sir, while we were clearing customs, that you knew nothing of my activities."

"Oh?" Jellison shot him a brief but penetrating glance. "Would it, in your estimation, be better for me to remain in ignorance?"

"I trust your discretion absolutely, Captain," Elijah said uncomfortably. "But as a matter of fact, I would prefer you to remain unenlightened, at least until the shores of home have been sighted and the chance of being searched at sea unlikely."

Ships from the United States were neutral carriers, transporting cargo in and out of European ports while France and England skirmished with one another on the high seas and in the travel lanes. But stopping neutral ships was not uncommon. The English searched for deserters, the French looked for foodstuffs to confiscate. *Susannah* would not be safe until she was in American territorial waters.

"Perhaps you can tell me why you need a ride home," Jellison suggested. "I gather that at one time you had a vessel of your own."

"I had to send her back without me."

"Really!" Jellison's interest was intense.

"Aye. We cleared for Spain with a load of flour, but were escorted to Brest by a French frigate. The prize master took my papers and disappeared with them. The cargo was offloaded, to feed starving people, I gathered. My crew and I were lodged in a flea-ridden hotel at the expense of the French government."

"Then what?"

"Two months later they came to me. It seems my case had been tried and that I was to be paid for the stuff taken besides extra to compensate for my capture. The vessel was mine again."

"Well, that's jolly good, I must say!" Jellison exclaimed, reaching for his pipe and motioning with it for Elijah to go on.

"They gave me my papers and said they'd pay me within sixty days. After the first sixty went by, I could see that it wasn't going to be simple. I sent my vessel and her crew home with the mate—in ballast, of course, because I had no money to buy cargo—and then I went to Paris to see if I could get some help from the French government."

"Paris!" Jellison whistled appreciatively. "That's a long way from Brest!"

"A very long way," Elijah agreed. "But in my case, it was fairly fast. I travelled with the mail, and we never stopped except to change horses." It was more than four-hundred weary miles, and dangerous ones, too. Brigands who were still committed to the cause of the executed King constantly disrupted and even destroyed the couriers and coaches carrying national dispatches. For three days and nights, escorted by no fewer than six and as many as two dozen armed guards, the mail and Elijah Merrick were carried over rough roads with nary a moment to sleep, meals consisting of such food as could be snatched up along the way. "When I got there and presented my papers, wouldn't you know they got lost?"

"Lost!" Jellison was incredulous.

"So I went back for another set," Elijah continued.

"To Brest?" Jellison asked, his pipe paused in midair.

"To Brest."

Jellison shook his head in wonder.

"This time I got two copies, and when I returned to Paris, the first of these was lost too. So I gave in—I paid the sons of bitches off, then bribed one of them to take me to Robespierre."

"Isn't he the man in charge of their revolution?" asked Jellison, awed.

"He was. He's dead now. The Paris mob decided he was becoming a dictator so—off with his head . . . ." A moment Elijah had witnessed and preferred not to remember, but one that would stay with him to the end of his life. Robespierre had been guillotined with a dozen of his compatriots, ironically in the same square where King Louis had met the same fate the year before. When positioning him at the block, a guard yanked off a rag that bound Robespierre's jaw and the victim let out a scream that silenced the gathered mob.

That scream!

He learned the jaw had been shattered the previous day when Robespierre had attempted suicide with a pistol to his mouth. To rip off the bandage . . . .

The manner of the man's death also haunted Elijah. Among the hundreds of others executed while he was in Paris, Robespierre alone was face up, presumably to better see the fate awaiting him. Elijah shuddered at the thought of it, then forced his attention back to describing the meeting he'd had when Robespierre was alive.

"When I got to his office, he pointed me to a chair, without speaking. There was a man already in the room, an interpreter, who told me that Citizen Robespierre wished me to commence my story from the time of my capture to the present. He would translate. When I was done, Robespierre waved his hand and the interpreter left. Then he conversed with me using flawless English!"

"Why did he use an interpreter, then?" Jellison asked.

"He knew he was in danger, because of being so powerful. Maybe he was not sure if he could trust this translator. Not sure if the man would distort the truth and tell him something different than what I was saying. If he did, Robespierre would know he was untrustworthy."

"Well then, what happened next?"

"He questioned me about some particular points, but especially about the loss of my papers. Usually he didn't interfere with mercantile matters, he said, but in my case, he felt he must. It's one thing to confiscate a ship for food, but another to steal off with the indemnification. He wants the support of the United States against the English, after all. Cheating one of us out of a small fortune isn't the way to go about it."

"I suppose not," Jellison shrugged. "Go on."

"At last, he instructed me to go to the office of a certain official and tell him who had sent me and warn him that if he didn't make good my indemnification, he would be hearing from Robespierre personally, and not in a pleasing way!"

Despite this assistance, it was hard not to be bitter against the very great dishonesty he had found rampant in France, dishonesty that required him to part with still more of his profit. His words sounded cool and composed as he talked with Jellison, and did not reflect the unending anxiety and frustration of those aching journeys over those endless miles. There were times when he wondered how he had kept his sanity.

"Robespierre did have a lot of power, then," Jellison observed. "All he had to do was issue an order, and it was carried out, aye?"

"Yes, indeed." Elijah nodded. "But even so, my trials weren't over. Imagine my surprise and dismay upon learning that once the money was mine, I might not take it out of the country."

"What!" Jellison nearly lost his pipe at this.

"It seems there is a law forbidding export of specie, which lay in useless heaps about me. No one had mentioned such a statute before."

"Rotten bastards!" Jellison bawled. "What did you do?"

Elijah laughed and leaned back in his chair. "That, Captain, is what I would prefer you to know nothing about. I will tell you, though, that I met your mate Pollard at an opportune time, in a tavern in fact, while I was pondering my dilemma. Without him I would be there yet. An able man is Jack Pollard."

"Aye," Jellison agreed. "He'll not be long getting command himself."

"Even though Pollard is Salem-born," Elijah observed, "and despite my prejudice in favor of Cape-born sailors, I think him as skilled as any mariner from my own village. In any case," Elijah said in what he hoped was a conclusion, "I'm sure you can appreciate that there might be some advantage to you if I don't relate the entirety of my story just yet."

"So be it!" Jellison pounded the table for emphasis, rattling the breakfast dishes. "Make yourself at home, young man. I'll share a few of my better yarns with you later when the watch turns."

They shook hands on it. "I have a few books yonder." Jellison pointed to a fenced-in shelf above his bunk, where some worn and battered volumes were pressed behind the slats, along with papers and charts all bundled together. "Rum's in that locker. Pen and ink and paper in the top drawer there. Let me know if you need anything else."

"This is just fine, sir. You must know how appreciative I am."

"Right." Jellison disappeared onto the quarterdeck while Elijah watched the cabin boy clearing the mugs and plates. He drummed on the tabletop, its shining patina reflecting his fingertips.

What he ought to do was start writing a report to Fuller. It would be a good report, and it would be a joy to write. Or he might take a book and stretch out on Jellison's bunk to read in comfort.

But he did not want to read, nor did he want to write. He wanted simply to be left alone with the moment, this moment, so that his thoughts, like the needle of a compass, could at last swing toward home and Molly. After signaling the boy that he wished a tumbler, he fetched spirits from the locker. Poured. Drank. And reveled in the freedom to think about her.

He was actually going home. Soon she would be in his arms. Stowed away for him in Rockford while his lifework in ships was carried forward, she was the fulfillment of his destiny, his dreams, his very being. Now he could think of her without unresolved longing bedeviling him uselessly, for they would be together in little more than a month. His own wife! His very own treasure!

She did present challenges, though. The confounded chaise was evidence of that! How preposterous, that she had even thought of foisting it on him unawares, forcing him to pay for it else he look like a fool there on the London waterfront. Had he really promised to buy one? He couldn't recall, in fact had paid her idea little real attention. For it was a whim, was it not? She had no real need for such a thing. Soon enough she would be too busy enjoying their child and tending the garden to even remember that once she had wanted to ride about like nobility!

No, the real problem, as he saw it, lay in the fact that she had used her own judgment without consulting him, had usurped his place. Even now, it was hard to believe his own wife would do such a thing. Not only did it go against the grain of tradition, and even law, there had been less money to invest in cargo because of it. If it had not been for her, he would be richer now.

It had not been easy to put aside his anger. He had struggled with it all the way back from London, but her willingness to admit her error and his own unwillingness to cause her grief had induced him to forgive her. And because of it, they had shared intimacy he had never imagined possible. Oh, they had been close. So close!

He drank deeply of the rum and in his mind's eye, happily drove her into the woods in the new chaise, stopping to lift her onto his lap, kiss and caress her.

Molly! Molly! How well he remembered following her into their bedchamber where he carefully removed the green silk dress, where the firelight flickered on her flawless skin, her firm hips, her full breasts, her legs parting as she lay welcoming him . . . . How could a man be anything but exhilarated, knowing such wealth awaited him when he returned?

His groin ached to think of her. To distract himself, he took up a pen and began writing his report for Fuller. It was dull business now, compared to thinking about Molly, but as he drank and became tipsy, and as he described the size of the profit, he was happy again. When the captain returned to his quarters, Elijah's welcome was as gracious as Jellison's own had been.

Ah! He blessed the captain's rum! With its help, and abetted by Jellison himself, Elijah coaxed time pleasantly by, sleeping in the hold with the crew at night, and by day drinking his way to Boston. At the wharf he was surrounded by the excited owners of vessels, all eager to know how he had got out of France. What was it like there? How much profit had he made? He was friendly and uninformative so that no one would gain information best known only by Fuller. Experienced now, he knew how to say little and make it sound like much. It was easy to divert them with descriptions of the guillotine, the French revolution, and his adventures on the roads.

Fuller was ecstatic over the extraordinary profit. They sat before the fire in his new Boston office while Elijah related the highlights of his trip. Fuller rubbed his hands together with glee.

"For so new a master, Merrick," he gloated, "you have done very well."

"I'm glad you're pleased, sir," Elijah replied.

"How would you like *Morning Star*?"

Morning Star! It was true that she was not the top of the fleet anymore, for New England was producing newer, better ships as rapidly as rabbits begat offspring. But only a few years ago *Morning Star* was the best, and she was still respected today. She would be a fine feather in his cap!

Containing his excitement, Elijah asked, "What did you have in mind, sir? When will she go out?"

"She'll start loading tomorrow." Fuller leaned forward. "I'd like to see what you can do in the North Europe route, Merrick. Rotterdam, Copenhagen, Hamburg. Why bother with the aggravation of England and France? Instead, let's build up a whole new German trade. I think you can do it, and I think *Morning Star* is the perfect vessel."

"But, sir," Elijah hesitated, his elation fading, "there are matters at home I need to take care of—a farm, bills to pay, a child I've hardly seen, and the family's provision to arrange before I go out again. I've been away from my wife for over a year," he pleaded. "Would you have me go mad?"

"Listen, young man, I understand. I hear she is a beauty." Fuller shrugged sympathetically. "You can have five days while the *Star* loads."

"Two weeks is what I'd need," Elijah begged, unable to turn his back on the prestige and adventure, but equally unable to forgo Molly's eager and waiting arms.

Fuller shook his head, thought, then countered. "I can give you two days extra if I hire the crew myself. Return in seven days, and *Morning Star* is yours. If you can't, I'll get someone else and you can have *Moppet*. She's being scraped down now and will be ready in three weeks."

Moppet was not in the same class as *Morning Star*. But she would give him twenty-one days. Twenty-one days to be with Molly, to hear her voice, feel her wonderful body close beside him. It was senseless to give her up now, so long had he waited already.

"I'll take *Moppet*," he said regretfully.

"Don't decide now," Fuller urged, then added, "but consider this— I'll increase your captain's share to eight percent if you'll agree to take *Morning Star* out."

Elijah's world spun. The three percent he had now was considered high! Such generous terms were hard to pass up!

"Send word to me within four days. If it's yes, you'll be back in a week, and I'll hold *Morning Star*. If it's no, then *Moppet* is yours. Agreed?"

"Yes. Thank you, sir." They shook hands on it.

"Pinch her bottom for me," Fuller chuckled.

Finally, Elijah was free to return to Molly.

The schooner cut through familiar waters, the distant coastline sliding by slowly, all too slowly. Would they never get to Rockford?

"Hear you've done big things, Elijah," said Will Robbins, skipper of Snow's packet. "The whole of Boston Harbor was talking about your arrival when I pulled in this morning."

"Had it been up to those French bastards, I'd be chasing around Europe yet," Elijah said depreciatingly.

"Well, it looks like you found a way around them," Will observed.

"I bribed a man. More than one, actually. That's the way it's done over there. Nothing happens without a bribe." It was expected that he would neither brag nor boast, that he would keep his comments as humble as he could.

Will prepared to set the packet on a new tack. For a while he busied himself with this task and then set his crew—two lads of twelve—to properly coiling lines on the deck.

"Bet your owner was pleased," he continued, as though their conversation were unbroken.

"Pleased!" Elijah exclaimed. "Fuller nearly ate me up. Nothing would do but I should climb aboard *Morning Star* and go right out again and make him another fortune." Humility be damned!

Robbins was impressed. "Well?" he asked. "Are you going?"

"Not unless he'll wait a bit. I'd like more than a few hours at home," Elijah growled.

Will eyed him speculatively, acquainted with the charms of Merrick's wife. Elijah paid him no further mind, his thoughts turning to the object of his greatest interest.

Molly. He could die, right this minute, for the very sight of her. She had the power to kindle him as a fire. She had wrought a miracle on his life, opening his heart as it had never been. His wife. Waiting for him. But he would have no time alone with her when he arrived, he knew. Many townsmen would meet the packet this afternoon. Probably a crowd would escort him home, eager to hear his stories. It would not occur to them that a man might prefer his wife's company to theirs. They would linger. He'd just have to wait it out.

There, in the distance, was the landing and, just as he had known, his townsmen. As the packet drew nearer, he could make out John Warden, now a Rockford resident. How splendid! In his joy at seeing his friend, he was able to set aside his preoccupation with his wife.

He and Will secured the ship and rowed ashore with the mail. Eager hands pulled the dory up on the beach while John pumped his hand and friends of the family crowded 'round and then thronged up the Rockford Road, laughing and chattering. They cut through the back pasture, past the well and the barn and to the back door, where his brother stood to welcome him with a broad smile.

Debby bustled out with little Sarah. "Here he is!" she exclaimed to the child, and thrust her into her father's arms. The little girl burst into tears at being held by a stranger, and everyone laughed while Debby took her away again and tried to comfort her.

But Molly was nowhere to be seen. His gut clenched, his hands became sweaty and his heart beat harder. Good grief, he thought, I have wrestled with the powers of the world, and the very thought of my wife makes me a gawky boy again.

Then a thought hit him, like the crash of a falling mast. Was she ill? Or injured, or . . . .

No. At last she appeared. Framed in the doorway, she was wearing the green silk grown, ravishing as never before. Her skin glowed, her hair shone, her lovely face and figure worthy of a portrait. She stood there quietly, and over the crowd and its din their eyes found each other. Thirteen months vanished as though they never existed.

The guests politely chatted, pretending not to notice as Elijah put his mother, his sister, his brother, and his daughter aside and made his way to her side.

"My darling, you are beyond believing," he whispered.

"Welcome home, beloved." She smiled deeply into his eyes. "I've waited for this moment a long, long time!"

"Mistress Merrick," called a voice from the yard. "Show him your new token of affection." The lot of them had guarded the secret carefully, and happily waited now, knowing Elijah was unaware that he had begotten another child.

"Come with me!" Molly laughed.

Puzzled, he waved at the group, then followed her into their chamber where she closed the door, threw the bolt, and reached up to him. They kissed deeply, oh so deeply. She was part of his flesh, her lips ripe, her body giving, giving . . . .

The beauty of their coming together was broken by a squalling and wailing that rose up from the far side of their bed.

"About that token!" Molly chuckled and left him to go to the cradle, there to lift up a blanket from which protruded waving fists and kicking feet. She set the angry bundle in his arms. "Meet your son," she said softly. Elijah thought his heart would burst, it was so full. Never would there be another moment to match this one. A son!

"What have you named him?" he asked in awe.

"Elijah! What else!" They laid the small Elijah Merrick on the bed, and his father knelt beside him. The infant, seeing this new and strange phenomenon, quieted and grunted and reached unsuccessfully for Elijah's nose. His tiny hand wrapped around his father's finger.

"Did he cause you suffering?" Elijah asked humbly.

"Only for a short time," she answered. "I'm getting the hang of it now."

What a good and uncomplaining wife! Elijah had never witnessed childbirth, but he had heard of its horrors. "I had no idea," he said at last. "I never got a letter from you. Or anyone."

"We wrote to you, of course," she told him. "We didn't hear from you ourselves until two months ago. Your mother was beside herself. Debby and Jon were already digging your grave. I never feared, trusting completely you'd soon return safely."

He smiled at that.

"I have forgotten to ask," Molly said. "Are you rich? Like you described in one of your letters?"

"Rich enough," he assured her. "Rich enough for you and me and little Elijah here. And Sarah," he amended quickly. "I had better go and sit with her so she can become accustomed to me. She screamed when Debby tried to give her to me, as if I was a pirate."

"Such a sweet child," Molly smiled. "She has made my days more pleasant; I am never alone now."

Just as he had hoped. Elijah was pleased.

"There are certain matters I must talk with you about," she said urgently. On the other side of the door their townsmen had entered the enlarged keeping room, and conversation and laughter was growing louder. No doubt rum was already circulating. She turned her hands upward in despair. "But I think we'll have to wait. Both to talk and to have our own private time." The sparkle in her eye told him she had missed him. And more: she wanted him.

All over again Elijah was flooded with the rising up, the great surge of impulse. He put it down manfully. Cradling her face in his hands, he kissed each smooth cheek, her lips, the swelling of each breast nestled in the curved neckline of her gown.

She stayed behind to attend to the baby while he faced the growing throng on the other side of the door. The keeping room table had been moved into the parlor to make room for everybody. Someone had brought cider for the ladies, and beer and rum to make flip. Clearly the crowd meant to stay a while.

Mother seated Elijah on the hearth bench beside Debby, Sarah on her lap. Jonathan took one of the chairs across from him, and Mother herself claimed the other. There would be no place for Molly, but he would take care of that when the time came.

John Warden pushed loggerheads into the coals, while one of the men poured beer into mugs all around, another added molasses to each, and a King cousin topped them off with rum. As the celebrity, Elijah was first to thrust a hot iron into his mug.

A cloud of steam instantly rose up, a furious hissing erupted, and the group burst into cheers and applause as the flip broke into a boil. There was much hilarity as the rest of the men grasped the heated rods and finished off their own flips. Old Elnathan King, up from his bed and carried across the street by friends, burned his shin when he drew too broad an arc with his loggerhead; the rum soon caused him to forget his pain. Sitting on the floor with his bevy of daughters, he remained happily drunk for the remainder of the afternoon.

All were eager to hear of Elijah's adventures. They wanted to know about France, and tears came to the eyes of the older generation as Elijah described the great admiration there for George Washington. Their tears turned to hard anger when he told how the French government tried to cheat him and trick him and wear him down. The crowd became irate when they learned he could not bring the money home.

"Unbelievable!" they cried.

"Bastards!" announced Uncle Elnathan with drunken rage.

"Believe me," Elijah regaled them, feeling happy and warm, full of flip and success, "they weren't going to let that money out of the country for anything. But I'm not going to tell you how I did escape with it until my wife is here beside me."

"Moll-ee!" they cried. "Moll-ee! Moll-ee."

She came to the chamber door, tried to hush them so that little Elijah would stay asleep in his cradle, and made her way toward the bench. Elijah urged Debby to move so his wife would have the position of honor. Molly curtseyed, the skirts of the silk dress swaying, first to the group and then to her husband. She slid in beside him, taking Sarah as she did so. How graceful she was!

"There I was," he continued, now that Molly was nigh, "with all manner of money. But there was nothing I could do with it. So I bribed a man to trade the silver crowns for Spanish doubloons which, being gold, reduced the bulk to a third of its original volume. I bought two stout belts and slit them open, stuffed the money in and sewed them back up. The rest I put into the soles of my boots—a skillful French farmer, whom I also bribed, fitted them with false bottoms. So there I was at a tavern in Brest worrying over my mug of rum about how I could get home when I met a fellow named Pollard, mate on the *Susannah*, a fine fellow! He introduced me to Cap'n Jellison, who offered me passage to Boston. Pollard wore one belt and I the other. No one was the wiser, including the captain. I will admit," he told his audience, "that one of my life's greater pleasures was watching the faces of the customs agents. They knew there must be money somewhere on the *Susannah* since I was aboard, but they just couldn't find it. They tore the ship to pieces searching. Nearly repaid all my months of trouble!"

"Terrific!" John Warden exclaimed. "Elijah, you are a credit to our calling!"

Molly was smiling. He could see she was proud of him, very proud. His mother was not. "That sounds dishonest to me."

"Nonsense!" John said without due respect. The rum was taking its toll. "We all do it, when we must. There is no one to help us. We have no way to bring force to bear. The United States doesn't even have letters of marque, let alone a navy. Bribe 'em all, I say!"

"Hear! Hear!" Elnathan King cheered from his now prone position on the floor, and a great chorus of Yankee Doodle was raised. From behind the closed door, little 'Lije could be heard.

"I must go to the babe," Molly told him. "I'll wait for you." She transferred Sarah to Debby's lap, made her way through the throng to their chamber.

He watched her departure with regret, then turned to his mother.

"Had I not bribed those bastards, excuse my language, I'd have come home empty handed. We'd have sustained the loss of a whole year's income. I think that's worth a little dishonesty."

"It may well be," his mother retorted, "since we are in debt."

"Mother!" Debby gasped. "We were to wait! So Molly could tell him!"

Fascinated, the guests watched attentively.

"Debt?" he asked, puzzled.

"Why, I suppose there has been no time for her to tell you. Molly has arranged for you to buy Samuel Sears' place," Mother simpered. "She has drawn up an agreement with him that only awaits your signature to make it legal."

An agreement to buy Sears' farm? He was speechless, but the crowd was not. A buzz of excitement rose up. Christ almighty, she had done it again! He could hardly believe it. And worst of all, there was absolutely nothing he could do about it until the crowd left. Taking a deep breath, he stretched his lips into a smile. It was important that he sound easy and genial, pleased to be able to procure the place, as though he had commissioned Molly to act for him in his absence. Of necessity, the wives of seafarers were often required to do so.

"How much did she get Sears to settle for?" he asked.

Instantly the guests were quiet.

"You'll have to ask her," Mother Merrick sniffed.

"Well, she must have seen a good opportunity," he declared. "She's clever that way."

Desperately he held fast to his pose of affability. He managed desultory conversation with his brother while his astonishment turned to rage and he seethed, his passion for his wife fading under the weight of this disobedience. Beneath that demure and gentle façade she was sheathed in an iron determination. She had learned nothing from the chaise incident.

There was no choice now, none at all. His wife must be made to understand that by committing his money in his name, she had dictated the course of his life for years to come. She would have to learn, finally and forever, that she could not run him into debt. And there was only one way to do it.

All available news having been covered, the citizenry gradually disappeared into the growing darkness beyond the door, carrying Elnathan King with them. They were not Molly's friends, he realized. In fact, they were families known to his mother and approved by her. His wife was still alone and isolated, he guessed, but he could not allow her to use that as an excuse for asserting her own will and judgement.

Sarah was asleep in Debby's arms. His sister carried the child up to the loft while Elijah shook hands with his brother, who had waited for the dispersal of the crowd so that he could go to bed. Turning away from his mother, Elijah bade her an abrupt goodnight over his shoulder, signaling his displeasure. She had sprung Molly's news on him before Molly herself could. She had done it deliberately, in order to estrange him from his wife. And, he observed ruefully, it had worked.

There was a cramp in his gut as he let himself into the master bedchamber; his hands shook at the prospect of confronting Molly, and most difficult of all, chastising her. But he would do both.

On the far side of the bed, her back modestly turned, she suckled the baby, a shawl draped across her shoulders for warmth.

"Finish up," he ordered. "I would have the babe satisfied before we talk."

Continuing as if she had not heard him, she did not turn around. Surely she knew what they had to discuss. There could be no doubt she had heard his mother relate the news of their debt. And from his tone, she must know he was seething. It seemed to him that she prolonged the nursing, and the effect was devastating. His anger grew and swelled, heightened by each passing moment.

Finally, she sighed and slipped the baby into his cradle. Refastening the green dress, she stood up, smoothed her skirts, and turned to face him. Her shoulders were straight, her head high, hands crossed demurely.

"All right," she said with composure. She had taken on the manner of a *grande dame*. While he admired the spunk it required, he pretended not to notice.

"Bring your shawl. We're going to the barn." He took the candle burning on the mantel of their fireplace and put it in a lantern.

"Wh—, what?" The *dame* disappeared.

He opened the chamber door, and the front door too. "Come along."

"And leave the baby?"

"And leave the baby."

"But he might wake and cry," she pleaded, reaching for her wrap.

"Then he will cry," Elijah said grimly. Taking her arm, he led her briskly to the barn and closed the door. He hung the lantern from a nail; the corners fell away into shadow. Hector snorted, then was silent.

Sternly, he asked, "How is it, Molly, that you feel so free to put financial burdens on my back?"

"It was wrong of Mother to tell you the news. She doesn't understand that it's a very exciting opportunity, to secure the land of your ancestors." The *grande dame* had reappeared; Molly stood straight and composed.

"It was not your decision to make. And even worse, you contracted with Sears before you knew whether or not I had succeeded in Europe."

"You wrote to me that you would," she said. "And I believed you."

He could see that she was pleased with her acumen, that she was not at all the shy and timid girl she pretended to be. Pausing for a moment, he thought about how he might best proceed, watching her as he considered it.

His silence unnerved her. Instead of waiting him out, she filled the void. "I admit I was afraid you wouldn't want it."

When he still made no reply, her tongue loosened yet further. "I was afraid you would say no because your mother would be upset, or your friends would think you were putting on airs with a handsome new house on 75 acres of land."

"A house?" He was incredulous. "So there's to be a new house, too?"

"Well, that is my dream. A house like John Warden's. If you aren't afraid of being ostentatious. If you are bold enough."

Bold enough! He, who had faced miles and miles of French roads ladened with danger behind every bush and boulder, in every valley and behind every hillock. Her words stung him, flicked him on the quick of his pride. Between clenched teeth, he asked, "How much did you tell Sears I would pay?"

"It's a wonderful property for us, Elijah," she said in a rush. "Your ancestral land!"

"How much?"

"There's even an old salt works, which I'm sure you'd be able to get into working order. Lots of room for animals—you could keep a riding horse, a good one. I know you have ever admired good horses."

Her feeble justifications were suddenly intolerable. The anger he had contained so far boiled over. He struck her, harder than he intended, and she staggered. In the lantern light, her cheek showed white.

"How much?"

"Two thousand, five hundred dollars," she quavered, then stood straight again and looked him square in the eye. "At first, he wanted three thousand but I got him to accept less."

Two thousand, five hundred dollars! It was four times what he had brought back from France! He would have to hire the entire sum so he could use his profit to reinvest in cargo.

Damn! Damn her!

"You're forcing my hand," he managed to say. "You have no idea how much I've brought home, whether there's enough to buy the place or not. You must know I cannot let this pass."

"You have the final word, Elijah. I told Sears that you might not want it. He would understand, I am sure."

"Maybe, but I'd have to explain it to everyone else in the village too."

"Because of your mother!" she argued, her own temper rising. "No one would be the wiser, if she had kept her mouth shut."

"That is beside the point. The point is you committed my money without my knowledge. The point is the rightful place of a wife." He started loosening his belt.

"I do know!" she insisted, refusing to look at his hands. "I know a good wife acts in the best interests of her husband and family, and I have." She stepped back. "It's a fine purchase, Elijah. But I've left you a way out, if you are stupid enough to take it."

The stillness of the barn swallowed up this insult as though it had never been uttered, but it echoed in his head, round and round. Stupid. Stupid.

She had gone too far. By denigrating his worth, she had sealed once and for all the outcome of this night.

Now he removed his belt. "All right, Molly. Hear this." He wrapped the belt around his fist, leaving ten inches free. "You may not decide the course of my life without my knowledge and consent." He moved toward her as she drew away. "You may not make decisions that commit everything I have." He was shouting now. "You may not call me names just because you do not agree with me. I am your husband. It's up to me to decide what we shall do, and when we shall do it. Take off your dress."

"My dress?" she gasped. "Take off my dress?"

"If you value it, you had better," he told her. "Else there will be nothing left of it." He drew back the belt.

"Please, Elijah," she whimpered. "Pray do not!"

The thrill of supremacy shot through him. "Obey me!"

She caught his arm with both hands. "Please, Elijah, I see now that it was wrong. I will not repeat it. Please. I implore you."

With his free hand he trapped her wrists and forced her to her knees. The belt hit her back smartly, its crack loud in the night stillness. She shrieked.

"If you have a shred of pride, you'd better not cry out. I will beat you in front of anyone who comes, I assure you."

There was a gap in the fragile silk; he had hit her too hard. It would not do to outright injure her. He must calm himself! Releasing his hold, he stood back. "Will you take it off now?"

Tearfully, she rose and complied, her stricken eyes on his. The garment fell in a billowing heap around her feet.

"Keep going," he commanded, steeling himself against feeling sorry for her. Quaking in the lamplight, she removed her undergarments and stood naked before him, her nipples dark and tight in the cold air. Disdainfully he looked her up and down so that she would feel the humiliation of it.

She broke and ran for the door.

Catching her, holding her away from him, he laid on a stinging, cutting slap with the belt. And then using utmost control, he continued, keeping the pace slow and cruel, while she struggled to protect herself, helpless in his grip as her eyes followed the belt. She gasped and panted and whined throatily as the pace of his strokes grew faster. He must stop himself!

Summoning more self-restraint, more strength than he had ever mustered before, he released her. She dropped onto the straw-littered floor.

Having punished men on ships, he knew that the establishment of authority after a beating was as important as the strokes themselves. "Leave," he commanded. "Quickly. I would have you out of my sight."

Without looking at him, she complied, wrapping up in her shawl and carrying her clothing, her weeping done, her swollen face a mask. He could find no pity for her. None. She had got what she deserved, and were it not for his ability to control himself, it would have been a lot worse.

Finding a moldering horse blanket, he settled on into a mound of hay, covered himself, and fell into a mercifully numbing sleep which only a shaft of morning sunlight dissipated. Hector was chomping on his oats, occasionally snorting to clear his nostrils of dust. Jon must have been in to care for the nag and had quietly left again. What had his brother thought of him sleeping here?

Brushing the hay out of his hair and off his clothing, Elijah reviewed all he had to accomplish that day. He'd done what he must so far—well, overdone it, perhaps, but many more tasks remained. There was his mother, his brother, Samuel Sears, and, Molly herself. He must speak to them all.

But first, he went across the road to ascertain the sailing of the packet. Snow agreed to wait until the last possible moment. Returning home, he saw his brother leading Hector to the pasture and hastened to catch up with him. Together they leaned on the fence, watching the old fellow graze.

"To be honest, Jon," he confessed. "I've had quite a session with Molly over this whole Sears debacle."

"A-yuh," his brother said unhelpfully.

"I need your help. I'm leaving today."

Jon accepted this news without a show of surprise.

"I can trust Molly with nothing, yet I am quite sure this situation wouldn't have happened if she hadn't felt a great need for a place of her own."

"Hmmm," Jon said.

"I think I must give her the house she wants."

"A house?" Jon seemed surprised. " Now?"

Elijah sighed. "I'm afraid so. Yet I cannot let her have any part in its construction. She's too headstrong."

"She has good ideas," Jon replied, turning to Hector who had come their way for fondling. "My forge, with the bow attached so I could pump it myself—that was her idea. Said she'd seen one like it in

Yarmouth. Knew it would help." This was a long speech for him, but he faced up to the task manfully. "Buying Sears' place is a fine idea, too," he added, for good measure. "And you're right. It's probably a good thing to build a house on it right away. At the rate you're going, you'll fill it up in no time." He chortled at the idea of endless babies.

"Will you oversee taking Sears' house down and putting up a new one in its place? One like John Warden's?"

"Ah." Jon was impressed. Not many people had two-story houses! "Sure," he nodded.

"I trust you'll keep the expenditures under control, as before. I'll send you money for it when I get to Boston. Just have the shell put up, the fireplaces installed, and the windows glazed. Use clapboard siding on the outside."

"Not shingles?" Jon wondered. No one in Rockford, besides the wealthy John Warden, could afford clapboard.

"No," Elijah answered. "Houses look more elegant when they are sheathed in clapboard."

"Well then, it should be painted, so the wood will be protected," Jon offered diffidently.

"Aye. Molly can decide on the color. But everything else is up to you."

"Very well," Jon thrust out his hand, already standing straighter.

Next Elijah found his mother, listlessly churning butter at the back door. "Good morning," he said.

"I suppose it is."

"And what are you so cheerful about?" he asked with annoyance he made no effort to conceal.

Mother worked with the churn for a few moments, then put it aside. "I suppose you'll buy Sears' place," she grumbled.

"I suppose I will."

"Molly has you under her spell," she observed knowingly.

"Hardly!" Never had he been so irritated with his mother! "She and I have talked about Sears' land before this," he lied. "I'll admit being surprised that she'd bargain for it now. It's a little sooner than I'd expected."

"Probably I shouldn't have brought it up in front of company, but it was uppermost in my mind," Mother said earnestly. "She would have preferred to keep it from me, I'm sure. But I saw Samuel Sears and his wife leaving our house—through the front door! I was just coming home from the Simmonds' and there was Molly, all fancied up in that green dress, waving goodbye and looking very pleased with herself. Naturally, I demanded an explanation." Mother shrugged. "I'm sorry I didn't give her a chance to talk with you first. It just slipped out."

"I'm sorry too, Mother but I don't believe it just slipped out, not at all." Not so very long ago he would have accepted her explanation whether he believed it or not. "It seems to me that it was part of your design to discredit Molly. I asked you to help her, and it doesn't appear that you have. So I've come to the conclusion that we should be on our own, Molly and me. I've asked Jon to build us a house over there, where Sears' place is now."

The wind spilled out of Mother's sails. She could but stare.

"It will be a spacious house, and there will be room there for you in your old age, should you need it. Until then, I think it would be wiser to separate the two of you. Naturally, this house will be yours always. We can discuss the details when I get back."

"Back?" she asked faintly. "You plan to leave soon?"

"On the tide," he said evenly. "I am going to master *Morning Star* and start a new route to Northern Germany."

He crossed the keeping room and rapped smartly on the chamber door. Facing Molly again would be one of the master performances of his life.

Beside her, the baby played with his toes. At the foot of the bed Sarah held a wooden doll Jon had made and watched her mother sewing a new dress for it.

Great hollows and shadows lay beneath Molly's eyes. Her lips were swollen where she had bitten them to keep from crying out last night. Glancing up at him, she said gently to Sarah, "Take this to Aunt Debby, Sweetheart."

Sarah refused in a rush of indecipherable words.

"Go," Molly said firmly to her. "Or your father will carry you out."

Sarah wasted no time. Elijah held the door for the toddler as she scurried away with her doll and its partially completed garment.

Molly picked up little 'Lije and held him to her as a shield, eyeing Elijah warily.

He sat heavily at the end of the bed. "I know you think I've been unfair," he began.

The injured look in her eyes made it clear she thought him enormously so.

"I'll not deny that the Sears place is ideal for us," he went on. "Your judgment was quite correct, as far as it goes. But that *is* as far as it goes, Molly. It must never go further. You must never commit me— ever—for anything—without my consent. Do not run my life, Molly. Do not run me. Do you understand?"

She nodded.

"I am leaving money with Jonathan for construction of a house on Sears' land. He knows what to do; you will have no part of it, save choosing the color of the clapboards. He'll put up the exterior; you and I will complete the inside together, when I return. Do you understand?"

There was no reaction in her eyes, which held his steadily. "Yes."

"I'll see Sears on my way out. Fetch the agreement, please."

Releasing her hold on the baby, she laid him down carefully. Slowly she rolled herself out of bed, painfully leaned over the trunk and withdrew a crackling parchment, handed it to him.

"You have already given him money, I see." He was astounded. "Where did you get it?"

"From Mistress Warden."

She must have asked for it, no doubt telling the Wardens why she needed it. Did the whole of Cape Cod know that his wife had taken on debt in his name?

"I'll take the agreement over to Samuel now and arrange payment. Then I'll catch the packet back to Boston this afternoon. I'm taking the ship *Morning Star* to Hamburg."

She listened without response.

"I need time to smooth over this breach, and I'm sure you do too," he said. "Perhaps, when I return, we will be able to meet as friends."

She did not ask how long that would be, nor did she express reluctance to see him go. After all, he reminded himself, why should she be reluctant? She must hate him!

"I'll be on my way, then."

She said nothing.

"Good-bye."

"Farewell," she said tonelessly, and did not watch his awkward exit from the room.

Wearily, he climbed aboard the packet. No other passengers were aboard, this trip, and he was thankful for the privacy. There was much on his mind.

Stern measures had ever been the only way of coping with Molly's headstrong determination, a way he should have chosen long ago. What the consequences would be, he could not predict. Would he ever feel the same way about her again? Would she ever love him as she once had?

The whole way to Boston he mulled this over. Reporting to Fuller, he was able to negotiate the loan. To Sears, he sent what was owed for the property. To Jon, he sent money for building the house and maintenance of the family until he should return. His own profit from the last trip he invested in cargo, including some on Sears' behalf, as Molly had offered. Damn! There was no end to her outrageous behavior—again, she had forced his hand. He refused to think about it further.

Within a couple of days, the onloading of *Morning Star* was complete. After checking the bill of lading carefully, he signed on the crew himself, since he had returned early enough to do so. One by one, the men filed into his cabin, signed their articles, received an advance on their pay. They went happily off to spend it in the nearest tavern while Elijah went over and over the problem his wife presented and his handling of it.

Granted, buying the Sears place made a lot of sense. Not only did it include 75 acres, most of them cleared, but also six woodlots scattered around Rockford, rights to pasture in the salt marsh when the field driver opened it in season, and rights to take hay there as well. There was nothing wrong with her reasoning except that she had committed him for more money than he had! And, again, she had usurped his place. Had he failed in France, he could not have honored the contract, for he would have been unable to obtain credit, a contingency she seemed unable to fathom. However bright she might be, she needed his wisdom and experience, whether she wanted it or not.

Exhausted, Elijah leaned back, remembering painfully the body he had loved and had not been able to touch. The curve of her buttocks, fitting his hand so well, the soft belly, warm thighs, generous . . . .

"All set?" Fuller asked, seating himself in the cabin.

Quickly he returned to matters at hand. "Aye. It'll be a good crew."

"Did you pinch her bottom for me?"

"Eh?"

"Your wife!" Fuller laughed.

"Oh, yes, I did." Elijah could feel his face getting hot. "She didn't think much of the message, though."

"Hah!" Fuller gestured toward the city. "I was about to go out for the evening. Care to join me, Merrick? My treat."

"Well!" Elijah forced himself to laugh. "In that case, of course!"

"I know a fine woman who'll fix you up in no time."

"I could use some fixing, I'll admit," Elijah grimaced.

There were other gracefully curving hips in this world, other breasts to fondle, other legs that would open for him. There were no tender kisses for sale, no softening of the eye, but certainly the will to please, for cash. It was an unencumbered and uncomplicated way to find one's ease, and exactly right for him in his present state.

Let her be cold! Granted, he had used her in his rage, but she had caused it herself. She must know that she deserved whatever he chose to do, in abundance. Enough! Now he must build up a trade route. He could not allow himself to be distracted by the situation at home. His brother would manage everything while he, Captain Elijah Merrick, would open an office for Fuller in Hamburg, using it as a base for other cities in northern Europe. His captain's share was at the top of the scale, and he had bought a large portion of the cargo. True, he'd had to borrow for the Sears place. But if the Hamburg route was a success, he could well afford the land and the house that Jon would build on it. And he would succeed. He knew it.

Until he came home again, that would have to be enough.

CHAPTER

The House

The new nation was quickly becoming locked into regional power struggles. New England remained conservative, influenced by the traditions of the Church of the Standing Order, and was still controlled by the Federalists in Boston, patrons of the trans-Atlantic merchant trade.

In the Middle and Southern States, centers of the country's agriculture, Americans were fast forming ranks around the Virginian Thomas Jefferson who favored government by the people rather than by the powerful. Their support for him was bolstered by an increasing number of landless workers, called mechanics, who congregated in the cities, and by the settlers pouring over the mountains into territory previously denied them by England. The Federalists and the Standing Order meant nothing to them.

Meanwhile, on Cape Cod, the fishers on the South Shore prospered, feeding the expanding population and exporting the surplus. On the North Shore, the fortunes of the mariner rose with those of Boston's merchants. As of one accord, the fleet worked the European route where its captains could haggle and bargain, a practice that suited their salty and parsimonious souls completely.

In their company sailed Elijah Merrick.

✦✧ I ✧✦

UPON HIS RETURN from Hamburg, he took the packet to Yarmouth, for he did not wish to be met by his townsmen as had happened the last time. With a rented horse from the inn, he took the County Road as he had done so long ago when courting Molly. He urged his mount to a faster pace as he passed the tidal marshes he remembered, houses and barns and ponds, familiar bends in the road.

The land was nearly deforested now, and the sun beat mercilessly down on it. Yet the trees that remained were magnificent, growing without being crowded, attaining a symmetry and beauty they had never possessed before. The bay was in view much more, too, and he liked that. He was lonely for it whenever away, and reveled now at being back on the Narrow Land. This was where he belonged.

Aside from the pleasure it gave him to see the old places, approaching Rockford from this direction would give him a chance to look at the new house, to inspect it at his leisure, and know the state of its construction exactly.

Molly's house.

That was how it had stamped itself on his mind. It was stupid to think of it as hers, especially since he was paying for it. But there was no helping it—the house was Molly's. A house exactly like the Warden's, reminiscent of a brig under full sail, with its great height and balanced spread of windows. Only such a house would satisfy his ambitious wife. Given the choice, would he have elected the usual Cape cottage instead, low to the ground and modest, more in keeping with tradition? He no longer knew.

Riding into the west of town, he saw that new homes were being built, and across from the ford was rising an imposing square-rigged structure like his own must be, right here in the middle of all the cottages and industries. Warner Hall, chief of the clan, must be doing well, he reflected. Downstream of the gristmill was a new tannery, distilling evil smells. No doubt the land upon which it stood had financed Hall's grand new mansion.

It was apparent that Rockford was gaining wealth which, twenty years before, no one knew even existed. Farther toward the center of Rockford was John Warden's place, sitting beautifully on its crest of land overlooking the bay. And there—look—another two-decker! Not only complete, but lived in, judging from the chickens that strolled about with a proprietary air. It was incredible, really!

He cut off the highroad to the low, so unused as to be merely a trail. It began to widen and became less rough. Then there was the boundary boulder that had once marked Sears' land. Now Merrick's.

Although he had expected to be indifferent, his heart began to pound. He saw a glimmer of glass in the sun. There was a flash of bright yellow! He dismounted, tied the horse to a tree and walked the next hundred yards so he could approach gradually, letting the new house reveal itself.

There it stood, proud and gleaming, its windows shining, paint glistening on the clapboards that sided it all the way around.

Clapboards! In his mind he could hear his mother intoning: *clapboards are an invention of the devil. They reveal excessive pride, as though the person who uses them thinks he is better than his fellows. We have always used shingles, and I hope we always shall. Shingles are simple and the Lord favors them.* He smiled grimly. Mother.

Putting her out of his mind, he lingered and admired his new home. Granted, it was tiny and insignificant compared to the mansions of shipowners in Boston, but it well fitted Cape Cod. Such a home announced to the world that a man of success and substance lived there, satisfied that his needs were met in a manner suitable to his station, yet disdaining ostentation. It was perfect—especially in view of the fact that other houses just like it were now being built in Rockford. He would not feel foolish, as he would if his were the only one.

Atop the roof was a fenced deck, like a crown on the golden house. Why, he thought, from up there I'll bet you can see the whole bay. It must be a beautiful view!

But he could not think about the house without facing the fact that he and Molly would have to live in it. Together.

It had been ten months since he left, and he knew there would be no surprise token of affection awaiting him this time. Not once had he written to his wife, nor informed her that the ports of Northern Europe had yielded immediate success. The way was open for trading there without interference from France or England, and he happily exploited the opportunity. With hard work and concentration on the task at hand, he had eliminated thoughts of Molly, visiting willing women in the ports of call when he could contain himself no longer. But now he and his wife would be in the same place at the same time; he could not avoid her, nor she him. How would their relationship be, given her coldness, her unwillingness to even converse with him before he left?

He peeked in a window, its glass a purplish rainbowed hue. Within was a pile of lumber, neatly stacked. The floor consisted of rough-cut boards, and only lath was nailed to the walls and ceiling. Yes, it was a shell, just as he had instructed Jon to build. It would require many hours with Molly, selecting wainscot and molding and flooring and later, carpets and draperies and wallpapers. Being cold and uncommunicative would work against her; if she refused to speak to him, she would lose the chance to have exactly what she wanted, for by God, he'd select the furnishings himself, if he had to!

There was no need to hurry back to sea. He was in a position to bargain with Fuller, having just earned *Morning Star's* owner an almost unheard of profit, and he'd asked Fuller for a corner on the Hamburg market. It was a city he was coming to love. Assuming Fuller would concur, this would take time to arrange. In that interval, Elijah would have the opportunity to firm up his position as head of the Merrick family.

Until now, he had been gone too much of the time. Unavoidable, but a large factor in the trouble between Molly and himself. What kind of marriage was left to them?

Slowly, he walked back to his horse and led it toward the highroad, the surface of which was much improved since he'd last used it. A carriage came bustling by—a carriage!—driven by old Reuben Hopkins!—and then he was home. He took the horse around to the barn and tied it there, moved quietly to the keeping room door, rapped smartly, flung it open.

"Elijah!" his mother shrieked and looked as though she would faint.

"Elijah!" cried Debby, and snatched up a terrified Sarah whose screams could surely be heard clear to Provincetown.

Jon came limping in from his forge as fast as his damaged legs would carry him, brandishing a musket until he saw the cause of the commotion. Little 'Lije, not yet steady on his feet, toppled to the kitchen floor and wailed.

"It's your father, little one!" crooned Debby. "Hush now."

"Dear son!" His mother's face was streaming with tears; his brother pounded his shoulder in greeting.

Elijah laughed and scooped up the baby, patting his back side and offering a finger to be clutched. Sarah watched curiously.

"Fadder?" She pointed. "Fadder?"

Molly was not there. As he turned to ask why, he saw her walking slowly from the garden with a basket of carrots. His heart hammering his ribs, he gave 'Lije to Mother and left them all, to discover what sort of reception his wife would offer.

Her face was just as expressionless as it had been the last time he saw it. "Welcome, husband," she said, without a smile. He took her hand, bowed and kissed it as though she were a lady of distinction.

"How well you are looking, Molly." It was like a play, rehearsed, and like a play, was being watched from the kitchen door. He did not wait for a response, but offered her his arm. She hesitated, then took it while keeping some distance between them.

So that's the way it was!

"I have gifts for everyone in my saddlebags," he tried to smile. "I'm sure you'll enjoy seeing them."

"I'm sure I will."

With disinterest, she accompanied him to the rented horse, where he removed his packs. She followed him into the house and watched while he presented a china doll to Sarah, whose joy could hardly be contained, and a small wooden gun to 'Lije, which the little boy promptly began to chew on. Each of his women received a lace-edged handkerchief.

"Such finery!" Mother exclaimed. "To blow your nose on! I shouldn't think the Lord would favor it."

Jon received a small silver-plated tinder box, in honor of his successful forge.

"I came by the low road, so I could check on the house," he told his brother. "It is magnificent! You've done a great job."

"Thanks," Jon ducked his head modestly. "I made all the nails."

"We hoped you would like it," Debby exclaimed. "It was such fun to see it abuilding. Molly and I took the children over every day to watch it going up."

He glanced over at his wife for confirmation. Her expression was pleasant but impenetrable.

"You'll need to decide what to do next, Elijah," Jon said. "We—me and Pat Mayo and his men—we stopped with the shell, just as you asked."

"First of all, lets return my horse."

They laughed uproariously, drunk with relief at his return.

"Then Molly and I shall have to make some decisions straight-away." He smiled at her, and her lips curved up in what he took to be a smile in return. "I've asked Fuller to give me exclusive rights to the North Europe route. It will take him a while to work it out. So we can take our time, consider carefully what we want."

"And you have so much money that you need not work for a while?" Mother asked.

"Oh, yes. We are richer than before!" He looked straight at Molly. "There is plenty, and I'm sure we can finish up the house in any way we wish, and buy all the furnishings for it that we desire."

"How nice." Molly's voice was right, her smile was right, though her eyes were not. She was still resentful, he guessed, and determined to stay aloof. But he could outlast her, he was sure.

The rest of the day was spent at the kitchen table, getting to know his children, talking construction with Jon, waited on by his mother and sister and wife, being welcomed by neighbors who, having heard that he had returned, dropped by to welcome him back. They listened to his news of America's fight against the Moslem pirates, in places they never heard of before: Morocco, Algiers, Tunis and Tripoli.

As the day wore on, there was time to tell them about the cultural life of Hamburg, his favorite city, its music, literature, theaters (the worth of which was still questionable in the Puritan mind), and the passion of its people for learning. His neighbors were enchanted to learn about these things, though it was difficult for them to conceive of an opera, having never heard one.

After relating all the major stories, the children were fed and put to bed. The adults went home for supper and then returned with rum. More and more townsmen arrived. Molly excused herself and disappeared behind the chamber door.

When at last he came to bed, Elijah carried a kitchen coal and lit the fire in their hearth so that he and his wife might see one another.

But he need not have bothered. She did not stir; the light did not disturb her slumber, and he did not feel free to rouse her. For a long time he looked down at her in the firelight, willing her to wake up. She did not. And if she had, he wondered, what then?

The next morning he found that his brother and sister and even Molly were waiting to show him the new house, its generously sized rooms, every one of them kept warm by the double chimneys, and the multitudes of windows that would make it bright, even in winter.

Jonathan showed him the especially tricky places where expert carpentry had saved the day. Debby led him upstairs to the bedchamber he would share with Molly and to another directly across the hall, nearly as large. "For me," she laughed. "When I come to visit." In the back were two smaller bedrooms, with hearths in both. A flight of narrow stairs led down to the keeping room, where Molly listlessly waited.

Wasn't this the house she had always wanted? Wasn't she getting exactly what she asked for, a mansion like Mariah and John Warden's? She should be dancing up and down these stairs, leading him everywhere, overjoyed, laughing, planning how each room would be used.

But she did nothing of the kind, placidly standing by until they decided Mother had been left long enough with two tiny children. She did nothing to bring the house to his attention that afternoon, apparently had no opinion about how they might finish it, or what colors she might favor or what sort of wallpaper she might want to use.

She was lost to him.

To escape her silence, he walked the land later that day. Roaming the fields and woods, he went back to the little pond where he and John had often fished and trapped muskrat as boys, hiked down to the beach to look over the remains of Sears' salt vats, walking until he came to the packet landing, back up the Rockford Road to his mother's little house. The little house that he would leave in favor of another place so much more grand. But how could he do that in the company of a woman who appeared to have died inside?

It was nearly suppertime when he returned. Sarah had been fed; Molly was nursing 'Lije by the hearth. Jon was waiting with blueprints and details to discuss so that he and Pat Mayo could resume work the next day. As the women of the house worked together, serving supper and cleaning up, Elijah observed that there was peace between Molly and his mother, but as he watched more carefully, he could see that his wife simply complied with whatever his mother wanted—a fact fully as alarming as her lack of interest in the house.

Going over the drawings and questions that needed to be answered, he sat with Jon late into the evening. Mother, Debby, and the children were asleep in the loft, his brother ready to retire when Elijah lit a candle and let himself into the front room. Molly was asleep, as she had been the night before, and he could see that this would be the way of it, day after day and night after night until he left again . . . .

No! He would make her care! He would force her to care! All she needed was a little firmness, gently applied to be sure, to break through the barrier between them, and she'd be restored to her normal self. Yes!

The candle guttered on the mantel as he climbed into the bed and shook her awake.

"Molly!" he whispered boldly.

Slowly she roused. "Elijah?"

"Molly! I would be intimate with you."

"Oh! Very well." She shed her nightgown, a very modest one that buttoned up to her throat, and lay back beside him. Pulling her unresisting body to him, he felt for and found her breast. She was quiet as he reacquainted himself with the feel of her, the small waist, the abundant hips, the smooth thighs. Despite her passivity, he became hot and ready and took her. But there was not the pleasure he remembered.

Slipping her nightgown back on, she took the candle and left the room; he heard her climbing the loft ladder to check on Sarah. When she came back, she tucked a light cover around 'Lije and slid under the blankets, asleep in an instant.

So much for gentle firmness. Elijah willed himself to lie quietly, trying to cipher it out like a problem in navigation.

She is compliant enough, he thought. Perhaps she does not hate me. Yet what else can she be feeling? She is caught, snared in a trap too complicated to escape, and I have put her there.

He must speak, must tell her how sorry he was that he had lost control, that it would never happen again, that he would take her up to Boston to shop for clothes and furnishings which, he knew, women so dearly loved to do, that he would ride around in the chaise with her and call on John and Mariah, even go to Yarmouth and Mistress Warden, if she liked . . . .

But how to start?

Perhaps he could initiate a high style of living right here, right now, without waiting for Jon and Patrick Mayo's crew to finish the house. She had converted the parlor before, just to please him and give him an idea of what elegance looked like. He would encourage that, and he would start with a small party for her to orchestrate. Tony Gray was due home soon; perhaps the young Merricks could have a little gathering to welcome him. Debby could join them, and they would sit in the parlor and the ladies would drink tea and he and Tony would drink rum and the four of them would converse pleasantly about something, he knew not what. But Molly would know, or at least act the part. He remembered her little charade down by the mills, bowing and conversing with the trees. Oh! What he would give to have that Molly back! He needed her, needed her to be the way she was. Oh, Molly!

⋈✦⋈

"A party?" she asked. "In the parlor? For Tony Gray?"

It was morning, and she was sitting in their bed with Sarah and the new doll.

"Tony's arrival would only be an excuse," Elijah explained. "But it would give me practice at being a host, which I have never done. I need to learn, since we will be living so grandly."

She looked at him with more interest than she had exhibited since he'd come home. "Hosting a party," she mused.

"I remember that you fixed up the parlor once, and it was lovely. And we could get some new things, too, if you like. Chairs that are more comfortable, for one."

Then she smiled. "Yes, that might be a good idea. How do you know Tony is coming home?"

"Because I saw him in Boston when I was there just a few days ago."

"Really! You didn't mention it."

"I didn't want to say anything that would get Debby's hopes up. She would fain see him, I know. At our party she'd be able to talk to Tony all she . . . ."

"When will he arrive?"

Her eyes were brighter already, he saw, and rejoiced.

"He had trouble with his return cargo, customs and tariffs and such to straighten out, and he has to square up with his owners, and get himself another voyage. I'm not sure exactly when he'll be back, but we can get everything in readiness and then, when he does arrive, invite him."

"Do you think we could go up to Boston now and buy some nice cups and saucers and a tea pot? Later we can use them in our own house."

"Indeed, if that would please you," he agreed. "And those chairs I mentioned."

"Maybe we could find Tony, and learn of his plans."

"Yes, I'm sure we could."

"I'll have to take 'Lije with us."

"Of course. When would you like to go?"

"Today?" she asked.

"Why not! Do you think we should take Debby along? She could mind 'Lije while we go shopping, and perhaps buy herself a pretty dress so that she is at her best when Tony comes acalling."

Molly was suddenly watching him.

"What is it?" he asked. "Have I said something wrong?"

"No, of course not." She looked at him searchingly now, as though wondering how much she could say. "Sarah, sweeting, can you go to Aunt Debby and show her your doll? Can you ask her to make a dress for it?"

"Mommy make."

"Well then, could you ask Aunt Debby if she has any cloth I can use?"

"Me go," Sarah agreed, and ran out of the room.

"I'm never sure how much she understands." Molly closed the door and sat beside him on their bed. "I must tell you about something concerning Debby."

"I'm listening."

"If it makes you angry . . . ."

"Considering how I behaved the last time I was home," he put in quickly, before he lost his nerve, "I can understand your concern. I promise, I will not be angry. I've been wanting to tell you how sorry I am that I was so harsh."

"You did what you felt you had to do," she said, looking down at her folded hands.

He covered them with one of his. "But now you are unsure of my temperament. And to tell the truth, I can't say that I blame you."

Again she was silent. It was like stalking a deer in the woods, he thought. You dared not make a sound, and once you spied the quarry, you dared not move until it came within range.

"You wanted to tell me something about Debby?"

"Yes. It has to do with the chaise."

"Well?" he probed.

"It was before 'Lije was born. I was out riding with Olive Snow and we encountered Tony. It seems that he never really had a chance to get to know Olive before then, and he was taken with her. And she with him."

"Olive Snow?" The girl was a Hall, and Tony was a King!

"Yes. She's my only friend." Molly looked him squarely in the eye.

Damn, this was complicated! "Would you invite Olive to our party, and not Debby?" he asked gently.

Her gaze returned to her hands. "If you are willing, Elijah."

The compliance was back. But he had lured her a little way out of her fortress, and he was not about to lose her again. "If you believe that Tony and Olive Snow are a good match and will make each other happy, I wouldn't try to interfere."

"That's very generous of you," she responded cautiously. "But what about Debby?"

It would mean arranging a party in which Tony Gray and Olive Snow were the primary participants, leaving his sister out entirely. But he would make it up to her somehow, later on. "We could get together in the parlor without Debby even knowing about it, if it was late enough in the evening."

Her eyes sparkled. It was the first time since he'd been home that he'd seen that mischievous look. Now he knew he was on the right track! Remember the doe in the woods, he told himself. Stay still and let her come to you.

And so it was that he was able to interest his wife in a plan that appealed to her. She was still cautious, watchfully assessing everything he said and how he said it, still careful not to offend him. But she was more present to him than before.

They took the packet to Boston, with the baby dressed warmly and wrapped in many layers of blankets. They shopped for a tea service, two padded chairs, silver candelabrum, a box of sweets, and a new dress. The green silk one was ruined, she confessed, as though it were her fault. He cringed, and said abjectly, "I'm so sorry, Molly."

Tony returned on the packet with them. He cordially greeted

Debby who had heard the canon and was there to see who was returning, hoping against hope, as she always did, that it would be him. He
politely declined her invitation to linger at their house and refresh
himself, explaining that he must get on home to his mother and sister;
there were details to which he must attend. Perhaps later?

But he did not visit Debby. Instead, he came to the party in the
parlor, there to court Olive Snow as he had done every time he had
been home since he'd ridden with her in Molly's chaise. Elijah called
for the girl himself, and he would take her home again later. Her family
would not know that she had been with Tony Gray.

It was a quiet party, and very beautiful. Fresh from Boston, the
china tea service shone in the light of the candelabrum, one on either
end of the mantel, five candles each, creating brilliance heretofore
unknown in anyone's house! Molly poured gracefully, and Elijah
served the sweetmeats they had hidden under their bed for safekeeping.
Everyone kept their voices low so they would not be heard by Mother
or even Jon, certainly not by Debby, in an unspoken conspiracy that
was disquieting but necessary.

Molly and Olive encouraged Tony to tell them all about his tra-
vails with the customs house and the details of his next voyage. All of
them discussed the Moslem potentates that sabotaged shipping in the
Mediterranean.

After an hour, Elijah escorted Olive home, so that she would not
return too late and arouse the curiosity of her parents. When he came
back, Molly gracefully excused herself so that he could enjoy Tony's
company man-to-man.

"I've been wanting to ask you how to go about being married by
a justice of the peace," Tony began without preamble. "Like you did."

"Has it come to that, then?" Elijah asked, retrieving the jug of
rum and two mugs concealed in the kindling basket. They drank deeply.

"I don't know how much Molly has told you about Olive and me,"
Tony said. "Old Snow will have nothing to do with me. He wants Olive to
marry into their family—God knows there are plenty to choose from—
and he forbade me to come calling."

"How have you managed to see her?"

Tony grinned. "When I'm home, Olive walks over to visit with Molly. This is fine with her father even though you're a King. Molly and Olive stroll around your place, usually with a child or two, and then Olive just slides into the barn, where I'm waiting."

"And Jon?" Elijah could hardly fathom the logistics.

"Is at his forge, or if the weather's fine, fishing. We're careful to check. So far no one has seen us, but your mother and sister are always somewhere nearby. It's nerve-wracking!"

"I can imagine! You're bound to be discovered if this goes on much longer."

Tony looked morose. "Indeed! But Simmonds can't marry us if our parents object, since Olive is not yet 21. Mine would be content if she is the woman I want, but Snow would refuse, and carry the old King-Hall rift forward to the next generation."

Elijah nodded. "My mother would, too, if it were up to her. They're on opposite sides, but they're cut from the same cloth." He poured another tot of rum, and they pondered.

"If we marry out of the church," Tony said, "we'd be cut off from our families. At least for a while, until the furor died down. But I could build a house on the low road, near yours, and Olive would have Molly nearby. If you're willing. You two would be all we'd have." Maudlin tears filled Tony's eyes and he helped himself to more rum.

Having experienced firsthand in France the power that money could yield, Elijah offered, "Maybe I could arrange a tribute larger than Snow's so Simmonds would marry you. I don't like to brag, Tony, but I've managed to do well in the last few years. I'm sure there's some-thing Simmonds wants badly enough to forfeit Snow's contribution of firewood and hay."

"That's really swell of you to offer. But wouldn't that publicly humiliate Snow? Olive couldn't condone that. "

"Yes, yes." They drank while considering the problem. "How about holding the ceremony in my new parlor? The house won't be finished for a while yet, but we can get the parlor and dining room presentable pretty soon. The rest won't matter."

Tony whistled. "A dining room! You are coming up in the world, Captain."

"And I'm a member of good standing in the church. My contributions to its maintenance might rise substantially, were I to continue to be a member of good standing."

"Damn!" Tony laughed, softly so that no one would hear. "It would work, wouldn't it!"

"I think so. If you can stay home long enough. How long have you got?"

"Believe me, Elijah, as long as it takes."

"It takes three weeks for the banns to be read."

"I'll go up to Boston and arrange for a different ship," Tony declared.

Three weeks. Elijah hated to wait so long, but if Fuller agreed to give him a monopoly on Hamburg, he could fill the time by sailing up to the city a few times, organize cargo, hire crew, encourage Fuller to write letters of introduction to the North European merchants he wanted to capture in his exclusive net.

"Three weeks it is!" he declared. "You rearrange your next voyage and I'll pay a visit to the parsonage tomorrow."

✦⚬⚬ 2 ⚬⚬✦

He left the house at dusk, having spent the day with Jon and Pat Mayo and his crew. Plastering of the lath had begun; trim and moldings had been installed in the spacious front door entryway, and Elijah had applied the first coat of paint to them. The parlor and dining room would be ready within the allotted time, Pat Mayo assured him.

Building a house was hard work, Elijah had to admit. Standing on a quarterdeck was quite a lot easier! But his painting tasks kept him out of the way at home, which seemed like a good idea just now, while the balance between himself and his wife was beginning to right itself. He needed to be very still yet, so the doe would come fully out of hiding. If he wasn't there, hanging about, it would be less likely he'd blunder in his effort to bring her back.

His knock at the parsonage door was readily answered. Simmonds straightaway took Elijah into his little parlor and cordially poured them both some rum.

"Merrick!" the minister exclaimed. "I am honored by this call. It's a pleasure to see you here, sir!"

"My pleasure to be here, sir," Elijah dutifully returned, and they drank to one another's health and chatted for a while about doings in the town and within the congregation of saints in Rockford. It was not difficult to nudge the conversation to the matter of Ben Snow's vendetta against Tony.

"A troublesome thing, this feud," Simmonds sighed, then drank deeply of his rum. Ministers of the Standing Order, Congregational, did not spring from the villages they served, so Simmonds did not always know which families belonged to which bloodline. He was continually in danger of being squashed between the millstones of the Hall-King family dispute.

That had been the case when young Tony Gray had asked if Simmonds would perform his wedding to Olive Snow. Innocently, the minister explained to Elijah, he had congratulated Benjamin Snow on his daughter's good fortune when he next saw him. Snow, beet red with the veins in his forehead standing out, as good as forbade him to perform the ceremony, implying he would become a Baptist and attend church in the South Parish, taking his multitudinous family members with him, should the marriage take place.

Baptist! Even Elijah understood the magnitude of this threat. When the faithful opted to leave the Church of the Standing Order, they no longer paid their taxes to support the minister. Schism was the beginning of the end for men like Simmonds, leaching away their income and power. It was important the pastor keep the counsels of the rich on his side, thus perpetuating his own sphere of influence. Benjamin Snow was Rockford's business leader and had more money to give to the church than most. But Elijah, recently rich, perhaps would become more wealthy even than Snow. And Tony Gray was a captain too, and one day would be well off in his own right.

"The situation concerning Mr. Gray is exceedingly delicate," Mr. Simmonds pointed out.

"I believe Tony's family would not object, and they also support the church, do they not?"

"Aye," Simmonds said uncomfortably. "They are always very prompt with my firewood and hay." Though not so generous with cash contributions, he did not add.

The two sat in silence while Simmonds poured more rum. If they kept on at this pace, the minister would shortly be drunk. Elijah held his liquor well; Simmonds, with years of surreptitious drinking under his belt, did not. His eyes were starting to glaze.

"I believe Tony and Olive are thinking about marrying outside the church, as my wife and I did," Elijah stated. "What if all our young couples just took it upon themselves to marry so? Once out of the church, they might stay out. They would, then, object to paying taxes to support the ministry. Can you not see this distinct possibility?"

"Yes," Simmonds answered morosely. "I can."

"Is Snow worth it?"

"I'm not sure, Captain. As I've implied already, he is a generous supporter of the church and the Hall clan is very numerous."

"Perhaps there are other members of the parish who are ready to be generous, also. Who are prepared to fill in the gap, should Snow make good his threat."

"How generous?"

"Perhaps generous enough to erect a steeple on the church."

"A steeple!"

"With a bell in it, so that we wouldn't have to hang ours from a tree anymore."

"And a ball on top, perhaps? With a vane? That would be most impressive, and uplifting, reaching to heaven itself!" Simmonds, aided by the rum, could see it, touch it.

"How much?" Elijah asked.

"It would cost 500 dollars." Simmonds, having wanted a steeple for years, had the figure ready.

"We would be second to none on Cape Cod, with a steeple like that," Elijah said slowly, contemplating the cost as well as the spiritual impact. "The Baptists would be quite overshadowed."

"Yes, yes."

"I am prepared to underwrite such a project," Elijah said. "But I cannot do it if you are discriminating against my friend by honoring Benjamin Snow's wishes. It would look as though I support the continuation of this feud between the Kings and the Halls. And that I am not willing to do." After pausing, he pointedly asked, "Sir, are you prepared to perform the marriage of Miss Snow and Tony Gray? We could conduct it in my new home." In exchange for a steeple with a ball and weathervane, he did not add.

Simmonds sighed and thought about it. "There is another complication," he admitted at last. "It has to do with your children."

"My son and daughter? How is this so?"

"They have not been baptized," Simmonds explained. "Your support of the church's holy mission is very much compromised, Captain Merrick, since you have not troubled yourself to see to this matter. It might appear to some of our members as though you are trying to buy your way into heaven instead of attending to the spiritual requirements of faith."

A more heretical idea could hardly be conceived!

"Have you and your wife considered this matter?" Simmonds persisted.

"Not exactly," Elijah hedged. He had never discussed baptism or even the church with Molly. "There has not been sufficient time, with my having been gone almost constantly since we were married." In truth, these matters had never seemed particularly urgent.

"Perhaps this would be a good time to think about it," the minister said. "If you intend to be so generous as to donate a steeple, Captain, you would become a prominent member of our church. Perhaps the most prominent. It would be unbecoming, indeed, for so upstanding a member to appear unconcerned about baptism."

"Well, then, shall we baptize the children this Sunday, since I am home just now?"

"Alas, we cannot." Simmonds looked abashed. "Because your wife has not been baptized either."

The complications were beginning to weigh heavily. Elijah helped himself to the rum. "Pray continue," he sighed.

"In order to receive baptism, your wife would have to perform public confession and humiliation. That would take longer than just one service, sir. It would take several."

Elijah shook his head. "What in God's holy name is she supposed to confess?"

"Bastardy," Simmonds said.

It was late when he returned to his mother's house. The night was clear and quiet, and he lingered in the back field, leaning on a tree and looking over the distant moon-spangled bay that stretched for an infinity to meet the stars.

The devil! What a rotten time Molly had had in life! Some while ago, Henry Hastings of the Yarmouth church had come to Simmonds, to tell him about an interview between himself and Molly in which she had asked for baptism in order to be married in his church. Hastings had not wanted to risk the criticism that would certainly ensue had he done so, but the sacrament itself had saved him. It required public confession. The girl's mother had lived in sin with a reprobate who had never darkened the doors of any church. Miss Molly had claimed that Seth Adams was not her father, but there was no way to prove it, of course, and she was probably some man's illegitimate child in any case. Hastings had wanted Simmonds to know, so that he would be prepared if the subject came up again, in Rockford. And now it had.

Simmonds had pursed his lips with sanctimonious certainty, and Elijah had clung fiercely to his self-control. The two of them sat and drank for a time.

"Very well," Elijah had said finally, and put his mug down, leaning forward in his chair so that his face was not far from that of the pastor. "Let me tell you this, sir. Molly is my wife, the mother of my children. To withhold baptism from her is an outrage. To withhold it from my children is a sacrilege. I know that Molly is innocent of anything Hastings may have charged her with, and if you persist in pursuing the same course he did, I will be forced to conclude that the will of God is not being carried forward by our church. I may, like the Baptists, have to also to conclude that my tax dollar is not being used in support of a godly enterprise. Do I make myself clear, sir?"

Simmonds swallowed with difficulty, seeing that his church was in danger of losing more than its steeple. "Perfectly."

"I will take responsibility for raising the requisite sum of money for a spire and will make up the difference, if there is one. If you would like clapboards for the church, I will be glad to supply them, too, and the labor to apply and paint them."

Clapboards! Paint! Simmonds' face was a portrait of elation.

"I hope this will free you from any pressure that is being brought to bear as a result of Benjamin Snow's stubbornness," Elijah continued. "I also hope it frees you to publish the banns for Mr. Gray and Miss Snow and in three weeks, join them in holy matrimony. And I hope it frees you to baptize my wife without benefit of confession, and baptize my children, too. Can you, or can you not, do these things?"

Simmonds bowed his head as if in prayer. Long moments dragged by. "Yes," he said. "I can."

Now Elijah understood why Molly had fought back so hard against exclusion, why she had wanted a chaise, why the new house was so important to her, and why she was willing to sustain his displeasure the last time he was home. He saw that it would have been too humiliating to tell him how low she had been cast by Hastings, too mortifying to admit how badly she needed a place to be safe from the opinion of the community.

Well, he would do what he could for her. Simmonds was only the beginning. The fine house would be an important part. Their role, together, played from the setting of the house, would allow Molly to pick and choose the people with whom she wished to share her life. It was high time that it came to pass.

The kitchen was heavily shadowed in the moonlight; the bedroom was pitch black. He went back for a candle, and using its light, fetched one of the candelabras from the parlor. The room jumped into brightness and Molly was instantly awake.

"Oh!" she exclaimed. "Isn't it pretty, all lit up! Are we having a another party?" A little smile hovered at the corners of her mouth.

He sat beside her. "I wanted to tell you that Tony and Olive will be married in three weeks, in our new house."

Taken by surprise, she blinked. "Good gracious, Elijah! How did you do it? Olive will be thrilled!"

He took her hands. "Did you know that Pastor Henry Hastings of Yarmouth once visited our own Pastor Simmonds?"

At the name of Hastings, her face changed. In her eyes he read shame and fear and suppressed rage.

"The question of baptism came up, for Sarah and 'Lije," he explained.

"And so it came up as regards me, too."

"Yes."

She trembled; her voice shook and became a strained whisper. "Hastings—he was so . . . insistent. He said that to earn the privilege of membership, I would have to go before the congregation on my knees because my mother had offended their morals. She who voluntarily put herself in servitude so that I might be safe. Oh, Elijah," she wept. "I could not bear it. The cruelty of it." Then suddenly her face froze in pure terror. "Are you saying that I am required to go through it here, so the children can be baptized and Simmonds can perform the marriage?"

"God, no! No, Molly! No!" It was excruciating to see her so broken, so humiliated, defenseless. He gathered her to himself, cradling her gently. His own tears fell onto her hair. "My darling, my Molly, it is over and done. Put it behind you; let it torment you no longer. Simmonds will baptize you and the children, all on the same day. Whenever you desire."

She was utterly still, and then pulled away from his embrace so that she might look him in the eye. "He will what?"

"He will baptize you, and the children. And he will marry Tony and Olive in three weeks. At our new house! We can have a real party—a reception!"

"Elijah," she cried, laughing between each word, irrepressible as a bubbling spring. "What did you do? Hold a musket to his head?"

"Henry Hastings is dead and gone now, so Simmonds is safe from any criticism he might have raised. Besides the church needs a new steeple. In addition to that, it's going to get clapboards and white paint. You can't have a steeple without white clapboards."

"Clapboards!" She pressed her hands to her mouth. "Mother will positively wither," she giggled. "Everyone knows the Lord favors shingles."

They collapsed on the bed in gales of laughter. 'Lije woke up and laughed with them, then snuggled into Elijah's unaccustomed arms and went back to sleep. They sat cross-legged, facing one another.

"Now, Mistress Merrick, may I invite you to participate, by my side, in seeking solicitations for the steeple?"

"I thought you were going to donate it," she smiled.

"I was. And I am. But the church belongs to everyone who attends it, and I believe it would be a good idea to include all of the members in the process."

"Well, surely."

"You and I shall call on the citizenry of Rockford. We will drive up to each member's house in the chaise, request contributions for the steeple, and work in a few details about our new home with its furnishings from Boston. By the time we're done, every woman in the church will want you to invite her to see it. And no husband will refuse to accompany his wife."

Sober now, she looked at him for a long while. At last she said, "So you really do understand."

"Yes," he said humbly. "I really do. And I'm sorry, Molly, that it took me so long."

"We could have a good time together, soliciting."

"I hope we shall, my dearest, because I love you so."

"Elijah, Elijah, I am the most fortunate of women, to be married to you." She leaned over the sleeping 'Lije and kissed her husband's mouth softly, caressed his cheek, smiled into his eyes. "Let's put the baby back in his cradle, shall we?"

8

The Rise of
Molly Deems

Elijah Merrick was at sea when the nation elected Thomas Jefferson President of the United States in 1799, and the second time in 1803 as well, when even Massachusetts supported the Virginian. The Federalist powerful languished and lost control, and a Jeffersonian was elected as governor of the state.

America had settled these differences peacefully. The nation of the people, by the people, and for the people had acted as prescribed by her constitution. She prospered and was content. A certain smugness settled in.

In Rockford, as in the rest of coastal New England, mariners could see no harm in Jefferson, who had not meddled with the tariffs that favored American sea-going commerce. They grew wealthier than ever before, and at home, their women-folk thrived.

✦✿✦✿✦

MOLLY MERRICK HAD WORN beautiful gowns in the past few years. Some of them had been made for her in Boston, and some had been sewn right in Rockford, but she never had one to match this new rose brocade! Turning this way and that in front of the glass, she assessed it, a daring combination of low-cut bodice and full skirt starting just below her bosom. Its deep and rich folds suggested the drapes of ancient Greek statuary; its simplicity and elegance created an illusion of regal height and classical loveliness.

Pinning her hair high, she was ready for her newest prize. As she had done innumerable times this day, she peeked into the leather jewel case lined with satin, in which settled resplendently the ruby necklace Elijah had given her last night. Gleaming darkly, it would adorn the expanse of bosom that the rose brocade left to public view. The dress and the jewel together would make a dizzying combination. She clasped it around her neck and turned to the mirror. Despite the fact that her hair resisted its pins and escaped untidily, she could see that she was right. Oh, how beautiful the ruby was, its richness intensified by the depth and texture of the gown.

Enraptured, she admired herself a little longer.

In the dozen years since they'd moved into the house, the Merricks were in a position to decide between satin or brocade, damask or lace. They served their guests using crystal goblets and delicate china, and during all that time, Elijah had provided jewelry to complement every gown that she owned.

The Hamburg run had brought him fine profits and with them, many luxuries. When the British blockaded the Elbe last year, Molly worried that her new life would be restricted. Why, Elijah had even suggested they augment their income by converting the dining room and pantry into a bedroom/sitting room and hire it out to the schoolmaster of Rockford's newly-built academy! Concealing her horror, she had countered with the suggestion that Elijah see what the Mediterranean route had to offer. It would be safe now, since the Moslems had been recently defeated by the new American navy.

This, too, proved lucrative, and Elijah did not again mention the preposterous notion of taking in a boarder. Objects of value continued to appear—rugs and fine furniture, books and laces and jewelry—borne to her in proud homage.

And now the ruby, yes, the ruby! She unclasped the necklace and reverently held it up to the sunlight.

Her first party had been the reception she held for Olive and Tony when they married. It was the first time she had worn a dress made for her in Boston. At each subsequent gathering she had worn a new gown, more beautiful than the last. And, she noted with satisfaction, the dress of her carefully-chosen guests had been correspondingly more elaborate, too. All of them had been able to pursue the good life as the wealth of European trade accumulated at their hearths and the rise of the Rockford captains, accompanied by the rise of Molly Deems Merrick, continued. The competition to be Rockford's most beautifully-dressed woman was more intense than ever, and Molly thrived on it. Her clear skin glowed in the excitement of knowing that even after carrying five children, she still could hold her own.

"Mrs. Coy? Mrs. Coy?" she called from the top of the stairs.

"A-yuh?" came Lottie's voice from the depths of the kitchen.

"Can you help me, do you think?"

"Be there in a minute, Mrs. Merrick."

"Don't hurry!" she called back and returned to her mirror, to gaze upon herself while waiting for Lottie Coy. She would not hurry, would Lottie Coy. She and her husband, Thomas, were South Shore folk and not inclined to hurry anywhere, for anyone. None of the North Shore families treated their South-side hired help as though they were servants. No, they were guests in your house, willing to assist if you remembered that they were not mere hirelings, but folks who were willing to lend a hand, if they were paid well enough to do it. So if Lottie took her own time to mount the stairs, Molly would say nothing. She needed Lottie far more than Lottie needed her, and she would do anything to keep her content.

The South Shore folk made leisure possible in the homes of all of the captains. If one did not hire household help, and did not have interests and style like Molly's own, one would not be part of Molly's circle. One would not be allowed to take dinner between Sunday services at the Merrick's house nor take tea there when the afternoon service was over. Only those couples living in large, well-appointed houses much like the Merrick's were eligible to attend Molly's parties, like the one she would hold tonight, timed to coincide with the greatest number of captains home from their voyages. Unspoken rules for entry into her group also required that clothes must reflect the current style; the candidates must have at least one servant and a carriage, and must have read or seen something recently that would make for lively conversation. Their numbers had grown over the last 12 years.

Lottie Coy's heavy footfall thundered on the back stairs and down the hall toward Molly's room. When she arrived, Lottie would complain that not fifteen minutes before, she had climbed those confounded stairs to lace Molly into her corset and stuff her into that dress, and if Molly insisted on running her helper up and down the stairs all day, she could not expect to also have the refreshments ready for the party tonight.

But Molly would pacify Lottie by putting the beautiful ruby around that wrinkled and scraggy neck and letting the woman admire herself to hers heart's content. She was not immune to beauty, nor to Molly's charm. She well knew the important place she held in Molly's life. She had delivered Elizabeth, two stillborn babies, Susannah, and little Sonny. She had held Molly's hand, and sponged her brow and nursed her through the fever that followed Sonny's birth two years ago. She had organized the house and all its occupants single-handedly then, including Elijah when he rushed home. And throughout her years of service, she had never complained about anything until she and Molly were alone together and she could do so privately. She was one in a million, and Molly loved her.

Lottie bustled in.

"Here, Mrs. Coy," Molly said, holding the ruby out to her. "Try it on."

"Oh, no, Mrs. Merrick," Lottie protested. "It's too fine." But her eyes were soft at the sight of it, and she turned so that Molly could fasten the clasp.

"My husband gave it to me yester evening. I haven't had a chance to try it on with the dress until now. Is it not lovely?"

"Beautiful." Lottie inspected its reflection in the glass. "And perfect for the dress." She took it from her throat with a sigh. "You will do it justice, Mrs. Merrick!"

Lottie almost never issued compliments; Molly was inordinately pleased. Turning around, she allowed Lottie to undo the buttons on the dress and the laces of her corset, and sighed with relief.

"This corset is too tight, you know."

"Well, I sag."

"Hmmm." Lottie could not contest the point, for Molly did sag. There was no avoiding it as she stood there clad in only her chemise.

"I'll come down with you, Mrs. Coy, and help you put the icing on those cakes."

"No need. My sister will come by later. She'll finish them if I can't." Lottie extricated a robe from a pile of garments on a chair and helped Molly into it, patted her shoulder. "I think you should lie down, Mrs. Merrick. You're not as strong as you wish you were."

There was no arguing with Lottie, who was already removing the bedspread and holding back the blankets for Molly to crawl under.

"Take your ease while you can. Miss Debby will be returning soon with the children, and then there'll be no peace." Debby had dutifully taken the brood to Mother's. It was the usual Saturday arrangement, designed to stop Mother Merrick from complaining that Molly had taken even the grandchildren from her. When they returned, the chances were good that Debby would feed them and scrub them up and put them to bed, without bothering Molly at all if she was not feeling up to being bothered. It was nice to know they all would work together so she could save her strength until the last possible moment.

Snuggling down happily, she drifted with her contentment and the anticipation of an enjoyable evening. When she arose, she would be fresh, an important step in keeping her looks. She wanted her husband to think she was the most beautiful woman he had ever known, wanted to be everything he would wish in a wife. Since he was so infrequently home, it was easy to maintain a façade of devotion and seductive admiration.

Her husband doted on her, contributing in manifold ways to her well being. Shielding her while helping her to take the spotlight, he had unlocked the doors of Rockford that she could never have opened by herself. He had that nasty Pastor Simmonds in the palm of his hand so there were never any complaints about the Sabbath noon gatherings that lasted so long her guests were often late for afternoon service, nor about the rather elaborate dresses Mrs. Merrick wore to church.

Elijah had been gone when she contracted the childbed sickness. The infant Sonny (officially named Kingson) was given out to a wet nurse; the children stayed at Mother's and Debby cared for them there. Molly's elegant friends put on old clothes and mob caps and swept floors and dusted furniture and polished silver, leaving Lottie free to take care of her as she burned with fever and lost all consciousness of time and place.

When Elijah learned of her illness, he left his ship under the command of his mate and sailed home instantly, sick with fear that Molly would die before he got back. He had wept with relief to find her alive still, though very weak and tired. It had been a long, slow recovery and even now, two years later, she tired easily and needed to rest often.

Oh, yes, he loves me, she thought, lying there in her bed, the feather mattress puffed up around her, the ropes that held it squeaking and rasping slightly as she burrowed deeper and drew the blanket up higher. Once she had made her husband miserable by being so submissive that he could not reach her—retaliation for that beating after she'd bargained with Sears. Her intention had been to use that cool distance for a long, long time—a fitting punishment for what he had done to her.

But then he had bribed Pastor Simmonds and bought her acceptance into the church, without which she could not make her way. When she saw that he truly understood why she so needed control of her own destiny, when she saw his compassion for her, and his love, her anger melted away and she was able to take up her role as the wife he desired. She made sure he was happy when they were together, and was available for love-making as circumstances permitted. It was an unbeatable combination. In return, he had worked hard to prepare the parlor and dining room of the new house for Tony and Olive's wedding, and he had given Molly free reign to plan the reception in honor of the controversial couple.

She'd done it with Debby's help, recalling her enticement of Elijah's sister with satisfaction. They had been alone in Mother's house when she had set the snare.

"We'll have a wonderful reception," Molly told her. "One that will serve as a house-warming. Or a least, one that warms the parlor and the dining room."

"Do whatever you want," Debby balked. "I shan't come to their reception, and I won't help you plan it."

Debby turned her back and sighed shakily into the silence. "I wanted him myself," she said at last, trying not to cry. "And I thought I had him, too. But Olive Snow ended up with the prize."

"I'm so sorry."

"So am I."

"But Deb," Molly continued gently, "I don't recall that Tony ever came to see you. You weren't really even courting. Isn't it time you looked elsewhere? He's not the only man in Rockford."

"He is as far as I'm concerned."

"Nathan King would have you in a minute."

"But I will not have him!" Debby said fiercely. "He is old and boring. I would spin the rest of my life in the household of another woman before I would marry Nathan King. Besides, maybe Olive will die in childbirth. Then Tony will be free again."

"Debby!" Molly whispered, horrified. "You must never say such a thing." Death was never far away from a childbearing woman.

"I hate her! When we were young, I watched her eating candy and reading books and wearing pretty dresses. Her father could afford to give her whatever she wanted, while I wore homespun and we ate turnips, and I didn't even have a father. I really hate her!"

"Shhh, shhh," Molly soothed. "Have a cup of tea with me, sweetheart, and calm yourself." She did not want to trap the vulnerable and broken-hearted girl in an argument over Olive Snow. Her need of

Debby was too great. Seating her sister-in-law at the hearth, Molly set out the cups with a pinch of tea in each and filled them with hot water from the kettle hanging in the fireplace. They sipped quietly.

Then Debby set her cup down abruptly. "And she took you. You were the only interesting thing that ever happened in our house, and she took you away from me, just like she's taking Tony away from me."

"Whatever do you mean?" Molly demanded.

"When you got your chaise, remember? I always wanted to go out with you, but she went instead."

"We went together, you and I, more than once."

"I think you preferred her."

"I needed her," Molly said softly. "That's different."

They drank a second cup of tea in profound silence.

At last Molly offered, "This reception is a golden opportunity."

"Oh?" Although deeply desolate, Debby's curiosity was aroused.

"To build a new way of life for me, for you, for Rockford," Molly carefully explained. "You can't deny, Sister, that people in Rockford have spurned me from the minute I arrived. Is that not so?"

"Well, yes, I suppose it is," Debby answered, squirming at this admission.

"But now I have more than they do. A new house, built in the new style. And it will be furnished in a way no one has even dreamed about here in Rockford. Everyone will be eager to see it. They wouldn't hesitate to visit me if I asked them. But I shall not open my doors to just anyone who wishes to enter."

"You won't?" Debbie asked, interested despite her wounded heart.

"No, indeed. Once they have come and seen and admired, they might be tempted to continue to ignore me. But I won't give them a chance. I'll invite only a few people at first. Ones who exhibit enough intelligence or taste or both to enjoy what I have to offer, ones who will never ignore me."

"And what is it you would offer?" Debby asked, mystified.

"A stimulating atmosphere. Since our men trade in overseas, they are in continual contact with Europeans. We could discuss politics, and listen as they share what they learn about the capitals of the world, once we convince them that these things matter."

Debby looked dubious. Perhaps a more familiar approach was needed. "We can get a dancing master and learn something besides reels." Molly added.

"Like what?"

"I'm not sure," Molly admitted. "But if we hired an instructor, we could find out. Maybe minuets. And folks here play musical instruments. Many sing. We could entertain each other, as genteel people do."

Her interest was piqued, but Debby was still reluctant. "Don't you think it's unwomanly to discuss politics and such?"

"Indeed not. Being womanly is a state of mind. I watched Mistress Warden talk with male guests about such things, and they listened. They admired her!"

"Truly?" Debby wondered.

"Oh yes. Naturally, females have to be careful. We have to do more listening than talking. Our men know so much! They've seen the world! We shall, of course, respect that and at the same time benefit from their great experience, develop our own minds and talents. Be able to express opinions that have worth. Wouldn't that be more interesting than crops and clams and the weather?"

Debby had to laugh. "Of course!"

"And dancing and learning to sing well? Wouldn't that be fun?"

"Indeed!" Debby's eyes lit up at the prospect, then dimmed with self-doubt. "But I don't believe I'm suited to such things—singing and dancing." She could not dance at all, never having had the opportunity, and her singing was confined to the tuneless psalmody of Rockford's church.

"You are very graceful, Debby," Molly lied. "You could dance well, if you knew how."

"There's a master in Barnstable, I've heard," Debby speculated. "Perhaps we could contact him."

"That's the spirit!" Molly took Debby's hands in her own, looked earnestly into her face. "To create the group we want, Debby, we must select only the people we are sure will accept our lead, and we must begin with a very small set, with people we invite to Olive and Tony's reception. I'd like everyone else to feel that their company leaves something to be desired. Then, one at a time, we'll invite a new person to join us on Sundays, when we'll serve dinner between services."

"But everyone brings their own food. Serving a meal sounds like a party," Debby argued. "We don't have parties on Sunday, Molly."

"If we don't call it a party, it won't be a party," she grinned. "And then, once our guests see what we require of them, they will become better informed and more open to new ideas in order to be invited again. Our group will grow, and we will direct its activity."

Debby shook her head. "Pastor Simmonds may have something to say about it."

But Molly knew that Pastor Simmonds would say nothing. "The rewards will be wonderful," she went on. "You'll be glad of such a stimulating environment, and you will play an important role because you are on good terms with everyone in the village. You are accepted, as I am not. No one would refuse an invitation if you were the one to issue it."

Debby blushed at this compliment. "Do you think so Molly?"

"I do." She smiled, playing Debby like a trout nibbling at the bait. "And you will help me select the people we'll invite, because your judgment is very acute."

Debby giggled, but her smile faded again. "I am not sure I'd like to be around Olive so much."

Molly held tight to her patience. "Olive is important because there are other Halls we might want to invite, and they will follow her lead. With Tony and Olive's marriage, the families begin to merge. It's the beginning of breaking down the barriers that have separated the Kings and the Halls for so long."

These grand social changes went right by Debby as she focused on the primary object of her interest, Tony. There was a pause. "Well, I suppose I'll be able to see him more often if they're included in your circle." She shrugged. "That'll have to do. So tell me who you'd like to include at the wedding reception. I will tell you whether or not I think they would suit us."

Us. Debby was hooked!

"Solomon and Phebe Denning?"

"Yes. Phebe is very smart. She learned to read long before the rest of us at dame school. She has a very pretty singing voice, too."

"And Solomon?"

Debby laughed. "He can't be stupid, or he wouldn't have chosen Phebe for his wife. Elijah likes him, too. Always has."

"What about Solomon's brother?"

"He is married to a Hall—Ruth. I've never associated with a Hall."

"Perhaps the next party?"

Debby nodded. "How about Martha and Tim Stone. Martha can play the mouth harp."

"And her husband?" Molly asked, trying not to cringe.

"Well, I think he knows how to dance. Jigs and all."

"Do either of them think about anything besides the weather? Tim is a farmer, is he not?"

"Yes. But do we want a group that is exclusively mariner?"

"The advantage to being a mariner is that the men are going to be interested in foreign affairs and politics and, if we are lucky, European culture. What is your opinion about the Wardens? John is Elijah's best friend, and his wife has been very pleasant to me."

"Ah, the Wardens." Debby sounded impressed. "I would love to get to know Mariah."

"Then you shall! And who knows what captain might come walking through their door one day, looking for a wife, when you are visiting at their home."

Debby stiffened at this reference to her unmarried state.

"Or what about inviting your cousin Nate?" Molly suggested quickly.

"I'm not sure he is cultured enough," Debby said. "Considering what you have in mind. And if we invited him, we'd have to invite the girls too, wouldn't we?"

Debby had not been in Melissa King's kitchen when Mother and Molly had visited there. She especially hated the King girls, and she would enjoy seeing them clamoring uselessly for entrance to her parlor. If their brother were invited and they were not, she could imagine their dismay. Gleefully.

"Those girls don't like me," she said. "Because of my mother. I can never invite them to my house, Sister. They are not my friends."

It was not an easy position for her, yet Debby must declare herself, be willing to leave them behind. "If they dislike you, Molly, then they are not friends of mine, either." She tossed her head, tossing her lot in with Molly as well.

The voices of the children and Debby, returning from the afternoon at Grandmother Merrick's house, could be heard downstairs now. No one came to fetch her; it looked as though Molly would have more time to rest. Too excited for sleep, she reminisced further, and remembered when she had moved into this house.

Elijah had left for Hamburg in the fall. The following spring, when she was seven months pregnant, the house was finished, and she made haste to move in before the child arrived. But Mother refused to leave, knowing very well that Molly could not go there alone.

"Nobody is going to force me out of my home," Mother announced. "I'm going nowhere. I don't want a new room. I like my old one. I don't want to mind the hearth of another woman and take orders from her, as though I were a servant, and especially not from you, Molly Deems. Besides, Elijah told me to stay here."

"Mother!" she cried. "It's Elijah's house! These are Elijah's children. I can't manage such a large place by myself and care for the children and deliver a baby. I need you. The children need you!"

"You should have thought of that before," Mother sniffed. "I could have told you it would be too much."

"But it isn't too much," Molly shouted. "It's only too much if I'm alone." She had not meant to cross swords so openly! She walked away and calmed herself. "Forgive me for raising my voice, Mother. But I am defeated if I have no help. The very thought has undone me."

"Well, get used to it, Mistress. You aren't getting help from me."

Molly turned to Debby and Jon who were watching the battle, and took as deep a breath as the baby beneath her heart allowed. "Please, help me!"

Sarah, who had been sleeping on Debby's shoulder, awakened and squirmed down. "I will help you, Mama," the child declared, taking her hand.

Debby sobbed, for she loved Sarah dearly. "What shall I do?" she moaned, casting helpless eyes at her brother.

"There is no question, Sister," Jon said from the distant corner where he had been whittling a boat for 'Lije to sail in a puddle, come the next heavy rain. The little boy played with the wood scraps as Jon continued working with his knife, not even looking up. "I know who it is that gives me a room of my own. I know who pays the bills. Our brother decided to buy the Sears' farm and put a fine new house on it. If his wife needs our help so that she can live there with his children, then I don't think we need wonder what we should do."

"Don't you see?" Mother Merrick shrieked. "She has torn our family apart. She has inveigled one son into marrying her and the other into involuntary servitude, leaving me destitute. And now she would take my only remaining daughter, the comfort of my old age."

"What do you mean, 'servitude'?" Jon asked indignantly. His mother had insulted him.

Likewise, Debby was displeased at being the daughter designated to comfort her aging parent. It would be infinitely more interesting to be a spinster in Molly's house, rather than stay at home with her mother and her mother's ancient friends. With surprising firmness, she said, "We'll have to find out, when Elijah returns, whether or not he can support two households. Meantime, I will go with, with . . . Sarah!" She opened her arms, and the little girl joyfully ran into them.

Debby and Jon decided they must move the next day, leaving behind the person who had done her best to keep Molly down and out of sight. Whisking their belongings and those of the children from the old Merrick house to the bright new one with its shining crown, they settled in to await the arrival of Molly's third baby.

And then they awaited Elijah.

Molly had met him at the packet, disregarding her usual policy of making him come to her. It was necessary to get to him before his mother did.

"We must talk right away," she said as they walked up from the landing.

"Oh hello. And how are you?" he teased. An auspicious beginning.

She laughed too. "I'm sorry," she said. "How are you?"

"Very well. And you?"

"Elijah, listen!" Lowering her voice so that the others walking up from the landing could not hear, she began. "It's your mother."

"Is she ill?" he asked quickly.

"No, unfortunately."

Inspecting her face closely, he saw that her quip was a cover. "Let's have it," he said. "The last time you wanted to talk to me, we were in for a farm. What is it now?"

"She refused to move into the new house with me," Molly told him, unable to keep her voice from trembling. "I didn't know what to do. I didn't want to offend you by leaving her but I couldn't wait. Debby and Jon agreed, so we went, and she is very irate."

"Yes, I can imagine she is."

"I hired help—a couple from the South Shore. Jon can't manage the place by himself and I, I needed a woman to help me when your new daughter was born."

"A daughter!" Elijah loved Sarah and was delighted to have another little girl.

"I didn't know if you'd approve of my hiring help, either. Have I done wrong, Elijah?" A tear spilled down her cheek. "Have I made you angry? I have tried so hard. I named the baby Elizabeth, after Mistress Warden, and she is beautiful, and I know you'll love her," Molly wept.

"Oh, darling, dearest, precious one," he soothed gently, taking her in his arms, disregarding the gaping public. "It sounds to me as though you did the only thing you could. I'll take care of Mother."

"And Lottie and Thomas Coy? They come up every morning and go home in the evening every day except Sunday, and I pay them each a dollar a week. Is that all right?"

"Definitely not," Elijah declared, and she shrank back. "They must have more than that, woman! How do you expect to retain their loyalty with so little money?"

It took all her self-control not to wrap her arms around his neck and kiss him in the manner he deserved.

The very next day, he went to Mother, to remind her it was he supported her in her old age, and that he would tolerate no further insults to his wife, public or private.

Thanking his brother and sister for coming to stay at his house, he commissioned Pat Mayo to build an addition on the back of the place, so Jon would have a ground floor room of his own instead of sleeping in the pantry. He endeared himself to Lottie and Thomas Coy by raising their wage and by taking the time to know them and to discuss their suggestions for running the house and the farm. And he did everything he could to help build the new Rockford.

The wedding reception had indeed been the beginning of a whole new society, as Molly had hoped. Sunday dinner was served in the dining room each week, with a new person or couple added now and then. Saturday soirees were given every month, and a large party that included everyone once a year, each more lovely than the last, and so enjoyable that the men tried to get back home for them.

As the years went by, Molly acquired more and more china and silver and stemware and tablecloths and *objets d'art* to enhance the house, and encouraged gracious manners and deportment among the increasingly elegant guests. When Elijah was home, he too enjoyed the fruits of her industry and grew to be a gentleman of sorts, or at least what passed for one on the Narrow Land.

There were sad times, of course, disconsolate times. A year after moving into the new house, Jon got wet while catching herring. A catarrh turned to pneumonia and he was gone within a month, snatched away as quietly in death as he had comported himself while he lived. Molly and Elijah had done their best by him, giving him a place of his own and a family for him to love and be loved by. He had been so good with the children! They all truly mourned him.

And then there was the repudiation by Elizabeth Warden that cast a pall over Molly's days for rather a long time. Mrs. Warden refused to attend a Saturday soiree that Molly had arranged especially with her in mind. She would not, she wrote Molly, despite her love for her foster daughter, lend her presence to a place and an event that was centered on display and affectation. It was a blow, and rocked Molly deeply until Mariah told her that Elizabeth Warden never visited her house either, for the same reason.

Once she recovered from the shock of it, she told herself that she would go to Yarmouth sometime soon, so she could visit quietly as befitted Elizabeth Warden's preference. But she never went, and time rolled on by, and her life of display and her rise within it absorbed her completely.

❊❊✦❊❊

The rose brocade bewitched him, as she had known it would. He had waited to see it as she dressed her hair, winding a rose-colored velvet ribbon in it and pulling little clusters of curls down in front of her ears. Then he watched Debby settle the gown around Molly's shoulders, fastening its myriad buttons in back. Finally, he hung the ruby pendant around her neck, and then all three of them admired it in the mirror.

Debby curtseyed. "Your Highness!"

"You'd grace any court in the world, Molly. You truly would!" Elijah's admiration was gratifying and she basked in it, knowing already that the evening would be a success. She would reign, her court would assemble around her, homage would be paid. Surely everything was just as it should be!

And it was. The parlor and dining room buzzed with spirited conversation, the kitchen throbbed with heat and activity. The pantry provided a logical overflow for those guests who were not as yet comfortable with the mighty, in this instance, Jackson Pollard, Elijah's fellow conspirator from Jellison's ship, *Susannah,* and the academy's newest schoolmaster, only six months in town.

In the crowded parlor, Molly offered her guests an array of sweet things and sandwiches on a silver tray with grape leaves embossed around the edge. By doing so, she could circulate through the gathering, chatting with each person and each cluster of friends, moving the party in the direction she wanted. Tonight, a new woman was here. Tabitha Bradley, who accompanied the Dennings while her husband was at sea. The newcomer was chatting with Nathan King and Tony's sister Hope, now married to Captain Daniel Blake. From what Molly could hear, Tabitha had recently returned from a voyage to Spain in her husband's ship and had seen wonderful paintings there, which she was describing with spirit. She seemed quite able to hold her own in the present company, and not once did she speak of her interest in knitting.

Molly smiled secretly. She had rescued Rockford from the cultural desert that it once was. Her group was accomplishing everything she had hoped for, she thought proudly.

Mistress Blake took the tray so that all of them could admire the dress and ruby. "Just beautiful. Don't you think so, Dan?" she asked her husband.

Captain Blake pretended to appraise Molly critically. "Yes, yes," he said finally, helping himself to a tiny sweetmeat. "Yes, I think you might say that our Molly is beautiful."

"I thank you," Molly beamed. "You may be called handsome, Daniel, in exchange for those kind words."

"But mine, Madam, are true." He bowed over her hand. She was happily aware of other admiring eyes.

"Where did you learn pretty manners like that?" she demanded saucily.

"From you," Daniel and Hope chorused. Everyone laughed.

Molly retrieved the tray and moved into the entry hall where Captain Will Robbins, now in Continental trade after his service on Snow's packet, was talking loudly with Tony Gray and Desire Snow, another stranded wife brought to the party by other members of the group while her husband was overseas.

The heated, though cordial conversation of the men was plainly a grievance session against President Jefferson and his recommendation to impose a full embargo on trade, to which Desire listened with interest. Molly moved on to Debby and Olive who were positioned by the front door to welcome late guests. They were friends now, the two of them, though Debby still cast secretive glances at Tony. All these years, and she still loved no other!

"John and Mariah haven't come yet," Olive reported. "Once they get here, that will be the last of the guests."

"I don't want you and Debby to spend any more time at the door," Molly told her. "John and Mariah know the way. Come, Deb," she directed. "There's something you can do for me." She led Debby into the dining room where Elijah chatted with a half dozen other guests who were picking at the meats and cheeses and breads on the sideboard, arrayed around the punch bowl, then went on into the keeping room where soiled dishes and goblets were piled everywhere.

"I'd be glad to help here," Debby offered.

"Washing dishes was not what I had in mind," Molly assured her. They filled the tray with more sandwiches. "Come now!" Debby picked it up and Molly led her over to the pantry door and threw it open.

Jack Pollard and the schoolmaster were within, fairly advanced on the road to inebriety. "Would you boys like a sandwich to soak up some of that rum?"

"Miz Molly!" Pollard exclaimed. "An' Miz Debby! With san-wiches." Steadying himself with a hand on a pantry shelf, he took one.

"A morsel would be fine," the schoolmaster rejoined. "But I must refuse, Madame. Your rum would be ruinated by food."

"Aye," agreed Pollard lugubriously. "Ruinated. But you must take one, because Miz Debby brought it."

"Carry on," she instructed Debby, who made a face at her, knowing that Molly was deliberately stranding her with the unmarried males.

She picked up a new tray that Lottie had made ready and backed up to the swing door and into the entry, where the discussion now focused on women's suffrage.

"Women already have the power of the vote," Tony proclaimed.

"Whatever do you mean?" Desire Snow demanded.

"At the last town meeting, there was a warrant asking for thirty five dollars—thirty five!—to pay for the services of a singing master who would teach us sacred music. Is that not so?" Tony asked.

"Yes," Olive, now at her husband's side, replied in unison with Desire.

"And said singing master was approved by unanimous vote, was he not?"

"He was," affirmed Will Robbins.

Tony continued his peppering. "And might I suggest that the idea of a singing master originated in the heads of Rockford women, in fact, probably right here, in this very house?"

"You might," admitted Olive.

"And might I further suggest that this is plentiful evidence that our gentle ladies run the town as fully as we men do, and therefore, have suffrage!"

One day we must have a debating club, Molly thought. That would be something new. Everyone enjoys a lively discussion.

Something new seemed important, somehow.

The front door knocker rattled, scarcely able to be heard over the din of the party.

"Here, I'll take the tray," Olive said.

Her hands free now, Molly pirouetted in the direction of the door and flung it open. There stood John and Mariah, as she had expected. Mariah was very much pregnant with their fifth child. "Don't let anyone know I was seen in public," Mariah greeted her gaily. Pregnant women never came to parties, unless they happened to be friends of Molly Merrick!

John followed with open arms. He embraced Molly and stepped back. "You are looking wonderful, as always," he proclaimed. "It sounds like a splendid party. Oh, and we've brought a guest with us," he went on. "I hope you don't mind. My brother, Isaac."

Isaac.

She could scarcely breathe.

Isaac Warden.

"He has just returned from England," John was saying.

And there he was, as a visitation from the past. Crossing the threshold of her house. Of Elijah's house.

Mind? She couldn't even think, let alone form an opinion.

Isaac!

John's voice was quite distant, as though he were far away. "He's on his way to a post in New York City."

She must conceal her shock and dismay. Holding out her hand, she managed to say, "How nice."

Isaac took and kissed it, the candlelight catching in his golden hair as he bowed. When he stood straight again, his eyes met hers with an impact that appeared not to be noticed by anyone else. A profound passage of time seemed to occur right then; in her ears rushed the sound of her heart.

"Mistress Merrick," he murmured.

"Welcome, Master Warden," she heard herself say as she withdrew her hand. He had entered her house, this bastard who had raped her when she was yet a girl, as though he were a visitor like any other. Deep, deep down, something like anger was rising and something else as well, something that threatened to overwhelm her. Turning to John and Mariah, she asked, "Will you please show Isaac to the dining room? Elijah is there, master of the punch bowl. Excuse me—I must see to something in the kitchen."

She fled. Debby and the two men of the pantry were drinking coffee with Lottie Coy. "Privy," she murmured by way of explanation, and snatched up a wrap hanging by the back door.

She let herself out into the night, past the well and beyond the privy. The darkness was cold and still. Sounds of her party, the best party ever, floated faintly in the air, but it was no longer the focus of her attention.

Isaac Warden.

Why was he here?

He could have excused himself from accompanying Mariah and John, but instead he had come along with them, this man who had so nearly ruined her. It was not a simple and casual act, his coming here. The depth and command of his eyes had deliberately held hers in an intimacy that shocked her and had taken her back to the girl she had been, a maid in his mother's house, vulnerable.

It was clear that he had done it deliberately.

He deserved only her scorn, her anger. Both were present now, but there was also a deep response to that intimacy, unlike anything she had ever shared with Elijah.

She reeled.

Stop this! she told herself. Think on it later, not now! Your own party is going on without you. Your friends are inside, as is your husband, so steadfastly devoted to you. You are no longer a maid, nor a girl; you are a woman with a position to maintain.

Staunchly putting aside her confusion and turmoil, she marched back to the festivities and her role as hostess, settling in the dining room at Elijah's side, conversing and laughing with her guests, hoping there was no flaw in her performance that her husband might detect.

Would Elijah remember that their flight to Provincetown, so long ago, was an avoidance of Isaac Warden and the implications of his gifts and trinkets?

Leaning elegantly against the sideboard, she decided against a glass of the punch for fear her hands would shake. Will Robbins was expounding on the chances of the extended embargo passing in the legislature. Jefferson's previously benign reign had lulled the Federalists of New England into apathy. There were not enough of them left in Congress any more to champion the nation's mariners, upon whose shoulders rested American credit in Europe.

Molly had never let a topic get out of hand like this, overtaking all other social intercourse. When individual concerns threatened to dominate, she had always redirected them, and she was good at it. But not just now.

Fortunately, of its own accord, Will's diatribe turned into a debate as to whether the impending embargo would put a permanent end to British impressment. Hundreds—even thousands—of American sailors had already been taken off United States' merchant ships and forced to serve in the Royal Navy. Everyone gravitated to the parlor to discuss it, and Molly was left alone at the punch bowl with Elijah.

"Well!" she said brightly, testing his reaction to their unexpected guest. "Isaac Warden looks as though he prospered in England. And whoever would have thought it, wastrel that he was?"

"It is a surprise to see him," Elijah frowned. "Did you know he was at John's? That he would be coming tonight?"

"Not I!"

"Would it have mattered to you?" He looked at her closely.

"No, darling," she said in what she hoped was a dismissive manner.

"Well," Elijah said, trying to make his voice light as hers, but failing badly. "He's still a handsome devil."

"So are you! I'd prove it to you right here and now, if it weren't for so many people in the house!"

He guffawed then, just as Tony and Olive came in for more punch. Then the bowl was moved into the parlor to slake the thirst of the debating guests.

By three o'clock in the morning the party had ended. Exhausted, the Merricks climbed the stairs and fell into bed, and Elijah was soon fast asleep. Now Molly could concentrate on the challenges presented her.

Her husband would say nothing more about Isaac Warden, she knew; it was beneath his dignity. Yet, he would be watching her, watching very carefully. And she must not, for a minute, let him see that Isaac had dismayed her in any way.

You were drawn to him back then because he offered something you never before had, she told herself, something exciting, arousing, mysterious. But now you have Elijah.

Yes. Elijah.

That was where the difficulty lay, was it not? Elijah had done everything for her, and he was exactly what she'd needed him to be. But he was not exciting, certainly not mysterious, and he had never aroused her passion as Isaac once had. And, it seemed, still did.

A ridge of the feather mattress, like a bundling board, was humped up between them. Except for her husband's soft snores, she was encased in a warm cocoon of privacy. He shifted in his hollow on the other side of the bed and she froze, waited to see if he would waken. He did not, and she relaxed, lay still.

Isaac's eyes haunted her, his shimmering hair haunted her, the memory of what it had been like when he had kissed her long ago, and the response deep within herself, haunted her . . . . But then he had taken her and used her, and the passion had disappeared instantly, replaced by humiliation and fear. But she saw now that it had not vanished. It had been lying in wait, that passion, all this time. The years of parties and gatherings and social supremacy were triumphs that had not really touched the heart of the vulnerable girl she had once been. A lonely girl, eager to be not only loved, but to love passionately in return. That heart still waited.

It would have to remain hidden, for it threatened to ruin everything. She could not acknowledge these feelings, must make them disappear again, put Isaac from her. If she could keep her time and her mind full, there would be no room for him. A new accomplishment, she thought, would occupy her, restore the balance of her world. And she must come up with it now, before Elijah awakened, so there would be something to hide behind that would conceal her distress from him.

What could she conjure up? The ladies' choral society had been practicing diligently under the direction of the singing master, who came twice a month from Barnstable. A performance by the group would attract people from Yarmouth and Dennis as well as the other towns. The choral society would be acclaimed, she was sure, but Molly Merrick would be a participant like all the others, not a star. It was not enough to keep and hold her attention.

A dance wouldn't work. Most of the men, in town just now for tonight's fete, would be gone. She considered and discarded several other ideas, trying to shut her mind to the knot of panic that lay within her breast, the panic that told her she was in even more trouble than she realized.

Think, she admonished herself.

It must be something out of the ordinary, something that would put her back in stride, so her pursuits would once again be exciting, full of promise and pleasure, and would single her out as special.

At last, she had it!

Eagerly she waited for Elijah to wake up, to see if he would agree.

"Good morning," she said brightly as soon as he stirred, kissing his cheek over the center mound of mattress. "Have you slept well?"

He yawned, sending horrendous fumes of stale alcohol through the room. "Hruuumph."

She squirmed out of bed and crossed the room to her dressing table. Until he was more fully awake, she would engage in small talk. "Tony and Olive are coming over tonight, to help us finish off the remains of the party."

"Hmmmm." He propped himself up on one elbow. He was awake enough. She must act now.

"Elijah," she said, turning abruptly on her bench. "Do you think I might have my image painted?"

He blinked once and looked over her lovely face and the cloud of dark shining hair that framed it. "Of course you may," he said. "I should love to have a picture of you with me on my trips."

"Mmm, yes. Well, I have something a little larger in mind. Perhaps I could have a miniature done for you and a full portrait for the house?" She turned back to her mirror, watched him watching her. "One day I will be old. No matter what I do or how careful I am, I will have wrinkles. My hair will turn white. I'll look terrible. But I'm not old yet, Elijah, and I'd like a picture done before it's too late."

"You'll never look terrible, dear Molly."

Her light laugh acknowledged his compliment, then she pushed on. "I should like something that will remind me, every day of my life, what we hold, together, right now. It would include things that we love, like the candelabrum we bought so long ago, and that little statue in the curio cabinet—the horse one. With a curtain in the background, pulled back to reveal a ship, standing for your success."

"In the middle of the orchard?"

"In the middle of a seascape, you ninny!" They chuckled at the thought of a brig in the back yard. "I would be sitting in the parlor beside the table full of treasures. It would present the life we are leading at this time, when everything is so fresh and lovely."

"Even as you are," he said loyally. Then he scowled. "I think it would be quite expensive. Perhaps we should wait to see if this damned embargo is going to come to pass."

"Well, naturally, if you think that's best." She could fairly feel her face falling into the lines of sadness as she saw her opportunity to have a wonderful new show for Rockford slipping away, along with a necessary diversion for herself.

Elijah relented instantly. "I will do it if you smile," he said. "And if you will come right here, right now, so that I may inspect your loveliness more closely than, I trust, a limner will."

"Oh, Elijah!" She bounded into bed with him. "Thank you! Thank you!"

"At the beginning of the week, I'll be catching the packet up to Boston to check out my next voyage with Fuller. If I can, I'll find a good painter there and engage him for you," he promised. "Won't all the other Rockford ladies be furious that you thought of it first?" He looked pleased at this prospect, always at her side in her perpetual conquest of Rockford.

Molly smiled. "You are the world's most generous husband," she murmured into his ear.

Yes, it would help, she thought, snuggling closer to Elijah in what she guessed would be a lengthening embrace. In her mind, she was already sitting for a grand full-length portrait with elegant props surrounding her. She would invite the Rockford women in small, carefully-chosen groups, to take tea and refreshments with her while the artist worked. As the painter put her portrait together and she chatted with her guests, she would tell them that her husband had insisted on it. Indeed, they would envy her and then would badger their own men-folk to demonstrate the depth of their affection as Elijah Merrick had demonstrated his. The painting would absorb her attention completely. By the time it was finished, Isaac would be gone to New York and she would be free again.

It was so happy a prospect, so beautifully resolving everything, she nearly laughed aloud. But she restrained herself just in time to receive Elijah's kiss in a properly devoted fashion, and return it as he expected, so he would never guess that her whole life was held in the balance, with joy on one side and disaster on the other.

The Embargo

IT HUNG OVER THEIR heads as a sword. The captains hastened away, intent on getting in as many voyages as they could before the sword dropped and commerce would be cut off.

Elijah had orders to go to Philadelphia, load the *William Tell* with flour and take her to Cadiz. No sooner had he arrived than Fuller's agent brought the word: Jefferson's embargo had passed in Congress and would go into effect on Sunday morning, December 22, at ten o'clock—just one day away.

Until it was lifted, which could be months or years from now, no one could leave an American port, and no merchant trader, still on the high seas, could go out again once he returned.

By cutting off the services of American carriers, the president hoped that England and France, who were again at war, would discontinue searching neutral merchant ships, confiscating goods that could be construed as aiding and abetting the enemy, and in the case of England, removing crew members who were thought to be British citizens, forcing them to serve in the her navy. Britain had used this practice, called impressment, for many years in order to man her enormous fleet. But it had intensified during the war with France, and United States citizens were being illegally taken as well. Several thousand Americans were presently serving the Royal Navy under duress.

Jefferson believed that an embargo would force the British to abandon this practice altogether.

But it would throw the port towns along the whole Atlantic coast into disarray. It would bankrupt New England, and if it were prolonged, the wealth and security that had been built up since the end of the Revolution would be wiped away. The Boston merchant and Cape Cod mariner alike would face ruin.

Enraged, Elijah was determined to make the trip to Cadiz. The profit was bound to be high because this would be among the last shipments of flour entering Spain, and with luck, he and Molly could ride out the embargo. They'd need to be careful, of course, have to do without luxuries, but they'd be comfortable enough—if he succeeded.

In the twenty-four hours before the embargo would become law, he hired a crew, supervised the loading of 3,000 barrels of flour, cleared customs, and took on a pilot. Then he waited for the ebb tide, which he needed in order to slip down the Delaware River.

In that interval, he was able to write to Molly, explaining that Congress had just passed the cursed embargo, and this was the last trip he could make before it took effect. They would have to conserve their savings because future income was uncertain. She must send the portrait painter back to Boston. Pat Mayo should be asked to start building vats so they could make salt to sell inland next winter. Thomas Coy should plow a larger garden; they would need to grow as much food as they could. The Coys might remain in service for now, but the situation would have to be reassessed when he returned.

'Lije, now 14, could perform many of Thomas Coy's tasks, he thought. Sarah and Elizabeth, at 15 and 12, were quite capable of doing the wash and sweeping the floors. Susannah, who was 6, could watch 3-year old Sonny, and Molly could join Debby in cooking and baking and tending the kitchen garden.

She would hate it, and so he did not enumerate these things. Instead, he ended by promising to have the portrait finished later, when their lives returned to normal.

He sealed the letter and left it with Fuller's agent. By then the tide had turned, though the breeze had dropped. The *Tell* worked her way downstream and did not arrive at the mouth of the Delaware until well past 10:00.

Embargo be damned—nothing was going to stop him!

The sunlit sails of a ship were breaking the distant horizon— possibly a government revenue cutter coming up from Baltimore to enforce the embargo. Farther out to sea, a breeze ruffled the water. It well might reach him ahead of the cutter, allowing the *Tell* to escape. Hoisting all the ship's light sails, he let the pilot off with a handsome reward and waited.

It was indeed a government ship approaching. Through his spyglass, Elijah could almost see the faces of the crew before the breeze filled the *Tell's* sails and allowed him to pull away.

Yes, he had broken the law. But the law would break him and those like him, not unlike the British laws that would have broken their forefathers thirty years ago had they not rebelled. Delivering the flour now was no different than smuggling, at which the colonists had excelled. And it would be worth a small fortune.

There were so few ships plying the waters that he toyed with the idea of staying out. His trade would no doubt be welcomed anywhere. Both Britain and France would wink at their own restrictions, for now there was no neutral party to carry for them. Other Americans would do it, he was sure. They would stay out until the embargo was over, and they would make a lot of money for themselves and their owners. But Elijah would not, for the crew had signed articles binding them for no more than this voyage, and the ship belonged to Fuller, who would never favor breaking the law.

In Cadiz, the flour brought an even higher price than he'd guessed. He took the *Tell* to Boston in ballast. Despite the risk, it had been a surprisingly uneventful trip.

The absolute still of the coastal waters, with only a few packets about, spoke eloquently. In the harbor, protective barrels hung upside down on the masts of vessels, shielding them from the weather. He walked along the wharf, under the bowsprits of the empty ships, riding high above his head like drawn swords. The ropewalks were silent, the warehouses abandoned. Damn that Jefferson!

Snow's packet was getting ready to sail with the mail. Simon Hopkins, the young captain who'd replaced Will Robbins, was delighted to have a passenger. "By God! A fare!" he exclaimed. "How the hell are you, Elijah!" They shook hands with vigor. "Weren't all of us glad to hear about your voyage. Molly told us about it."

Elijah nodded appreciatively. "Luck was with me. I suppose all the men are back?"

"Everyone. Pastor Simmonds is beside himself with joy; there is a full house each Sabbath morning and most afternoons. He howls about the iniquities of the Jeffersonians and the congregation loves it!"

Elijah watched the coast slip by as they headed home, hugging the shore so no revenue cutter would suspect them of trying to steal out to deep water. It was a choppy, uncomfortable, cold March voyage, but he did not seek the warmth of the cabin. The bleakness of the day suited his spirits as they left one and then another village behind, the smoke from scattered chimneys blending with the sullen sky.

Well, he was home, at least, and not stuck forever in a foreign port as he had been in Paris under Robespierre. Waiting out the embargo would not be pleasant for any of them. There would be no carefree entertaining any more, no luxuries. The saltworks he had instructed Molly to have built would pay for themselves with the first harvest. They would keep him busy all summer. In the spring he would sow; in the fall he would harvest; in the winter he would rot, along with everyone else.

Keeping the Coys was out of the question. He would rather enjoy taking over Thomas' tasks himself, for they would keep him occupied. But Molly's dependence on Lottie would present a problem. She would hardly enjoy taking over Mrs. Coy's role, even with Debby's help. It was difficult to picture her laboring at the hearth or at the wheel, and impossible to imagine her being happy about it. Perhaps he'd just have to keep Lottie, after all.

Molly, Molly, Molly, he thought. You are my joy and my burden! When he was in Cadiz he had bought her a lovely Spanish comb. It might well be his last gift to her for a while, and he had chosen it carefully, hoping it would assuage her disappointment at being thrust back into the archaic life they had left behind.

"How long will Ben Snow run the packet, Simon?" he asked.

"Good question. I go up for mail once a week, and pick up whatever I can get for his store. But supplies are hard to find and the mail can come overland if need be. I may be out of work soon."

If supplies were hard to find, then the Boston folk must be hoarding, convinced the government was prepared to wait as long as it had to. Elijah thought of Molly again and sighed, then began to look for his own stretch of beach, where he hoped to see his new saltworks. Yes! There they were—a series of large wooden boxes with cone-shaped square lids. They were not attractive, but he did not care. Within lay the promise of income, and he believed he would need it before the end was reached.

No one had known of his coming, but there was a crowd at the beach waiting to see if the packet brought any news from Boston, and Elijah's boots no sooner touched dry land than Tony Gray and Sol Denning were upon him, slapping his back and congratulating him on beating the embargo. They urged him to come and see the new armory right away.

"What are you talking about?" he demanded.

"The armory of the Second Regiment of Rockford," Denning told him cheerfully.

"We commandeered the academy," Tony announced with pride.

There had been only one regiment when he left, composed of farmers and fishermen who mustered a few times a year. Although all able-bodied males were required to participate in the militia training, men who could afford to, including himself and the captains he knew, avoided service by paying the fine that was imposed by law. Now his friends were regulars, Elijah guessed.

"We've been stockpiling arms and ammunition," continued Tony. This was beginning to sound serious.

"An impressive stash," Solomon assured him. "Come look!"

They tucked their arms beneath his and began to walk him up the road, clearly eager to show off their prize.

"Hold on!" he begged. "I'd like to check my new saltworks. And I'm sure my family will be waiting for me; they'll have heard I'm back."

"But there are important matters you must hear about," Tony insisted. "You'll have plenty of time to check your vats and family later."

"I'll have plenty of time to see the armory later, too." He freed himself and waved them farewell, taking the path off the Rockford Road that would lead to his houses, the new and the old.

Tony and Solomon continued on to the former academy, no doubt disappointed that they could not prevail over Elijah's devotion to his wife. They'd get over it, he thought. Tomorrow he'd drop in. Just now he must see Molly with his own eyes, hold her close, and find out how much progress had been made toward the necessary hunkering down.

The path from the old house to the new was well trampled by the feet of his children on their way to visit their grandmother. The old place was holding up well, he noted, and hurried on to his own domain, past the outbuildings—the woodshed and privy, the well and the hen coop which, he noticed, was larger now to accommodate an expanded flock. Good!

"Molly!" he called. "Molly?"

"Elijah!" She burst from the barn, a dust cap on her head, a huge apron over her coat, her face smudged and her hands dirty. He opened his arms and she flung herself into them, laughing and kissing him joyfully while he held her as close as her bulky clothing would allow. Such a spontaneous and happy an embrace was not possible in public; he was glad she had not been at the shore.

Debby ran to him now, garbed much like Molly and, like Molly, full of happiness at seeing him. "Come with us, Elijah!" his sister cried, grabbing his arm. Molly secured the other. "We'll show you what we're doing." They dragged him to the barn door and gestured grandly into its dark and musky maw. In the dust-clouded depths he saw Thomas Coy cleaning the stalls right down to bare wood, piling the soiled straw onto a sledge in the middle of the central open space that usually accommodated the chaise, not present at this moment.

"Good afternoon, Mr. Coy."

"Afternoon, Captain," Thomas responded with his countryman's brevity.

"Where's the chaise?" Elijah asked. "Where are the horses?"

"We took the carriage over to Captain Gray's place," Thomas told him. "And the beasts."

"Do they really need such immaculate stalls?"

His womenfolk giggled like girls. "We're going to have a dance," Molly explained. "I wanted the horses gone for a while, so we can air out the place out."

A dance? Was she demented? Were their friends really willing to cavort around in a barn at a time like this? He would have to put a stop to it, for he could not afford such idiocy. Yet, here was Molly, holding onto his arm, eagerly looking up at him in her most engaging manner.

"Will you be my partner?" she asked prettily, and he smiled at her uneasily, aware that Debby and Thomas were watching, waiting to see what he would do next.

"I hope I may have that honor." He took her grubby hand and bowed grandly over it.

"The dance will be very modest, Elijah. The ladies are going to make over their older gowns. New ones are banned. Each couple will contribute a refreshment. A fiddler and a caller will cost something, but we expect to find a bargain, since no one has any work these days."

With Thomas Coy in earshot, Elijah was reluctant to pursue the subject of frugality. "Is a cup of tea possible? I'm cold after my trip down on the packet."

"Of course, my dear!" she exclaimed. "Forgive us for not insisting on it first thing!" They left Thomas to hauling the sledge out into the newly enlarged garden. Molly and Debby cleaned up at the well, followed Elijah inside and prepared tea. They bore the china service on a tray into the parlor, which they used all the time rather than saving it for special occasions, like a visit from the minister.

Molly's portrait was hanging between the two front windows. It was beautiful, showing her clad splendidly in a gown he had never seen, wearing the ruby he'd given her last fall. One of her hands was holding a beautifully painted fan. Beside her, on an inlaid mahogany table, was a load of luxuries that seemed so real he could touch them—the silver candelabrum, a small ship model, the horse statuette that Molly loved so well, a pile of books, and a golden frame that held an embroidered, unreadable motto. The sitter and table drifted in vague mists of gray, as though in a dream.

"Do you like it?" she asked.

"Of course I like it," he said.

"We couldn't decide on the motto. That's why you can't read it."

"I wondered about that," he admitted. "How much did it cost?"

"Excuse me, please," Debby put in. "I'll fetch some cake. You must be hungry, Elijah." She hastened away without waiting to find out.

"Yes?" he asked his wife.

"Twenty dollars," she answered. "Had I received your letter sooner, I'd have sent the painter away before he started. But since he was so far along when I heard from you, I had him just finish off the bare canvas with fog and then leave."

Debby came bustling back carrying a tray with cake and plates that matched the china tea pot.

"Thanks." He devoured his piece and sliced himself another.

"It is a splendid portrait," Debby offered.

"My friends admire it profoundly," Molly told him. "Everyone wants to get theirs done, too, when this silly embargo business is over."

He was disquieted, because from the sound of it, neither Molly nor Debby realized what the embargo could do to them, that their days of spending and acquiring were over.

"Beloved ladies," he said slowly, "We don't know when the embargo will be lifted. Until we do, we must plan very carefully."

"Oh, we've been careful!" Molly explained. "When the group comes here on Sunday, Debby and I serve only the most economical of dishes."

"Well, my darling," he said firmly, "from now on, our friends will have to bring their own dinner when they come."

Molly's eyes opened wide with shock. "Bring their own! In a bucket, you mean, like a farmer going out to his fields?"

"They can use any container they please, but we cannot provide the noon meal for them, Molly. I'm surprised they would let you do it these past months!"

"Oh, everyone raised a great fuss, but I assured them that the voyage you made, getting away from Philadelphia and all, would be very profitable and there was no reason that the Merricks, at least, needed to change their ways, and surely not at the expense of their friends." Her head was high, her eyes bright, her back straight, a determined pose he had seen her take before.

Setting down his empty plate, Elijah turned to his sister. "Will you excuse us please?"

"Oh! Of course!" Debby exclaimed, as though she had not known he would want privacy. She departed, no doubt intending to listen from the keeping room.

Turning back to Molly, he said, "It's not a question of excluding anyone. They'll still be welcomed here."

"Bringing a dinner bucket!" Her voice was full of disdain.

"Dearest, the embargo is on us. It is damnable. We mariners, all up and down the coast, are the ones who will pay most dearly for it, but we must face that. Pretending things are just as they have always been will do us no good, because nothing can be the same while our ports are closed. Soon, I expect, there will be shortages of necessities and certainly of luxuries. By the way, I brought you a Spanish comb."

"Thank you." She was tense and poised as though for flight, uninterested in his gift, he could see.

"We can't live as we have been, sweetheart."

"Sunday dinner doesn't cost much, Elijah. And I had the portrait stopped, and there is a fine profit from your successful voyage. Surely there'll be enough."

"There's no way to know if it'll be enough, because there's no way to know how long the embargo will last. We do have a good profit, but

I'll have to insist that we spend nothing we don't have to until the damn thing's repealed."

"I was afraid of that." Her cake uneaten, she rose and went to the front window, to look out on the low road and the trees and the path to the house. "I had hoped I could keep everything going and when you came back with all that money, we could continue with our entertainments and everyone would be happy." Her voice quavered. "And then the men would just forget about separating from the South Side."

"What? What do you mean, separate?"

"They want the North Shore to be a different town than the South Shore. Two villages, no longer just one."

Good grief! "Whatever for?" he asked, puzzled.

"They blame everything on Mr. Jefferson, the embargo and all."

"But what does that have to do with dividing the town?" he asked impatiently.

"Our district went for Mr. Jefferson in the election."

"When all the captains were gone?"

"Yes. The South-siders voted for him to a man and helped him win. Now your friends would cast them off, force them to go their own way and pay their own taxes and support their own church and eat sea worms if nothing else is available. To punish them."

"Your view seems rather harsh," he observed. "Are you sure?"

"That's how Lottie and Thomas will see it. They're proud people and would never settle for such insulting treatment. They'd leave us. And I wouldn't blame them!"

He led her back to the settee and sat beside her, hoping to calm her and learn more. "When I came ashore, Sol Denning and Tony wanted me to come with them to the academy. The armory, I mean. What can you tell me about that?"

"Oh, the armory!" she scoffed. "After all the entertainments that the ladies and I dreamed up, after the choral society had sung and an instrumental evening was conducted at Mariah's and a declamation and oratory contest held here so they could bellow to their hearts' content, they dismissed the singing teacher, formed the Second Regiment, fired our school master and took over the academy. The children all have to attend district school now. And the men want us, the ladies, to make uniforms so they can march around and look impressive."

She was very distraught now, frightened by what she saw as the erosion of the things she set such store by.

Perhaps he should leave, give her some time to calm down. "I think I'll run over there now," he said, patting her clenched hands. "Hear what they have to say."

"They'll talk you into it, I know they will. You'll fall in love with the idea, with the armory and the militia and the Committee for Correspondence and Safety . . . ."

"A Committee? What for?" Surely she was mistaken!

"It's the War for Independence all over again," she said sardonically. "They plan to secede, along with the rest of Massachusetts. The militia, led by the Committee, will defend secession if anyone tries to stop us. They have it all worked out."

Good God! "I'd better be on my way, then. There's a lot to learn."

"Don't let them petition for a new town," she pleaded. "I know they'll listen to you, Elijah. See if you can't get them to be reasonable."

"I'll do what I can," he assured her, and let himself quickly out of the house and into the clear air, away from Molly's distress. If she was right, it was obvious that the whole situation had got badly out of hand. A Committee for Correspondence and Safety, designed to defend secession, was dangerous, very dangerous, for secession could not be defended, however advantageous such a move might be for commerce. The New England states could not feed themselves, for one thing. They depended on imports, and if the southern and middle states decided to charge extortionist rates for foodstuffs, they'd have to pay it or starve. Their small hill farms alone would not be able to produce enough to satisfy the hunger of the cities.

And, then, what exactly was the seceded maritime fleet supposed to export? At present, trade involved carrying produce from the agricultural states to England and France and bringing back European refinements unavailable in America. If they seceded, the

United States might decide to carry its own commerce and boycott New England.

And then, once New England was starved into submission, there was the issue of retribution. Secession was treason, when you stopped to think about it. Secession could bring the whole American self-governing experiment down. And what would the penalty be? He didn't even want to think about it.

His mind reeled as he walked to the armory. There was too much idle time for the men because of the embargo, too much frustration at being made helpless by the government. There must be something else, he thought, to engage the minds of his friends, to divert them from pursuing secession. They were captains, accustomed to action, lots of it, all the time. Separation of the parishes, the task of organizing and running a new town, would keep everyone busy for a while. But there was Molly to consider, and all her friends whose hired help came from the South Shore. Just as Molly had said, that help would leave and the way of life they had made possible would go with them.

Was there anything else? Something to relieve some of this pressure? That would prevent angry men from making arrogant fools of themselves? Something as challenging as secession, as dangerous, as compelling, as . . . .

He stopped in his tracks and pictured the revenue cutter from which he had escaped, its sails rising up from the edge of the sea, its might and power neutralized by the escape of the William Tell. What if . . . .

Solomon Denning and John Warden were at the armory, along with Nathan King and Tony Gray and David Bradley and Jack Pollard, who had married a Denning girl two months ago when Debby again refused his suit. There were half a dozen others, and everyone had been drinking and gambling. They rose now in hearty welcome at the arrival of the newcomer, putting aside their cards, finding a chair for him, launching into a description of their plans to rectify their plight.

Secession.

"Seems pretty drastic to me," Elijah said.

They turned on him with scorn.

"Planning it, having it to rally 'round, keeps us sane is what it does," Bradley pointed out. "And it's exciting to have contact with other Committees of Correspondence, just like they did in the old days."

"There are other Committees, then?"

"Oh, yes. Many!"

It was even worse than he thought.

None of them had been old enough to fight in the War for Independence, which was taking on the patina of a hallowed cause now that its depredations were smoothed over. They clearly liked having a revolution of their own to participate in. And not just the Rockford mariners either, from the sound of it!

"And we have to think about separating the parishes too," declared Nathan. "The South Shore will oppose secession and they outnumber us. Cast them off, I say, so that our vote for secession can be heard."

Loud agreement and cheers went up.

Elijah saw that the plan to separate from the South Shore was not entirely about punishment, but in the main, Molly had conveyed it all quite as it was. Of course she wanted him to talk them out of separating the towns, but it was more important to try to dissuade them from fomenting secession. Oh, it was a good thing that he had gone home first, for it had given him time to take it all in and prepare.

"New England will not be allowed to secede," he shouted over their excitement. "The Navy has twelve ships. And now that the Barbary pirates have been brought under control, the government has nothing else to do but patrol the coast."

"We know about that," said Sam Hall. "They're patrolling it right now."

"But just think," Elijah urged, "New England's coastline extends unbroken from the Long Island Sound to New Brunswick. We can't possibly defend ourselves, and I don't believe we could secede without a fight. Think about it!"

"Secession is our right," declared Sam Hall. "Why should we allow ourselves to be crushed? The Democratic-Republicans and Thomas

Jefferson have taken our livlihood away from us. That's unconstitu-
tional!"

"Whether they have a right to do so or not, the South Shore will
never support secession," Tony said. "Why not concentrate on creating a separate town on the North Shore? Then, at least, we can vote for
secession if it comes to that."

A roar of approval rose and the captains jumped up and stamped
their feet, causing patches of ceiling plaster to flake down on them.

"Wait! Wait!" Elijah thundered. "Listen to me a minute, will
you?"

He did not want to oppose separation of the parishes. It would be
senseless to do so, since the men had obviously examined the proposi-
tion and probed it for quite a while, and everyone present was in favor.
Separating in this way was foolhardy, though, and there was Molly
to placate besides. He must try to divert their aim. "Here, Sam," he
begged, "sit down with me. David, Jack, Nathan, come, listen to this
idea."

Gradually they subsided.

"I don't oppose separation of the parishes," he told them. "But
to do it now, in the heat of this embargo fiasco, is unwise. You'll look
back and see that you've acted out of anger because the South Shore's
political views don't jibe with yours. We'd create an enemy next door,
and the bitterness between the towns would last longer than our own
lifetimes. The North and South shores will split eventually anyway,
because Rockford is getting too big to administer from one location.
So let's not lose sight of the real foe—the embargo. My friends, think
on this: might we not rally 'round a plan to escape it?"

They stared at him. The room was so quiet that the whisper of one
last twirling flake of plaster could be heard when it landed in the middle
of the table.

"How?" asked Nathan King.

"By outrunning it," Sol Denning said in a hushed voice. "Like
Elijah did."

"Omygod." John Warden took the name of the Lord in vain without even knowing he had done so.

"We don't have a ship," objected Sam Hall, ever practical.

"That," Elijah ventured, "is exactly what I meant when I suggested we might rally 'round a plan. If each of us contributed what he could, I believe there'd be enough to build one of our own."

"Build a ship!" Abner Denning, well along in drink, fell on the floor, laughing. "As though we were rich!"

"It'll repay us if it can be got to sea. We can build it in Plymouth, in an upriver boatyard where it can't be seen from the bay. We'll design it ourselves—a ship with a sharp hull and a stretch of canvas that could outsail any brig afloat and outrun the guns of the government. To carry between European ports. And keep on carrying until this nonsense has come to an end."

"Merrick," Jack Pollard sighed. "I followed you to Rockford because I thought you were a genius, but now I know. He's a genius!" he shouted to the others.

"Huzzah!" they shouted in return. "Huzzah! Huzzah!" They passed a jug of rum around.

Elijah filled with pride, with the glow of happiness that awaits a man at the center of the group he most wants to impress.

"A ship with a sharp hull wouldn't be able to carry a lot of freight," Nathan King mused. "But she'd carry something, which is a lot more than anyone's carrying now."

"And we could make up her crew so we don't have to hire one. I'm sure there are a lot of us that don't want to sit around Rockford until the end of this mess. We can all take shares in proportion to what we give, and that will be the proportion of the profit each of us gets."

"We'll all end up ahead, when the embargo is done!" David Bradley proclaimed.

Tony drew a rough sketch on the table top with a piece of charcoal. "No frigate could ever catch us if we built a ship with this much sail."

"Like a Baltimore clipper, you mean. But bigger," John exclaimed in wonder. "Of course!"

"She'd be tender with so much canvas," Elijah offered, pleased to see his inspiration greeted with so much enthusiasm. "None of us has ever mastered a vessel that large and tender."

"We can master anything," Tony bragged. "We're the best sailors in the world." This was not, they knew, a groundless boast. Immediately, they got down to business, each declaring how much money he could put into the ship. They would solicit absent captains for contributions, undercover, of course. On the spot, Elijah was picked to oversee the building of the ship at Plymouth.

Solomon Denning jumped up onto his chair and waved his mug of rum. "I move we call the new ship *Dennington!*"

"Dennington?"

"The name of our new town!"

"Wardensboro," John roared.

Well, at least they weren't talking about secession any more. But the separation issue had not left their heads.

"On what grounds would you separate?" At least he could give it another try!

"Why, you provided the reason, Elijah—Rockford's become just too big to manage. We'll separate gracefully, as you suggested. See, you are a genius," Pollard offered.

The enthusiasm filling the room made any further protest Elijah might have raised on Molly's behalf futile. It was true he'd tried, and he'd tell her so, hoping she would not hear that it was he who had provided the rationale for the split. Ruefully, he reflected on the wild course a gathering of men might take. Control of a mob was not an easy thing. Not at all. He remembered Robespierre and wished he had not.

"It's got to be Waterford," Sam Hall declared, pounding on the table. "Otherwise, someone's precious family pride will be aroused, and personally, men, I've seen enough of that. I think we've all seen enough of it."

"I certainly have," said Tony. "Why, Ben Snow hasn't once entered my house to see his own daughter."

As one, they toasted Waterford. David Bradley offered to draft a petition for the separation of the parishes.

"Can it wait until the herring have run?" Elijah asked. "I'd like help with that, and Molly is sure our South-Siders will leave when they learn we would separate parishes."

"She's probably right," John admitted ruefully. "Sure, let's keep it quiet for now."

Elijah could not help being excited about their own ship, a new design, a dream come true for any mariner. But now he would have to face his wife, convince her he had tried to prevent the formation of the new town. Acknowledging cowardice, he detoured to the beach on his way home so that he could, at last, see his new saltworks.

As he approached, he saw the sails of a U.S. frigate far out, watching Cape Cod Bay as a cat might watch a giant mouse hole.

Damn Jefferson!

Under the March sky that scowled at him, in the breeze that did not admit yet of spring, he hunched further into his coat and stared up at the vat closest to the high tide water line. Standing on stilts, twenty feet square, it was covered in its entirety with a hip-roofed hat. Rails lay to one side of each vat onto which the roof could be slid to expose the seawater to the sunshine, then slid back again to protect it from the rain. The next vat was lower, connected to the first by a trough, so when the time was right, water from the first could drain off into it, left to evaporate, then be drawn off to the next and then into the lowest vat, where the salt of highest commercial value would finally be left to scrape up, break up, haul away, and sell inland.

It looked like quite a project! Hopefully the salt would be as profitable as everyone said. If it were, he would build more vats one day, and windmills, too, so that water could be pumped instead of hauled up with buckets. He did not know how much Mayo would charge for construction, but it would be considerable, he guessed, and there was the cost of the blockade-runner to consider, too. Surely Molly understood that a big dance at this time was a foolish way to use their savings.

"Well, my dear," he announced genially upon returning home, "it was an interesting reunion with the boys."

"What was the outcome?" she asked breathlessly.

"We are going to build a ship to beat the embargo."

"What do you mean?"

"We're going to built a fast ship—very fast—then get out before any government boat can stop us. I am going to oversee it," he bragged.

"Elijah, surely that's against the law."

"Yes," he admitted, "it is."

"And if you are caught?"

"A fine, I suppose. Maybe jail for a while." This he offered calmly.

"But you wouldn't be hung, drawn and quartered?"

"This is America, Molly! Not Britain!"

She laughed a little, but clearly she was worried.

"Meanwhile, it's not a crime to build a ship. The only crime is in trying to sail her out. But no one will catch her. We're going to load her with canvas so she'll fly. And once out—well, you needn't know the details. Most people won't know them. She'll pay for herself and make money besides. That I can guarantee you, so that once this embargo business is done, we won't be poor after all."

Not being poor was a pleasant thought, and Molly latched onto it firmly, pushing her worry aside. "Well, that's a relief!" she smiled. "Was it your idea, Elijah? I'll wager it was!"

"Well, yes," he admitted modestly.

"And I'd be very surprised if you didn't do it to keep their minds off separating the parishes."

"Well," he hedged, wishing the topic would go away. "I did try to divert them, that's true. But I was unsuccessful, Molly. I'm sorry, but they're hell-bent on both—the new ship and the new town. They've decided to call it Waterford. Honoring our ford, by the mills."

"Waterford," she repeated flatly. "How nice."

Her relief over being rescued from penury was short-lived, he saw. "Sweetheart, maybe not every South-Sider will desert," he said as gently as he could. "Maybe the Coys will stay."

"I doubt it," she snapped. "I hope you look forward to pitching hay."
Turning away, she made to leave him. But it would lead to greater difficulty, he reasoned, if he let her stalk off now; the facts had to be faced,
and there was no point in being childish about it. She was half way up the
stairs before he caught up with her.

"Stop it," he commanded. "I will not have you running away
like a three-year-old child, Molly. You have had a good life and have
enjoyed it. I think it's not asking too much to support our friends now."

"Leave me alone, Elijah. I don't want to talk about it anymore.
It's too late for talk. The issue has already been decided, has it not?"

"Sweetheart, there's no point in sulking. We are face to face with
their decisions and need to do our part. We live here, after all, and must
be seen as one with them."

"Lottie will never come back." Molly nearly wept as she spoke.

"That's probably true," he admitted, "and I'm sorry. I really am.
But after the embargo is lifted, I'll bring a girl down from Boston—a
redemptioner, maybe, —and you'll be able to live stylishly again. We'll
be able to afford it if our plans to get out succeed."

"Yes, yes, it would have to be a redemptioner," she pouted. "No
farmer's daughter, North or South, would stoop to serve us once we're
rich again. They envy us."

"Probably they do." He led her back to the parlor. "I'm sure we
can get a lot of herring in before the division is made public. I'll help
when the Coys leave. The children will do much of the work around the
house. Salt will provide us some cash, and even after I pay my share of
the new ship, there'll be some of the profit left from the *William Tell*.
We'll be able to get through next winter, Molly. My guess is that the
embargo will be lifted by then. Meanwhile, let me cheer you—please,
darling, don't look so sad! The petition to divide the town is not yet
written, not yet approved by the General Court, and the Coys haven't
left yet. I'll tell you what, my beloved," he proffered, reversing his
thinking of only half an hour ago. "Hire the dance master and a fiddler
for the ball you and Debby planned. We'll have a splendid occasion,
and we'll provide the food and drink for all our friends—anyone you

want to invite. A gala event just now would be good for us all and a fit christening of our new ship. We'll show the world that we don't give a fig for Jefferson's embargo."

Her face brightened. "Really, Elijah? It won't be cheap if we pay for the refreshments."

"We will disregard the cost," he said manfully, shutting his mind to the portrait, the soirees and the Sunday repasts of the past few months. "It's the last time we'll be able to do anything like this for a while, and I think we should do it in style as only you, Molly Merrick, can! What say you?"

"I say, thank you," she smiled tremulously. "I say that I admire your spirit, and I shall try to be equal to it. Our dance will be remembered for years!"

He enjoyed the light of admiration in her eyes, her happiness with the upcoming festivity, her gratitude to him for allowing it. She had come through better than he had thought she would, and he could see that she was truly trying to live up to his expectation of her. Perhaps she had finally adjusted herself to the idea of a simpler life, to the idea of the new town and the change it would mean for them all.

Perhaps she was growing up.

The Dance

IMAGINE! Homemade decorations! Indignant, Molly laid out scissors and thread. Her needles and pins were skewered to a strip of muslin and each one was counted, for their price had risen; Snow declared he could get no more in Boston. In the middle of the dining room table she piled brightly-colored snippets of cloth: red, blue, yellow, pink, green. Her guests would cut out circles, gather them in the middle, bind them with thread, fan out the edges and hitch them to lengths of twine. Thus were garlands of flowers produced for Molly Merrick's dance. Six delicate teacups were laid out on the sideboard, beside the Merrick silver service. Tea, at least, was still available; she would serve it to her friends without the accompaniment of pastry or cake, for Elijah had forbidden it. Really! How much did cake for six ladies cost? He was going too far!

Her scorn turned to tears, which she tried to blink away.

The women would come to her house today dressed for a party because there were no other occasions where fine clothes could be worn. They would drink tea and make flowers and talk about the things she liked to hear. All of them would carry on as if nothing at all were wrong, just as Molly had tried to do before Elijah came home. But when the dance was over, they would have only the dinner breaks on Sundays with everybody bringing their pails. There would be nothing to plan and talk about besides the oppression of miserly husbands and demanding children, whom the women would most likely have to care for without the help of their South-Shore servants, once word of the separation got out. They could compare their pregnancies too, for more than likely a new crop of babies would appear within the year.

That, at least, was not one of Molly's worries. The doctor told her she would conceive no more children as a result of the fever following Sonny's birth. Probably she should be thankful, but a new baby just now would have occupied her attention and helped to distract her.

When she had received Elijah's letter four months ago, written before he set sail for Cadiz, she had understood he'd wanted all her entertainments stopped, just as he had wanted the portrait stopped. But she could not obey him. She dared not face the endless march of days with nothing to occupy her mind, for she knew Isaac Warden's presence would fill her thoughts, even though he was far off in New York. So she continued the sittings, with her circle gathered around admiringly. It had worked like a charm, just as she expected. But she had known better than to allow the painter to complete his work and had him fill in the background with swirls of gray instead of the landscape she'd envisioned, then unhappily dismissed him.

A handsome portrait, even if unusual.

As the captains came home, one by one, she had kept right on with her Sunday luncheons and Saturday soirees. With the members of her circle, she labored incessantly to devise entertainments for the men—recitals and readings and debates. But as men will, they persisted with their own interests anyway, organizing the militia and ruining the school, dismissing the choral society's director and quietly agitating in favor of dividing the Parishes, which was sure to alienate their South Shore servants.

With aplomb she had managed the Sunday noontime meals and Saturday soirees, assuring her guests that Elijah could afford them because he had beat the embargo and his cargo would realize a fine profit. And indeed she had foolishly hoped the profit would make possible the continuation of their life as it had always been, holding her attention and shutting thoughts of Isaac out as it had done these past few months.

But there was no hope of that now. A builder for the new ship had been found near Plymouth. Elijah had forbidden everything but the dance and Sunday dinners. He had tried to be companionable when he was at home in the evenings, but he was so absorbed in the ship—where much of the profit from his last voyage had been squandered—that he paid her little heed. Ignored, like an unwanted child, her anger smoldered.

Now he was netting herring at the run. The men had delayed their work on separating the parishes until the spring migration was over. Thomas and Elijah had gone to the millstream every afternoon this week. Lottie was in the barnyard, slitting and cleaning the creatures, their offal in a pile for Thomas to take out to the fields.

The only bright spot was the dance—thank God for the dance—and into it Molly threw herself with vigor. She had sent elaborate invitations, writing them on her elegant stationery, sealing them with wax on which she stamped a curlicued letter "M". She hired the dancing master who had initially taught them their steps, and, of course, his preferred fiddler from Yarmouth. At this afternoon's tea, the most favored of Molly's circle would make as many garlands as they could. Thomas would hang them strategically so that the herring, drying in the rafters, would be hidden. The effect—if not the odor—would be one of having entered an immense garden filled with passable, if unidentifiable, blossoms. Thomas had cut down young maple trees, not quite in leaf yet, and set them in pots of sand. Their branches would be adorned with the cloth flowers, and together with the garlands, would complete the effect of making it seem as if spring had arrived early in the Merrick barn.

A platform had been constructed for the fiddler and the dancing master, a table set up nearby for the punch. Refreshments would consist of cake and wine—the former baked by Lottie and Debby with ingredients bought out of Elijah's reluctant largess. The female guests had happily pondered the problem of clothing. Their dress could not be too formal for such an atmosphere, and must be easily handled, too, for the dancing would get very lively. Since new dresses could not be bought, they had set to making over their old ones. This effort made Molly Merrick's dance even more interesting, for it was a matter keenly important to them, to see who could compose the best garment of the lot all by herself. No one could afford a seamstress.

To Molly's dismay, this very morning Elijah mentioned that representatives of the Committee for Correspondence and Safety would be going to Plymouth for the week, to review the blueprints and any contractual changes with the shipwright.

The Committee involved most of Rockford's captains.

"Will you be back in time?" she demanded. "I can't very well have a successful dance if you're not here to be my host and partner. And if everyone's husband is in Plymouth with you." It was hard to keep the aggravation out of her voice, and she knew she was unsuccessful.

"Only Jack and David and John will be going with me," he explained patiently. "If they don't make it back in time, Tony can bring their wives."

"Elijah! Who will they dance with?" She knew her voice had become shrill.

"Now, now," he soothed. "If the men are satisfied with the blueprints, I'll send them home early. If changes to the agreement are needed, I can draw them up and bring them back to the Committee."

"So they'll be here, but you might not?"

"The dance is Friday, is it not? I'm quite sure I'll be back by then." He was overly genial, probably due to a bad conscience.

It would have done no good to suggest the Committee wait until the following week. Men are only grown up boys, she thought. They'll do just what they like, and they'll do it when it pleases them. Resolutely, she put these rebellious thought away and tried to smile. "Very well. I expect Cousin Nathan can escort both Debby and me, if need be."

Fortunately the dress she would wear absorbed her attention; she worked on it avidly to avoid fretting. It would be the finest, most beautifully-designed outfit in the barn. The bodice was made from one old garment, the skirts from another, with lots of lace from this gown and that. To complement her jewelry, she trimmed her shoes with gold braid. Many of her dresses were defaced in the making of just this one, but better times to come would allow her to replace all of them.

The doorknocker resounded through the house; afternoon tea was about to begin. It would be fun—they would make it so. Fun is what we do best, Molly thought bitterly, and hastened to the door, threw it open.

"Welcome," she cried. "It's flower making time!"

※※※

The intoxicating lilt of the fiddler warming up filled the early evening as she made her way to the barn on Nathan's arm, with Debby on the other side. Its gaiety allowed her to dismiss the fact that although the other Committee members had returned from Plymouth, Elijah had not. They would dance without him; however, because of his absence, there would be an uneven number. All the men would be gallant and attentive, and would dance with her if need be, but Molly could not allow any of her friends to be left out. There'd be an odd person, and that person would be her. She'd have to be an observer for most of the evening.

Still, it was a party. A grand party! The excitement of it lured her out of her vexation. Behind her, the beautiful house glowed like a lantern, with candles in all the windows. Its dining room was set for the refreshments that Lottie would serve later. Candles standing in little boxes of sand, which Thomas would light later, lined the path between the house and barn. Within the barn, a table ablaze with fabric flowers held two huge bowls of punch to slake the dancers' thirst; one with rum, one without.

Debby and Nathan took up places at the double-wide door to bid welcome to the guests. Nearby, Molly greeted them and showed them to the now-pristine stalls where they might hang up their cloaks. Their beaming faces and excited voices told her that the evening was one they all looked forward to. While the guests warmed themselves up at the punch bowl, the fiddler continued to play happy tunes. An adequate supply of punch was on the platform for him and the dancing master, but with only a small quota of rum added. Both needed to remain sober for as long as possible.

Most guests had arrived and the barn looked full. She made her way over to the master.

"I believe we can begin, sir," she called up to him.

He conferred with the fiddler while she turned to the crowd, raising her hands high. "It's time!" she cried. At that moment, she noticed latecomers in the doorway. Ah! John and Mariah, tardy as usual. Then she saw him entering just behind them, impeccably dressed and impossibly handsome.

Isaac Warden.

Shocked, her arms dropped. The dancing master took this to mean that the first dance should start this instant.

"Form the Round!" he announced. "Ladies on the inside, gentlemen on the out." The fiddler struck up the introduction.

She could hardly think as the group arranged itself along the perimeter of the dance floor. Isaac Warden joined the circle; she must join it too, else there be an uneven number. Her heart beat hard, and her hands were suddenly cold as the fiddler soared off, finished the preamble and held the final note.

The women lifted their skirts just high enough to reveal a tantalizing inch of ruffled petticoat, and curtseyed. The men bowed and the circling began. Molly dipped to David Bradley, took his hand and changed places with him, balanced, passed back to the inside in a twirl beneath his arm. The men moved left; she now faced Sol Denning. He bowed, she curtseyed, they changed places and balanced, and she was twirled back to the inside circle, her skirts flaring wide, her gold-trimmed shoes flashing. All the while Isaac was moving closer as the women wove in and out through the circle of men.

"Good evening, Mistress Merrick." He bowed as she dipped. His smile was easy and assured, his eyes assessing her dress, her face, her hair.

"Good evening, Master Warden," she said as cheerfully as she could, over the pounding in her ears.

Was there ever a man so handsome?

"I am visiting my brother," he explained. "Mariah assured me you wouldn't mind if I came along with them."

They took one another's hand and changed places with the little step-hop-step the master had taught them all, something Isaac seemed to do quite easily. As they balanced, she said politely, "We are always pleased to have you," then twirled beneath his arm and dipped to Nathan King.

How can it be? she asked herself, repeating the steps with Nate and moving on to Jack Pollard and then to Tony. She had worked so hard to put him out of her mind! All that effort was undone now by the fact of his presence.

Here he was coming 'round again. The dance was acquiring new steps, now that the initial circling had been completed. This time, they would dip, promenade, balance, promenade in the opposite direction, circle 'round their partner, and then the women would be double-twirled to the next man.

When he met her again, Isaac said in a low voice, "You're looking especially lovely tonight, Mistress Merrick." His eyes looked deeply into hers.

"Thank you," she responded, properly.

They promenaded.

"I see that your husband is not present," he observed as they balanced and promenaded again. "When the master calls the first minuet, I hope I may have the honor of being your partner." They circled 'round and he twirled her twice, spinning her so vigorously that she had no opportunity to answer.

The first minuet called for husbands and wives to dance with each other, and here she was without a husband. And so it was that when the master, having done himself proud by his circle dance, announced the minuet, she could not refuse John's brother without everyone noticing and wondering why she was being inhospitable to him.

"Mistress, may I?" He held out his hand and she took it. The master called the steps before the music began in an effort to refresh the memory of those who had forgotten, but Isaac needed no instruction, Molly saw. He had probably been in great demand at dances in English society, and in New York.

"To what do we owe the pleasure of your company, Master Warden?" she asked as coolly as she could. "When we last saw you, a career in the big city awaited you."

"Ah," he smiled. "It seems I have lost my situation. I thought I would wait a while in Yarmouth with my parents, until the embargo lifts. Employment is hard to find these days."

This was not true for lawyers, she knew. They were in great demand, with the embargo creating a mass of unpaid and unpayable debts, and much litigation surrounding them.

"In any case, it is pleasant to have your company, sir," she made herself say with lilting gaiety, "but I must hope we do not have it for long. If Mr. Jefferson persists in this folly, we all shall be consigned to the poor farm! No dancing there."

"From the looks of it, you and Elijah are not going to perish." He glanced at the ceiling. "Or go hungry. You've put by a lot of herring, and are having a great party. Knowing you, there will be many more to come."

"It's a farewell party, I'm afraid. There won't be another until shipping starts up again. But we will go out in style!"

"I'm glad I was here to witness such an occasion," he returned as they finished the dance, he bowing, she curtseying. She hastened to the refreshment table and her duties as hostess.

For the rest of the evening, she dodged him. When the guests left the barn at last, strolling to the house along the path lit by candles, there to indulge themselves in the refreshments, she kept herself busy helping Debby serve their friends. She was her usual witty and charming self, and was careful to treat Isaac no differently than anyone else. No one would be able to detect the slightest evidence of any feeling she might have about him, she was sure.

When the door closed on the last of the guests, she set to clearing away the remains with Debby and Lottie, chatting about the party as they did so. But then she was hit with the full impact of knowing she must never mention him, and be equally prepared to have no reaction when someone else did. Even now, Debby was saying she would marry Isaac Warden herself if she had the chance, and wasn't he so very good-looking? And Molly must laugh along with Lottie, pretending to heedless abandon.

Claiming fatigue, she left them, crawling upstairs and burrowing into the hollow on her side of the bed, there to lie and stare blankly at the curtains swaying in the breeze of the spring night.

How often would he be visiting John and Mariah, she wondered? The masquerade of not caring would have to be maintained at all costs, especially if he were present.

But even more difficult was the problem of keeping him out of her thoughts, which would be harder knowing he was back on Cape Cod. For the first time, she found herself glad that the Coys would be leaving soon—she would be submerged in the endless work of housewifery, too busy to worry about her fear of Isaac Warden and the power he yet held over her.

✦≈≈ 2 ≈≈✦

Elijah became even more involved in the new vessel and the Second Regiment. Nearly all his time was spent at the armory, where he huddled with the Committee for Correspondence and Safety, communicating with other Committees and making plans for the *Swift Avenger,* their name for the ship.

Small groups of men continually journeyed by land to Plymouth, simply to gape at the rapidly-building vessel, admiring her lines and curves as they would those of a naked woman. The *Avenger* became the mistress of each mariner who had a stake in her, and she had captivated Elijah completely.

When the petition to divide the town was approved, Lottie and Thomas packed their bags. They left even before a formal protest from the South Side was filed in Boston and conveniently lost, with the assistance of a Federalist sympathizer. Within a few weeks, every South-Sider who served a North Shore mariner was gone. It was their retaliation, leaving the wealthy to tend their own land and their own hearths, shovel their own manure and pitch their own hay, gather their own eggs and polish their own boots and care for their own children.

"They'll be back," Elijah assured her. "The embargo weighs on them, too; they're hungry. Lottie and Thomas will be back, Molly."

"They'd starve first," she said sadly. "And you'd probably feel we couldn't afford to pay them, even if they were willing to return."

Clearly he was heartened by this evidence of her understanding of the exigencies of the situation. Kissing her hand, he said, "I'll try my best to help you, sweetheart. There must be some household chores I can do."

She could not help smiling at the image of Elijah with flour up to his elbows, kneading dough.

"I'll spin and weave," Debby declared. "I'm good at it. Or, at least, I was until you spoiled me, Molly!"

"Mother can do the weaving," Elijah put in quickly. Into the silence, he said, "We'll have to bring her over here. I can't run two households. She can take Jon's old room; we'll set the loom up in there."

Mother! Not only would they all work like indentured servants, but Mother would be here, too!

"I'll take care of the fields and the barn, with boys' help, if you ladies will attend to the children and the house. And I'll carry water for you," Elijah told Molly, trying to cheer her up.

"Thanks," she said lamely. "That will be lovely."

He gave her a long look, but wisely said no more.

Again she was a maid, scrubbing and cleaning and baking, cooking at the hearth and scouring the pots. Mother, for the most part, avoided Molly even as Molly avoided her. Sarah and Elizabeth helped with dusting and sweeping. 'Lije fed the horses and hens and gathered their eggs and brought in wood for the fire. Elijah made an effort to be home more; he lugged the wash buckets into the house and lugged them out again when they needed emptying. Debby helped her mother; everyone minded Sonny, and Susannah followed her sisters, whining and complaining because they would not play with her.

All of them were like the ox in the Bible that went around and around, pulling a millstone. Pastor Simmonds talked about that once in awhile, Molly knew not why. But there they were, going 'round and 'round, doing the same things day after day. Elijah went 'round and 'round, too, but for him, beneath the labor of farming and making salt, there lay the dream of *Swift Avenger*, while beneath Molly's unceasing chores, there was only the secret place wherein dwelt Isaac Warden.

It was a struggle, trying to keep her mind on her tasks to stem the drifting, drifting of her thoughts as each day passed, warmer than the one before, and summer slowly arrived.

❋

It was high noon and hot the day she was wrestling with the decapitated hen. The larger feathers had stripped away easily, but the down of the breast stuck to her bloodstained hands and sweaty face. Her hair drooped and tickled her nose, completing her misery, and she was ready to cry when behind her, his voice, cool and refreshing, cut through the heat and wretchedness.

"Mistress Mariah wishes you would come for tea."

Jumping up in alarm, she dropped the hen in the dust, turned to find him laughing at her. He was dressed casually in an immaculate white linen shirt, full-sleeved to the cuff and open at the throat, his nankeen trousers tucked neatly into calf-high riding boots of lustrous leather.

Mute and mortified, covered with sweat and feathers, she was again a servant in the household of Elizabeth Warden, lowly and humble. She stooped to retrieve the partially plucked bird.

"It's amazing. No matter what you're doing, Mistress Merrick, you are beautiful."

She would have been glad to expire on the spot, but straightened her shoulders and held her head high. "I've always been partial to feathers," she said airily.

"I'm staying at my brother's house for a few days. Mariah thought it would be pleasant if you could visit with her and sent me to ask you. I have her chaise, and can fetch you there now."

The Warden house was filled with Mariah's relations who visited continuously and helped her with the work so she could wile away an hour when she chose. Lucky girl!

"I am unable to accept the invitation," she said formally. "I have an engagement with this bird. Please convey my regrets." Brushing the dust off the hen, she examined it closely so she would not have to look at him.

"Would tomorrow be better?" he asked softly. "When you can plan it?"

Elijah was in Plymouth for the week. Around one thirty Mother would take her afternoon nap. Her hearing was much diminished with age and she would never hear the chaise leaving.

"All right," she heard herself say as she fought the undertow. "Around two o'clock. I'll drive over myself." She refused to watch him leave, which would suggest that it mattered. It did not.

It must not.

Furiously she pulled off the remaining feathers, flinging them into the air to drift and fall like early snow. Eviscerating the bird, she threw it into the stew pot hanging over the fire, gathered the clean shirts from the orchard where she'd hung them this morning, and plucked green beans from the kitchen garden for supper. As she worked, she tried to sort through her confused thoughts.

Isaac was behaving very well, courteous and respectful. Yet she had known him to be wholly untrustworthy once, taking unfair advantage of her when she was still so innocent. Could she believe that he really was the person he presented now? And even if he had changed, what difference did that make? Her loyalty was to Elijah—she was a married woman. Tomorrow she would go to Mariah's house for a welcomed interlude from this ceaseless round, and that, she told herself, would be the only reason. She could only hope that John's brother would have already gone back to Yarmouth by then.

The next afternoon she parked the chaise and Florida, the Merrick trotter, in the shade of the Warden's backyard. It was quiet throughout the house. "Everyone's asleep," Mariah explained. "The heat is tiring. But no nap for me! It's my time to enjoy myself!"

They took their ease together, drank tea, talked about their children and the Committee for Correspondence and Safety and Pastor Simmonds' latest sermon, which they agreed was more excruciatingly boring than usual.

Isaac was not there.

Both relieved and disheartened, Molly sipped her tea and finished mending a skirt she'd brought along.

"It's so refreshing to get away," she told Mariah as she rose to leave. "Let's get together again sometime. Do visit us—Debby would enjoy seeing you, too."

"With all she does, I'm sure she could use a respite," Mariah agreed. "So first, I shall invite her to come here. Then I'll visit your house—with my mending in hand, so your mother-in-law won't complain." All of Molly's inner circle understood the menace that was Mother Merrick.

She kissed her friend's cheek and left by the keeping room door.

He was waiting for her at the chaise, patting Florida, feeding her carrots from the family garden. This day he was clad in disreputable clothes—baggy pants, a shabby shirt, mud-caked boots. At his feet was a satchel of fish.

"I thought my catch would spoil before you came out," he said. "I could hardly go in and get you, seeing as how I'm not fit for the parlor!" His smile lit the landscape of her soul.

"You look fit enough," she said, and thought it remarkable that he still seemed like a prince for all his disarray.

"I have caught a lot of bass. Would you like some for supper?"

"Thank you very much. We would enjoy them."

He slipped several onto the floor of the chaise. "No chicken feathers today, I see."

"What a sight I must have been!" She could not stop herself from giggling, both because he was there, waiting, and because she must have looked ludicrously awful yesterday.

Bowing, he said, "You are always a sight to behold, my dear Molly." Her laughter allowed her to avoid acknowledging his compliment. "Today I shall exchange feathers for scales when I prepare your fish for supper!"

"Even better. You'll be head to toe spangles, shining in the sun." In the warmth of the afternoon, his face reflected affection, and she thought that she had not felt so happy for a long, long time.

"I'm always finding scales in my hair. And there are always more left on the fish than I take off."

"Your hair is lovely as ever."

"I . . . " She stopped and looked at him honestly for the first time, neither hiding nor pretending to, and found to her surprise that he was not hiding, either.

"The years have not touched you," he said softly. "You could pass for twenty. The gamble—has it worked?"

"Gamble?"

"Of being Elijah's wife. Did it work?"

Her husband's name brought her back to the role she must play. "That it did, Isaac," she replied, her gaze level. "That it did—until the present, of course, when all of us gamblers have lost the game and must wait for the cards to be dealt out again."

"I'm glad it worked for you." His sincerity could not be doubted. "You deserved it," he added as he helped her up into the chaise, checked the bit and bridle, patted the mare and murmured soothing words to her that Molly could not hear. Florida was quiet, breathing moistly, her head pressed against his chest as she was wont to do with men. Isaac fondled those fuzzy ears, then looked up, the message in his eyes causing her blood to stop its coursing, muffling the sounds of the summer afternoon.

He stepped back and watched her drive away.

Her brain was a hurricane: joy darted here, despair dashed there, excitement leaped up, trepidation brought it low. Finally home, she detached Florida from the chaise and led her to the enclosed pasture, released her from the bridle and reins, leaned on the fence, remembering. Because of the message in his eyes—a message she understood only too well—it would be harder, if not impossible, to put Isaac out of her mind. But really, she decided, there was no harm in just thinking. It provided a pleasant contrast to reality, just as the new ship gave Elijah pleasure. She needed a little! And so she stood a while longer at the fence and watched the swallows darting and diving in the afternoon sun and allowed herself the pleasure of further recollection.

∞✦∞

Without having planned it, the men gathered the following Saturday evening at the Merrick house, drifting in after supper, all of them bone tired. Molly and Debby filled the punch bowl with tepid tea and added the contributions of the guests who had brought a little something, alcoholic or otherwise. Mother Merrick looked askance at the concoction and retired with a sniff to her room where she knitted sanctimoniously, freeing them all from her depressing presence.

Elijah was looking weary, Molly thought; the strain of planning *Avenger* besides all his field chores and salt making was beginning to tell. Waiting for him to catch up with her at the buffet, her smile was warm and encouraging, but he was so immersed in thought that his returning smile was a distracted one.

Then he looked into the hall. Entering with John Warden was Isaac.

"Look who's here," he grumbled, frowning.

"Hmmmm," she murmured with what she hoped sounded like boredom.

"Being John's brother, there's not much we can do about it," Elijah said glumly. He left her side to welcome them both, as Molly had taught him to do. She did not join him, but stayed in place at the buffet and spoke with the men who wandered in to get punch, collecting herself so she would be cool and unflurried when Isaac came by.

Eventually he made his way there. "Mistress Merrick, good evening."

"Good evening, Master Warden. Visiting your brother again?"

"I never left," he answered, watching her.

"Would you enjoy a libation, which has no name as yet?" she asked, gesturing toward the punch bowl.

"I would indeed." He filled a mug. "May I say something rather private to you?" he asked softly.

Conscious of the men around her, she murmured, "I'd rather you didn't, Isaac. I'd rather you went back to the parlor."

But still he stood there beside her; he did not go, and Elijah's friends were starting to glance their way.

"Please! The men are staring at us."

"Will you forgive me, Molly, for my mistake so long ago?"

Startled, she replied with blunt honesty. "How can I? You nearly destroyed me. Excuse me, please."

Obligingly, he stepped back as she edged past him and into the keeping room where she put the bean pot on the warming shelf for tomorrow's breakfast and escaped up the kitchen stairs.

The sheets were cool on her cheek when she drifted back from sleep the next morning. Elijah's side of their bed was an empty hollow; he had already left, to ride up to Plymouth with John. Air stirred the white muslin curtains and smelled fresh. Land breeze, she thought, and lay snuggled and content, feeling clean as the morning. Listening for the sounds of the household, she heard Debby's voice chatting with Mother and the children, no doubt making porridge for them all. There was no immediate need for rising; the moment was hers alone, a rare occurrence since Lottie had left. She luxuriated in it, and allowed her thoughts free rein.

Of course they were of Isaac. How could they not be?

It seemed that he really had changed, that he was no longer a selfish and spoiled youth. He was sorry for what he had done, found her beautiful still. Creeping up her spine was a tingle of anticipation, as though her life still held promise; she knew why, and knew she must turn from it.

Into the busyness of the day she hurried, briskly organizing the children into a brigade of window washers while she and Debby beat carpets and polished brass. Then it was noon and time for dinner, after which Debby took the littlest children upstairs to rest while she read to them. The older ones were sent to the garden to unhappily hoe weeds.

Molly poured Mother a cup of tea, and then heard knocking. Guardedly, she went to the front door, knowing who would be there.

"Good day, Mistress Molly," Isaac greeted her.

"Master Warden," she returned, and waited to see what would come next.

"Mariah wishes Miss Debby would come for tea tomorrow."

"I'll ask her," Molly answered, quickly turning toward the stairs.

"Wait! Please!"

She stopped.

"There's more I must say," he pleaded. "I want you to know that my apology last night was sincere."

Looking at him, she saw admiration reflected in his eyes, and longing too, his handsome face sober and his mouth grim in his determination to let her know that his heart held her to him even if his arms did not. She could not contain the rising up of hope, irresistible, the soaring up of happiness, irrepressible.

Isaac! Isaac!

"You must leave," she whispered.

"Oh, Molly, there is so much I wish to tell you. Could you meet me somewhere that we could speak privately? I'll lose my mind if I can't talk with you!"

"I can't meet you," she said simply.

"John went to Plymouth with Elijah and they will spend the night in the tavern there—is that not so?"

She could not deny it.

"Meet me at Elijah's salt vats this evening."

"No," she replied softly.

"There will be no moon. Wear dark clothing; no one will see you."

She shook her head.

"I'll be there, Molly, waiting for you."

He turned and left, mounted his horse, rode off without waiting to find out if Miss Debby would visit Mariah the next afternoon.

He had come for her.

As surely as the tide rose, as surely as the summer wind came in from the southwest, as surely as the small dark ducks appeared each winter, riding the swells of the bay, he had come for her. She knew it with certainty, in the manner women knew such things.

And he would be coming to her tonight.

Would the house ever settle down? Would the whole night waste and wane while she, trapped upstairs, was helpless to prevent it? Sonny said he was hot and could not sleep. 'Lije complained that Sonny was keeping him awake. Susannah had a bad dream only an hour after she went to bed and then demanded one drink of water after the other, with subsequent need of the chamber pot. Elizabeth complained that Susannah's needs for the pot were disturbing her, while Sarah said they were both bothering her and would Mama do something about it?

Molly sat fully clothed in the darkness. If you're not able to leave, she told herself, because everyone's awake, that would put an end to it, would it not?

Perhaps, she mused. Or perhaps he would simply reappear at the front door. The decision to meet has been taken out of my hands, she thought. I am forced to comply lest he come again and corner me and we be discovered. Maybe it will be all right. We will simply talk, as he so wants to do, and maybe that will satisfy him.

But she was afraid it would not satisfy her.

It was very, very late when at last she let herself out into the night, moving stealthily past Mother's door, past the barn where, thankfully, Florida must have been dozing and whickered no greeting. Once she reached the crest of land behind the house, she started running toward the village of vats, then slowed as she drew near so she could catch her breath.

At the vat closest to the water and furthest from the house, he was waiting for her. It was a quiet night, she realized; all she could hear was her own labored breathing. He said nothing, allowing her to catch her breath; he did not hurry. Isaac Warden never hurried.

At last, his voice low, he spoke. "I can assure you that I will not impose on you this way again, Molly. I know the risks it involves for you. But I must know . . . I wanted to ask . . . I needed to find out . . . if you can forgive what I did, if there is any way I can make it up to you."

His stumbling over words surprised her; he was normally so composed. "Such a thing cannot be rectified," she heard her voice saying into the quiet darkness, and marveled that she could speak so dispassionately. His very presence beside her was as a magnet; she fought its pull. "If you care about me, you will leave me alone." It broke her heart to say it, yet she knew she must.

In the distance, far over the bay, a gull laughed.

"I had that coming," he said at last. "And you are right. If I continue to pursue you in this way, I prove that I love only myself. But it is not so. I love you, Molly. I have loved you for years, and I shall prove it. I shall just wait, instead."

He had loved her for years! He must have loved her when she was yet a maid in his parents' house! Her head swam.

"What will you wait for?" she managed to ask.

"For you to come to me."

And be ruined.

"I will not," she forced herself to say. "You need not wait, Isaac."

He drew a deep breath, let it out again. "In London, and in New York, I had tried to forget you, and all that time, I failed. All these years, I've searched and searched and can find no one like you. So I came back to tell you that I am sorry for what happened so long ago in the woods. It was not simply the act of a cad who forgot it as soon as it was done. When I saw you at your party, Molly, with that ruby around your throat and your gown gathered beneath your breasts and ribbons in your hair, I was sure."

"It is too late," she mourned, desolate. "It's too late. Go away. Now."

"Very well," he said calmly. "I shall, for only then will you believe that I would not harm you, that I regret deeply what I did to you."

"Thank you for telling me," she said, her voice low, barely audible even to herself.

"Remember. I will be waiting."

"Just go!" she cried desperately.

He did. There one moment, he melted away into darkness the next, while Molly lingered a long time beneath the vat, gathering up the disordered pieces of her life.

✦∞ 3 ∞✦

The days that followed were unreal, and her presence in them seemed insubstantial, like a shadow, as she tried to keep a steady course.

There were two worlds, one inhabited by herself who ran the house as before, who scrubbed the clothes and hung them to dry in the low-slung branches of the young orchard Thomas Coy planted several years before. The homely world where she set the children to gathering bayberries for making candles, which she could no longer buy at Snow's store. Where she helped Elijah reap the harvest, burying the root crops in boxes of sand to store beneath the house, hanging onions and herbs in the keeping room, drying beans and corn and peas for soups and chowders during the winter to come.

The other world lay deep within, without definition or limit, where no breath was breathed, where no breeze stirred, where everything was hushed and stilled, peaceful, yet on the narrow edge of erupting uncontrollably, awake to all nuances, beating with the very essence of life. Yet so well concealed that no one could find it, not even Molly herself, until she paused in her rounds of chores. Whenever she had a few minutes alone, she was suddenly in the middle of that other world. In its fathomless depths, she did lose herself, stealing quietly into its hushed stillness where Isaac waited.

Unencumbered now by the past and its pain, she was free to dream. That of course, was all she could do. Nothing would ever come of those dreams. Ever.

She clung to the safeguards of her life, all of them more precious than before—to her children, to Debby, to Elijah and the loyalty she owned him. Even to Mother Merrick, who would keep her on the strait and narrow path whether she wanted to follow it or not.

The hull of the *Avenger* was ready, her masts stepped. The men of Waterford, having shipped their salt inland, having stacked their hay and wood for the winter, set up camp in the Plymouth woods so they could help with the painting and caulking and rigging. Soon they would draw lots for crew. Elijah must lose! Then he would be home for the winter and the duration of the embargo, and surely his increased presence would be sufficient to tame and finally extinguish the inner world that lured her away. There would be no hope for it to feed upon, and it would not be abetted by loneliness. Her husband would be attentive again, probably more amorous, certainly more entertaining than this distracted man who came home now only when he had to.

The day they pulled names out of a hat, she knew he had not been selected; his shoulders sagged, his head hung low with disappointment when he came back from the drawing to tell her.

"Dearest, I must confess that I'm not sorry at all!" she said, clinging to his arm, trying to make him look at her so he would see that she needed him to be with her, and that she wanted him here. "With all the field work done and the ship gone, why, we'll have time to spend together, snug at our hearth this winter. Won't that be pleasant?"

"Of course, of course," he nodded, patting her hand but avoiding her eyes, most likely hoping to hide the truth of the matter: he would rather be out with the ship.

"You say John will be home, too, and Sam and Sol," Molly continued. "Lots of the men, as many as will be leaving. You won't lack for companionship, and the Committee can still correspond."

"Yes, yes," he agreed absently, and drank large quantities of rum that night.

All of the men, even those not sailing, camped in Plymouth now, waiting on the wind and tide. The ship was ready. It would be a tricky departure, south, to clear the Duxbury peninsula, then northeast across Cape Cod Bay and out to open water. That was where they would be most vulnerable should a government vessel be cruising near Boston or Provincetown. Tony, who had won captain's spot, would need a night tide and an off-shore breeze. At home, the women waited. They would not know the outcome until their men retuned. Olive visited daily, to pass the time and to stem her anxiety.

"If he's caught, what do you think will happen to him?" she wondered.

"Elijah says jail, until the embargo is lifted," Molly reported.

"Will they punish him? Beat him?"

"I think jail's considered punishment enough." Molly replied, assuringly.

"All the others will go to jail too, won't they?" Olive fretted. "He won't be the only one, even though he's captain?"

"I'm sure they'll all be together," Molly soothed, without knowing anything of the kind.

A week passed, the weather slowly deteriorating. Then the thunder began, and the skies darkened as the wind shifted. Everyone huddled around the hearth—the children and Debby and even Mother. The change in wind direction meant the ship could leave. They waited, and waited, then rain was flung against the windows and the wind became stronger. Still they waited until, at last, the door latch rattled and John Warden stumbled across the threshold.

With exclamations of joy and concern, they jumped up to greet him, fetched a blanket, poured hot tea, located Elijah's rum, and crowded 'round.

"She's gone, I trust," Molly said.

"Aye. Around five o'clock this morning. We didn't spot a sail; it was dark enough to hide ours, and the storm drove the ship right out into the bay and deep water before sunrise."

He laced his tea heavily with the rum. Something was wrong, out of alignment.

"Why isn't Elijah here, with you?" she asked.

"Well, hummm, he went out," John told her.

Molly stared. "Out with the ship?"

How could it be? She glanced at Debby who said loudly to Mother, "Let's bring the children into your room and read to them."

"Is Elijah well?" Mother asked.

"He's fine," John assured her.

"Good. Come then, children," she bid them. "My bible is ready."

"Noah!" the little ones chorused, following their grandmother. 'Lije and Sarah waited to see if they would be allowed to stay and listen. Molly signaled her assent with a nod; they were old enough, now, to share the adult doings of their parents.

"I put my horse in Hector's old stall," John mumbled. Hector had departed the earth the year before. "Gave her some of Florida's oats."

Molly said nothing, not wanting to encourage John's stalling. Finally, shame-faced, he started. "Dan Blake broke his leg. Tony was a man short."

"So they drew lots," Molly filled in. "And Elijah's name was pulled out of the hat."

John looked away. "There wasn't much time for debate. We had to decide in a hurry."

"And he volunteered," she concluded slowly.

John was silent, trying to form a response.

"How did he manage it?" she asked, fairly quivering with rage. "Did he offer all of you a bribe?"

"He just said the idea was his to begin with, and it was only fair that he should go." John looked miserable, yet he had done nothing wrong. The wrongdoer was Elijah, who had as good as abandoned her.

"Want to play checkers?" Sarah asked her brother, sensitive to the tension in the room.

"Sure," the lad agreed, and they fled.

Molly and John sat silently for a while, neither one knowing what to say to the other. Elijah has done what he wanted to do, she thought. And who could blame him for that? She quieted, her anger subsiding. Indeed, no one would blame him, since going out with the *Avenger* was so important.

More important than staying here with her.

The ramifications were interesting. If he wouldn't be home this fall and winter, leaving her to face the embargo's hardship alone, if it were more important to him to do as he pleased, then perhaps she had the right to do as she pleased, too?

No, she reminded herself. Women have no rights.

"Now then," John said after a suitable interval, "there's the matter of your protection and safety to consider, without a man in the house."

"I'm sure we'll be fine. We always have been."

"The United States Marshal is going to be looking for culprits, and he'll bring troops with him. Until we better know what they're going to do, you shouldn't be here by yourself."

"What do you mean?" she demanded in alarm. It had never occurred to her that the *Swift Avenger* would put the women and children in danger.

"Well, after all," John said grimly, "we've aided and abetted an act of treason, all of us. Everyone will double up, in the houses of the men who are still here. Elijah trusts me to bring you and the family to our place."

"Why?" she asked. "From the sound of it, no one even knows the *Avenger* exists."

"They do now. Once she sailed, she broke the law. Before then it was just a group of unemployed captains having themselves a good time. The Plymouth Selectmen will report it to Boston. They'll have to, so they can't be charged with complicity. Boston, of course, will have to notify the federal authorities. At the very least, they'll be by asking questions. If you are with us, I may be able to shield you, lest you be forced to lie or inadvertently reveal information. I'll be back by mid-afternoon with our wagon and someone to ride Florida over. In a trice, all of you will be snug at our hearth."

"If it must be," Molly acquiesced, her heart somersaulting within her breast. Would Isaac be there? If so, John and Mariah's house was the last place on earth she should be! But what could she do except comply, allow herself to be protected in the absence of her husband?

Once at the Warden's, she saw no sign of Isaac. Mother read the bible to all the little children, Merrick and Warden alike, while the older ones brought in wood or helped in the keeping room. After supper, the younger ones played "I Spy" and "Button, Button." Then the children went to bed, the women arranging sleeping quarters in the attic for the boys, except for Sonny. The girls would use one back bedroom, Molly and the little boy in the other. John waited in the parlor until they returned so they all could rehearse what they would say to any Marshal who might show up. Despite the difficulties presented by Elijah's sudden disappearance, they were hardly able to contain their excitement over the escape of the *Avenger*. Their pride rose higher and higher as they practiced their responses to the marshal.

Into their merry rehearsals, Isaac flung open the front door.

"Good news!"

Luckily Molly was seated near the hearth; no one noticed the sudden flush suffusing her face. "The Committee has learned that the Marshal has been called to Buzzard's Bay," he announced.

"Buzzard's Bay!" they marveled. It was far away!

"Luck was with us," Isaac explained. "A skirmish had the Marshal and his men busy last night. They intercepted an English ship on Buzzards Bay, trying to smuggle in machinery for the new cotton mill at Troy. And that's not all! The smugglers were thrown into jail, then rescued by a bunch of ladies."

"Women?" they cried.

Isaac continued, chuckling. "Turns out they were really townsmen in bonnets and skirts." The very thought sent them all into gales of hilarity as they reveled in their good fortune.

"Finding the culprits is going to challenge the lawmen," he told them. "How are they going to identify the men without their ladies' garments on? We needn't expect the Marshal for a couple of days."

The girls upstairs were giggling now, aroused by the noise in the parlor. Debby excused herself to calm them and retire for the night. Mother too turned in, taking the borning room. "I'm afraid you'll have to sleep in the attic with the boys," Mariah told Isaac.

"I'm charged with delivering the news further down-Cape," he told her. "I'll be back later tonight."

"I hope you'll forgive me for not waiting up," John yawned. "It's been a long and exhausting week away from home, and the last two nights I've had hardly any rest at all." He started for the stairs.

"Is there anything you need?" Mariah asked Molly.

"No, no. But I am so excited by all of it," Molly replied, "I swan, I'll never get to sleep."

"A night ride always calms me down when I'm all wound up," Isaac said easily. "Why not come with me?"

Before Molly could protest, Mariah added, "That's a fine idea. I sometimes ride out at night with John, and I went with Isaac once too. Exhilaration turns to exhaustion every time."

"It does the trick," John agreed, smothering yet another yawn.

"How about it, Molly," Isaac asked. "Will you come with me?"

The question meant more than the others knew. But Molly knew, and Isaac waited.

"Oh, do go, Molly," Mariah urged. "If any of your little ones wakes up, we'll settle them back down."

She avoided looking in Isaac's direction. "Very well," she said. "Since you all recommend it so highly."

"We'll see you in the morning, then," John called and waved as he disappeared up the stairs, Mariah in tow.

The house was suddenly silent.

Wrapping up in a cloak, Molly followed Isaac to the barn. It's destiny, she told herself. You tried hard, and it would have worked if Elijah had done his part. Isaac quickly saddled Florida and boosted her up, mounted his own horse. "We're off, then! Follow me, Molly Merrick!"

It was a wild night, the wind rollicking, tumbling her emotions and whipping her passion, drawing her further and further away from the constraints of her daily life and its expectations. The clouds were flung headlong across the sky, and the moon raced with them as they rode to the home of the next town's Committee chairman, where Isaac delivered the news. Then he turned to the shore and the flats, fully exposed now at low tide. She knew they would stop at Elijah's salt works on the way back, and they did, stopping at the nearest vat.

"Let's rest the animals," he said, dismounting. He reached up to catch her as she slid off Florida, then looked down at her. The moonlight on his face illuminated his features, sculpted as in marble by the blue and eerie glow.

"Well!" He smiled, a gentle, intimate smile. "Shall we take a walk? Or shall we stand here just looking at one another? What would you like, Molly? It's all up to you, as I said it would be."

She thought for a brief moment of Elijah, away at sea, doing what he wanted most. And here she was, beneath the vat, with a chance to do the same.

"You are moved by me, are you not?" Isaac's face was inscrutable in the light.

"You know I am," she said unevenly. "You have always known it."

"Yes," he said softly. "I always have." Surely he sensed the desire that rose in her as a flood, rising, rising with nothing to stop it. "If you tell me we must go back to John's, we will do it. It is not too late to turn back."

"Yes, it is. It is much too late."

He took her in his arms very gently and held her close. He kissed her eyelids and the bridge of her nose, his strong, taut, body close to hers at last, after so long. Their lips met, gently at first, then with frenzy so intense she thought she would die of it.

"We could go into your house, if you are willing," he said finally, his breathing quick. "No one is there, after all."

"I cannot wait so long," she confessed. "We can lie here, under the vat."

He laughed then. "Molly, Molly, let me teach you how to savor pleasure." Yet he was not mocking her. "Starting now. We shall not avail ourselves of the vat but shall walk, hand in hand, to the house. We must have a bed to lie upon so that we may have our pleasure in comfort. For all we know, there will not ever be another opportunity."

Somehow her feet carried her there, dizzy, her head spinning.

The back door to Mother's room was unlocked, as was the rest of the house. No one locked doors on the Narrow Land.

"Perfect!" Isaac led her to the window, where the incredible moon hung over his shoulder. He kissed her, oh, he did kiss her mouth with his mouth so strong, his lips so firm, kissed her with longing and loving, and then he released her to unfasten her bodice.

Suddenly worried, she put her hands over his. "I am not a girl anymore," she whispered, fearful. "Not the girl you remember. I've had five children and I'm not young now, as I was before."

"I would not have you hide from me," he said quietly. "I would not have you think I want you because you have pretty breasts or a small waist or a cute fanny. I would have you understand that we belong together, we always have, and that what you look like has nothing at all to do with it. That I will love your body, whatever it has become, because it is yours." Gently, he gently took her hands away. Somehow she untied the strings of her skirts while he undid the lacings of her bodice. She thought she could not bear it when at last nothing was between herself and him, and he could see that her breasts were heavy now, her stomach no longer flat, her hips wide with childbearing. "D-Don't you see?" she stammered, ashamed.

"I see that you have ripened," he said. "I see that you are a woman, well ready for being truly loved." His clothes rough and scratchy as he drew her to him, smelling of leather and tobacco and horses. His wonderful face was full of command, of intent, and of pursuit. Deeply afraid of his power over her, afraid of the path she had chosen, Molly shivered, but could no longer turn back.

The moon smiled on them, and then disappeared behind a cloud.

He carried her to the narrow cot and knelt beside her. "You are meant for me, for my loving. Just lie here." His hands and lips moved carefully, without haste, causing within a sweep of urgent need. It took all the discipline she had to keep still under his touch. Finally, unable to endure more, she seized his hand.

"Isaac," she gasped. "I am so full of need for you, so full. Come to me! Come to me now!"

"Gladly," he whispered, rising easily from his knees and quickly stripping off his clothing. She knew she was disgraceful, so ready for him, her very flesh aching, throbbing.

Then, ah yes, then he swung above her and entered her slowly, so slowly, so deliberately that it was a torture to her. She must have more; she strained to meet him but could not make him thrust more quickly. No, his assault was measured and steady, drawing her from herself, drawing her farther out than she had ever been, while he slowly entered, slowly left, again, and again, drawing her out and out.

"Let it take you, Molly!" he urged. "Let it take you away with me." His voice was as strong as a caress. His speed began to build. "I'll be there, on the other side and we'll come back together." His beautiful face twisted as the beat built. "Molly! Molly!" he called at the exquisite spill of seed, and thrust hard so that she, too, was cast far out into the embrace of climax, never before known to her, now carrying her away to a place so mysteriously different that she could not put words to it.

They lay together, returning from the world they had shared, and when she dared to open her eyes, she found him watching her with tenderness and pride and possession.

"There is nothing left. You have it all," she whispered. "Everything."

He caressed her cheek. "You have, as I have always known, extraordinary passion. How well I will love you, Molly. I will take you, all of you, hold you to myself, sustain you. There is much to share."

"We cannot," she said sadly. "My family will return to this house soon, and Mother will lie on this very bed."

They were quiet for a time. "What about the other house?" he speculated. "Where she used to live."

Of course! For as long as Elijah would be gone, and the embargo in effect, the old place would be perfect! Molly's cup ran over. "And we need not worry about being found out. I cannot bear children now."

"I knew that," he admitted. "I heard Mariah say so to John. I wouldn't have sought you out otherwise. Just tell me that you have never been loved as I love you, my darling! Tell me I can do things to you no one else can." His voice was vibrant with his own joy; her exhilaration knew no bounds.

"No one, no one, no one," she cried. "I am like the clouds out there, high and serene above the night and able to see the whole world, because of you!"

They could have stayed and spoken words of love a long time, but, of course, they did not. For there would never be time enough, and already they had tarried too long.

CHAPTER

The War

❋᠈᠊ I ᠊᠈❋

THERE WAS NO WAY she could prolong her stay at the Wardens. The United States Marshal had come to Waterford; no sooner did he arrive than another attempt to evade the embargo was reported at Falmouth. A few questions were asked, and then he hurriedly left town to attend to this newest insurgency. With no reason to fear further investigation, Molly and her brood would be returning home.

But she hated to leave!

Isaac had traveled back and forth between Waterford and Yarmouth, delivering messages and meeting with each town's committee, but he managed to end most days in his brother's house. Molly loved being under the same roof with him, where she could hear his laughter and his voice, see his perfect face, and at the end of the day say goodnight to him and know she would see him again in the morning. She loved watching him play hide and seek or blind man's bluff with the children, or debate the political situation—especially the possibility of secession—with John and the other men who dropped by in the evenings. Then she could covertly observe him to her heart's content.

Now, she must go. But how could she simply leave him behind, having not spoken intimately with him since they had lain together? How could she just ride away in the Warden's wagon without arranging to meet again?

The morning of the family's departure, Mother Merrick provided the answer.

"Do you think you could take me back in your chaise?" she asked John. "That wagon is a little rough for old bones like mine."

"Oh, gracious, my dear Mrs. Merrick, of course we can!" John replied loudly so that Mother could hear him. "I'll drive you myself." With a flourish, he brought the Warden chaise around and settled the old lady in, wrapping a blanket snugly around her, attention she loved.

When the wagon rolled up, the children and Debby settled themselves in back. Isaac handed Molly up to the front seat, climbed in beside her. They bid goodbye to Mariah and the Warden children, then set off.

Looking around at the scenery, Molly pointed at a tree on Isaac's side of the road, as though she were bringing his attention to a bird in its branches. "What shall we do?" she asked as quietly as she could over the rattling of the vehicle and the trotting of the horse's hooves.

"I will come to you." He nodded vigorously, as though the invisible bird were indeed a marvel. Debby started a song with the children.

Soldier, soldier, soldier, will you marry me, with your musket, fife and drum? chorused the younger ones.

"When?" Molly sang.

"This Wednesday?" he asked. "At midnight?"

How can I marry such a pretty girl as you when I have no hat to put on? Sonny and 'Lije answered.

She was prepared. "I'll put a candle at my window. If it's lit, go on by. If it's not, I'll be at the old house. At midnight."

Off to the haberdasher she did go, As fast as she could run. . . .

He pointed across her, to the other side of the road. "If it's lit, shall I come the following week?"

"Yes, please!" she caroled to the treetops.

And the soldier put it on.

How badly she wanted to hear words of love, and to say them! But it was enough just to be sitting beside each other, their thighs pressed tightly, hidden beneath the fullness of Molly's skirt, knowing that soon they would be as one. Already Isaac had taught her to savor the waiting.

ⓧⓧ✦ⓧⓧ

And so it was they met most Wednesday nights after that. Sometimes he would be waiting just inside the door of Jon's room at the back of the old house. They would start slowly, embracing lightly, their lips moving against each other's as their words and their kisses met. He would caress her, unclothe her as she lavished on him her love, on and on until delirium struck them.

Isaac!

Sometimes he simply snatched her into his arms, tore her gown from her, and ravished her with silent and joyous abandon. Sometimes she arrived before him and hid in the shadows until he found her. Then not a moment more was allowed to pass before their bodies were one body as their souls were one soul. Sometimes he made her lead him, shyly at first, then with more and more confidence as she learned the ways of love. When the chill of winter crept in, they spread out blankets and made a tent over the little bed, trapping their own heat so that they might lie unclothed in each other's arms.

There was not, and there never would be, anything to match his loving. There was no part of her that was not his; nothing mattered but him.

Isaac!

Her chores were no longer burdensome, for within their repetitive isolation her dreams were undisturbed. For the first time in her life, Molly Deems Merrick was glad to be a woman, engulfed by the peace that a woman, loving and loved, can know, seeing beauty where she had never seen it before. In her enchanted world the barnyard puddles were a mirror for the sky, flakes of infrequent snow were jewels to adorn the bosom of the earth, and frost on the windowpanes was the deft touch of a fairy.

Then dawn began earlier, little by little, and the hens started laying, and in March of 1809, the embargo was half-heartedly lifted. As long as cargoes were not destined for Britain or France, the American merchant might once more take to the seas. Celebrations were held all along the Atlantic coast.

But there was no rejoicing in Molly's heart.

Swift Avenger would be coming home.

"We won't be able to meet any more! Oh, Isaac!" He had just come down from Boston with the news, which he had delivered to the Committees. And now to her.

"Hush, hush. It'll take a while for the *Avenger* to hear about it," he soothed, holding her closely. "But it's true that soon I'll have to seek employment."

Bravely, she determined not to present him with a weeping woman destitute at their impending separation. She would accept his departure with dignity, a mistress he could be proud of. "I shall recall you fondly when we are absent, one from another," she told him, trying to hold her voice steady. "You have given me so much, Isaac!"

"You make it sound as though everything is finished," he said, holding her away from him so he could see her face in the darkness.

"Is it not?"

"Not unless you wish it to be. It's not easy to bed two men, but if you can manage it, I think there is a chance for us."

Her heart began to beat hopefully. "How?"

Nuzzling her throat, he revealed his plan. "If I'm working in Boston, it won't be hard to keep track of Elijah's coming and goings. I'll know when he's at sea; I'll know I can come to you then, if you will allow it."

He would come all the way down from Boston!

"How will you get here without anyone seeing you?" she asked. "Simon Hopkins knows everyone on his packet."

"I won't use the Waterford packet," he answered. Clearly he had been thinking. "Instead I'll take the one to Barnstable. I'll rent a horse there, and come to you. The next day, I'll return the horse and catch the packet back to Boston. It won't be often, I'm afraid, but it will be all the more wonderful for that."

"Oh my dearest, it seems like a lot of work!"

He smothered his laughter so it would not carry through the quiet of the night. "You are worth a lot of work, Molly! If your mother-in-law comes back home—here—we may have to lie beneath a vat, like once you wanted to do. There'll be nowhere else we can meet, but you're worth that, too!"

A month later he left. Now she must face her husband. How could she do that, having betrayed his trust? Would she seem like the wife she had been? Or would her heart reveal her secret?

She reminded herself that she was not the only party to betrayal. Elijah, after all, had disappeared in the middle of the night. Had left her, alone, without a word. Had chosen his beloved ship over her.

Yes—to assume the role of the abandoned wife. That would do the trick. It would ease her past any reticence when she met her husband behind the closed doors of their chamber. Welcoming and pleasant, she would also be the injured party whom he must win back.

Having settled her apprehensions as best she could, she waited for Elijah's return.

✦ఌ 2 ఌ✦

The embargo had accomplished nothing. Friction with Britain was as high as ever, and most likely only a war would resolve it. All the Waterford captains made haste to prepare for that day. They must voyage while they were able, where they were able, and any money they made must be hoarded. They all knew who would pay for a war!

Avenger returned to Boston with her profit in a Hamburg bank and a cargo of inferior Spanish wine in the hold. This, as her owners had known, would be confiscated by the customs authorities as punishment for violating the embargo, but at minimal loss to themselves.

Once the men had settled their accounts with each other, they had to decide who among them should master the ship. She'd paid for herself and earned them money besides. All of them wanted her, but again they drew lots. Her quarterdeck was given to David Bradley, and first mate to a young mariner who had been shore-bound throughout the embargo and needed the experience she could provide. They renamed her *Sweet Charity* and re-registered her, then secured voyages for themselves and sailed again nearly as soon as they got home.

During the week that Elijah was back, he briskly set his family on course. "Mother will continue to use Jon's room," he decreed. "It's wasteful to maintain two households. We must save as much as we can."

"But she won't want to stay," Molly pointed out, keeping firm hold on her excitement. Mother's house would remain empty!

"I'll arrange to have an outside door installed," he promised. "Then she can entertain her friends privately. That should put an end to any complaints she might have."

"What about my friends?" Molly allowed herself to pout.

"If you can find hired help one day a week," he cajoled, "I think we could afford that, and then there'll be a little extra time to have your friends in for tea. Will that help?"

Sometimes a little pouting went a long way!

Their bedroom posed the greatest challenge.

"Is something wrong?" he asked the first night they were alone together.

The time of testing was now upon her, and she went instantly into battle.

"Why do you ask?" she replied politely.

"Well, you seem a little, ah, distant."

"Perhaps it hasn't occurred to you, Elijah, that it's not easy to just put aside the fact that you deserted me."

"Is that what you thought? That I deserted you?"

"Is that not, in fact, what you did?" she accused.

There was a long silence wherein she saw he was struggling, frustrated that his desires might not be soon satisfied but required to take her concern seriously.

"I'm sorry you feel that way," he apologized. "I hope you can forgive me."

Primly, she replied, "I shall try. It may take a while, is all."

"Allow me to help." He drew her to himself, and did not mention her reticence again. If she seemed different than the wife he'd left behind, now there was an explanation for it. The effort it took to participate in the marital embrace was well hidden, just as she'd hoped it would be. In the remainder of the week, Elijah hired a Waterford man, too old for farming, to tend his vats, directed Pat Mayo to build Mother's door, met with the Committee and the Second Regiment, reacquainted himself with his children, and then was off.

Molly nearly wept with relief. She found a young and compliant girl, Sally Nearing, the daughter of a local farmer, to help with the chores. Her father, like the rest of his kind, had come to resent the wealth of the captains and, like other farmers, had been gratified by the sight of the wealthy folk toiling through the embargo. Now he relented, as most of them did, allowing their children to fill the vacancy brought about by the departed South Siders. They, too, would need extra money to get them through the privations of war.

Because of Sally, Molly could see her friends and spend more time with the children, helping them with their studies, reading to the younger ones. In the late afternoons, the house clean, supper prepared, she taught all her daughters fancy stitches and the art of conversation so that they would be ready, when the time came, to continue the tradition of fine living. In the evenings they practiced the minuet with their brother 'Lije, while Sonny watched, too young, yet, for dancing.

All the while Molly waited, keeping her worries and longings and impatience firmly out of sight beneath the busyness of these things. Three months passed, each day a struggle with her pent-up passions and her fears that Isaac would not return.

But then, one Wednesday, the Warden chaise was driven to the door for a ladies' gathering. There was Isaac handing Mariah down, escorting her into the house, kissing the hostess's hand in greeting and smiling into her eyes, as though he had never been away.

"Tonight," he murmured as he left. Molly staggered through the tea, nearly unable to converse at all, violating her own rule about edifying conversation.

She waited, waited, waited until very late. Finally, she fled down the stairs in the darkness, her hair streaming behind her as she ran to the old house, and without breaking stride, flung open the door of the little room and threw herself into his arms, unable to restrain her tears of relief and not caring if he saw them. It was so wonderful, his arms around her again, his lips on hers, his whispered words of love in her ears, his body close—Isaac!

Knowing he would return, she could wait forever; she could outlast the moon and the stars and the tides. Now she could allow herself the luxury of being confident, knowing that he would come to her whenever he could, however he could, and that she held his heart's happiness as he held hers.

She could wait in peace.

With her friends, Molly laughed happily and was much more thoughtful and considerate. With her children, she was more affectionate and tender than she had ever been. She cosseted Elijah's sister because she was sorry that Debby had no lover of her own, preparing the little cakes that accompanied Mother's tea parties so that Debby would not have to, and scrubbing more than her share of pots.

On the days that Sally came to the house, Molly worked willingly, singing as they washed clothes and kneaded bread and ironed dresses, because she was the beloved of Isaac Warden and life was a joyous thing.

In quite a different way from before the embargo, she was on top of her world, and if her friends noticed any change in her, they attributed it to the tempering experience of hardship. She was loved the better, and followed as before, her ways and conversation and interests emulated, as she waited for Isaac.

Swiftly, swiftly, the summer ran by, and autumn came around again, then winter. Elijah's infrequent visits were easy and effortless. Deceiving him no longer disturbed her; she concentrated on his abandonment and reminded herself he had not earned her fidelity. Knowing that Isaac was watching for his departure, knowing that Elijah was never in Waterford for long, she could be more than cordial, even in bed.

Then dawn came sooner; buds swelled on the apple trees in the young orchard, animals rutted, new seed was sown, and the beach plum bloomed, rising in joyous sprays along the dunes. Through all the seasons, Isaac was hers, hers alone, hers forever.

Elijah continued his comings and goings, away nearly all of the time, intent on gleaning everything he could before another embargo or even war could arise and put an end to maritime trade. He reported the English were still impressing American sailors, a fact that made Molly worry, for if there was a war, her husband would be perpetually present. Meanwhile the axis of life in Waterford remained steady while her very being was centered in a universe known to no one else, while her heart and her hope and her joy bloomed like a garden in the confines of Jonathan Merrick's back room, tended by the sure and devastating hands and heart of the man who gave her so much.

Until a cool, late night in April, 1812. The day had been unseasonably warm and the little room still held its heat. The window was open and the night air occasionally breathed on them as they lay naked in the little bed. Moonrise was just beginning; in the marshes the little toads peeped incessantly, calling out their annual song.

Molly was filled, filled to the brim and overflowing as Isaac always caused her to be. Dared she be so happy?

He rose from the cot and pulled on his breeches and boots, then sat on the edge and lightly kissed her.

"I will miss this." In the shadow, she could not see his face. His hands took hers and in the stillness, she heard him take a deep breath. "I am going to be married next month." The words, so softly spoken, disappeared into the darkness.

Married! She tried to take her hands away, but he held them more firmly. "I will miss you more than I can say, Molly. But her father is rich, and he will pay my debts."

"What debts?" she asked stupidly, as though it mattered.

"Gambling. These several years I've spent foolishly and gambled besides, mostly losing. A lot. Her father will give us a house in Boston to live in and set me up in a law practice of my own."

It was not possible to be lying here, naked as the day she was born with the man she lived for, and listen to him tell her he was going to wed another woman! He, who not many minutes before, had loved her so well and so completely.

"Let me up," she commanded, and he did. She ignored the hand he courteously extended. Finding her dress, she slid into it and faced him across the widening chasm between them. Panic welled up within her, which she masked with hautiness. "Perhaps you'd be so kind as to explain yourself, sir."

"Mr. Madison has issued a non-intercourse act against England. There's no doubt it's a prelude to war, so once Elijah comes home, he'll stay. That alone would finish our pleasant dalliance. War coupled with debts—that's hard to beat. This provides a way out, and I'd be foolish not to jump at the chance. Don't you agree?"

Hugging herself against the encroaching chill, she asked, "How long have you known this woman?"

"Long enough," he answered in the dark.

Oh, the hurt of it! Long enough he had known, yet still he had taken her down the long and intimate paths of passion with him. He had gambled himself into marriage while pursuing a "dalliance" here in Waterford, and now declared it done.

"Isaac, do you love her?"

"It doesn't matter, whether I do or not."

"It matters to me," she cried, forgetting to keep her voice low.

"Hush!" he commanded.

"You have loved this woman all the while you were *dallying* with me?" she hissed.

"Of course I don't love Marian." He turned away, walked over to the window and she must follow, else he would have to to raise his voice to be heard. Leaning on the sill, he said softly, "Once I told you I could not forget you. Do you remember? When we first met, by the saltworks?"

Molly nodded in the dark. "Yes," she whispered.

"It was true. I could not forget you. But there was an added reason I sought you out." He looked out the window, then back. "If there is a man anywhere in world whom I hate, that man is Elijah Merrick. If I could repay him by cuckolding him, I was not going to refuse the opportunity. These two things—my very great hatred of him, my very great desire for you—drove me into your arms. And it has been worth it, my sweeting, chasing from tree to tree in the middle of the night." As through to touch her, he reached out; she recoiled. "I didn't dream that such a grand passion would come of it, but I accepted it happily. Being your lover, Molly Merrick, has been a privilege. Does that answer your question?"

"Why do you hate Elijah?" Her voice, caught in her throat, was barely audible.

"I believe I never told you—and I'm sure he did not—about the night he took you away to be married, so long ago. He and I were drinking in the taproom in Yarmouth, to celebrate your impending marriage. I was quite drunk when he dragged me out behind the inn and beat me— yes, Molly, he beat me—surrounded by his friends who laughed, who enjoyed seeing me pounded to a pulp! And I dared not lift a hand, lest I injure him. You had threatened to tell my parents that I had violated you unless Elijah carried you away—do you remember? So I let him thrash me, but I swore I'd get back at him. And I have done it, done it most pleasantly! I have had his wife, and not just once behind the bushes, either." He stopped, as though coming up for air. "Sometimes it's better not to understand everything, is it not? But, perhaps knowing will make parting easier for you. I'm not a nice man, Molly. Not at all."

She shook her head from side to side, took a step back, her legs weak. Oh, if only the night were not so still! If only she could cry out with her pain, instead of having to smother it. If only she could regain some shred of self-respect. But there was nothing she could do except submit to the final, devastating humiliation of being used once again by Isaac Warden, and used unsuspectingly for nearly four years.

Finally, in a softer tone, he spoke again. "Yes, I was hell-bent on having you, hell-bent on repaying Elijah for that beating, but the rest of it did not depend on revenge. The rest happened because of you, Molly. It has never been like this for me, and it never will be again. Does that satisfy you? Knowing I will never forget you? But I cannot have you anymore, my beloved. Elijah is coming home. I do not care to get shot, as I would surely deserve. And since I do not care for debtor's prison, either, I will marry next month."

All her questions had been answered. There was nothing more to be said. It was over. With a clear, steady voice that did not betray her devastation, she said, "Just leave, Isaac."

He complied, tucking his shirt into his breeches, pulling on his boots, moving to the door. "Good-bye, then," he said, and waited.

She offered no reply, and he left, disappearing forever from her life.

✦≈≈ 3 ≈≈✦

Mr. Madison's request for war passed in Congress on June 18ᵗʰ. When coastal New England learned of it, the church bells sounded the death knell, and flags were flown at half-staff. For the mariner, it meant disaster.

By going to war, the United States aimed to put an end to English blockades in Europe as well as the continued impressment of American sailors by Britain. With her tiny navy and a considerable fleet of privateers, the young nation proposed to capture and destroy the merchant shipping of the world's greatest sea-power.

But for the mariner, war was too high a price to pay. War would put him out of business; he would rather deal with blockades and searches. Yet this was not the only reason for the tolling bells. Included in Madison's plan was the annexation of Canada.

Canada! What had Canada to do with it? Three of the five New England states shared a border with her, as well as a very lucrative trade. Now their neighbor was the enemy? To make the situation even worse, the state militias were called out to join the federal army in Michigan Territory, where the invasion would be launched, leaving the coast open to the British navy.

Almost everyone in New England was opposed to the war; Massachusetts and Connecticut outright refused to send their troops rather than leave their shores undefended.

The church bells indeed tolled truly.

Elijah returned home just before the hostilities commenced. On the way, he secured the rank of Brigadier General from the State House, and was consumed with militia business from the moment he set foot in Waterford. He was too preoccupied to wonder about the despondency his wife exhibited, attributing it to the departure of Sally Nearing.

Olive Gray, however, was worried.

"Molly! All of us are burdened with household chores! Nobody likes slaving at the hearth, but you seem especially brought down by it. What's wrong?"

They were walking back to the house after Sunday morning Meeting. Carrying their dinner pails, more friends of the Merricks trailed along behind.

"You must think me a spoiled child," Molly offered weakly. She could not tell Olive or anyone else that her life had lost its meaning. "I know everyone is working hard, but I have Mother Merrick, too. She takes most of Debby's time and attention, so I have to do it all myself."

"Most of us do it all, my love," Olive chided, squeezing her hand.

But Molly was lost in misery, and Olive's well-meant scolding told her only that she must hide her feelings better. "You're right, of course." Trying to brighten her voice, she added, "I'll stop complaining this instant!"

How could she go on? When the things that meant so much to Elijah meant nothing to her. When the children were just five more burdens added to everything else. When nothing mattered.

She tried to forget about the love she had shared with Isaac, but it circled endlessly and remorselessly through her brain. Never again would she know laughter. Never again would the world be a magical place. She must plod through the repetitive round without anything to lighten her days, no way to find ease beneath her burdens. Her children complained incessantly about the tasks they must perform, now that Sally Nearing had been dismissed to save money, but Molly paid little attention.

Early that summer, the pride of Boston—the USS *Constitution*—escaped a British squadron off the coast of New York by hauling itself out of range of His Majesty's guns, towed ignominiously by kedging, until a breeze favored her escape.

In August, the war struck closer to home when the *Liverpool Packet* of Nova Scotia captured nearly a dozen vessels off Cape Cod's Highland Light. But spirits rose when the *Constitution* defeated HMS *Guerriere* 600 miles east of Boston.

At these events, Molly feigned alarm and joy, but in fact, she did not care. While the army was defeated at every turn in the Michigan Territory, while skirmishes in the state of Ohio and the Territories of Illinois and Indiana ended in massacres by the Indians and retaliations by the Americans, she went silently about her tasks, unable to feel either horror or even sympathy.

The Waterford militia purchased a new cannon from Yarmouth, and with the aid of a keg of rum, towed it on a barge across the flats and secured it at the top of the Rockford Road.

"Capital!" Elijah crowed. "Now we can just run it down to the beach and fire if the enemy tries to land."

"Father! Can I learn to load it?" 'Lije asked.

"All of us will learn its ways," Elijah answered jovially, as though this instrument of destruction were child's play.

The men are just like boys pretending to be warriors, Molly observed scornfully, while she and Debby and the children washed clothes and tended the chickens and took trays of food in to Mother Merrick. Every hour of every day, she tried to avoid memories of Isaac Warden—his hands that had caressed her with such love, his eyes that had seen so clearly into her soul, and especially, his cruel deception. The obligations of the hearth covered over her desolation, but rising in the morning after a night of fitful sleep, responding to her children as a mother should and to Elijah as a wife must, was exhausting.

She plodded on.

Bits of war news arrived daily, often muddled and usually a few weeks old. In November, the ports in South Carolina were sealed. By the end of December the British closed the strategic Chesapeake Bay. Winter passed. The herring ran. By then, Molly accepted her lot, like the ox hitched to the grinding wheel, going 'round and 'round and 'round.

ΚΟΟΦΚΟΟ

In the spring, they heard that the harbors from the Mississippi River to Long Island Sound were closed, but there was no alarm in Waterford. Everyone knew that New England's ports would remain open. The British needed the Yankees to carry supplies to her troops in Spain, fighting Napoleon. A few American merchants were willing, reaping great profits.

During the summer of 1813 Maine seethed with coastal encounters, and privateers on both sides captured their prey. Good news was provided by a captain from Rhode Island, who defeated the British on Lake Erie in September, but over the winter and into the spring of 1814, the army lost one battle after another on the Canadian frontier. In March, adding to the humiliation, the USS *Essex* was captured and added to the British fleet.

Then, at the end of May the British blockaded all ports, and included New England. In Europe, where war with Napoleon had finally drawn to a close, British troops made ready to sail to America.

The time for worry was nigh.

"They're closing in on us!" Desire Snow wailed.

"Up until now, they probably hoped we'd fight on their side," Molly contributed listlessly.

"As if we would. Just because we're against the war doesn't mean we'd turn traitor!" snorted Tabitha Bradley.

"Well, I think there's real trouble ahead," Mariah told them. "Their troops aren't needed in Europe now. The whole English army will be brought over here. And their navy too. Can you imagine what it would be like to have a ship of the line firing on us?"

They shivered.

"Do you think we should bury our valuables?" asked Hope Blake.

Valuables! At last Molly began to pay attention. "What do you mean?" she asked .

"That's what they've been doing in Maine," her friend told her. "When they think the enemy is going to invade, they bury their silver and jewelry, or if they're in a hurry, dump the valuable stuff down their wells before hiding in the woods."

Invasion? Here? On Cape Cod? Worry replaced desolation. Her jewelry alone was worth a king's ransom!

"A fellow near Portland sent his servant out to bury the family valuables," Olive teased. "But after the English raid, the servant couldn't remember where he put them. They're still looking."

Molly was not amused. Her jewelry was important to her; she would preserve it. Some energy returned to her shuttered world. She could hardly wait for her friends to leave.

When they were gone, she gathered her sons. 'Lije was 20 now, Sonny, 8. Between the two of them they could dig a fine hole, she was sure.

"Six feet deep?" 'Lije asked incredulously. "Mama, all you need to do is keep the things out of sight, not send them to China!"

They compromised on a two-foot trench, which they would disguise with scattered leaves and twigs.

It seemed that her precautions might prove necessary after all, for the war moved closer, early in June, when an American schooner from Maine slipped into the harbor at Beverly, north of Boston, carrying armaments to reinforce the militia. A British warship, anchored nearby to watch the coast, dispatched soldiers to set fire to the vessel. Militiamen gathered by the hundreds, and after an exchange of cannon fire, forced the British back.

That same month, HMS *Bulwark* and HMS *Nymphe* burned private vessels in Scituate harbor, south of Boston. After that, British troops and artillery were sent to neighboring Cohasset. The militia faced them down, having mustered twelve hundred men from surrounding towns. A less fortunate fate met the townsfolk of Wareham, just to the west on Buzzards Bay, when HMS *Nimrod* fired upon ships and buildings along the harbor, inflicting losses up to $40,000.

The British turned north, harassed the coast of Maine, then came back in July. HMS *Nymphe* arrived practically next door, demanding $1,000 in exchange for sparing fishing vessels in South Yarmouth's Bass River. After much frantic hustling, the town produced the money.

"I used to think our men spent too much time marching around and being military," Olive confessed. "Now I have to think they were right, all along."

"I hate to admit it, but you've got a point," nodded Tabitha Bradley grimly.

Eastern Maine was occupied early in September. Gloucester, north of Boston, was raided just as word reached the Cape Committees that only a few weeks before, Redcoats had landed in Maryland and, after routing the local militia, proceeded on to Washington City burning the Library of Congress and the President's House.

Then the war came to Cape Cod when HMS *Spencer*, under the command of Richard Raggett, arrived in the bay fresh from convoying troops to the fighting in Maine. In short order, the Spencer's tender was tricked by an enterprising captain from Eastham who had been forced to serve as pilot. The vessel was run aground and captured by the Eastham militia. Raggett retaliated by demanding $1,800 in exchange for not bombarding the town's saltworks; this was paid promptly.

But the *Spencer* did not sail away. Instead, she moved to the edge of the outer bar off Waterford and anchored.

For a day there was no action.

Molly had been on the rooftop porch, snatching a moment for herself after dipping the last of the coming winter's candles. The day was clean and crisp, good for their curing. She leaned on the railing and closed her eyes so that she would not see the enemy hovering beyond the flats, raised her face to the warmth of the early autumn sun, breathed deeply, wished that moment would last forever. When she looked again, the enemy was still there, of course, but a dory was now moving briskly toward Waterford's packet landing. It carried the white flag of truce.

"Elijah!" she called frantically.

Oh, God, where was he? She looked out from the porch on all sides, knowing he was near, for he had no plans for the day. "Elijah!" she screamed.

"What's wrong?" He came running from the barn.

"They're here!" she shrieked. "The British!"

The whole household heard and instantly the steep stairway was filled as Debby and the children and then Elijah clambered up.

Motionlessly, he looked through his spyglass at the approaching dory, rowed with precision by men in red coats.

In their innocence, Sonny and 'Lije were joyful at seeing the enemy in person. The girls were frightened, clinging to Debby for comfort, except for Sarah who moved close to her father.

"Papa?" Sarah asked him. "Will they shoot us?"

He drew her tightly to his side. "Don't be afraid, sweetheart. We're prepared! We won't let any harm come to you!"

Over Sarah's head, his eyes met Molly's and were not as reassuring. They both knew that in the event of an attack, the saltworks, shoulder to shoulder along the shore, would be targeted first. With their house so nearby, it too, could go up in flames.

Then Tony galloped into the yard, shouting, pointing toward the beach, and behind him was Sam Hall. Elijah motioned them to come up. They arrived, breathing heavily, and waited for a chance at the glass.

"There's a lot of Waterford men that would like to take a shot at them," Sam observed.

"Well, let's go and see what's on their minds." Elijah became the general. "We'll need something white—Molly, fetch a towel or a pillowcase, then keep the girls with you. Gather the Committee," he instructed Tony. "We'll meet at the armory. Sam, you come to the packet landing with me. 'Lije, you and your brother stay up here and keep an eye on the *Spencer*. Send Sonny to the armory if there's further action. Debby, please attend to Mother."

They scattered to do his bidding.

"The British are coming?" Mother roared from the back room. "They were here only a few years ago! You mean to tell me they're back?" Her memory was fast failing her.

Carrying a pillowcase, Sam and Elijah marched to the beach. The white flag was always respected; Molly did not fear for them. Yet. Watching from the porch with the girls, her mind whirled, her thoughts churned. Here she'd been, pining away and nursing her wounds, letting life pass her by and giving not a damn about anything when all that time, their lives had been at risk. All along it had lain in wait, this danger. Now it was here, threatening her family.

Never had they meant so much! Now, when it all hung in the balance, when everything depended on the message being given to Elijah and Sam, she saw the things that truly mattered. Her heartbreak over Isaac withered into insignificance. Fear took its place—for the safety of the children, her husband—even herself.

Feverishly she waited, and when Elijah came back, she ran downstairs, directing the girls to join Debby in Mother Merrick's room, thus sparing them any frightening news.

"What does he want?" she frantically demanded, before he had even had a chance to pour a tot of rum.

"Five thousand dollars," he told her. "In retaliation for the destruction our troops inflicted on Upper Canada."

"Five thousand dollars!" She was shocked at the exorbitant sum. "What if we can't raise it?"

"I don't know. I don't know if we'll even try. You heard Sam—there are some men who'd rather fight. Ones that don't own saltworks, anyway."

"But could the militia protect us? Or would . . . ."

Elijah did not allow her to finish. "There's not a thing we can do if *Spencer's* cannons can reach the shore from that distance. If they row ashore and attack us outright, our militia will engage them, and probably be able to turn them back. But there'd still be considerable damage. We'll discuss it at town meeting and decide what to do. The selectmen have called for one in the morning."

"And if enough men vote to fight . . . ?"

"That's what we'll do," he replied, calmly.

"But you're the General, Elijah! Can't you just command . . . ?"

"The military is always under civilian control," he reminded her. "But I believe we'll agree to pay. Here's your pillowcase."

She twisted it in her hands, fervently wishing it were Raggett's neck.

Elijah called the boys down from the roof.

"They rowed back," 'Lije reported.

"To their ship," Sonny confirmed.

"Very good." Elijah told them. "Carry on, 'Lije. Sonny, you're excused. Go to your mother."

"But. . . " Sonny began.

"Now," the General ordered, and left for the armory.

Molly struggled to maintain her composure, since losing it would be no help at all. There was nothing she could do but wait—but nay! Her valuables! If the house were destroyed, the jewelry could be sold and the family would have money. She left the children and ran quickly upstairs, emptied her pearls and diamonds and the ruby into the pillowcase, then added Elijah's cufflinks and rings.

Downstairs, she gave the bundle to Sonny. "Hurry," she told him. "Take this and bury it in the hole we dug. Then come right back."

She shooed him out of the house and called the girls to her in the dining room, where the silver serving plates and trays richly ornamented with raised leaves and vines, the tea service and extra candlesticks gleamed. "Throw everything down the well," she told them.

They stared. "But Mama," Elizabeth protested. "We overheard Father—he said we might pay."

"Do it!" she screamed. "In case we do fight! If our house burns down, at least we'll have something left."

They hurried to do her bidding.

Her mother's pewter porringers! Why, she hadn't thought of them in years, but Molly knew she must save them too. Simple and not even valuable, still important—more important than her jewelry, she now realized. By then Sonny had returned. She went back to the hole with him and tucked the little bowls into the pillowcase, then helped him disguise the hiding place.

Now that she had done all she could for her possessions, she must safeguard the family, make a plan for evacuation. The children were familiar with the nearby woods and would know of a good place to hide, if it came to that.

They conferred. 'Lije, solemn, and Sonny, puffed up with importance, would lead them to a clearing. Everyone made up a satchel of cornmeal and dried herring to take when they ran away, and lined up coats and blankets in Mother's room. Debby would be in charge of the old woman when—if—the time came.

Then, again, they waited.

The town meeting had been riotous, taking all of Elijah's skill to maintain order, he told her when he returned home. Having been elected moderator, it was his role to be sure all opinions were heard, and there were many of them. A large faction wanted to take on the British directly—the militia was ready. Another large faction wanted to meet the British demand rather than find out the hard way whether or not *Spencer's* cannon could reach them—that meant raising five thousand dollars in three days.

The meeting reluctantly voted to hire the money, taxing all buildings—saltworks, barns, dwellings, hen coops, even privies, to pay it back.

"I'm sorry, sweetheart, but our assessment is going to be very large," Elijah told her when he returned. "We'll have to sell Florida and the chaise. And Blitzen."

Losing his riding horse would hurt him, she knew. Letting the chaise and Florida go was no easy matter, either, but she only shrugged. Of course they must be sold!

"I know how much that chaise means." Elijah said sympathetically. "It worries me, what losing it will do to you."

Taking his face between her hands, she kissed him. "Thank you," she said softly. "I'll be fine. Let's consider the chaise—and Florida, and Blitzen—our contributions to the cause of freedom. And let's just hope *Spencer* goes away."

"No doubt she will. She knows there's no more money to be had from this town."

"I hid our silver and jewelry. Is it safe to retrieve them?"

He smiled. "You were afraid we wouldn't pay."

"Yes."

"Why not leave them where they are? We'll polish the silver up later, when this war is done." He stretched the tension from his weary back. "It'll be all over, one day, and we'll get another chaise and more horses, I swear." Taking her hand, he kissed it and added, with a grin, "And maybe a coach, for you to ride around in, like Lady Washington."

After the ransom was paid, everyone waited breathlessly until the *Spencer* left. The militia continued drilling, just in case the enemy returned.

✦᭜᭜ 4 ᭜᭜✦

Then a personal loss befell them. John Warden knocked on their door, and in a single glance, Molly knew.

"Mother's gone," he said. "Yesterday. She just didn't wake up."

Molly tried to take it in.

"You were ever special to her, Molly."

"And she to me," Molly wavered, then wept. "I failed her. I failed her miserably, John!"

"We all failed her. How could any of us live up to her example?" He broke down then. Elijah, coming in from stacking wood, found them in the hall, clinging together, and embraced them both.

"Please accept my sympathy," he said to John when their tears subsided. "What can we do?"

"There will be a memorial service tomorrow at noon. Burial afterwards."

"We'll be there with you." Elijah walked John to his horse, an arm across his friends' shoulders. Numb, Molly sat at the kitchen table for a long time, then made herself lay out supper.

She must keep going, but she was paralyzed by guilt. All these years, she had deliberately put Elizabeth Warden out of mind, careful not to dwell on the steadfast kindness and unwavering faith that her Mistress lived by. She had always known that her love of fine things ran counter to Mrs. Warden's values of simplicity. Even more had she labored to put Elizabeth Warden behind her when loving Isaac had become a reality . . . .

Her thoughts stopped dead in their tracks, a chill embraced her. Isaac! Surely he would be in Yarmouth tomorrow!

Stunned, she nearly dropped the soup plates. Quickly she set them down on the table, ladled chowder into them, called the family, and fled up the back stairs.

Elijah followed. "I know what she meant to you, dear one, and I'm so sorry," he murmured as he held her close.

He would comfort her! He whom she had betrayed, along with Elizabeth Warden!

"I'd like some time alone," she whispered. "Can you manage?"

"Of course. Debby will help."

He left, and when he retired much later, he did not try to speak with her, only kissed her forehead, smoothed her hair, climbed in beside her and fell quickly into sleep.

She was alone as she had never been, alone with worries and fears that overshadowed her grief. Isaac. Tomorrow she would see him. No hint of personal response could be allowed to pass between them, no glimmer of a shared secret. Could she do it? For more than two long years, since the war began, she had thought of him incessantly, even when trying not to. Could she shake the hand that had touched her with such sure intimacy, behold the eyes that had cruelly deceived her, without giving herself away? And Isaac himself—would he inadvertently reveal something? Her husband would be right there. If he saw anything that suggested an intimacy between herself and Isaac, it would wound him so deeply that there would be no possibility of forgiveness. She could not bear hurting him so.

Her anxiety rose intolerably; she tried to focus on Mistress Warden, that wonderful woman who had given an impoverished child a chance, who had helped Elijah's wooing, had sent money when Molly needed it. Whom Molly had never found time to visit, knowing that the Merrick way of life was centered on the wrong things.

She spent the night listening to Elijah's peaceful breathing, tried to cry but could not, tried to still her inexorable thoughts but failed, her only comfort gleaned now and then from the presence of her husband.

Leaving the children with Debby, they rode with Mariah and John in the Warden's carriage, rolling beneath the golden canopy of maples that reached over the high road, gradually giving way to the marshes and tidewaters of the bay as they approached Yarmouth. Beauty that Elizabeth Warden would never see now. Beauty she had loved so well, believing it a divine gift.

They took their seats in the packed Meeting House where everyone silently, respectfully, waited for witness.

There was not a sound.

Many minutes went by.

Then from the back of the room came the creaking of a chair, and a voice. "Our Lord was asked how many times we should forgive. He answered, seventy times seven. My mother forgave seventy times seven."

It was Isaac.

"I deceived her when I was young," his voice went on. "And I deceived her later in my life. But she'd have forgiven me if she had ever known." His voice broke, and a rustling suggested that he'd sat back down.

Molly sat in amazed silence. She'd heard his voice at last.

And it didn't matter. Nothing stirred within. Only what he said was important—yes, had Mistress Warden known of the transgressions of her children, she'd have forgiven them.

Could Molly forgive herself? She fought her tears. On his lap, Elijah opened his hand in invitation, and she took it, accepting his comfort. Oh, Elijah, she silently wept, would you still love me if you knew?

"She befriended me in time of need." From the far side of the room a wavering old woman's voice entered the Quaker silence. "After the war, I was destitute. I asked her for passage to Boston, where I might find work. She gave me enough money and more, even knowing that my husband had died at Yorktown." Died fighting, contrary to Quaker insistence on pacifism.

Again silence, quiet so thick it was as a presence.

"I will always remember her wisdom," said a disembodied voice. "She showed me the Way."

Silence.

"She was a fine helpmeet to her husband. They knew God's love together."

It went on until, after a lengthy pause, the congregation rose, wordlessly shook hands with one another, moved out and around the building to the cemetery at the back, where the Quakers buried their own in rows of unmarked graves.

There he was, with a homely woman, standing on the far side of the plain pine coffin that was smaller at the foot than at the head. He was watching her, over that infinite space, and Molly looked back steadily, easily, without any effort.

He did not move her.

After all this time, all these months, the hours of misery, the place in her heart where he had lodged was sealed up, and did not permit him entry. Instead, it opened now to her husband, standing beside her and ready to steady her if she needed him, and she was filled with a flowing gratitude, made deeper for the remorse of her betrayal.

Without fanfare, the coffin was lowered into the hole dug for it. The men stepped forward; then the only the sound was that of the earth falling onto the coffin's lid.

She watched as Elijah moved to help John. He was a good man, her husband. Better than she deserved. Over the years he had tried so hard to bridge the gap between the poverty she had known and the security she had so badly needed. He was a bulwark—her refuge, protector, provider. Her house, her possessions, even her social standing, were the result of his love. He had given her everything.

Elijah!

Molly and Mariah walked with each other to the house where Elizabeth Warden would never again welcome them.

"Do you believe in Heaven?" Mariah asked.

"I'd like to," Molly replied. They were close enough as friends not to worry about the heresy of Mariah's even having asked.

"I'd like to think she is with John's father," her friend said. It had been ten years since Abel Warden had passed.

"I'd like to think she's with my mother." Molly's eyes filled yet again, but she persisted. "And I'd like to think my mother would have a chance to thank Mistress for everything she did to help us." Their conversation would only lead her to greater sorrow; she changed its direction. "Mariah, I'd like to meet your sister-in-law."

"Certainly," her friend agreed.

They entered the house where Molly had been a servant so long ago. Family and a few close friends, subdued, milled about, spoke quietly. By the parlor fireplace Isaac stood with his wife.

Mariah led her to them. "Marian, may I present Mistress Molly Merrick?"

Molly curtseyed, as did Isaac's wife. "I'm sorry, so sorry," Molly murmured. "Such a great loss."

She turned to Isaac, took his hand in both of hers, looked deeply into his eyes. "I know that her death will leave a great void in your life, Isaac."

Then she turned away so that he need not respond. There was no shiver of passion, not even a secret sliver of attraction. There was only her sympathy, and she saw that he knew it.

He was gone from her heart and she was free, more free than she'd ever been, to love and cherish Elijah, to be the wife he deserved, to somehow make her treachery up to him, to be his and his only for many more years, years of happiness and peace as they grew old together.

If the war would only end.

CHAPTER

Africa

America's second war with England was finally done. Ships of the merchant fleet, at anchor throughout the conflict, were readily refitted and went to sea quickly, but new challenges awaited the mariner.

With the threat of Bonaparte gone, Europe now carried for herself. This unwelcome competition greatly reduced the profits mariners could expect. Even worse was the interference of manufacturing. Encouraged by the embargo and fostered by the war, America was producing cloth and casting metal of its own. Now in political power, the owners of factories and forges imposed protective tariffs.

Once again the mariner paid.

＋∞ I ∞＋

WHEN ELIJAH MERRICK RETURNED from his first post-war European voyage in 1815 and saw how high were the duties on wool, hemp and iron, he realized his financial future looked grim. Not only were the tariffs making great inroads into his profits, but the war had cut short the time to accumulate sufficient savings for securing his future.

It was true that soon he would have fewer mouths to feed. His daughter Elizabeth was to marry Tony's oldest son and would be leaving home soon; Sarah married in January, when everyone learned the war was over. Twenty-one year old 'Lije lived now in Boston, apprenticed to a tea merchant. Sonny, their younger boy, would go to sea in a few years. Susannah would surely take a husband in the foreseeable future. There was his sister, of course, who refused to marry anyone, and his mother, who required more and more care as she declined. But eventually Mother would fade away, and maybe he could persuade Debby to wed Cousin Nathan. That would leave only Molly and himself. Most likely they'd be comfortable, but would not be able to live as they once had, entertaining and dancing and setting the social pace of Waterford. Molly would hate that! And Elijah knew he would hate it, too.

Discouraged, he saw to the offloading of his cargo and its assessment, then reported to his owner, reviewing the dismal results.

"I was afraid of this," Fuller said. "While you were gone, I thought a lot about developing a new route, Elijah."

"As I remember, we did that once before. The Hamburg run."

"Indeed we did! Now it's American-manufactured stuff we need to get around, rather than French or British blockades." Fuller grimaced, then brightened. "I've been investigating the possibilities. Africa is the answer."

Elijah didn't even have to think about it. "I will not enter the slave trade, Benjamin." It was not negotiable.

"No, no!" Fuller exclaimed. "The trinket trade! A trade in trifles—beads and buttons, knives and colored cloth for the natives in exchange for ivory and gold dust, and ice in exchange for coffee."

"Ice?"

"White people have plantations off the Gold Coast. The demand for ice and fresh apples and grapes will be enormous there, on an island called Principe by the Portuguese, Prince's Island by English speakers," Fuller told him. "Your ship, *Sweet Charity* is very fast, is she not? And can use a light breeze that might becalm a larger vessel? She could get that perishable stuff to Africa before the fruit even hints at spoiling."

Fruit? Ice?

Africa. A whole new route.

"Her hold is somewhat small," Elijah reminded him.

"But such cargo as she can carry would be very desirable. They'd kill for ice, let alone grapes, on the coffee plantations, and you can trade with the natives on the mainland for gold dust and ivory. They love beads and knives and mirrors that won't take up much space on the way over—and coming back? How much room can tusks and dust and coffee beans take? No tariff, Elijah! I think we could get in at least two voyages before everyone else tries to cash in on trade there, but even when they do, they'd never be able to match us in perishables. A larger, slower ship would lose the ice half way across the Atlantic."

They pictured the competition's profit literally melting away, and laughed at so pleasant a scenario.

"She's not all mine, actually," Elijah explained. "I own her with some friends." Waterford's captains had not yet decided what to do with her. They were hell-bent on getting back into ships with large carrying capacity and were even now out on whatever vessels they could find, voting to leave *Charity's* destiny to Elijah, to do with as he saw fit. She was still in port. Being copper sheathed, thus protected, she could put out to sea very quickly with little restoration needed.

"What's your thinking, Benjamin?"

"Why don't we form a corporation with your friends, Merrick? You provide the ship, and I'll fund the cargo. We'll draw up shares to divide the profits. I think we'd earn a fine return."

If the plan worked, it would help greatly in rebuilding his savings. He'd take his profit as member of the corporation besides captain's share and could hire labor to plow his fields and shovel his salt. Very possibly he and Molly could enjoy the life they loved so well after all, given a few years.

Africa, he thought, could set the Merricks up for a lifetime! All he needed was *Charity*.

❧❀❧

But John had bigger ideas. "Let's buy them out, all of them, and go into partnership, just you and me. The idea of marketing perishables and ice is brilliant, Elijah! My hat's off to Benjamin Fuller! I'd heard about the African trade just now opening up, but I'd never once thought about trading in chilled American fruit!"

"I hadn't heard about Africa it at all," Elijah admitted. A couple of months at sea put a man out of touch, and this route was very new. But John had retired and got the Boston newspapers daily.

His friend went on enthusiastically. "My father's inheritance is still intact."

"How much would you throw into the venture?"

"Half the ship's value. Your credit's good—I'm sure you could raise the other half."

Elijah mulled over the sums. "We'll need to fund the cargo too. What if I asked Fuller for a loan for my half of *Charity*, and offered him the chance to invest in the cargo to whatever extent he wishes, as a way of repaying him for his idea, so to speak? I think the fellows right here in Waterford would purchase shares for the balance."

"Great idea! After the first trip, everyone will have a profit and you can pay back your loan for the ship and Fuller will be satisfied. We can get another loan for your share of the second trip's cargo, I'll buy the rest and after that we'll be equal partners!"

"That's even better! Do you remember how we used to talk of having a ship, the two of us?" Elijah asked happily. "Who'd have thought we could make it come to pass?"

"You're agreed then?"

"Indeed I am!"

"Thank God!" John cheered. "I thought retirement would be preferable to working for the miserable profit we mariners make now, but I was wrong. I want to go to sea again, and I'd be honored to sail with you."

They shook hands on it.

❧

"The land!" gasped Molly. "The house! You put them up as security for a loan?"

"Africa is a windfall, my darling! Everyone has agreed to sell their shares in *Charity* at a decent price and they'll join Fuller in putting up the money for cargo. We'll be tapping into the market before anyone else besides, and even when there is competition, we'll make a profit because of the ice! I'm confident you'll never have to smoke another herring."

"You won't hear me object to that!" Yet a guarded cloud of doubt remained in her eyes.

"I would never put our house at risk if I wasn't sure of myself. You must know that."

"Indeed I do. But why not let your friends continue to invest in cargo, instead of taking a loan for the second trip?"

"I'm pretty sure I can restore the life we have known and loved with this windfall. If John and I can finance the operation by ourselves, the profit will be much, much larger, and you and I will have what we need that much sooner."

"I see! I'm behind you all the way." She hugged him. "If anyone can do it, you can."

⋈✦⋈

"You never told me you had a rich friend," grumbled Fuller when Elijah presented the proposal. "But I'll take what I can get, and thank you." He put up money for a third of the cargo and Elijah's half of the ship.

⋈✦⋈

They went out together, he and John, as they had dreamed about when they were boys. *Charity* was a delight to handle; John's company was pure pleasure. Profit from apples and grapes, in season now, and trinkets and red cloth translated into a great amount of gold dust and ivory and coffee. The money they made from the first voyage was greater than he had even dared to hope.

"Tell you what," he said to Molly upon his return. They had wakened early enough for lovemaking before the household stirred, and were enjoying the morning, at ease, fulfilled. "I'll guarantee a fancy party when we come back from the next voyage."

"We'll be rich so soon?"

"Rich enough!"

"Oh, Elijah, you are wonderful," she said softly, showering him with kisses. "May I have a new dress, do you think? For the party?"

"Of course," he laughed. "Tell me the color you'll choose and I'll bring back tribal jewelry to go with it."

"Shall I pierce my nose?" She giggled as she used to, before she had seen so many dreams fall prey to disappointment.

"I'd wait on that," he advised. "Let me see if nose piercing is still the fashion in Africa." He trailed a hand over her, there before his eyes and lush as ever. Her response to his loving was wonderful; the intimacy they shared just seemed to get better and better.

Drat! He'd be gone all too quickly.

But back soon enough. And in just a few years they would rise, and Waterford would rise with them. He felt young again, with the promise of fortune once more within his reach.

"Oh, Molly," he murmured, "just hang on; the sky's the limit. Can you do it?"

"Can you?" she retorted, mischief in her eyes, and moved his hand to her breast.

✦✦✦✦✦

He strolled over to the armory, hoping to see some friends. There would be no time to go acalling, and most of his martial comrades were at sea in any case. He and John would take the packet up to Boston tomorrow, onload the ice and fruit and trinkets, sail as soon as the wind and tide permitted.

Sam Hall and Sol Denning were there.

"Elijah!" They shook his hand and clapped his shoulder. "When do we get to invest in shares again?" Sol asked.

"When I'm rich enough to retire," he replied.

They guffawed. "How about a hand of poker? Sam asked. "Sol and I were just sitting here, wondering what to do."

"Poker it is!" They dealt the armory's cards and poured the requisite rum. The game was well under way and Elijah was happily losing when they heard hoofbeats and a pause while a rider dismounted and came to the door.

"There's been an accident." It was a Warden servant, grave and deferential. "Master John was checking his salt vats. One of them collapsed, and he was beneath it," the man reported, his face grim with grief and worry.

Jesus! All that weight falling!

"He's asking for you, Master Merrick. My horse is outside. Please take it; I'll walk back."

Elijah was so stunned that his mind refused to function. He could only stare.

"Hurry, man!" Sol urged. "Hurry before it's too late!"

Too late. Too late.

"Tell Molly I'll be at the Warden's," Elijah called as he ran, mounted the manservant's horse, rode faster than he had ever ridden before. The Warden's door was opened by the young doctor who had settled in Waterford only a few months ago. "I'm glad to see you, Captain," he said somberly. "He's been asking for you when he's conscious."

"What is his condition?" Elijah's voice was not quite steady from the exertion of the ride and his shock.

"His vitals are crushed. He will die from bleeding inside."

"And the pain? There must be a lot of pain!"

"Yes. Try to keep him quiet; laudanum works better that way. If he must speak, of course let him, but don't protract your conversation."

"Does he . . . know . . . it is the end?"

"He knows."

"And his wife?"

"Yes. She won't want to leave him, but I know he wants to see you alone. I'll make sure she goes without a fuss."

Alone. John wanted to see him alone to say good-bye. They had been such good friends for so many years . . . .

Elijah's heart boomed in his ears, dread shuttered his brain. He followed the doctor, shaking all over, to meet his friend in his last hour.

In the darkened room, John lay still, very still, soaked in sweat, motionless in his effort to contain pain. Beside him knelt Mariah, her forehead on the edge of the bed, hands clasped in prayer, her tears an unending stream.

"Merrick is here," the doctor said softly, and John opened his eyes which were black, the pupils dilated. The doctor took Mariah's arm; she shook it off. They spoke together in whispers, the young man firm and insistent. Elijah helped her to her feet and embraced her briefly. The doctor took her away. The door closed behind them.

He took a chair to the bedside, sat down, and wiped his sweating palms on his trousers. He was terrified. Reluctantly he dragged his gaze to John's slate-colored face, steeling himself because he must behold his friend's inescapable agony. Oh, how he yearned to take some of its weight, relieve John somehow!

"We're not supposed to talk," he whispered, knowing his full voice would tremble if he used it.

"No," John whispered back. He lay silently for some time, looking at the moldings where the walls met the ceiling, then back at Elijah. "No Boston tomorrow," he said at last and tried to smile.

Oh, John, he grieved, John! That you should die this way! "Do you want me to sponge your brow?" he asked helplessly. Water and a towel were nearby.

"No," John said.

Did his presence give his friend comfort? Elijah wondered. A tear trailed down his face; he swept it away.

"My God, John," he whispered wretchedly. "I am sorry, so sorry."

"Me, too." John held his breath. "Something I must tell you," he gasped.

"Hush. Don't talk, my friend."

"Have to. It's Molly," John ground out. "She has betrayed you. With my brother."

The words hung there like a pall in the hot, heavy air of the room.

"Betrayed me? With Isaac?" Elijah waited and watched, rocked to the core. How could it be?

"Told me. Night before his wedding. Drunk." John's body arched in a rigid holding in of fresh pain. "He's bored. Now. Might come for her. Again."

Isaac Warden.

Molly Deems.

A new pain was growing, growing, deep in his gut.

"Should have. Told you. Before. Couldn't. Forgive me."

"You need no forgiveness," Elijah said as steadily as he could. "You have done nothing wrong."

Molly had betrayed him!

"After you left. With *Avenger*. Suspected. Not sure. 'Til he told me. You must. Prevent him. I can't."

Around his own intolerable pain, Elijah murmured, "Thank you, my friend, for telling me. I'll take care of it."

"Stay?"

"Here?"

"Parlor."

"Yes, of course."

Evidently relieved, John's eyes closed, and he allowed the laudanum to take him away.

Elijah could only grope his way from the room, down the stairs, seating himself in the parlor, defenseless, hostage to his friend's passing.

He anchored his mind there, to the indisputable, inexorable fact of death. The man he had admired when they were both only children, whose friendship had always meant more to him than the regard of any other, was now in his final hours. Through John Warden, Elijah's life had been altered—John had chosen him for a friend. His steadfast loyalty had sustained the young Elijah when he had lived with Farmer Crosby. John had taken him to his home in Yarmouth where Elizabeth and Abel Warden had encouraged and uplifted him by their attention and affection, and in their home the most profound change of all had occurred. . . .

There! Avoid it as he might wish, he could not. For the Wardens had been the instrument by which Elijah had met Molly, and John, now dying, was the instrument by which Elijah's life with Molly was over.

Within himself a cry, primal, enraged, desolate, sounded where only he could hear it.

Jesus! God! It cannot be! John is delirious, he told himself, fighting to keep steady. And yet, he knew miserably, if there was ever a time in their life together when Molly could have taken a lover without his even suspecting, that time lay during the embargo when *Avenger* was out to sea. If he recollected correctly, Isaac had been living on Cape Cod then, often visiting his brother.

He remembered that he had not trusted Molly when it came to Isaac Warden. There may have been something between the two of them, once. Long, long ago when they all were young and vigorous, when John Warden's life lay ahead of him and not, as now, behind. . . .

She had seemed so happy recently, he thought. Content at his side, loving and tender. And all the time she was hiding a secret from him, as well she might. There was no telling what he would have done if he had found out.

Around and around his mind circled, refusing to fix itself anywhere, wheeling about like a gull over carrion, looking at death and love and life all at once.

John! John, did you have to tell me?

But of course he had to. Isaac was bored with his wife, and might come after Molly.

And Molly—would she receive him? Oh, God, I don't even know, Elijah wept, broken. In time—minutes or hours, he did not know which—he realized he could not go home. His wife was the last person he wanted to see! He would stay here, as he'd promised, and when his friend had passed on, he'd go up to Boston to take *Sweet Charity* out by himself. But before he sailed, he would confront Isaac.

It took John until dawn to die, in the longest night Elijah Merrick had ever spent.

✦∞ 2 ∞✦

Isaac Warden's house in Boston was quietly fashionable, connected to other houses on either side, three stories high, three granite steps leading to its richly paneled and painted front door with a brass knocker.

Elijah was let in by a maid who bobbed him a curtsy and led him to the parlor where high ceilings and white-painted ornate moldings set off heavy cream and maroon flocked wallpaper. The floor was lushly carpeted with Turkish rugs, burgundy velvet draperies were held back at the windows with gold cords. There were paintings on the walls, and the fireplace was framed in white marble. Soft chairs and deep settees and small tables were artfully scattered about.

Isaac Warden was as well-appointed as his house, wearing a silken suit with long trousers and a jaunty cravat. He entered the room with curiosity, not knowing who had come calling. His handsome countenance was beginning to show signs of fleshiness, but his yellow hair was as abundant as ever and his face nearly unlined. This man had not spent a lifetime at sea! His curiosity turned to caution as he saw who was there.

They shook hands, though Elijah hated to extend that courtesy.

"To what may I attribute the honor of your presence?" Isaac asked.

It appeared that he had as yet no news from Waterford.

"I have come to find out if you have made a fool of me."

"Oh?"

"I would know, Isaac, whether you have ever been my wife's lover."

"Her lover?"

"You heard me."

A long, fraught moment passed.

Isaac laughed. "Great God, Merrick! I would never admit to such a thing! What makes you think I would dishonor your wife by confirming it, even if it were true?"

"You do not deny it."

"Nor do I admit it."

He's a lawyer, Elijah reminded himself, and can use words as a sword. Changing his approach, he said, "I have reason to believe that you and Molly have deceived me, and I need to know the truth so I may deal with it in my own mind. I think you owe me that much."

"I owe you nothing," Isaac Warden said coldly, now fully in possession of himself. "Nothing whatsoever."

Elijah had not meant to lose his temper, but this show of smug superiority overturned his resolution. "You son of a bitch!" He found himself gripping the lapels of Isaac's elegant suit coat before he even knew it, backing him up to the wall. "Tell me what I want to know!"

But Warden was strong and broke the hold. They faced each other, inches apart, breathing heavily. "Would you call me out?" Isaac sneered. "I warn you, I'm a good shot."

"I'm not bad myself," Elijah said. "And yes, I will call you out unless you answer me."

"Very well," Isaac returned, without moving an inch or giving ground at all. "Dueling is out of favor now, and I don't want to risk hurting my professional reputation. So I will tell you that I've had your wife. I will tell you that I had her when she was ripe, and I had her before, when she was a virgin. And if an apology is what you want, by all means accept mine."

Elijah stepped back. It was more, much more, than he had bargained for. Look proud, he told himself. Look as though it isn't such shocking news. He straightened his shoulders.

Smoothing his rumpled coat, Isaac asked, "Did you never wonder, Merrick, how it was that you could beat me up so easily behind the Yarmouth Inn so long ago? I was a match for you then, even drunk. But we, Molly and I, needed you to carry her away that very night. We needed you willing to wed instantly, rather than waiting for the proper time. Then if it turned out that she was carrying my child, it would not ruin her; you would assume it was yours. Which your eldest daughter well may be. Is there anything else you'd like to know?"

A sort of protective screen was suddenly in place between them, behind which Elijah felt nothing. "No," he said. "But there's something you should understand. I will shoot you if you so much as glance at her again."

"That sounds like a challenge, Merrick."

"If you accept it as such," Elijah returned firmly, meeting his adversary's disdainful eye with an intent that could not be denied. "I'd be glad meet you, whenever you require, preferably behind your brother's house. Once he is buried."

There was a pause while Isaac took it in. Buried.

Elijah spat on the marble hearth and turned.

"My God, man! What's happened?"

He did not answer as he descended the granite steps.

"Merrick!"

Elijah's voice broke as he called over his shoulder. "Your brother is dead, Isaac Warden. Go you to Waterford and lay him to rest. And leave my wife alone!"

✦∞ 3 ∞✦

It was a tormented, aching trip out to Africa, a trip that held Elijah Merrick prisoner in the lonely captain's cabin where there was no distraction, where he was isolated with misery and humiliation. After his confrontation with Isaac, there was nothing to shield him from the hateful knowledge that Molly had betrayed him. There was nothing he could do to forget Isaac's words and their awful implications, implications that multiplied and festered in his brain. To know that Molly had tricked him before they were wed, that after twelve years of marriage she had betrayed him again, was made worse because all the while he had believed, without ever doubting it, that she loved him. . . .

His isolation in the captain's cabin was unbearable. There was no one to whom he could speak, nor even anyone to whom he could write a letter about the burden now weighing upon him. But he would write, nonetheless, record his thoughts in order to keep them anchored to the reality of his life, rather than banging back and forth like a loose cannon in a hurricane. Lighting his lamp, he brought out rum and paper and ink.

February 12, 1816. I am on my way to Africa, to restor my fortune.
I will not share my windfalle with my wife. She does not deserv
to gain by my work. I long to punish her by forbidding parties and
dances and such, but if I do, everywon in town will know something
is wrong. It is bad enough, knowing how wrong everything is with-
out everyone else knowing it, too.

Bound in on all sides, he was helpless. There was no way to undo
the past and no way to escape the flail of frustration and mortification.

Of course, he could chastise her privately. In fantasies fueled by rum
and rage, he beat her without mercy, made her service his body on her
knees, made her sleep on the floor beside their bed where he could rape
her at will. Yes! He would rape her!

February 15, 1816. I know I will not do thes things. They would
make me into a beest, a brute. One more defeet, really. I must find a
way to live with her in an estrang'd state. I can not go home without
a plan.

Not go home. A glimmer of light showed there. Might he not live
elsewhere? In Hamburg, perhaps? The city he had loved so well when he
was young. Where, no doubt, he could make a living in business of one
sort or another.

He could just disappear.

February 20, 1816. If I us'd Charity as my home, sailing here and
there in trad, bas'd in Hamburg, I would never have to see Molly
againe. She would have to sell one treasur after another to support
herselfe. In a few years, she would lose everything. The hous would
be empty. The taxes unpaide. The paint peeling, the land gone to
weeds. She would have to live at the poor farm unless 'Lije took her
in. She would have nothing of her own.

That, at least, was satisfactory under the circumstances, an acceptable alternative to returning and hiding behind a veneer of normalcy. It was something else to think about, a release from the prison he was trapped in. Whether he would do it or not—that would depend on the manner in which time worked its way with him, if it weakened his resolve or strengthened it. He knew how to wait for the wind and the tide. He would wait now. Africa was close, and once he got there, he could seek the companionship of coffee plantation owners, of officers who manned the fort at the neighboring island of Sao Tome, of the women a sailor found in any port. Pleasure and distraction could be had; he need not hurry home. There might be other ships in the harbor at Prince's Island. He could visit their captains and invite them aboard *Charity*. Whatever he could do to enjoy himself, that he would do while he continued his bid for the windfall that lay on the Dark Continent and while he decided what to do about his ruined life.

When he anchored in the harbor at Prince's Island, he found, to his consternation, that the place was cluttered with all manner of vessels. Word of gold and ivory and coffee had gotten out, just as Benjamin Fuller thought it would. But never had Elijah expected this throng—ships from many nations all crowding in, hoping to cash in on his special trove.

There would be plenty of company, at least, providing much needed distraction. When he went ashore to sell the perishables, he discovered the reason for the mass of mariners. Not only had the word of riches got out, but the coffee crop was much delayed by unseasonable weather, and added to this, the gold and ivory had not arrived either. The natives on the mainland were busy with a war and had no time to bring these treasures to the coast. So each vessel that came in stayed, waiting for the coffee crop to ripen, hoping that by the time it did, the tribal difficulties would be over and the gold and ivory would be brought in, too.

Well, Elijah Merrick would wait with them! There was no hurry to return home, that was certain. He would put his wife behind him, where she must remain. He would go to work, right now, to rise above the hurt.

As before, the ice and apples were very welcome and yielded a solid profit from which he could support himself and the crew while *Charity* waited with the rest.

March 5, 1816. It ranes daily. The heate is awfull. Everyone is waiting. All the captains play cards together, either on board or at the dwellings of the plantashun owners. We set the watch with as few of our crew as possible so the men can go ashor and find such distracshun as they can.

Multitudes of visits were exchanged, countless card games played, much alcohol consumed. The days began to slip by instead of hanging motionless as they had at sea, and for this Elijah was grateful. He was seldom alone, drank to oblivion so that he could forget who he was or where he was coming from, denied himself nothing.

But then the Waterford contingent showed up. Bradley came in first on *Eventide,* and Pollard was only a few hours behind in *Raven.* They brought with them remembrance of himself as he had been, and forced on him the role he would have to play whether he returned home or not. He went to meet the challenge instead of waiting for it to come to him.

"Elijah!" David Bradley was delighted to see him. "I figured you'd be in these latitudes!"

"David!" They shook hands. "I see your owners discovered Africa."

"Indeed they did. Pollard's coming too. Those are his sails, yonder. We left on the same tide." Bradley gestured toward the horizon where, indeed, a set of sails could be seen. "Do you suppose everyone in the world is here?"

"Looks like it," Elijah said, helping himself to Bradley's rum. "A great crowd—you'll enjoy them if you decide to hang around."

David looked shocked, as well he should. Elijah explained the situation.

"Oh, God," Bradley moaned. "What else can we do but wait? Blast those natives." A burst of raucous laughter from a nearby vessel reached them. "Having a regular party here, hey?"

"Oh, yes indeed. But it would be much more enjoyable were John here." He must take this tack briskly; he knew his absence at his friend's funeral must seem strange.

Bradley examined him closely. The careful exploration began. "I heard you were in town when he died."

"I was."

"We missed you."

Elijah said nothing.

"You must be sore distressed to lose him."

"Yes."

"Mariah took your absence as an homage," David said looking somewhat embarrassed at so private a communication. "I heard her say, myself, that you could not bear to see him buried."

"Yes." Elijah gestured vaguely. "I'm much grieved. Fortunately there's a lot of mixing and mingling here just now, fellows to drink with and play cards whether they speak English or not. It helps keep me from dwelling on it."

"Ah, yes, of course!" David Bradley was happy for a change of subject. "And speaking of a welcome distraction, I have a letter from Molly."

It took all his strength to reach for it with a steady hand, slip it into his jacket pocket. "Thanks," he said with a voice he thought sounded normal. "How would you like to row over to yonder ship? It's from Lubec, in North Germany. The captain is a gentleman through and through who can empty your pockets quicker than you can blink an eye. And then lose it all again when he is drunk, which generally takes no longer than an hour in this heat."

"I'm game," Bradley said with a grin, making no remark about Elijah's apparent lack of excitement at hearing from his wife. "I'll leave word with my mate. He'll tell Pollard when he gets here."

It was nearly midnight by the time Elijah was alone in his cabin again, finally able to take the letter out of his pocket where it had been burning a hole all the time he lost at cards.

Dear Elijah:

The funeral is done—a very sad business. Mariah accepted your absence with grace. She appears to understand it.

I do not understand, but I accept. I realize that John was a friend of many years, going all the way back to your childhood. Perhaps your grief is just too deep. I would help to mend your broken heart if I could.

Perhaps knowing your devoted wife awaits your return and the chance to hold and comfort you—perhaps that, in its small way, will help to sustain you. For I do love you so, dear Elijah.

He stared at it, turned it over, picked off the sealing wax.

The letter brought it all back again. Her words made it even worse, reminding him that she used them well but did not mean them. Just as she knew the right postures to assume, the right way to entice him in bed, or to draw her eyebrows into a small frown of concentration when he spoke at length, as though she was listening very carefully, very respectfully.

He fetched a bottle of wine from his cupboard and sloshed some into his coffee mug. Not that he needed more to drink, but it was time to allow himself to wonder if the words in her letter described the state of her heart now. He needed to be fortified.

April 5, 1816. When I came hom after the embargo, she was different. She sayd she felt abandonn'd and I can see that it must have been hard on her. After that I was out most of the time until the war started, and then my oblugashun was to the militia. She was very quiet. I thot it was due to the lode of work she must carry. But after Raggett left, and after Mrs. Warden's funeral, she seem'd more abel to embrac our life no matter how much it had chang'd. She seem'd content.

Laying down his pen, he replenished his mug. He wished she had not written, wished David Bradley had not delivered the letter, because it admitted the possibility of hope. Because the letter and these confusing, muddled memories raised the question: had she come to love him after all?

But did it matter, really? Did it change anything?

He continued to labor with his pen.

The hole situashun is impossiblle. No matter what her true feelings are now, I can never accept her expreshun of them at face value. I will never be abel to trust her, ever. No, it doesn't matter how she feels. She offer'd herselfe to another man and pretend'd to love me all the while. The question is: am I going to confront her?

He drank deeply.

No man worthy of the name could let such an injury pass. No man worthy of the name would allow his wife to think she had fool'd him and got away with it. I must return long enough to let her know, long enough to punish her as I see fit, and then I will start my traid with Hamburg and never ever come back.

Then he again dived into the rounds and cards and rum. By now he had found the connections needed for carefully, discretely chosen women to be rowed out to *Charity*. In their merciful embrace, he lost himself, cherished them, paid them well, every one. They helped distance him from his difficulties. He would have given them every penny he had by way of thanks, except that he had spent more than was wise already. Unless he was careful, he'd be short of cash when the coffee crop did come in.

And so he carefully drank on, gambled on, whored on, and was totally unprepared for the mate who knocked one morning on his cabin door.

"Sir," the man called deferentially, "one of the boys is ill."

"Oh?" His head was heavy and thick; the heat, he thought, was too much! The previous night of revelry was too much! Did the mate have to awaken him so early?

"He's been feverish for a while, sir. I've been watching him and today thought I should tell you."

"Yes, of course." Somehow he rose from his bed. "Take me to him."

The seaman, only a youngster, lay in his hammock, covered by a blanket despite the heat. He was shivering, moaning, his speech rambling. The boy's lips were caked with the dried remains of his spittle, his eyes were glazed. Elijah became aware of an odor, hovering like a miasma, and knew there was trouble ahead.

"Has he a rash?"

"Yes, sir."

"Are there others in the crew who look to you like they are becoming feverish, too?"

"It's hard to say, sir," the mate replied, looking away.

"I didn't ask for a medical opinion," Elijah rasped. "I need to know if we're in for a siege."

The man shuffled his feet and then stood straight. "There are a half dozen that seem feverish. Exhausted. Can't climb a mast, sir."

In an instant, his hangover disappeared. "Well, then, let's provision the ship, take on full consignments of beef for a broth, and tea, and bread and butter, limes and lemons if you can find them, to use in water to slake their thirst. I'll warn the fleet."

He set off for Pollard's vessel, calling up to him from his dory, not daring to come aboard lest he be carrying the fever. "I must speak with the captain," he called up. Jack appeared in a trice. "Have you got any illness aboard?" he asked.

"I don't think so," Jack called back.

"Check and be sure. I have fever. If you don't, for God's sake get away from here!" he urged.

"Right. I'll check this instant."

"If it turns out you're going home, let me send a letter with you."

"I'll move farther out," Jack decided. "But I'll get back to you before I go."

He rowed over to Bradley. "David! David!"

"Come on up, for God's sake," Bradley urged, bleary eyed. "You don't have to hang around yelling like a fish monger."

"David! Have you any fever aboard?"

"Don't know, Elijah," he called back cheerfully. "Haven't asked."

"Best you check. I have it. If you don't, you'd better head out. And let me know before you sail, so I can send word back with you." A man never sent one letter if he could send two. Should misfortune overtake one carrier, there was always the second, who might get through.

Then he closeted himself in his cabin, marshaled his pen and ink, wax for sealing. To whom should he write, and how much should he reveal?

To John Warden's heirs, certainly, to whom he would owe the value of half the ship. To the bank, from which he had arranged a loan for his portion of the cargo. In the letters, he explained that the proceeds from trinkets had been small, and until the coffee crop came in, and the gold, he could not leave. In neither of the letters did he mention the plague, nor the fact that he had squandered much of the profit gained from ice and fruit.

The last letter he must write was to Molly.

In normal circumstances he would tell her about his worries, seek comfort from her distant presence and from the love he had always believed in. But now there would be no comfort, and that was the most painful loss of all. For he saw what was even worse than financial ruin, the real reason for anger, and the rage that pursued him: he loved her still.

It was nearly more than he could bear. He would not have minded dying just then, but he knew if he did, it would not be from the fever. In Surinam, he'd had a mild case of it, when he was a cabin boy. Once you had it, however briefly, you would not get it again. No, he would probably not die, though there was little to live for except *Sweet Charity* herself. If he could save her, he would at least have something with which to start again, pay his debts and build a new life, one without Molly in it. His love would fade away because it would have to, and he could move on in the years that were left to him, with whatever they brought.

Saving *Charity* was of an instant the most important task he had ever set his mind and hand to, and he did it with the whole of his heart and soul. He must contain the plague, and hope that no one else got it.

Slaves in the deepest South never worked so hard, breaking their backs to pick cotton and carry it to the wharves of their masters, nor had American sailors in the Mediterranean, forced to row the galleys of their captors, nor tin miners on the English coast of Cornwall, laboring deep in the bowels of the earth.

> *May 28, 1816. Many are sick. I hav mov'd them up onto the deck into freshr air, and have rigg'd a sail to protect them from the sun. We have nurs'd them as best we can. We comfort them, read the Bible to them, close their eyes when they dye. I preform the servic of bureall and then they are taken to a large dich east of here and put to rest in a mass grave.*

One man and then another slipped from his grasp and fell away into the mystery of death just as John Warden had, and there was nothing Elijah Merrick could do to stop it.

A week passed, a week full of weary, bone-aching work, and then another, time in which sleep was had only in snatches, food taken on the run. By the end of the third week he knew he was beaten. Ten men had died and new victims were even yet being struck down. A few had recovered, thanks to the care he had given them, but too few; the newly ill sealed it. He was numb, strangely numb in the face of knowing his labors had done no good. Hard work had always rewarded him before. It did not do so now.

Charity was lost. When he could, he would go back in ballast and the ship would certainly be scuttled by the authorities in Boston, for fear she carried the plague. Everything he had worked for would be sent to the bottom with her, and worse—there was no future. There would be no cruising the oceans, setting up in Hamburg, sleeping in whatever harbor he chose.

No. He would have to go home.

He must face what had happened to him, must somehow face it squarely, knowing there was no escape.

The sun was low in the sky now, approaching dusk. The sea was quiet, with only a slight swell running from a distant storm. *Charity* held peace and calm to herself as she rode slowly up and slowly down, her fittings leaning and creaking in unison, her sounds close and intimate.

He went out on the quarterdeck, leaned over the rail to watch the sun set. On the main deck, the crew, those who were well and those recovering, leaned on the rails, too, looking meditatively to the west where home lay, where the same sun would rise a few hours later. Then the deck lay in sudden shadow, with only the topmost spars and rigging catching the light that gleamed there, defying the encroaching night. And then the night fell, fast, as it always did in the tropics.

It was the hour and the time for mourning, and he mourned now. Over the men he had tried to save, who died in his arms. Over David Bradley who had been lowered into the common grave with the rest, only two days ago. Over John Warden, who had not been able to die without trying to square accounts and protect his friend from further shame. John! John! We wanted a ship when we were boys. And we got one. See, John, he grieved, see where it has brought us?

He grieved for the clean, unencumbered, shining love for Molly Deems that he had once known, a love that had carried him through more than half a lifetime, mourning, as well, the loss of the man who had lived with it so long. That man was gone, buried under the weight of knowing his wife had betrayed him.

My God, he thought. It has all come to naught! Anger filled him, an anger that began slowly and then soared in an instant as he thought of the unfairness of it all, the cruelty of it. He slammed his fist against the rail. Pain shot up his arm, brought him back to the quarterdeck; he must get out of sight of his crew.

Ducking hastily into his dark cabin, he felt around for the rum in his locker. There in privacy, in the dark, he could drink as much as he liked, fall off his chair, if it came to that, sleep on the unforgiving floor. But before then, perhaps, it would be a good idea to write the final pages of his journal. Writing had helped him to sort through his difficulties, and would help him now. He fumbled, found his tinderbox and lit his lamp. The light reflected softly on the polished surfaces of his cabin—the paneling, the bunk, and the small windows. It gleamed on the brass fittings, threw a calming glow upon the low wood ceiling, gave Elijah Merrick safe haven for this moment. Then the haven would disappear. It would be scuttled, and he would have nowhere to go but the Narrow Land, a penniless man facing old age with no protection against it.

> *July 12. It is over. I must return to my wife who has ever want'd only what I could give her. Now I have nothing to give. I must return to Waterford, the town I crownd with a steepel, with a ball and a vain, so my wife might gane acceptanse.*

He paused to admire his poetry—*the town I crownd*—nice! He drank deeply of the rum.

> *Now is the time to find out what I am made of. Now I must pick up the peeces and fit them into a pattrn that will make som kind of sense. I must stop hating and start thinking.*

Tipping his chair back against his bunk, he laid it all out.

Yes, he must return to a town that measured itself by the yardstick of wealth, a yardstick that would be put to use again as soon as there was something to measure. No longer would he belong to the group that held the yardstick. Those who held it would cast pitying glances his way as he took his seat at Meeting in the gallery because he could no longer afford a choice pew. The men would go to sea and bring back all the world had to offer, while Elijah Merrick would be plowing his fields and stacking his hay and shoveling salt, no longer in the company of captains, the American nobility.

> *I will be a farmer and not a captain, but I will not pine for what is gone. What, after all, have I lost?*

With another tumbler of rum, he scrutinized it.

He had been proud of himself for smuggling a fortune out of France, proud of his great house and his wife who led so brilliant a society there, proud of controlling Pastor Simmonds with a bribe of a vane and ball and steeple, of breaking the embargo, of leading the militia as Brigadier General, of owning *Charity*.

And none of it was worth a damn.

The life he had lived in Waterford—lived like a lord, with a woman who had used him—seemed now a sham, propped up by money but collapsed and utterly swept away without it. And Waterford, so proud of itself that it must separate from its less distinguished and politically unpopular neighbors—all Waterford had ever done was pay a bribe in order to avoid a fight.

Waterford, he thought wryly, had achieved about as much significance as he had himself.

> *A few old frends will continu to receeve us. The Grays. We have always defy'd convenshun together. Cousin Nathan, prob'ly, sins he has no family of his own. The Pollards. But the rest will graduly cast us off. Without welth a man does not count in Waterford. Not in the groop of people Molly and I have gather'd.*

But at least he would not have to pay for his place any more. That could be seen as a release, could it not? From the ashes of his ruin, he was free in a way he had never before been. From it might emerge a life that could stand on its own without needing the prop of riches. A life that did not depend on an exalted circle of friends for definition of itself. That, certainly, could not be called a tragedy! Rather, it might be viewed as victory, if he chose it, upheld it, and lived from its heart without apology or shame. If he was man enough.

He raised his tumbler in a toast: to choice. There!

It was the best bargain he could make with fate, and if he was not happy, he was, at least, satisfied. Besides, he thought with a quick rise of malicious joy, this disaster took from him the burden of having to live a lie when he returned home to his wife, took from Molly all the things she loved. Yes, she would suffer as he wished her to. It was perverse of him to take pleasure in it, but he did. Perhaps he *was* perverse. He had been through enough to make him so.

> *What will Molly Merrick do? How will she act, knowing that everything she has gain'd is gone, that she is permanentlee poor and lowlee and will remane so until she dies—which may be soon if I decid to punish her.*

At this, he laughed, but knew he would not harm her. There were better ways of making her pay. She would fight tooth and nail to keep her place with all its finery, pretending, if she had to, that the Merricks were not poor, and knowing Molly, probably getting away with it. But he would not let her do it. Self-respect could not be found in running after a prize that was slipping away, especially such an unworthy one. He was going to turn his back on the society of the mariner, and she was going to turn her back, too. He would see to it.

> *I will sell my hous and repay Charity's loans. We will return to the old plase. I will keep as much acrege as I can, and farm it, keep a right of way to my vats and make salt. I will not hate it as I did when it seem'd such a lowlee thing after the life of a captain. It is not.*

Inspiration hit through the alcoholic fog.

*I shall open a stor in the old parler and in the chaimber I add'd
on, and Molly will mind it in between helping Debby with Mother.
I shall sell her collecshun of fine things—her jewlry, the silver, the
china to buy stock for the store. Oh she will hate that!*

Oh, yes, it was a pleasant thing, was it not, to picture Molly minding
a store, humble before the folk she had once queened it over, having to be
nice to those she had once denied admittance to her circle!

It would repay those years she had cuckolded him, those years she
had wrung riches from him by pretending to love him.

They'd sleep in the loft, keep Mother in the back room. When
Mother no longer needed it, he would use it for an office, and Molly
would continue to sleep upstairs, as servants did.

This caused him to feel better than he had in weeks! At last there
was a course of action to follow in his marriage, and a course of action in
the town, too, where he would belong to a new nobility—the worker, the
farmer, the miller. The mariners would not pity him for long! Nor scorn
him. There would be a place for him after all, one quite different than he
had before, but perhaps more worthy.

He blew out the lamp, drank another toast, and fell out of his chair
and onto the floor, as he'd predicted earlier. Lying there, he determined
to tear up his journal and throw the pieces into the harbor, where they
would slowly sink and be gone. His writing had served its purpose. He
would notify his bank, the Wardens, and his wife, send his letters home
with the next ship departing. Meanwhile, he would not leave here until
there were no new cases of fever and until the men who had survived it
were strong enough for the voyage. And finally, he would return to the
house of his father, to do the best he could with it, and free himself from
and the devastation brought on him by both his ship and his partner in
life's voyage.

Then he sailed away in a ship of his own dreaming.

The Survivor

❖⚬⚬ I ⚬⚬❖

Through the long and wakeful night she waited, haunted by the image of John crushed beneath a salt vat. Had he lain there a long time until he'd been found? And now, this minute, was he in terrible agony? Elijah had not returned, which could only mean that John had not yet passed on. Oh, John, Molly crooned, oh John . . . .

That he should die this way was horrible, but there was the aftermath to worry about too, causing her to be even more anxious. For she would go with Elijah to their friend's funeral, and she would once again come face to face with Isaac.

When she saw him at his mother's burial service six months ago, she shook his hand and offered her sympathy without feeling any of the attraction she had once known. But seeing each other again now, in the midst of such upheaval and its maelstrom of emotion, might they inadvertently give themselves away after all? Such disclosure would be far more devastating to Elijah than even the loss of his oldest friend.

Would it never be dawn? She rose from her bed to look out the window. Yes, the trees were darker than the darkness surrounding them—the day would start soon.

Lying down once more, she waited and must have slept, for when she roused next, the sun was shining. The day had begun, in which she would see John dead in his coffin. She would go to his wife, to comfort her, and she would face Isaac once again. But it was less daunting, she found, now that the time for action was nigh. She was ready for Elijah to fetch her, or send word for her to come to him.

She brushed her hair, dressed, crept down the stairs quietly so as not to arouse the rest of her family, pausing by the tall clock on the landing to admire it. How she loved all the fine things in her house— the mahogany dining room set, the silver and crystal in the cabinets, the upholstered chairs in the parlor, the little tables scattered here and there. All of these had become like friends rather than just possessions and gave her comfort now.

Tiptoeing into the kitchen, she found Elijah's note, pinned beneath the salt cellar on the table:

John is ded. I cannot attend his funrale. I am leeving for Boston nowe and will put out with the tide.

Staring at the words, she was unable to believe them. John was dead and Elijah was leaving? He would not honor his friend by join-ing the community's mourning? Leaving for Africa without so much as saying farewell? Without giving her the chance to comfort him, to share the ordeal with him . . . .

Elijah Merrick, Brigadier General of Waterford's militia, leader of men and mariners, had run away.

It was unthinkable.

She tried a different tack. Perhaps he was not running, but was simply choosing to take *Sweet Charity* out; her cargo was ready to load, and time was critical. Or perhaps this was how Elijah felt he could best manage his grief.

At least he would not witness any slip between herself and Isaac. This thought soothed her as she made preparations to go to the Warden's, to be present for her friend, to help however she could for as long as she was needed. She would try to think of some story that would cover Elijah's absence . . . .

"No, no, Molly!" Mariah, sobbing, held her close. "You need not explain anything. Elijah has done his part—more than his part. He gave John solace in a way no one else could."

Molly quelled an instant rise of alarm. "I don't understand."

"John asked to speak privately with him. I don't know what was said, but when I went back into the room, John seemed able to bear his pain more easily," her voice wavered, faded. "Somehow Elijah made him stronger."

Truly alarmed now, Molly asked, calmly as she could, "They talked together? I wonder what they spoke of."

"I don't know. But whatever it was, it helped John so much! Elijah gave him peace."

Peace! What kind of peace?

Oh, so slowly, so painfully, she faced the awful possibility: if anyone had suspected her liaison with Isaac, that person was his brother. Why, both of them had been under John's roof when their tryst began. John would not—could not—have said anything, caught in the middle between his brother and his friend.

Until death forced his hand.

And once John was gone, Elijah left town so he would not have to look at his adulterous wife.

Molly did not want to think about it, would not. In panic, she shut her mind, fled it as desperately and as fast as Elijah had fled from her.

He will write to me when he gets to Boston, she told herself, and ask my forgiveness for leaving so abruptly, explain he was afraid of losing the cargo if he waited, and say that he hopes to put John's death in perspective, once he gets out to sea . . . .

Everything will be fine, she told herself, once she heard from him. Isaac and his wife attended the funeral and the internment in the Congregational cemetery. He did not look her way once, and left immediately after the burial. Molly did not care—truly she was free of him. Instead, she concentrated on Mariah, a welcome distraction from her crushing worry.

When she went home three days later, there was no letter. Even a week later there was nothing. She knew, then, that he had not written before he sailed. Resolutely, she continued to keep her mind shut tight. Everything must be as it always had been, and in her attempt to make it so, she wrote to Elijah herself, pretending nothing was wrong, entrusting the letter to David Bradley who was due to sail for Africa soon. Then she filled her days with tedious household duties, relieved only by polishing her treasures, her refuge.

He will write from Africa, she told herself firmly. There will be an outbound ship, and he will send a letter home on it. I know he will.

The early spring drifted into summer.

◖◖✦◗◗

Jack Pollard had followed Bradley to Africa. He returned in early July, his news shattering. Their friends gathered in the parlor to hear him tell it. Molly listened in frozen disbelief as he described the scene off the gold coast, the crowded port, the heat—and worst of all—plague. But he carried no letter from Elijah telling her about it.

She was stunned.

"Oh, Molly, he was very distracted," Jack said apologetically. "He had to provision *Charity* and prepare for siege. Why, he didn't even come aboard my ship for fear he might be carrying the fever."

Debby gasped.

"He's already had it," Molly told her. "In Surinam, when he was young. That'll be enough to keep him safe."

"No one knows what carries it," Jack continued. "Could be clothing, or maybe a miasma. He urged me to get out instantly, since no one in my crew was sick. But even though he's well, I can't tell you not to worry. He is certainly in trouble."

Molly listened with icy hands clasped tightly in her lap as Jack described the scene out there on Prince's Island.

Neither gold nor ivory had been brought in. Although their tribal war was over, the natives would not come near them, Jack related gloomily, now that the plague was there. It would be a profitless voyage.

Or worse. Now he was describing the possibility of condemnation proceedings once *Charity* came back to Boston.

Condemnation! Even the ship would be lost?

And her husband had not written either to comfort her or to solace himself. The Elijah of old would have sent a letter saying *"Cheere up!"* declaring that the fever would pass, the siege would lift, that he would get that coffee and perhaps even the gold and ivory if he waited long enough. Their fortune would be made after all. Even if he didn't believe it, he would say so in order to spare her.

But he had not written.

No longer could she avoid the implications. The buzz of discussion about disaster—plague—miasma—condemnation—pressed upon her mounting panic, chasing after her like a hound at the hunt. Dropping all pretense, she ran from the room without excusing herself and stumbled up the stairs to her chamber, shut and locked the door, flung herself down on the bed and burrowed into her hollow.

The group would assume she had lost control, which their very presence in the house was supposed to help preserve. It was a break anyone there would overlook, for any one of them might break, too. They would stay until Molly came back down to bid them farewell, so that the pretense of bravery could be taken up again, the breach repaired. Thus had the community of seafarers traditionally dealt with disaster. So would they deal with it this day.

Molly did not care, just then, if the group disdained her for losing her composure. Losing her composure was nothing compared to what she now knew she stood to lose. For condemnation of Charity was only part of it. Condemnation by Elijah—of his wandering wife—was implicit in his having not written after all this time and especially now, with ruin staring them both in the face.

Oh, God, she moaned into her pillow. It can't be! He has run away—from me—and might lose the ship and everything on it besides. She hardly knew which catastrophe was worse.

Ruin, she told herself, that is what you must face! That is what you must deal with! Ruin!

It was preferable to guilt and the impossible future with a husband who knew everything.

With determination, she rose from her bed, went down the hall and into the back chamber, looked out over the fields that Elijah himself had farmed on and off since the days of the embargo.

All right, she spoke within herself, let's sort it out. Condemnation is not a certainty. Let's assume that it will not happen. Even if the coffee crop doesn't arrive, or the gold dust, even if he has to come back in ballast, still he can borrow more for the next trip. But until that voyage is completed, there will be no cash.

We planted only a small kitchen garden in the spring. If he comes back empty handed, there will be nothing to eat once summer is over. How could the family get through the coming winter?

Well, she would just have to enlarge the garden and somehow earn enough money to buy what they must—oil for the lamps, perhaps a pig to fatten on slops and butcher later in the winter, molasses and flour and cornmeal . . .

Yes! This must be her course.

As though a breeze had picked up and caught her sails, she was steadier now. She went back to her own chamber, straightened her hair, smoothed her dress, refreshed her face with water from her enameled pitcher. Yes, she thought fiercely, I will fight. I will fight for myself, I will fight for Elijah, and I will start now.

When she rejoined her friends, no one mentioned her absence. Reassured by her demeanor, calm and quietly hospitable, they finished their tea and left, walking home because they had sold their carriages to pay Raggett's ransom. The wealthy of Waterford were presently humbled, but there was promise in the new ships a building that could haul more cargo, in quicker time like *Sweet Charity*, clipper rigged. They walked proudly, Molly's people, with whom she had shared so much. With whom she must keep pace.

Turning to her family, she announced, "We have some gardening to do! Best we change into our work clothes."

They turned puzzled faces to her.

"If Father does not have a return cargo, there will be no money to buy food next winter," she explained. "We must enlarge the garden."

"It's too late," Debby assured her. "The summer is too far along."

"We can put in winter vegetables, like turnips. Carrots. Beets. Parsnips. Once they're established, we can just leave them in the ground and pull them when we need them."

"Arrgh," Sonny groaned. "Turnips."

"And we will make salt."

"Us? You and me?" Debby examined her carefully, to see if she was serious and then, more carefully, to see if she was ill. "Whoever heard of women making salt?"

"Sonny will help."

"I will?" Sonny asked.

"Indeed! And Cousin Nate, too."

"Nathan!" Debby was less than pleased. "Really! Must we?"

Cousin Nathan's admiration of Debby had continued, unreciprocated, through the years. "There's no else we can ask ," Molly explained. "Besides, he's a relation, and Kings stick together, don't they? Be nice to him, please."

"I'll be polite, of course," Debby said. "But if I'm really nice, he'll think I'm getting soft toward him. That would be unfair to him, and it would put me in an awkward spot."

"Your spot will be a lot more awkward if we don't have some cash next winter!" Molly retorted, reaching for her bonnet. "Tend the house while I'm out, please. Children! Get into your old clothes and start working on the garden while I'm gone. Dig along the edge nearest the orchard. Sonny and Elizabeth, you're the biggest. Pry up the clods. Susannah and Sonny, you shake the dirt out of them." It was such a small, frail work force! Sarah would have been such a help, but she was married and living in Rhode Island. Molly could have used her now!

"Where are you going, Momma?"

"To Cousin Nathan's. Now get started."

King arrived the following morning, dressed like a farmer instead of in his usual elegant attire. With Sonny's help, he set up a windlass to raise buckets of water. The following day, when the tide came in, they filled and cranked up the buckets, and emptied them into the connected vats so that the seams would begin to swell, making them watertight.

"Mama," Sonny whined, lying flat on the sandy beach. "That was an awful lot of work."

"But we're only going to run one more batch through this summer, so there'll be only one more time that we'll have to lift buckets. Isn't that right, Nathan?"

"Yes, Ma'am," Nate agreed cheerfully. "With this weather we can start pretty soon. We empty the last vat, let the third into it, let the second into the third, the first into the second, and leave the roofs rolled back so the water can evaporate. Then we'll empty the last one out and fill it with water from the third, move the second and then . . ."

"All right." Elizabeth clapped her hands over her ears. "Enough!"

"I do thank you, Nate," said Molly from the bottom of her heart. "Now, about the garden. Once we plant it, we'll put seaweed on the beds and keep it wet. The seeds will sprout in no time."

"They'll need to be watered through the rest of the summer," Nate warned.

"Of course. You're right. We'll set up a bucket brigade," Molly decided.

"Like the firefighters do!" Sonny jumped to his feet, ready to have at the carrots and turnips and parsnips.

How wonderful to be young, Molly observed, ready to go with just a moment's rest.

"Will you help us with that too, Cousin Nate?" the boy asked.

"Surely."

Debby shrugged in resignation. Nathan would be hanging about all summer. But they needed him, and dutifully, with a grateful smile, she brought him refreshment when he was sweating in the sun, laboring with them all in the garden. And later, when they emptied seawater from the first vat into the second, where it would evaporate further, becoming more and more briny, and with Sonny, hoisted water for the next batch.

The heat of the summer sun and the unaccustomed labor wore them all down. It was too hot to sleep, too hot to eat. Everyone was lethargic and looking thinner, with circles beneath their eyes as, Molly supposed, there were beneath her own. She and Debby took turns managing the chores and caring for Mother, who slept most of the time now.

Under their care, the garden grew robustly and promised good returns.

The day of the storm was unusually hot as they sweated and toiled. Molly, Debby and the children worked the bucket brigade, with ten or more feet between each of them, for Nate had yet to appear to take his accustomed place. They lugged and poured, lugged and poured under a brassy, shimmering sky. Until Olive came by.

"You must rest!" she cried. "All of you are beet red. Come, sit with me."

They staggered to the shade of the orchard, happy for the respite. Sonny and Susannah stretched out in the grass and closed their eyes, their faces flushed and sweat streaked. Molly wiped her forehead with the hem of her skirt and sent Elizabeth to the well to fetch up the jug of cider cooling in its depths.

"You're working too hard, Molly," Olive said. "Really you are. Where is Nate? I thought he was helping."

Elizabeth returned with the jug. "Bless you, sweetheart," Molly smiled, sharing it with the rest of them. "Nathan does help. He was here just yesterday. We can't expect him to devote all his time to us."

"We should summon 'Lije," Sonny declared. "He's plenty strong, Mama."

"'Lije is busy in Boston. You know that."

"Well, at least you ought to confine your labors to early morning," Olive put in. "Dawn, if you can manage it."

"Dawn! We thought you were our friend, Auntie," moaned Susannah without opening her eyes. "Dawn! Help us, Lord."

"You'll all fall ill," Olive persisted. Her family would do well next winter because Captain Gray was even now bringing back spirits from Ireland; the profits would buy what they needed. "You shall stop right now. As soon as the sun rises tomorrow, I and my boys will water with you, and we'll continue to come here at dawn for as long as the garden needs us." Olive had three strapping sons at home; the arms of four more people would be sweet indeed , and Elizabeth, betrothed to the eldest of them, would be glad of his company.

"I can't ask you to do such a thing," Molly said, voice quavering, tears blinding her.

"I can ask, and thank you!" Debby put in quickly.

"There!" exclaimed Olive. "That takes care of that!"

Molly shook her head, unable to turn the offer down, unable to speak her gratitude, unable to do anything at all but bless Olive Gray and the friendship they had shared for so many years. "Go your own way, children!" she urged them. "You deserve the rest of the day to yourselves. We rise with the sun tomorrow!"

"I can't move," Elizabeth said. "I'm going to lie here and never get up again."

"Until an ant bites you," Susannah giggled, pinching her. "Like this."

"Mama! Make her stop."

"Go away," Molly laughed. "All of you."

The youngsters moved off toward the springhouse and its cool interior.

"Do I hear thunder over the bay?" Debby asked suddenly.

They listened.

There it was, a faint growl.

"Maybe the Lord will finish our watering today," Olive said hopefully, "and save us all from having to get up with the sun, at least for a while."

Far out on the horizon a gray curtain dropped. Yes! Rain would be falling on Provincetown soon! Would it come this way? They watched in silence and felt a very slight breeze, heard it whisper in the parched grass.

Blow in, Molly willed. Blow in. I cannot carry water much longer. Elijah must watch storms like this at sea, she thought, wondering if they would miss or hit. The breeze grew stronger and stronger on their faces. Suddenly Nate was there.

"We'd best cover the salt," he panted, for he was not in the habit of moving quickly.

The salt. Good grief, she had forgotten all about it!

"Where's the boy?" Nate asked. "I hate to have you ladies pushing roofs about by yourselves."

"The three of us can do it," Olive declared, struggling to her feet.

"We certainly can!" Molly affirmed, picking up her skirt and trotting along, with Debby bringing up the rear.

Now the breeze was strong and smelled of rain. The vats seemed an endless distance away as the four of them toiled across the field, the wind coming off the bay pushing against them.

"We'll cover the last vat," Nate instructed. The water in it had been the first drawn up, at the beginning of the project. Rain mixed with brine this far along in the process produced a very inferior salt, yielding little cash.

Thunder moved closer, and hard on its heels, lightening flashed. The storm raced to meet them as they reached the shore.

"Quick!" Nathan cried. "Grab the edge of the roof, anywhere you can, all three of you on one side. I'll take the other. Wait until I give you the word"

But Nathan had badly underestimated the strength of three determined women, and the roof was pushed unevenly. Over the wind, now howling, over the thunder, rolling ever closer, they did not hear his command to hold back. The roof pivoted on its rollers and jammed tight against the rails.

He came around to their side where the three of them were still pushing, Olive in front, Molly in the middle, Debby behind. "The other way," he yelled. "It's stuck. Push the other way. I'll hold my side steady. When you feel the roof give, lay off. Then we'll try again."

The rain was only an occasional splatter as they strained and panted and pushed with all their might. The heavy roof slid suddenly and jammed on Nathan's side. They heard him cursing and when he came around, meekly accepted his instructions.

"All right!" he ordered. "Push back—slowly—and when it starts to slide, reverse and push forward again. Now—easy—easy . . ."

They pushed. The roof slid a bit. They turned, and pushed again, steadily, steadily, and it began to move. Desperate to keep up with Nathan, they ran with it. The roof rolled home with a crash nearly as awesome as the thunder that shook the earth at the same time. At full speed, the three women sailed helplessly on by and landed in a heap of swirling skirts amid wild cranberry and clumps of sea-grass.

Thrashing and groaning, they tried to sort themselves out. Olive began to laugh and couldn't stop. "How funny we must have looked! Like witches, flying through the air," she gasped.

Molly and Debby giggled, picturing it, then became hysterical too.

"Next time we'll have to bring our broomsticks," Debby guffawed.

"How, how, how about a p-p-pointy hat?" Molly cackled.

The salt was saved! The bucket brigade was over, at least for a few days! Now the rain settled in. Lying back, they let it fall on their upturned faces, cooling them deliciously, and chuckling as the ludicrous picture of themselves in full flight presented itself now and again.

"Oh, Molly," Olive tittered between outbursts of laughter. "I haven't had so much fun since we intercepted Tony in your chaise so long ago."

"Yes, I remember! His feet stuck straight out from his horse. He looked like a scarecrow."

"And when you let him drive but refused to ride with him? Because he might hit a bump and cause you to lose your baby?"

Molly writhed in glee.

"Just so I could ride out with him, instead—" Olive stopped, and Molly's laughter died abruptly as she realized what her friend had just said.

"Oh, dear," Olive moaned.

Debby, sitting up now, looked Molly's way for confirmation. "I'm sure I can explain, Deb." Molly sat up too, wondering frantically how she could even begin.

"The two of you planned it!" Debby cried above the rain. "You took your chaise and rode him down."

"Not exactly . . ."

"You never gave me a chance."

Around them, the rain steadied into a gentle, thorough, life giving, summer storm. Nathan, who had been standing beneath the nearby vat, came forward. "What is it, Cousin Debby? What's wrong?"

Debby collected herself, and took his extended hand, got to her feet. "The exertion of our efforts has quite exhausted us," she pronounced in the manner of royalty. "We fear we cannot walk unaided. Will you escort us back to the castle, Nathan?"

"Of course!" Offering his arm, he glanced with bewilderment at Molly and Olive, who watched with mouths agape as the storm continued to drench them.

"They're fine," Debby assured him. "They like lying in the rain." She gently nudged his arm so that he would start for the house. "How would I manage without you to lean on, Nate?" They departed grandly through the downpour.

Olive stood and pulled Molly up too. "Oh, my dear, I can't tell you how sorry I am!"

"I know you are." Molly patted her friend's shoulder and shivered as the rain's chill found her.

"She must be very angry," Olive said as they started back to the house.

"I'm afraid so," Molly replied grimly. "Let's find something dry to wear." She wished she did not have to go inside where Debby would be waiting. "But Olive, if Tony had been interested in her, you never would have won him."

"I know. But she doesn't. Just give me something from the barn to throw over my shoulders. I think I'll go home."

"Coward!"

"Yes, indeed." They fetched an old horse blanket. "It would only be worse if I went in with you," Olive said, embracing her. "A final insult."

"I suppose you're right," Molly sighed. "Wish me well."

Slowly, unwillingly, she let herself into the house. The children were gathered about the hearth, heating cider. Neither Nathan nor Debby were anywhere to be seen.

"Cousin Nathan went home. Auntie is upstairs," Susannah told her. "Would you like some hot cider, Mother?"

"Surely I would. And I'll find out if Aunt Debby would like some." She climbed up to her chamber where she stripped off her wet garments and put on dry ones, pulled a blanket off the bed, wrapped up in it, and with trepidation went to Debby's room across the hall.

Elijah's sister was wrapped in a blanket of her own, curled up, facing the wall.

"Would you like some hot cider?" Molly asked softly. "The children are making some."

There was no response to this offer.

"Debby . . ."

"Go away."

"Please. Let me explain."

"There's nothing to explain," said Debby's muffled voice. "It's all very clear."

Molly sat on the edge of the bed. "Look here, Deb. Olive simply wanted to meet Tony . . ."

"Will you go away?"

Molly jumped up quickly, stung. "We never meant . . ."

"Yes, you did." Debby rolled over so that she could face her tormentor. "Yes, you did!" She unwound herself from her blanket and stood up, her fists clenched. "He was planning to visit me that very day! You knew it. And I would have made him a good wife, and he would have come to love me! But you wanted Olive's favor, so you traded me for it."

"Debby! What a nasty thing to say!" Molly protested, her face growing hot.

"You are nasty," Debby hissed. "You got everything you wanted, didn't you? And if you had to be a bit ruthless in your pursuit of it, well, too bad!"

"I, I just wanted to tell you I am sorry," Molly stammered. "I never meant to hurt you." She started backing up toward the door.

Debby followed menacingly. "You never cared if you hurt me. You never cared about anything but yourself. All of us Merricks simply served your purpose, except my mother, who knew better." In her hostility and anger, Debby looked more like Mother with each passing moment. "You had my brother Jon wrapped around your little finger. I have been as good as live-in help ever since this house was built. And Elijah?" Debby laughed scornfully. "He provided it all. You used him to get what you wanted. That was the reason you married him."

"Oh, Debby, you mustn't believe that," she begged.

"Well, I do believe it. Are you going to leave this room, or do I have to throw you out?"

Molly fled to the kitchen and the children.

"Is Auntie all right?" Elizabeth asked.

"She will be. Rest is what she needs right now," Molly answered. "We can put some cider aside for her to drink later." How glad she was for their company just then, and during subsequent days, too, when Debby spoke not a word, glowered and was as a black cloud in the house.

Then the letter came. It was without salutation, and trembled in Molly's hands.

The voyage is lost. The fever keeps braking out. I beleeve Charity will be scuttled. This daye I have writen my creditors. They will arrange an apprasle of the hous and ajasent land so I will know how much can be raised to pay my det. We'll keep Mother's house to live in, and some land. Show the appraser around and give him any information he needs.

Elijah

"What does he say?" Debby urged, coming out of her sullen shell.

"We are bankrupt," she told them all, her voice sounding like a bird trapped in a well, a distant echo unrelated to herself.

They all stared.

"The ship will be sunk because of the fever," she explained. "A man will come down to appraise the house and land."

"Appraise them?" Debby asked.

"Yes. To see what they're worth."

Debby was incredulous. "You mean, in order to sell?"

"Probably."

"Good grief!" Debby exclaimed. "I had better hustle." She reached for her bonnet.

"Where? Hustle where?"

"Across the street. Nathan has asked me to marry him again. I shall tell him yes, and as soon as we are wed, move over to his house. Hopefully, before this one is gone."

"Why Debby," Molly protested before she had a chance to think, "you would desert me now?"

Debby laughed without humor. "I would indeed, Molly Merrick," she called over her shoulder. "The sooner, the better."

As in a dream, Molly turned back to the cold, unmoving letter that contained not even the least vestige of warmth or comfort but only announced the destruction of everything they had worked for.

"Well, at least Father is alright," Sonny observed. "And with this rain, the garden will grow fast."

"Will we have to sell the house before Father returns?" Susannah wondered.

"He only says to have the appraisal done by the time he gets back," Molly told her.

Elizabeth frowned. "Where would we go?"

"The old house, I suppose." All of them shuddered. It was small, woefully dank and dreary.

"Maybe Mr. Snow will buy back the hunting knife Father gave me," Sonny said hopefully. "I know he bought it at the store. I'd be glad to give you the money, Mama, to help repay the debt."

"All of us have gold necklaces and bracelets that Father has brought us. We could sell them, couldn't we?" Elizabeth chimed in.

Sell necklaces and bracelets—and jewels. Sell the clock and the crystal and the Turkish rugs!

"Yes, yes!" Molly laughed, excited for the first time in weeks. "Thank you, my dears. From the bottom of my heart. That's a wonderful idea."

If everything were sold, it might be enough to save the house and at least the lot it stood on.

For they could never be replaced, never. The way the house overlooked the bay, shaded in front by trees grown large with the passing of years, commanding the whole of Waterford yet aloof from the common way of the highroad, all the more alluring for that— she could not lose it! Only a shell would remain, but a shell could be refurnished some day. Some day when Elijah would not be so cold as he was now, telling her they were ruined, offering not even a shred of comfort . . .

She put away his coldness and Debby's hatred, put away her calloused hands and her pride and set herself to the task of saving what she could.

He was an oily, unctuous man, and she hated him. Disdainfully he looked about, at the outbuildings and the spring and the salt vats, as though everything were crude and rustic, beneath contempt, jotting things down on paper with a stubby lead pencil.

"The house and outbuildings ought to cover your husband's debt," he announced when the inspection was done. There was no warmth in his insincerely smiling face.

"Would the land—apart from the parcel this house sits on, and that old house over there—would they cover it?" she asked carefully.

With a distasteful look, he replied, "I'm told your husband does not wish to sell more land than is necessary. And besides, the instructions were to save yonder cottage."

Clearly the appraiser did not want to deal with a woman. On to the next alternative.

"There are other valuables here that might fetch the requisite amount."

"Oh?" A cunning look crept into his eyes.

Woman or not, she had piqued his interest.

Bracing herself, she asked, "Won't you come in and have a cup of tea?" And with her best smile, added, "Or something stronger?"

"Well, now, I suppose I might," he answered, tucking the pencil and his notes into a small pouch.

She took him in by the front door, its brass knocker polished only yesterday. Inside, everything was swept and dusted, the white painted trims immaculate, the Turkish carpets glowing in the mellow afternoon light.

"What a pleasant place!" the appraiser exclaimed. "I had no idea that you folks lived so well down here!"

"We live very well," Molly assured him. "Let me show you around. But first, sir, some refreshment."

After serving brandy for the gentleman, tea for herself, they started on the parlor with its silver candelabrum on the mantel, a Chinese urn by the hearth, its fine furniture and bookcases filled now with first editions from England and France. Next, they went across the hall into the dining room and the mahogany table with its set of eight chairs, the matching sideboard and its silverware and china contents, the glassed cabinets with their hoard of sparkling crystal. Finally, they proceeded upstairs to look at the chests and bedsteads and rugs there. And her jewelry. He virtually licked his chops.

Once again, they sat in the parlor.

"You have lovely things, Mrs. Merrick. Of very high value."

"Let me offer you more brandy," Molly urged. "Tell me, sir, would the furnishings in this house cover my husband's indebtedness?"

Over his crystal snifter he reviewed his notes. "The captain made no mention of them, but it's possible they would. Perhaps your husband isn't aware of the value of your furnishings on today's market. It has been a long time since goods like these have arrived on our shores, what with the late war and poor conditions of trade, and now tariffs. You would be willing to sell them? And your jewels, of course."

"If they'll cover the debt, yes. I would," she managed to say.

"Buyers from Boston would come down if they knew such a treasure trove were here."

"Come down?" she asked, curious.

"Yes. Buyers would come to acquire finery for their homes, and dealers, too, will want to procure goods for their clients and warehouses. Set dealers against private buyers, Mrs. Merrick, the price will go up accordingly," he explained, his voice warming. "And probably there are people right here in Barnstable County who would avail themselves of such a splendid opportunity. Because they could haul the items away themselves, they'd avoid freight charges and might drive the prices even higher. If all goes well, your husband might still have the land, which he intends to farm, as I understand it."

An auction. He was talking about an auction, right here, with strangers walking unbidden into her house, Rockford folk at last allowed to enter, pawing through her belongings, able to touch her little porcelain figurines, her fans, her lace trimmed dresses, even if they couldn't afford to buy them, and Waterford people, who could.

One day, she might see the ruby lying on another woman's breast.

But she must put all that aside and focus on what the auction would bring. "Would it be enough?" she asked again.

"I believe it will be more than enough, yes, I do."

The house would be theirs, that was the most critical thing, and the land, which was so important to Elijah.

She recalled the last time she usurped Elijah's authority. But she must risk his wrath. "All right. We'll sell everything. Except for the kitchen essentials, if you please—pots and pails and such—and my portrait," she added, "and perhaps a few trifles of a personal nature." Like her porringers.

"They had better not be trifles of value, Mrs. Merrick," he warned. "Or the point of an auction will be lost."

"They will have no worth to anyone but us, I assure you," she said meekly.

"Yes, then, that's fine. Kitchen utensils, portrait. Trifles. And I'd suggest you hold onto your mattresses and blankets so you have something to sleep on." He noted the items. "How soon can you be ready?"

His eyes gleamed, Molly saw, no doubt at the prospect of a healthy commission for himself. And he was probably itching to get at it before Elijah came back, in case such an arrangement should not accord with his wishes. Evidently, brandy and the prospect of a good sum for himself were what it took for the appraiser to make a deal with a woman, and gladly at that.

"I'll be ready whenever you are."

"You'll never regret it, Mrs. Merrick, I'm sure."

Oh, *you* may be sure, she thought, watching him mount his horse and ride away. I am not. I may always regret it. But I'll have to do it anyway.

⊠⊠✦⊠⊠

"Come Molly," Olive begged. "Stay at our place until everyone is gone. This madhouse will haunt you."

Madhouse it was. The yard was filled with chaises and horses, wagons and carriages; the house was filled with people—strangers and ones she knew only remotely and many whom she had once disdained.

That morning, the packet arrived chockablock full of Boston folk, and another came in right behind, also full, chartered especially for the outing. The Merrick auction was a great occasion—a grand outing for Bostonians on a fine day, a local holiday for the Barnstable County citizens who had begun to gather early. Just after sunrise, they started to pull into the clamshell driveway, and now vehicles were parked all over the lawn and the bordering meadows for a mile down the low road.

At this very moment Tabby Stevens might be pawing over the what-not with its collection of china birds, carved boxes, enameled flowers. Strangers were most likely combing through her closets. Her sterling silver was at this moment being held in the hands of dealers who tried to guess its weight. The crystal was being tapped and rung by who knew how many dirty fingers, to hear the purity of its tone. Behind the house, a large platform had been thrown up upon which the auctioneer would stand and a phalanx of strong young men would bring out the furniture, one item at a time so the throng might see what was being offered.

Now she stood with Olive in the middle of the road, watching. The children had gone to the Gray's for the day, but Molly had lingered despite Olive's urgings. She must see in order to believe.

"If someone from our crowd espies you, it will embarrass them," Olive persisted. "They might want to bid for something, but they would not, if they knew you could see them do it."

"Well, we certainly wouldn't want that to happen!" Molly declared acidly, her eyes hot and dry, her head splitting. A crowd on the rooftop porch waved gay greetings, mistaking her for a visitor. "Of course you're right, Olive," she agreed, and slowly they returned to the Gray's kitchen where they brewed tea. The children were upstairs. Molly had no idea what they were doing, but thankfully they were quiet.

"What shall you do?" Olive asked. "When all this is done, I mean."

"We'll stay where we are. We'll eat right out of the garden, and sleep on the floor. We saved our mattresses and blankets."

"And then?" Olive gently probed.

"Then I wait," Molly said wearily. "Wait, as I have been waiting all these months. For Elijah."

✦∾ 2 ∾✦

She had no pride now. She had no anger, no bitterness, nor even despair. There was only fear, so crushing and overwhelming it left no room for anything else.

Elijah was coming home.

He had sent word by yesterday's packet that he would settle his accounts in Boston and come down on this evening's tide. Soon he would walk through the front door, into this house now stripped and shorn of everything that had once adorned and graced it.

What would he do? Would he embrace her, because she had worked so hard? Or berate her, or beat her as he had done before, for imposing her own decision on him?

But even greater fear loomed in the near certainty that he had found her out. All other terror paled before that one. If he did know, the future would have nothing to redeem it. He would make her lot in life so miserable that it would not be worth living, and he would be justified in doing so.

Weary and anxious, she sat at the bottom of the staircase, with a tallow candle a few steps above her. There was no oil lamp to light her way; there were no oil lamps anywhere in the house. There was not even anywhere else to sit, because all the furniture was gone. It must be late—ten or eleven o'clock—she was not sure because the clock was gone and there was no way to mark the time. In the darkness the candle fluttered and looked very lost, very lonely, even as she was lost and lonely. Nor was there anything left to give her courage, or pride. She had thought her portrait, the lone survivor of this debacle, would give her comfort, but it only reminded her of what was lost, of a time gone forever. The gray clouds that swirled about the lovely woman she had once been now seemed ominous, threatening to obliterate the sitter.

Upstairs, the children were asleep, their clothing about them in heaps and piles because the clothes presses and chests had been taken away by the auctioneer's men. Debby had left to be the wife of Nathan King, taking Mother with her. Molly tried to tell herself that she had done Elijah's sister a favor at the vats, freeing her to marry at last, but that poor attempt to gather a remnant of fighting spirit fell in defeat before Debby's contempt. How she longed to run to Elijah, to be held by him, comforted by him. But she could not even approach him, not until she knew his mind and mood. If his anger got out of control . . . .

She drew her legs up so she could lean on them to contain the cramping in her stomach. Head on her knees, she wept. Oh, Elijah, please don't. Please don't break me; I am so broken already.

Unwillingly, she was in the barn again, in the small circle of light cast by the lantern. Again she saw Elijah's hard, expressionless face, heard his command to unclothe herself and felt the devastation of facing his anger.

The latch clicked and slowly the front door swung open. On the step above her the candle guttered in the draft. He stood silently on the threshold, then moved to close the door behind him. Quickly she wiped her eyes and, with the aid of the newel post, pulled herself to her feet.

"They told me about the auction," he said, without greeting her. "How you arranged to sell everything." His voice was low, but in the barren hall it echoed and was enlarged and she had no difficulty hearing him. Glancing into the parlor and then into the dining room, he could see, even with only one dim tallow candle lighting the way, that they were empty. He looked past her to the landing where the stairs curved 'round, bereft of the clock.

She looked down at the bare floor from which the Turkish rug had been removed and heard the rustle of his clothing. Slowly he came nigh and tipped her chin up so she must meet his eyes, whether she wanted to or not. They questioned, probed, looked into the depths of the misery in hers.

"Why? Why did you do it?"

Quailing, trying not to tremble, she said, "To pay your debt."

"You sold your beautiful treasures to save me?"

"I thought it would help. They weren't much good without a house to put them in."

She could stand still no longer, and tried to back away. Quickly he reached behind her and grasped the banister, blocking the path of escape.

"You sold everything to pay the debt." It was a statement, as though he were trying to get it through his head.

"Was it enough? Is the house still ours? Yours?"

"Yes." He released his hold on the banister, gestured toward the stairs, and sat there with her, putting as much distance between them as he could contrive. Elbows on his knees, hands clasped, he stared sightlessly at the floor.

"I'm told you even sold the jewelry," he said at last.

"The girls contributed theirs, too. And Sonny took his pocket knife back to Mr. Snow for a refund."

He did not respond.

"Before I knew Charity would be condemned," she struggled to keep her voice steady, "I was concerned only with getting us through the winter, until you could get back with another voyage. I never thought of selling things then. I aimed to get some cash with salt."

That got his attention, and he looked at her. "You ran through a batch of salt?"

"Nathan and Debby and Sonny and I, yes. We made a bigger garden, too, and watered it so there are lots of winter vegetables—parsnips and carrots and turnips."

"Your favorite foods," he remarked.

Was he teasing? If so, might it mean he wasn't angry?

"And then it rained," she hurried on. "Nate didn't think we'd have time to do any more salt, and then we learned about *Charity* being sunk, and he and Debby got married."

"Married."

"To each other," she explained.

"Ah. And Mother?"

"Went with Debby, to Nathan's house."

"The children?"

"Sleeping. Upstairs, on the floor. Not on the bare floor," she hastened to tell him. "We kept the mattresses."

In the candle's glow she saw disbelief and, perhaps, a flicker of admiration. Hope stirred.

He looked away again. The stillness of the house hovered, settled.

Finally he said, "The auction earned more than enough. There is even some surplus cash. It seems to have bought us a chance to start over."

There was a long, long silence in which he appeared to be mulling over his choices. "I'll have to be a farmer, now that the ship is gone. We'll both have to work very hard, just to keep going. You as well as me."

You as well as me. That meant both of them. Together. That must mean he was not going to confront her about Isaac. Yet he was so cautious in the way he sat there, carefully holding himself apart from her....

Tentatively, she offered, "I'll do whatever you think will help."

"In Africa, when I believed this house would have to be sold," he said, "I figured we'd move back to the old place, and open a store in the front rooms so there'd be a steady cash flow, even if not a lot. Farming is very uncertain." He turned toward her and said firmly, "But since we still have this place, we can open a store here."

"Here?"

"Yes. We can live in the back, use the front for trade and rent out the old place for a few extra dollars." He paused, watching, waiting for her reaction. "What do you think of that, Molly?"

She thought it was an abomination. Yet how could she object, just as the husband whom she had betrayed seemed to be planning for a shared future, without reference to her infidelity?

"Why not?" she asked gamely, sick at heart.

"I wondered if old Ben Snow would like to retire. We could buy him out, move his stock over here, pay him a little now with the cash left over and the rest as we go."

She managed to nod.

"I have in mind that you will tend the store," he said.

"Me?" Surely her ears deceived her!

"While I am plowing and planting, you can take in the money and keep inventory. I'll help you with heavy lifting, of course, but the day-to-day operation would be yours."

Their friends were bound to advance in the next few years. They had started already, and there would never be a way to catch up with them if she were relegated to being a woman in trade.

"Do you think you could bear it, Molly?" he asked, searching her face now. "Are you too proud?"

You have run a bucket brigade, she told herself, and shoveled salt. You have sold everything at auction, and in the public eye you are destitute. There will be no chance to undo that impression if you are a common shopkeeper, but what choice is there?

She met his gaze. In his eyes were pain and hurt and longing, despair and courage and something else, as if there were more to his wanting her to mind a store than simply maintaining a cash flow.

"Are you too proud?" he asked again.

It was what she must do.

"My dear," she said quietly, "There is nothing left to be proud about." In her heart she pleaded, oh, Elijah, know that I love you, that I will do anything to be worthy of you. Please understand! "Certainly, between us, we can drum up pride in our work—you as a farmer, me as a shopkeeper. Surely we can do it if we're in it together?"

Oh, his face then! It seemed suddenly to crumble, and quickly he looked away, took a deep breath then slowly released it as he stood, holding out his hand. She reached for it and rose. He brought her fingers to his lips, searching her face, his eyes deeper and more compelling than they had ever been.

They were close now, so close, and she willed him to embrace her, to show her that they were as one. As if he had heard, he carefully gathered her to himself, giving her weary head haven upon his chest. She could hear his heart, beating heavy and strong, and felt his body shaking, ever so slightly.

"Molly! Molly!" he whispered fiercely.

He kissed her deeply then, possessively, as though to set his mark upon her, then held her quietly. Within her, joy welled up, rising from the detritus of what once were her dreams. For he was not angry about the auction, and perhaps, after all, he did not know about Isaac, else he never would embrace her so, comfort her so, kiss her so. And if he did not know, if they made a new life together, and if she waited for the right time, some day there might be a chance . . . .

Some day the store might hold more than basics. It might contain fine fabrics, and fashion books, and a little tea table in the corner where a customer might linger and chat about one thing or another—an interesting book or newspaper article, an upcoming musical event or dance. The proprietress would be well dressed, even elegantly dressed by way of displaying the potential of the materials on the shelves . . . .

Yes, a chance. One day.

There in the front entry, clasped tight, they lingered many moments, listening to the late summer night beyond the open windows, to the frogs bellowing occasionally down by the pond, to the beating of their own hearts, to the sigh and shift of the trees that overhung the house, while the candle on the stairs swayed in the gentle air of evening.

THE END

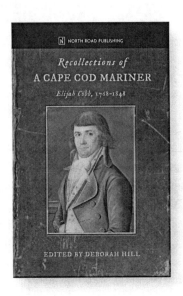

Read the memoir that inspired
This is the House

At the age of 75, Elijah Cobb wrote a memoir for his grandchildren, describing his "advenchurs." Cobb tells of his captures and escapes as he dodges the French and English who close each others' ports in their wars against each other. The Captain relates creating alternative trade routes, taking contraband gold back to "his owners" in Boston, meeting Robespierre, smuggling rum, and beating the embargo of 1807.

This is the House is based on these recollections, which provide historical and personal authenticity to a fictional Elijah, whose wife "ran him in debt for a Cape Cod farm" just as Cobb's did, and who, like the fictional Elijah, built her a house that still stands today.

The weaving of fact and fiction is so close that Hill herself has trouble keeping them straight. "It could have happened this way," she tells the reader, "at a certain time and in a certain place on the Narrow Land."

CPSIA information can be obtained
at www.ICGtesting.com
Printed in the USA
FFOW02n0911040914
7123FF